MW01098891

May 2016

To Roger

Thanks - hope you enjoy!

FIRST CLASS PASSAGE

A Jack Sterling Novel

The sea is everything. Its breath is pure and healthy.
It is an immense desert, where man is never lonely,
for he feels life stirring on all sides.

— Jules Verne, *Man of the Sea*

ALSO BY JOHN C. SMITH

The Scarlet Sentinels
ISBN 978-1-897435-76-2 (hardcover book)
ISBN 978-1-897435-80-9 (paperback book)
ISBN 978-1-897435-77-9 (ebook)

ABOUT THE AUTHOR

John C. Smith is a retired member of the Royal Canadian Mounted Police and lives in Victoria, British Columbia. Much of his service was served in 'front line' policing. He was a lecturer at the Canadian Police College and is a graduate of the University of Waterloo, Ontario.

First Class Passage is his second Jack Sterling novel. His first, *The Scarlet Sentinels*, is a realistic portrayal of life at a large RCMP detachment in British Columbia.

His insight into police work, and his cruise ship journeys, have enabled him to combine the two experiences into an intriguing tale of murder at sea, and the difficulty of investigating this kind of crime.

FIRST CLASS PASSAGE

A Jack Sterling Novel
by
JOHN C. SMITH

Agio
PUBLISHING HOUSE

Agio Publishing House
151 Howe Street, Victoria BC Canada V8V 4K5

First Class Passage
ISBN 978-1-927755-45-7 (hardcover book)
ISBN 978-1-927755-44-0 (paperback book)
ISBN 978-1-927755-46-4 (ebook)
Cataloguing information available from
Library and Archives Canada.

Printed on acid-free paper.
Agio Publishing House is a socially-responsible enterprise
measuring success on a triple-bottom-line basis.

10   9   8   7   6   5   4   3   2   1

ACKNOWLEDGEMENTS

I have the following to thank for their assistance:

Prof. Gail Anderson, School of Criminology, Simon Fraser University, Vancouver, BC

Hal Mueller, Sailwx, Orlando, FL

Prof. Kate Lewins, Faculty of Law, Murdoch University, Perth, Australia

Charles Mandigo, FBI (retired), Seattle, WA

Dr. Eric Milne, GP, Victoria, BC

Jenny Ray, International Satellite Radio, London, UK

Fernando Romero, ship's pilot, Port Authority, Cabo San Lucas, Mexico

Jeffrey J. Smith, Barrister & Solicitor, Ottawa, ON

Jamie Swan, Pacific Disaster Centre, Victoria, BC

Capt. Roger Williams, BC Coast Pilotage Authority, Victoria, BC.

DEDICATION

To Jean Smith, for her valuable assistance and patience while I wrote the story, and to my three sons, Greg, Jeff and Brad, for their continued support and encouragement. As well, to the many people I have had the good fortune to contact for their advice and guidance.

Staff Superintendent Jack Sterling sat behind a large, cleared desk in the Metropolitan Toronto Police Service headquarters building on College Street. It was the last working day of the month, and also his last day to occupy this chair. He'd reached thirty-five years of service and, as the uniformed officers would say, today was his *'End of Watch.'* Tomorrow, Saturday, he would no longer be Chief of Detectives.

As he sat reflecting on his service, there was a knock on his door. Looking up, Jack saw Chief Constable Bill Forsythe enter.

"Got a minute, Jack?"

"Sure, Chief, have a seat."

"Just dropped by to say my unofficial goodbye before your party next Friday evening. How do you feel?"

"Not sure, to be honest. Bit nostalgic, I suppose. No doubt my retirement will hit me in due course, but life goes on, as they say. Some new and different challenges lay ahead for me and I look forward to that."

"Yes. If you take their offer, I wish you well with your new job at Sentinel. Good outfit, I believe. Your depth of experience with Metro should help you make the transition smoothly. Sentinel Corporation is lucky to be getting someone of your calibre. You know, it's too bad about the 35-year mandatory retirement limit. Most people are really at the peak of their knowledge and efficiency when they are forced to leave their job."

"Yeah, Chief, I suppose you're right but there has to come a time for everyone to go. Maybe it's just as well. Makes room for promotions up through the ranks and maybe a newer way of looking at the job. Really, I feel I've done all I can. I've enjoyed my police career and look forward to the next phase of my life."

"Just left me say privately and sincerely, that I have enjoyed my association with you. You've done well with the Detective Division and I hope that Chief Superintendent Elliott can do as good a job. Thank you, Jack, and best of luck. Enjoy your cruise too, wherever you and Jean decide to go," said the chief, standing and shaking his hand. "See you Friday evening at the Astoria."

His thirty-five years with the Toronto Police Service had seen him rise from constable in the Patrol Division to the rank of staff (chief) superintendent. It felt a long, long way from his days as a recruit in training, then walking the beat for five years, mostly in the busy downtown area, and his subsequent rise through the ranks, with their various responsibilities in policing. The last fifteen years he'd been a detective, finishing up as the top-ranking detective, in charge of over 500 men and women. Toronto didn't have anywhere near the number of murders as large U.S. cities—40% of New York City's per capita rate, one-ninth of Chicago's—yet he'd personally investigated about seventy-five murder cases, and lately, reviewed many more. If anything made leaving the Service attractive, it was to get away from the sad, tragic and sometimes macabre events that were the *raison d'être* of a big city police detective. Jack Sterling was feeling a bit nostalgic, and relieved at the same time.

Jack Sterling and his wife Jean got home from his farewell party a few minutes after one a.m. He had been picked up and driven home in his black detective patrol car by his regular driver, Sergeant John Chisholm. On getting out, the man gave his boss a crisp salute. Under the streetlamp light, a glint of a tear was visible in the man's eye.

Jack returned the courtesy, then stepped forward to give the sergeant a brief hug and pat on the back. "Thank you, John, it's been a pleasure," he said. "I'll miss our little chats."

The party had been a memorable affair, the grand old hotel packed with 300 police officers, their spouses and other guests. He couldn't get over the genuinely warm feelings everyone showed toward him and, in his farewell speech, he found it very difficult not to choke up. The standing ovation was loud and long.

He removed his police mess jacket and black bow tie, hanging them over the back of a chair at the kitchen table. As he yawned and stretched his arms above him, Jean snuggled him from behind and murmured, "You wanna know how I feel, sweetheart?"

"Yes, tell me."

"I'll use just one word: *relieved*. No more urgent calls about deaths—no more danger—no more long days and restless nights."

Turning around, he looked at her face for a few seconds and, seeing her moistened eyes, replied softly, "I know you are relieved, and in spite of some mixed emotions, I feel that way too. It's a helluva way to feel—to be sad at leaving this job and happy about it too. Glad too, that I never had to shoot someone, although that came close to happening on occasion. I'm sure I'll remember this day for the rest of my life—just as I remember my first day as a cadet.

"You know, a civilian at the party asked me this evening how many dead bodies I'd seen in my career. I couldn't tell him. Except to say, 'probably hundreds.' Made me think, that did. If I'd had some comprehension of what I was getting into way back then, when I joined the Force, I might not have been removing my Chief of Detectives uniform tonight."

They stood, quietly holding each other for a minute before his wife said, "You must be tired."

MONDAY, APRIL 10
Toronto

Jack sat down in his upstairs, third-bedroom office, and googled *'cruise lines.'* When the results came up, he started clicking on the variety of companies and destinations listed. He and his wife had taken two previous cruises, both in the Caribbean where most people from the Toronto area doing boat trips, especially in wintertime, chose to go. It was a relatively short flight to Miami. On both occasions, they'd travelled on large ships, with Carnival and Holland America Lines. While both voyages—10 days each—were enjoyable, each ship carried over 3,000 passengers, and seemed *busy* and too noisy, with many children aboard. He and Jean had discussed this and were determined to avoid a repeat.

Today, he was looking for a smaller vessel, a cruise line that catered to older folk and no screaming kids. He was impressed with the Holland America line but continued scrolling, until he stopped at a company called World Cruise Lines, registered out of the Port of Road Town, the capital city of the British Virgin Islands, in the eastern archipelago of the Caribbean Islands. This company, WCL, seemed to be relatively new, its ships carrying a maximum passenger load of twelve hundred. Just right. Fare prices were comparable with other major companies and included return air fare. The photos showed one of the ships, MV *Seascape*, to be well appointed on eleven decks—six cabin decks, two activity levels and one for meals and snacks, a casino and shopping area, plus crew decks below—instead of up to 16 decks on the biggest ships. Even the lowest deck cabins appeared were quite acceptable, judging from the photos. Also appealing was the itinerary for a 17-day trip from Barcelona in Spain to Miami that including a nice long interval of crossing the Atlantic, after the last port of call at Santa Cruz de la Palma in the Canary Islands. Eight days of no stops—time to relax.

Jack called Jean over to have a look—he really did rely on her female view of things—and together they read the details.

"What do you think?" he asked.

"Seems good to me, honey. I like fewer people, especially fewer of the smaller variety. I know these cruise lines all glamorize their ships and cuisine but, hey, nothing ventured, nothing gained. What's the price comparison on the Barcelona–Miami voyage that we're discussing?"

"Well, I've checked four companies offering that cruise and the price differences are narrow—all within two hundred dollars. I've been trying to read between the lines about what each has to offer and my intuition tells me that this company will be our best bet. What departure date did we agree on?"

"I wrote it on the wall calendar. Let me check."

She went downstairs to the large calendar tacked up on a kitchen wall, found 'Leave for cruise!' tentatively written in the May 12 week block and called out the planned date range.

"Should be a good time to go," Jack yelled back. "Let me narrow in on the departure date for a WCL cruise closest to that. I think I'll book a verandah stateroom. I'm going to look at the Atlantic weather for that time of year too. Don't want rough seas!

"Also, I'll check on the conditions for flying to Barcelona two days early, before joining the ship, and then back to Toronto 3 days after we dock in Miami. I believe there's a surcharge to go early. Be nice to spend a bit of time in Barcelona at the start and then see the Everglades after we return to Miami. Hope we're not too late doing this."

"Alright, sweetheart, dinner'll be ready in half an hour."

He found that World Cruise Lines offered a May 16 sailing for the 17-day voyage from Barcelona, with three ports of call en route: Seville and Cadiz, together, in the south of Spain; and Lanzarote and Santa Cruz de la Palma, separate stops on the east and west sides of the Canary Islands in the Atlantic, off the coast of Western Sahara. From there, the ship heads out into the Atlantic for the remaining eight days on the open seas to Miami. 'Good. No other ports of call. This trip will give me just enough time to think about my new job,' Jack thought. 'We'll have to book right away though. Two full days in Barcelona means we'd fly out on the evening of the 13th.'

Going to the weather site, he'd found that May's weather was usually good for a trans-Atlantic crossing. The cyclone season generally started around the beginning of June, by which time they'd be in Miami.

On the *Expedia* website, he was glad to see that Air Canada flew to Barcelona, with a quick stop in Montreal and London in the United Kingdom. He hoped that was the air carrier the cruise line would fly people on from Toronto. Other airlines required a change of plane in Madrid and switching to the Spanish airline Iberia Air within Spain.

"So, Mrs. Sterling, are you okay with that cruise?" he asked.

Replying from the kitchen, she agreed. "I'd still like to see their brochure though. Is there an online version or a PDF we can download?"

♦   ◊   ♦

With his 60th birthday coming up later in the year, Jack Sterling was still fit and healthy. He was a member at a local recreation center, where he went at least five days a week, running on the treadmills for half an hour and swimming lengths in the pool for the same amount of time. He'd been offered a good job with the largest private security company in the city, discussions the chief had been informed about and cleared. Jack had accepted an offer the day before his retirement party, after carefully reviewing the matter, but was not 100% sure it was right for him. He was not at all sure he wanted to continue with enforcement work, even low-risk stuff. Maybe he really needed a complete change. The pay offered was generous, equal to his recent salary, and not easy to turn down. He could defer starting his pension, making it higher when he would draw from it later. Sentinel wanted him to start as soon as possible, but he'd asked them to wait until mid-June.

TUESDAY, MAY 13
Palm Beach, Florida

"It's eight a.m. and this is NPR news for Tuesday, May 13, with Dwight Howard. Good morning, everyone. Here's a roundup of early events making the news today. The president is scheduled to appear at 10 a.m. before the Congressional Committee on the economy...."

A hand appeared from under the blanket, reached over and slapped the button down on the radio/alarm clock. The large red numbers glowed 8:01 in her darkened bedroom. She was just not mentally prepared to hear about whatever the president was going to discuss. Not today.

Rebecca Gessner—née Abramowicz—rubbed her hands over her face in a quick massage, pulled the blanket back, rolled to the side of the bed and put her feet on the floor. She usually rose no earlier than nine, and more often at ten. Today, however, was her last busy day at home prior to departing from Miami International Airport for a seventeen-day cruise vacation from Barcelona, back across the Atlantic. Hannah Goldman, her secretary/companion, would be arriving at 9 a.m. to help with her packing and clear up her business mail.

She pressed Maria's call-button, said she was up and to put the coffee on. It was the beginning of another hot, sultry day on the Florida east coast, at Palm Beach, with a slight onshore breeze. Rebecca could see a number of early beach strollers as she opened the blinds on her second-floor balcony window. Her house, as she called it, was, by any other definition, a mansion—six thousand square feet on two levels, Spanish style, painted in two shades of tan and light brown with thick, red-ochre roof tiles, and occupying one acre of prime beach waterfront on South Ocean Boulevard. She and her husband, Solomon, had lived there for ten years before he died suddenly, five years ago at 63, of a heart attack. They'd had no children. He had been president and CEO of the Gessner Insurance Brokerage Corporation, with offices in Los Angeles and Miami. It was a lucrative business and they were multi-multi-millionaires. While she did not assume the CEO position upon his death, she did serve on the company's board of directors. Given her majority share ownership, her word understandably carried a fair degree of authority at the table.

Rebecca had recently turned sixty-five and was in good health. At five feet, six inches, her figure was still quite shapely, due in part to having been 'under the knife' a few times, as only her closest friends knew. She was due to go under the knife one more time. Soon. She worked out daily in the fully-equipped gym on the ground floor and swam in the large backyard pool, in heated water in the winter months, when she was not traveling to L.A. on business, or elsewhere on pleasure. Her Puerto Rican-born maid, Maria, lived in.

Rebecca was sitting in the kitchen bay window, mug of coffee in hand, looking at the Atlantic Ocean, when her thoughts were interrupted by a knock on the door. She knew it was her secretary.

"Come in, Hannah," she said and called to Maria to bring the young woman a coffee.

Hannah said, "*Hola*, Maria," to the maid and sat down at the marbled bay window tabletop, facing her employer. "How are you today, Mrs. G.? Sleep well?"

"Okay, until the damned helicopter woke me at 3:30. I thought it might have been the police and was correct in thinking that because Maria told me she'd heard a report on the local radio at eight o'clock. An armed robbery in the downtown area at an all-night deli. The lone employee was shot but is okay, mercifully."

Ordinarily, it was a quiet neighborhood. Few people living in the vicinity had regular day jobs and there was very little traffic noise.

Ms. Hannah Goldman did not like to be 'familiar' with her employer and in spite of being asked to use her Christian name, she stuck to the formality of 'Mrs. Gessner' or 'Mrs. G.' With an undergraduate degree in business administration from the University of Miami, she felt somewhat under-employed in her duties here. Her father, a long-time friend of Solomon Gessner, got her the job, or 'position' as he liked to call it, after graduation, and while it was interesting, paid quite well and involved some traveling, it was not challenging. Hannah knew she'd eventually have to find a more demanding career job to fit her personality and academic training.

"Well, you ready for our cruise, Hannah?" Rebecca said lightly as Hannah joined her for a light breakfast of toast and marmalade.

"Yes," said Hannah, "very much so. I've only done one, short, seven-day Caribbean trip, with Carnival. It'll be interesting to see what this ship is like in comparison, and I've never been to Spain. Travel arrangements and documents are all here," she added, patting her black leather briefcase cum purse. "I've confirmed our airline reservations and departure time, on American Airlines with a one-hour stop in Lisbon, a nine-hour flight. No changing planes, thank goodness. Our flight arrives at 11:30 a.m. tomorrow, local time. So, to reiterate, we leave Miami at 6:30 p.m.—1830 hours—tonight. By the way, that will be on the new Boeing 787 Dreamliner plane. Our fare in first-class seating will be $17,830 total, return, of course.

"Also confirmed is the cruise reservation. You'll be staying in a so-called Crown Suite on deck seven and I'm on the deck below you. With regard to departure today, we need to check in at Miami airport by no later five o'clock, which means we'll have to leave here, let's say, by three-thirty. I hope that's okay with you?"

Hannah looked up from the itinerary at Mrs. G., who nodded her reply. "I've arranged for Clifford to have the limo ready by then. I will need to slip home to pick up my things this afternoon and say goodbye to Mom and Dad, but I will spend some time with you now, reviewing company correspondence and your mail, if that's okay? May I take it that you've briefed Maria about our trip and she has a copy of the itinerary and my cell phone number?"

"All done," replied Mrs. G. "Maria seems very excited for us. Thanks for your efforts, Hannah."

◆ ◇ ◆

Seven hours later, Hannah and her employer were sitting in over-sized black leather chairs in the VIP Lounge at Miami International Airport, with a vodka martini and a sherry, respectively, in front of them on the low, oval glassed-topped table, watching the news on CNN delivered by Anderson Cooper. They had about an hour until their flight would be called. Cloudless blue sky could be seen through the high, panoramic windows overlooking the runways. They could also watch their gleaming new American Airlines 787 at the gate, being prepared for flight. Hannah hoped it would leave on schedule. They didn't have too much time in Barcelona before leaving on the cruise—and Hannah was keen on seeing the European fashions in the shops.

◆ ◇ ◆

Same day, Toronto, Ontario

"So, don't forget, Mom and Dad, you can use the skype app on your new Blackberry Passport Z10 that you received at your retirement party. It's a great little gadget and it'll do anything you want it to do in communicating. And, after my superb instruction session, I hope you've got the hang of it! Just to remind you, Barcelona is five hours ahead of us, so don't call me until *at least* after noon local time," lectured the Sterlings' daughter, Avery, as she shepherded her parents into the main concourse at Toronto's Lester B. Pearson International

Airport, two hours ahead of their departure time. It was 6:30 p.m. "I really hope you have a wonderful and memorable cruise. Wish I could go with you."

"Thanks, sweetheart," replied Jack Sterling. "We both are really looking forward to this trip. Good of you to drive us here. Don't hang around on our account. You'll have to move the car if you do, or risk getting a ticket."

With hugs and kisses, Avery departed, taking one look back at her parents before exiting through the revolving door. She wasn't 100% sure they would remember how to use skype, but surely there would be younger passengers or crew members to help.

After getting their boarding passes and checking in their bags, Jack and Jean walked to a nearby Starbucks in the Concourse and ordered two lattes with biscotti biscuits. Jack reviewed their flight itinerary, noticing they were flying on a Boeing 747, an older plane but very reliable and comfortable. He was ready for this trip—overdue in fact—and very much hoped for an interesting and, especially, a relaxing time. He'd booked their seats online weeks ago, reserving spots with the most leg room.

At 8:25 p.m., the announcer called their flight. "Air Canada flight 287 for Montreal, London and Barcelona is now boarding. Please have your boarding pass and passport ready for presentation at the gate. Rows 35 through 45 will be boarding first."

Sitting in the holding area, Jack said, "Here we go, sweetheart." They stood and joined the line, each with a maximum-allowable-size carry-on bag. Jack had checked the airline's website for the dimensions and had measured their suitcases and carry-ons twice. Best to be extra certain. It was the start of a four-thousand-mile trip.

WEDNESDAY, MAY 14
Barcelona, Spain

"There it is, Jean, Barcelona spread out below us," said Jack, sitting in the window seat, leaning back so his wife could get a glimpse through the big oval window. "You know, it has the same size population as Toronto, about five million. I didn't realize that. Notice the green hills on the north side," he continued, as the plane circled to land, "and the mid-blue of the Mediterranean Sea to the south. Feeling a bit excited, honey?"

"Sure am," she replied. "Looking forward to spending our two days in the city. Lots to see and do."

The plane made a smooth landing, on time, at El Prat airport, eleven miles west of the city center, at 2:35 p.m. Plenty of daylight left. Customs clearance was a breeze and they did not have to wait long at the baggage carousel. Their clean-looking taxi and polite driver, with little proficiency in English and rather distracted style of driving, deposited them at three-thirty, after a forty-minute ride, at their hotel, the Catalunya. It overlooked a beautiful square—more like a circle—of the same name, close to the city center. Barcelona sprawled under a clear-blue sky with a comfortable temperature of 25 degrees celsius—77 Fahrenheit. With a slight onshore breeze, the air was just right for strolling around the square and the old downtown area a bit later, after arranging a day tour for tomorrow.

At five, they left the hotel for a walk around the large plaça, window shopping, looking at the locals and how they were dressed, and trying to get the feel of being in España. It was warm, the sun still high in the sky, altogether pleasant. They went for dinner at the Restaurant Visual, at the top of the Hotel Torres, with a magnificent 360-degree view of the city. A good start to their vacation, they agreed.

◆   ◇   ◆

In spite of all her travels, Rebecca 'Mrs. G.' Gessner had never been to this city. Their residence for the next two nights was the 19th century Hotel Palace, close to Catalunya Square, one of the most elegant buildings in Barcelona. The high, cupola-style ceiling in the lobby was supported by four huge, flecked-marble columns, standing on a white marble floor. The painting on the ceiling was somewhat reminiscent of Michelangelo's Sistine Chapel at the Vatican in Rome. On their way up to their large, two-bedroom, beautifully-appointed suite, renting at $1,500 a night, Hannah picked up a handful of tourist brochures from the lobby rack. One of them showed a photograph of a stately theatre built in 1847, the *Gran Teatre del Liceu* in the city center. Giuseppe Verdi's opera *Aida* was currently playing, with none other than the talented soprano Cecilia Bartoli. Hannah knew that Mrs. G. dearly loved opera. After securing her enthusiastic consent, Hannah commissioned the concierge to get two of the best seats for tomorrow evening's performance. "The absolutely best seats possible, you understand," she told him, making it clear that price was not an issue.

In their suite at 12:30 p.m., Hannah reviewed the rest of the tourist brochures and read out recommendations of what they should visit for their one full-day in the city. When their suitcases were delivered by the porter, they unpacked a few change of clothes items. Mrs. G. placed her jewelry, in its soft grey leather bag, in the lock box in the armoire, using her date of birth as the combination. She then set her watch to the local time—Greenwich Mean Time +1—and the two women retired to their separate bedrooms to nap.

When they got up two hours later, they ordered a light meal:

cheese and avocado on whole-wheat crackers, a bowl of mixed fruit and a pot of camomile tea, served in the room. Reviewing the sight-seeing brochures again, they booked the seven-hour, *Grand Tour of Barcelona* by limousine, for the next day, covering most of the tourist sights. As it was mid-afternoon, with lots of sunny daylight left, both women wore large sun hats as they ventured out onto the busy streets.

Rebecca Gessner noticed it first: how many of the women, young and older, wore some form of black. Jeans or narrow slacks seemed to be the order of dress in daylight, with tops or shawls, and bright silk scarves also worn as a headdress, and shiny black, patent leather high-heel shoes. Pointing this out to Hannah, she wondered if it was the current fashion, or somewhat of a tradition.

Hannah said she thought it was fashion. She'd been glancing at a magazine in the hotel lobby called *Mademoiselle* which showed black to be the prominent color in Europe. Looking at what they were wearing, Mrs. G. said, "I guess we're out of fashion," and her younger companion agreed. They'd simply have to do something to rectify that.

"Elegant women like you and I, Hannah, *must* be in style. Let's do some shopping."

Catalunya Plaça had a high-end fashion mall with Bally, Diane Furstenberg, Louis Vuitton, Tom Ford, Internationale and others, all open until 9 p.m. The square was connected to La Rambla, a long, tree-lined boulevard, very popular for shopping and restaurants. Their day was made.

THURSDAY, MAY 15
Barcelona

At 7:30 a.m., the Sterlings were having breakfast in the *Cuarto de la sol*—the courtyard of the sun—restaurant, part of which extended outside the rear of the hotel onto the pool deck. Sitting under large, green and white striped sun umbrellas—provided by the Canada Dry corporation—with the warmth of the morning sun on their backs, they were enjoying *huevos revueltos*—scrambled eggs with thick, pan-fried potatoes—with a baguette and large cups of strong, black Spanish coffee. While a bit tired from the long flight, they were also feeling good about being in Spain and upbeat about seeing some of the sights of the city.

On their arrival in Barcelona, they had set their watches to the local time, reviewed their proposed itinerary for the next day's activities, and made tentative plans. There was much to see and they couldn't do it all in the day and a half before their ship sailed. "But enough for us to get the feel of the place," they had agreed. Today would be their big day. At 8:30, they would join an eight-hour sightseeing trip around the city, with a quick stop for lunch. Back to the hotel at around four-thirty for a brief rest, followed by a quick dinner, then dress up and off by taxi to the *Gran Teatre Nacional de Catalunya*, in the Plaça de les Arts.

Their bus arrived on time, almost full. One more stop and they'd begin the tour.

"*Buenos dias, mi amigos,*" their female guide said, after the last tourists boarded. "My name is Consuela Barrientos, 'Connie' for short, and our magnificent driver is called Pedro Mazon. Both of us were born and raised in this beautiful city, so, unlike other non-Spanish, European guides, we can give you the benefit of our personal experience showing, and telling you about, this wonderful city of Barcelona. I hope you have your tour pamphlet which contains a *'plan'* as we call maps, so that you can follow our course of direction. Before we start, let me briefly take a few minutes to describe the tour. Our fabulous, eight-hour journey will include one hour for lunch at the *Casa Tejada*, which has excellent food, specializing in Spanish and Portugese dishes. I always like to suggest to our guests that they try one of their soups and specialty sandwiches, for two reasons. They are delicious and, of course, we get quick service. You will also note, as we drive around the city, that little bits of modernization have crept in—like Ronald McDonalds, A&W, Starbucks, Subway, etcetera—a must, it seems, in today's society. All to make our visitors feel at home! I know, I know," said Connie, "most of you could do without them. It seems the world is becoming homogenized, which I don't care for. Anyway, to continue....

"This city was originally a Roman village—not surprising as we are part of what we call the 'Mediterranean complex', since most of the area was under Roman rule at some time or other. Our city was founded in the third century BC and was called *B-A-R-C-I-N-O*," she spelled out, "by a man named Hamilcar Barca. If you don't know this, he was the father of Hannibal the Great of ancient times, on a par with Caesar and Alexander the Great.

"We will explore three main parts of the city...."

A few minutes of description later, Connie said, "Okay, Pedro, start driving! So, sit back and relax and I hope you will enjoy your wonderful time with us today."

"Sounds like a good tour, Jeannie," whispered Jack. "I wonder if the guide's training includes schooling in the use of hyperbole. I have a feeling it's going to be heaped on us. Not complaining though."

Jean squeezed his hand and nodded.

◆   ◇   ◆

By 3 o'clock, they had almost completed the tour and covered much of the greater city area. The last part took them to Guell Park, designed by Spanish architect Antoni Gaudí, one hundred years ago. "Place took fourteen years to build," noted Jack. "I can see why."

"You know, I could easily spend a week here. Barcelona is a beautiful city, with so much to see and so much heritage. How many pictures did we take, do you reckon?"

"I can check that on the new camera. It keeps score of photos taken. I'll check later but at a guess, I'd say well over a hundred. I don't think I have to ask you what your favorite site was. Certainly the iconic Sagrada Família Cathedral would be at the top of my list—it's hard to find the right words to adequately describe its magnificence—and, it's not finished yet! Mr. Gaudí was a very inspired individual. We need to return sometime and stay longer, like you say."

At 5:30 this evening, their second and last in Barcelona, Jack and Jean Sterling sat in the hotel's elegant dining room, with high, narrow, Gothic-style windows framed with red velvet drapes, pulled back in the center by tasseled gold ropes. Their table was covered in a white, starched tablecloth and set formerly with fine Oneida silver flatware and English Waterford crystal stemware. On the mezzanine, a male pianist was playing classical music from a black Steinway Grand. They had decided to 'live it up' by doing dinner and the show in formal attire. One advantage of being on a cruise vacation, was bringing one's fanciest clothes. Jack wore a tux with a cream-colored cummerbund and matching bow tie.

"Lookin' good!" Jean assessed with a wink. Her formal gown was of silver lamé with a deep neckline, worn with a long string of cultured pearls. As they ate dinner and drank champagne, poured into the appropriate fluted glasses, they wondered what delights the evening and tomorrow could bring to top this grand setting.

When they arrived at the theater, it looked a bit like a modern, scaled-down version of the Parthenon in Athens, with massive faux stone, fluted Doric columns on the outside of the glassed-in building. The big marquee announced, in bold letters, *BOCELLI IN CONCERT.* Jack had reserved their seats before they left home, and had splurged on the best location. Jean and he looked forward to hearing Andrea Bocelli sing his signature song, *Time to Say Goodbye.*

During the performance, Jack turned his head slowly, left and right, and looked at all the people in his row of seats, most eyes fixed on the singer. Judging from the jewelry on display around women's necks and dangling from their ears, some of the audience were very, very wealthy. He thought how fortunate he was to be sitting in this wonderful theater, listening to the beautiful words and music, next to his elegant companion.

Jack also realized that he'd been methodically memorizing faces and other identifying features, a habit from his patrol days that he'd found useful throughout his career. He had looked for clues about income level, deviousness, and anything out of the ordinary. He was also wondering about security to prevent thefts of all that conspicuous wealth. 'How long in retirement before I stop being a detective?' he wondered.

Jean loved opera whereas her husband could 'take it or leave it.' But on this occasion, he thought it prudent that he should 'take it.' Besides, he liked Bocelli. It was a beautiful opera house and he did appreciate magnificent buildings.

When they got back to the hotel, Jean said, "Thank you for arranging that. I'm so glad we were able to see and hear him so clearly."

After a light snack, they retired to bed, tired but very satisfied with the day. Tomorrow, they would *'set sail.'*

◆   ◇   ◆

Earlier the same day, Barcelona
MV *Seascape*'s new captain, John William Stuart, was born in

Edinburgh, Scotland at the Western General Hospital on March 28, 1958, the second son of Alexander and Mary. At age 12, he was admitted to Bourne Grammar School, founded in 1638. By virtue of that, he was relatively assured of preparing his brain for admission to a university at age 18. His brother, Gordon, six years older, a Bourne 'old boy' at 18, was about to enter the University of Edinburgh to read classics and archaeology.

In John's infancy, his parents had taken him and his brother on a day trip by boat from Edinburgh toward the North Sea along the estuary of the Firth of Forth, passing under the huge bridge of the same name, built in 1890. The sights, sounds, smells and the feel of sea spray against John's young face, as he was held in his father's arms at the bow of the small, bouncing tour boat, was something that lingered with him and eventually became instrumental in his choice of a profession —sailor.

His apprenticeship to things naval started when he joined the Sea Cadet Corps at age eleven, in seven years rising to the rank of chief petty officer. In 1976, at age eighteen, upon graduating from Bourne and leaving the Cadet Corps, John did not please his father with his decision to skip university and instead enroll at the Britannia Royal Naval College in Dartmouth for their two-year Naval Officer Training Plan. When he graduated, it was off to sea, as an acting sub-lieutenant in the Royal Navy, as an apprentice deck officer aboard a destroyer escort, wearing one thin gold bar on his shoulder board.

In 1982, he was on his way to the Falkland Islands, in the far South Atlantic Ocean, as part of Britain's Naval Task Force, sent to reclaim the islands from the dastardly Argentinians. His ship took part in shelling one of the enemy ships, stopping it in the water, out of action. He also witnessed an Exocet missile strike HMS *Sheffield* in May of that year, causing a great loss of life and its eventual sinking. He'd stayed in the RN, rising to the rank of commander and captain of his own destroyer escort.

John Stuart retired in 2004 with 28 years navy time and a row of medals on his chest. He was a big man, tall, weighed 220 pounds ('near 16 stone'), dark wavy hair, ruddy complexion, ice-blue eyes, with a 'command presence'. At the time, the British government was reducing the size of its armed forces and that meant 'marking time' in his present rank for an unknown length of time. He was not prepared to do that. Especially with the lure of commanding grander vessels.

He continued his life at sea by first acquiring a position as a staff captain—a second-in-command position—with World Cruise Lines. The company had actively recruited him, and implied in the interview that he could eventually become a ship's master. WCL operated out of the Port of Miami, the corporate home of many other cruise lines. Because of that, John had to deal with U.S. Immigration and Naturalization Services for a work permit and understand the rules governing part-time residence in the U.S.A. He was a U.K. citizen, working for a Florida-based, Delaware-incorporated company whose ships were registered in the British Virgin Islands. Ships are registered under flags of convenience to reduce operating costs or to avoid regulations of the owner's country.

Four years after joining WCL, he'd been promoted to full captain, sporting four gold bars on his epaulettes. The salary level was much higher than his former Royal Navy income and in addition, he was drawing his modest military pension. As with all cruise ship companies' crew positions, he was not a standard employee but instead worked under a contract which required him to be at sea for certain specified periods of time. In his case, this meant four-month stretches, with two months off in between. During his down time, he kept busy writing his memoirs of service in the Royal Navy, especially as it related to the Falklands campaign aboard HMS *Viceroy*. He had tentatively titled them *The Bloody Falklands*—a play on words of sorts since typically 'damned' was inserted before 'Falklands'—to describe that deadly little war.

He did not much care for the short cruises, stopping in a port somewhere almost every day, though he did enjoyed his command position. He much preferred voyages that included successive days on the *'open blue.'* Nowadays, many cruise lines allowed wives and children of officers to be aboard ship for limited periods of time. Captain Stuart's wife, Susan, a renowned fiction writer of sea stories, would accompany him on this upcoming trip. Today, they had arrived one day early, from London where they now lived, taking a direct British Airways flight to Barcelona, arriving in the afternoon. He was to take command of the MV *Seascape*, a two-year-old ship, with a capacity population of 1650 passengers and crew, due to dock there at 8 a.m. on the sixteenth—his first time as master of this particular vessel. It was a much larger ship, in every aspect, than his Royal Navy destroyer escort. His spacious cabin and office was directly behind the bridge.

Now in Barcelona, he and Susan checked into the old but nicely appointed Hotel Catalonia Ramblas, where WCL always booked its senior incoming crew members, roughly two kilometres from the Port facility. He and Susan had dinner in the hotel, followed by a beer in the lounge and watching a cricket test match between England and India, in Bombay. Back in their room, he re-read his orders for the next cruise, while Sue watched a bit of telly. They turned in for an early night. Tomorrow was to be a special day for him.

♦ ◇ ♦

Michael O'Hara Donnelly—the 'O'Hara' from his paternal grandfather—was born in Dublin, living on the east side, in the Ringsend District, just off East Wall Road. As a kid, he often rode his bike, alone, to look at the freighters docked along Tolka Quay Road. His young mind imagined becoming the captain of one of those massive ships one day. He'd stand by the open gate to the dockyard and look, thinking how much he'd love to go aboard one of these ships. One day, after checking for a guard, he decided to venture into the dock area. Locking his bike to the chain link fence, he strolled over to a rusty iron bollard and sat down on its wide mushroom top, twenty feet from the edge of the dock, the nearest ship less than fifty yards away. He took his customary apple out of his pocket and began to munch away. He didn't hear the man come up behind him.

"Hello, son. Admiring the ships, are you?"

Young Mike was startled. He dropped his half-eaten apple and stood up.

The big man wore a dark blue windbreaker jacket with the word 'SECURITY' in large white letters across his chest. "Sorry about the apple," he said kindly. "Didn't mean to startle you. I see you at the fence sometimes. You like ships? My name is Andy—what's yours?"

After Mike told him, Andy said, "Okay, Michael, look, people are not allowed in here by themselves. You need an escort. Would you like to go aboard for a look sometime?"

Mike said, "Oh, yes, sir!"

"Alright. Here's what you need to do. When you get home, ask your mum or dad for permission to do that. Tell them my name. I'll write it down for you. Next time, if I'm here, I'll get you on a ship."

And he did, sealing young Mike's career path.

Right after leaving Glenmore School at 17, Mike found a job as an apprentice deck hand with the Cosco Shipping Line, on a bulk carrier. That was a dirty, dusty job and he managed, after two years, to transfer to a container ship, traveling the world in a somewhat cleaner environment. One ship's captain talked to him about getting his merchant seaman ticket. Mike enrolled in a two-year-long, Coast Guard approved, largely self-study program and had his ticket endorsed with the EDH level—Efficient Deck Hand.

Young Mr. Donnelly eventually found himself on the deck of a Maersk vessel, another container ship, and, over a period of four years, got his AB ticket—Able Seaman—requiring him to perform watch keeping duties. He was a bright and energetic individual and in his off-duty hours, he often spent time on the bridge, observing the ship's operation. The first officer talked to him about upgrading his credentials toward becoming a ship's officer—in this case, a deck officer. In three years, capably passing his tests, Mike was promoted to a third officer position, requiring him to wear a white uniform and a peaked officer's cap.

At age 29, he married an Irish lass named Moira, with whom they now have two sons: Sean Michael, aged 6, and Ryan Niall, age 4, the latter who, as his wife said, "is the spittin' image of you, Moikle Donnelly," in her broad Kilkenny accent.

They lived in Dublin, though Mike was off at sea for sometimes months at a time. Over the years, he had learned to distillate his thick Irish brogue into more understandable English, as he'd had to converse with people from around the world at sea and in the many ports he visited.

Mike had faithfully read the monthly *Merchant Marine Newsletter* and in one copy noticed an ad for security officer positions with Holland America Line out of Seattle. He'd had a latent interest in police work but did not want to become a police officer as such, at least not in Ireland. Security positions were considered to be part of the deck crew aboard cruise ships. After reading the short job description, he discussed the matter with Moria for her thoughts and, as a result, applied for a position. The *terms & conditions of employment* seemed quite good, the main difference was that he would have to 'contract out' his work, rather than be an employee. It also meant reducing his status to the apprentice level for a year, and taking a two-week course in law enforcement procedures as applied to cruise ships, but he'd had enough of the container ship business and looked forward to a complete change of shipboard life.

Now, seven years later, after transferring to World Cruise Lines, he had risen to the rank of chief security officer. His position was a responsible one, in charge of 12 men and women. They were employed largely in passenger safety which included a multitude of jobs: embarking and disembarking people, patrolling the decks, and tactfully checking unruly behavior by any drunken guests. While they did wear a white uniform, short sleeve shirt and long pants, they were not blatantly identifiable as security. Security personnel wore a discreet small brass nameplate on the left chest, with the word *SECURITY*. The company did not want an obvious and ominous police-like presence aboard ship.

Luckily, there was little serious crime committed, and life aboard, at sea, was mostly well-ordered and peaceful. After doing this job for seven years though, it had become a bit mundane, repetitious, and Mike felt he needed to upgrade his knowledge and skills again, to get to a higher position with more challenge.

Moira was proud of him, dressed in his pressed whites, two and a half gold bars on his shoulders and a white naval cap with some 'scrambled egg' on the peak. Jokingly he told her he could still make captain before he retired.

Sincerely she replied, "I know you can. Go for it."

Company policy allowed a crew member's family along once every two years. Mike, of course, had to pay the cost of the family's transportation to the port of departure, except for himself as a member of the crew. Moira had accompanied him on one cruise, through the Caribbean, two years ago with the two young lads. The four of them had enjoyed the trip immensely, especially his wife and sons.

While Mike was busy in his daily responsibilities and activities, he badly missed the company of his family when they weren't with him. He was happy then when his wife found employment as a clerk in a prestigious insurance firm in downtown Dublin. She felt better now that she was *'contributing to the family coffers'* and not stuck at home. She had also found a reliable sitter/tutor for the 3-hour period in the afternoons on school days until she got home.

For the most part, the two were contented people. He was due to go to sea again for a three-month term, and that usually meant flying to Miami, where the company and its ships were based, to start. This time, however, he had a short Dublin to Barcelona flight on Ryan Air to join the MV *Seascape* and begin the rotation.

Mike was looking forward to being at sea again, meeting his new captain tomorrow and, hopefully, another uneventful trip. He called Moira in the evening to let her know he'd arrived okay.

Captain John Stuart and his wife Susan arrived by taxi at 'D' jetty of Barcelona's Seaport Terminal Dock at 0745 hours, and watched the World Cruise Lines Motor Vessel *Seascape* approach, beginning its docking procedures for an 0800 arrival. The ship had transited overnight from Monte Carlo. It was to start a new, 17-day cruise later today. He'd arrived early so as to spend more time with the ship's captain he was relieving, especially as it was his first time as master of this vessel. The turnaround time from docking to departure was exactly ten hours. While the *Seascape* was very similar in design and handling to other WCL ships he had 'driven', each vessel had its own idiosyncrasies that needed to be reviewed and handled.

There were a great deal of administrative duties to do, going over the ship's log, its recent performance at sea, items requiring to be fixed, provisioning, bunkering (fuel), reviewing weather charts, discussing any crew problems, health issues if any, meeting his 'change of command' bridge crew, the staff captain, chief engineer, the hotel manager and chief of security. Lastly, he'd check the passenger count for this sailing, before getting underway at 1800 hours.

Guests would begin to arrive for boarding starting at mid-morning and the ship would have to be spotless. Passenger lifeboat drill had to be held just before departure.

When the ship's dockside gangway was lowered, Captain Stuart and Susan walked over with their travel bags and were met and saluted, by the outgoing chief security officer. The ship looked massive from this perspective. A baggage porter took their luggage and together they boarded the ship after being issued boarding passes, called *CruiseCards*, like everyone else, and going directly to the bridge. The two masters exchanged salutes. Captain Samuels greeted Susan cordially and instructed an attendant to escort her to the captain's living quarters.

Today was a complete rotation of the officer ranks. As each relieving officer arrived, he or she was required to review their area of responsibility with their outgoing counterpart.

By 0845, all the bridge officers and other department heads, of both crews, were assembled on the bridge. Captain Samuels thanked his departing crew members for their loyalty and good work and wished them a safe trip home and a relaxing time off, dismissing his people. Captain Stuart introduced himself to his key people and gave a brief description of his seagoing experience, saying that he looked forward to working with them. These officers were then dismissed by the staff captain to continue their discussions with the officers they were relieving. This procedure usually took an hour or two, before the departing crew left the ship.

The two captains retreated to the master's quarters to continue the takeover proceedings. Security Officer Mike Donnelly learned from his opposite that the cruise had been relatively uneventful, with a few minor and not unusual problems, like the odd drunk to escort to his cabin, or loudness in the passageways after midnight, a couple asked to leave the forward deck pool for nude swimming at one a.m., and two people who missed the boat, arriving dockside from a late, private, day excursion after the *Seascape* had sailed.

"Hope your trip goes well, Mike," he said, shook hands and walked down the gangway. "One hopes the guests will behave and not be at each other's throats!"

◆   ◇   ◆

Same day, Hotel Palace, Barcelona

Hannah Goldman got dressed in her blue and white striped running shirt and blue shorts, and left the hotel at six-thirty a.m., for her usual run, this time, doing five laps around Cataluyna Square. She tried to find time five days a week to do this, regardless of where she was. The sun was just peeking over the old buildings and it was still cool. She felt energized and really looked forward to joining the ship today, planning they would board at eleven.

She helped Mrs. Gessner finish her packing and had the porter take their bags to the hotel luggage room. At breakfast, they talked about their two days in the city and how enjoyable it had all been; shopping, their tour of the sights, and the theatre. "It's a good thing we dressed up for the opera last night. I didn't realize it was a black tie affair here," said Hannah.

"Yes. Bartoli was superb, wasn't she?" replied Mrs G. "I love that opera. It's a shame we don't have more time here. Nowhere near enough time to see the whole place. We've *got* to come back again."

Their white limo picked them up at 10:15 and dropped them off twenty minutes later, at the entrance to the cruise ship wharf. Their ship looked enormous from the forty-five degree angle looking down the jetty. Presenting their credentials, they were allowed through the security gate by Port Authority police, to join the people in the line-up on the quayside, waiting to board, looking like a long line of ants beside the ship.

◆   ◇   ◆

The Sterlings were about halfway down the dock, having arrived around 10:30. They were waiting in the open but it was a nice, sunny and comfortably warm morning. They entered a long, white marquee to register, deposit their baggage, and get their all-important boarding card. It had to be guarded like a credit card as it was used on a daily basis aboard ship: entry to their room, purchasing items, reserving for shore trips, boarding and leaving the ship. By the time they got to the registration desk, the line had stretched right up to the entrance gate and they were glad they'd arrived when they did.

While they waited, they spoke with the couple in front of them and behind, from Vancouver and Miami respectively. Jean was more chatty than Jack and he let her do most of the talking. He was more reticent largely because of his background. He'd found that when people learned he was a police officer, they tended to want to talk about nothing else, or sometimes complained about what they thought was an unwarranted ticket they'd received at some time. He'd had enough of that and tried to converse in generalities. The two women behind, a mother and daughter, he thought, were well spoken and not overly inquisitive.

♦ ◇ ♦

The three largest suites on the ship were at the aft end, on decks 5, 6, and 7. When Rebecca Gessner and Hannah Goldman stepped through the double doors of *Crown Suite 7001*, they were surprised and delighted at its size and elegance.

"Now don't you wish you were staying with me?" asked Mrs G. rhetorically.

Hannah had discussed her cruise sleeping arrangements with her mother, who accepted that her daughter would feel a bit uncomfortable sharing the suite. The mother offered to pay for her stateroom, so as not to impose the cost on Hannah's employer. When the issue of sharing accommodation was raised, Hannah politely declined the offer, saying that she felt that Mrs G. needed her 'space', and that her mother would cover the cost of her cabin.

Mrs. Gessner was adamant about paying for Hannah's cruise, so in order to keep the cost down, Hannah booked a very basic stateroom for herself, one deck below. While she liked the woman, she did not want to be 'in her face', as she told her mother. And besides, Hannah didn't intend to be in her stateroom except to sleep—"There will be too much to do on board. Maybe I might strike up a romance with a rich young European aristocrat."

After helping to unpack and hang up her employer's clothes, Hannah asked to be excused so that she could go and do the same, agreeing to meet back in the suite in an hour. They had heard the announcement about life boat drill, and would need to be back in the suite, Hannah bringing her life jacket with her, well before 4:20 o'clock when they would go to their stations on deck 3. Before then was ample time for a late lunch and a stroll around some of the ship.

◆ ◇ ◆

In the Security Operations office, Mike Donnelly had ensured that passenger lists had been distributed to the officers in charge of each lifeboat station. Embarkation and debarkation were by far the two busiest events for crew members, especially his security section. Part of his team were new to him and there was little time go get acquainted, but most of them knew their respective jobs thoroughly, having been through this many times before.

All twelve members were on duty. There were always a few passenger stragglers who held up the proceeding, but today, things went quite smoothly, to Mike's relief. All but two had checked in. He disliked having his crew chase down errant passengers but the personal attention was a hallmark of WCL. An assistant searched through bookings and began phoning the missing passengers' hotel.

He had much to do before departure at 1800, including checking with the various heads of departments to confirm that they were ready to sail, at least from the security point of view.

◆ ◇ ◆

The Sterlings checked into their stateroom, on the seventh deck, midships on the starboard side, at 11:30 a.m. It was high up in the ship, nicely appointed, and complete with a balcony. A super king-size bed, with a beautiful dark rosewood headboard and matching night tables, took up much of the floor space not occupied by a dressing table with vanity lights, and a large flat screen TV sitting in the middle of the armoire. The floor was covered with a pale grey rug, and the bathroom fixtures finished in brown-streaked, white, faux marble, and complemented with fluffy white towels and similar dressing gowns.

On the bed were a number of documents. A *'Welcome Aboard'* message from the captain, a list of the ship's various amenities, dining room menus, information about the MV *Seascape*, activities slated for tomorrow and information about upcoming land tours. Included in the literature were two notices, the first of which Jack found interesting:

WORLD CRUISE LINES – MV SEASCAPE

SHIP SECURITY

*We are required to provide information to our guests about ship **safety and security**. This is our highest priority. Medical emergencies, unruly behavior, or acts of a criminal nature are taken seriously, and are the responsibility of our ship's Security Section.*

If anything like this comes to your attention, please report the matter or incident immediately to any member of the ship's company, or by the emergency telephone number posted on the inside door of your stateroom.

Any criminal activity is reported to law enforcement agencies at the next Port of Call, so they can investigate, and if necessary, and take appropriate action. As well, criminal incidents affecting American citizens are reported to the Federal Bureau of Investigations (FBI), the United States Coast Guard (USCG) and Homeland Security (DHS).

Please respect other persons' rights and privacy. Note that there is a Medical Center, staffed by two doctors and three nurses.

The second notice dealt with hygiene, which he was pleased to see:

PASSENGER CONDUCT

Recent health events aboard a few cruise ships (including outbreaks of Norovirus) have led us to ask passengers to kindly observe a few 'rules' to avoid such occurrences.

Shaking hands – many cultures engage in this form of greeting. Unfortunately, it does tend to spread viruses and we ask you to respectfully avoid this practice. You will notice many hand cleaner stations on every deck.

Coughing and sneezing – with regard to this, we suggest the use of handkerchiefs or paper tissues. If neither of these are readily available, please cough/sneeze into the inside of your bent elbow – to stop cough spray from spreading.

We thank you for your consideration.

"We should remember to comply with this, Jean," said Jack, giving the sheet to her. "The not-shaking-hands bit might take a day or two getting used to."

"Yes, sounds like a good idea though."

They left the unpacking to go for a walk on the upper deck, and some lunch. Jean said, "You know we're both going to have to watch what we eat. Remember the last cruise and the weight we put on? We need a daily routine of exercise. Having said that, let's get something to eat! This sea air is making me starving and I could eat a horse."

At the deli counter, they made their own salads, got one bowl of oxtail soup and one of minestrone, two Montreal smoked meat on rye sandwiches with hot mustard and two black, sugared coffees.

"Delicious," they both pronounced.

While he was munching on his sandwich, Jack looked at the *Personal Log Book* he had brought with him from the cabin. It contained some stats about the ship, a list of their ports of call, distances between them and on to Miami. After leaving La Palma, they had eight days at sea – 'Good time to be able to relax,' he mused. Reading about the ship, he was impressed and wondered about doing a ship tour if that was possible.

Included in the information sheets left on every cabin bed cover, was a description of the *Seascape*, called the *Cruise Log*. The ship was launched two years ago, and was one of World Cruise Lines' smaller vessels, weighing 66 thousand tons, carrying 1156 passengers and over 450 crew members. For the mechanically minded, it had four diesel generators and one gas turbine engine, and was propelled by two Azipod propulsion units that can rotate 360 degrees for extreme maneuverability, and very quick and short distance stopping capability—within one nautical mile at full speed—comparable to a car leaving skid marks. It seemed a hungry ship for fuel consumption, measured in gallons per mile, not the other way around, guzzling a combined fuel load of 65,000 gallons per day, with a maximum speed of 23 knots. It was able to produce its own potable water and used up about 155,000 gallons daily. Its culinary capabilities were massive and extremely varied, offering plain to exotic meals with fruits and vegetables from around the world, as well as of course, wines and liquor. The bakery department worked two shifts every day.

Finishing their lunch, they took a walk around the upper deck, Jack noticing the flags flying from the upper masthead: the flag of Spain on one side and a pennant with the World Cruise Lines logo—a blue WCL on white background, within an elongated diamond shape, with a dark blue border. There was a flag too, at the stern. He did not know the nationality of it, except that it had the Union Jack in one corner and from that, knew that it was a former British colony, probably where the ship was registered. British Virgin Islands, wasn't it?

They took the wide, dark blue carpeted stairway down to the next deck below the promenade. There were three different lounges, one with a small stage big enough for a jazz band—very glitzy. Further along was a well-appointed library and coffee bar with big tan leather armchairs and a huge metallic bronze globe of the world. Off to one side was a closed-in smoking room. No TV present.

♦   ◊   ♦

In the security office, all of the section were engaged during the day in some aspect of quick disembarkation of departing passengers, and the slower embarkation of a new group. Admitting over eleven hundred passengers in the space of a few hours demanded a strict set of procedures and the production of a lot of paperwork, including passenger lists for each deck corresponding with their lifeboat stations. Nowadays, random checks of baggage were conducted and all of it went through scanners, on the orders of the U.S. Homeland Security agency. Overseeing all this activity kept Mike Donnelly on the run, from 0800 until midnight. He had a new captain to report to and a largely new bridge crew. While his position carried with it some fair degree of responsibility and respect, he had to be circumspect in how he interacted with the senior crew. Having the captain 'on his side' would make life a bit easier. He'd be meeting Captain Stuart in his quarters, with others, at 1400 hours, 30 minutes before the lifeboat practice would start.

♦   ◊   ♦

At 3:45 p.m. (1545 hours), the ship's loudspeaker system announced, "Ladies and gentlemen, my name is Steve Marks and I am pleased to be your cruise director for the next sixteen wonderful days you have aboard this World Cruise Lines vessel, the *Seascape*. All guests have now arrived.

"As you may not be aware, International Maritime Law requires that there will be a mandatory life boat drill, on deck three, for *ALL* passengers," he emphasized, "commencing at exactly 4:30 p.m., or to use nautical time, 1630 hours. I would like all persons to be in their cabins by 1615, thirty minutes from now, to await instructions. As you've probably already noticed, your life jackets are stored on the top shelf of your closet. When you leave, please take one with you as you will be instructed how to wear them. As well, an announcement will be made concerning your respective life boat station, which is also posted on the inside door of your cabin. Once again, it is important that ALL passengers go to their stations. When you return, I will have further announcements for you about tonight's activities. Thank you for your attention."

◆ ◇ ◆

Back in their cabin at 4 o'clock, the Sterlings got their life jackets out, ready to leave. Jack checked inside the door and noted they were assigned to Station D12 on deck seven. When they left just before 4:30, there was a steady stream of people walking down the inner stairwell—no one could use the elevators—but it was orderly, with directions being given by crew members. At their station, it quickly became crowded and people had to squeeze together. No one could leave until two things had been done: name checks and cabin numbers responded to, and the life jacket demonstration and donning of them, for practice.

After the drill, over at 5 p.m., they shuffled their way back up to their deck, threw their jackets on the bed and finished unpacking. A little later, they headed to the promenade deck, for fresh air, a drink and then over to the starboard rail, to wait for the undocking procedures to begin. From this height, they could see quite a bit of the city of Barcelona, and the top spires of *La Sagrada Família*. Next, they planned to take a quick walk around to check out the facilities available on the upper decks before going to dinner at seven.

At 5:30, Jack, leaning on the guardrail, noticed a man in white navy type uniform arriving and boarding the ship. "I believe the pilot's just arrived, Jean. Appears we'll be leaving on time. That's his flag on the mast, the red and white square one. When he leaves the ship, it will be lowered." He pointed out the other flags and told Jean about them.

"How'd you know that stuff, Jack?"

"It's in the information package left on the bed. Do you want to wait and watch the proceedings for leaving the port, or go for a stroll first?"

They elected to do some more walking.

◆   ◇   ◆

After the lifeboat drills were concluded, the Officer of the Watch was advised that the pilot from the Barcelona Port Pilotage Service was coming aboard ship and when he reached the bridge, his presence was announced: *"Pilot's on Bridge."* This was duly recorded in the ship's log with his name, the time, date and location of the ship. Signal flag 'H' was hoisted up the mast. The pilot would review his departure procedures with the captain, after which the undocking orders are given to the helmsman and the ship begins its movement away from the dock.

On the dock, at exactly 1759 hours, two dockworkers would be given the command, "Let go forward, let go aft." The fore and aft rope hawsers would be let go by unhooking from the bollards—with the words "all gone forward, all gone aft"—and pulled into the ship's bow and stern. On the pilot's order, the ship's engines were slightly advanced to start moving the vessel away from the confines of the dock, at a very slow speed, gradually turning into the direction of travel needed to navigate out of port. At the same time, 1800 hours, three deep and loud blasts from the ship's horn announced it was underway from the Port of Barcelona. Many of the passengers were crowding the upper deck rails to look at this maneuver and to wave goodbye to friends.

Jack Sterling said to Jean, back from their short look around the deck, "I wonder how people felt a hundred or two hundred years ago when they were leaving their home country to immigrate to a foreign land, knowing they would never return. Must have been very nostalgic, a mixture of sadness and anticipation."

"Yes, I remember my grandfather telling me as a little girl much the same thing when he left the U.K. for Canada. I think we were lucky to have been born when we were, Jack, that we can travel like this, knowing we live in a great country and can return to our home, don't you?"

It was a beautiful May evening. After finishing dinner at seven-thirty, they stood looking over the side of the ship at the south coast of Spain, and the evening sky, a collage of pastel colors worthy of a John Constable canvas. The Sterlings felt very contented, and the ship's crew and guests settled into their first night at sea.

Captain John Stuart was on the bridge and had been, much of the morning.

His intention was two-fold: to get acquainted with the deck department crew, especially the staff captain, Henk (Hank) Bernhard, his second-in-command, and to see how they were operating the ship. While ships today, like passenger aircraft, are largely self-driven by instruments, they still very much require the presence of human beings on deck, to make sure that certain rules and procedures—international and company—are followed and that safety lookouts are alert even though the ship is equipped with 'over-the-horizon' radar vision. So far, the master was pleased with what he saw and heard, though he also knew that his presence may have had some influence over that. He noted that the gauge showing the current quantity of fuel and the amount of consumption, indicated a slightly high rate of fuel use per nautical mile, the DPG or distance per gallon. Consumption had been rated during the ship's trials at sixty feet per gallon at the usual speed of 18 knots. Pointing this out to his second, he wondered about the cause. It was not much perhaps, but over distance, would add up to higher fuel use and cost. "Why do you think this is, Hank?" he asked.

"Yes, I notice that too. It's not much, a little over one hundred gallons per hour. It could be due to hull resistance, tide conditions, and we've had a constant westerly headwind—or that the engineers had slightly under-calculated fuel usage during trials. I've already made note in the bridge log book, sir."

"Hmmn. Keep an eye on it. What's our ETA passing the Rock tonight?'

"0300 hours, sir."

"Too bad, so late. Passengers won't get to see Gibraltar lit up at night. Who is joining us dockside at Cadiz?"

"Holland America—the *Noordam*. 0830 time of arrival, in from Lauderdale."

"Gonna be a busy place. Pilot transfer time set for 0730?"

"Yes, sir."

"Very well. I'm going for a goodwill stroll, then to an early lunch in the staff section. All yours, Mister Bernhard."

"Aye, aye, Sir. *Captain's off the Bridge.*"

♦ ◊ ♦

It was their first evening at sea. The Sterlings had spent much of the first full day exploring the various decks, getting to know their way around and, as much as anything, to get to know their way back to the stateroom.

For most passengers, it generally takes a day or so to learn that. During their walkabout, they noticed crew members constantly spraying and cleaning handrails, public area door handles, vacuuming stairwells and the carpeted passageways. A very obvious display of cleanliness.

The main restaurant, on deck ten, called the *Sea Buffet*, was quite big and well laid out, with tables for two, up to ten people. Large windows gave a great view outside. The food, offered at all three meals of the day, was enormous in choice and well presented. "Nice change from having to cook at home," Jean remarked. The two swimming pools and whirl pools were not too busy and they enjoyed some time in them, afterwards lying on chaise lounges in the sun, on the top deck.

There were no kids and it was peaceful. "Not like our first cruise," Jean reminded Jack. For that one, they had picked the American Thanksgiving long weekend to start a Caribbean cruise. There were 900-plus children on the ship.

Before a planned dinner at seven in the grand dining room, both decided they needed a walk around the upper deck exercise track. Most people seemed to use it for running during the day only. The sun was still relatively high with about two hours left before disappearing over the horizon, under a cloudless sky. It remained warm, with a slight breeze from the west flowing over the bow. Heading west, the south coast of Spain was about thirty miles off the starboard, or right side. In the distance, to the northwest, they could see a ridge of snow-capped mountains. Jean expressed surprise at this, not familiar the geography of the area.

"Let me check my trusty little smart phone," said Jack. "Surely there is an app for that." He fished the instrument out of his trouser pocket, tapping on 'Google Earth' and entered 'spain' in the blank space. Earth quickly spun around to Spain and he zeroed in on their present location. "See, Jean, that's what we're looking at—the Sierra Nevada range, about 35 or 40 miles inland. The highest peak reaches 3,500 meters or 11,000 feet. Who knew the country was this mountainous this far south?"

"I note that we pass by the Rock of Gibraltar," she said. "Do you think we'll see it tonight, Jack?"

"Let me think. I figure we have about 150 miles to go to reach it, or about 8 hours from now at our present speed—say 20 mph—that would be around 3:00 a.m. Unless you want to wait up or get up for a look, I don't think you'd actually see the rock itself, just the lights on it. Too bad. I'd like to see that historic place. Lot of ancient history attached to that piece of granite. I looked it up yesterday while you were having a snooze. There is evidence that it was occupied thousands of years ago by our ancestors, Neanderthal Man. Today, it's owned by Great Britain."

They had stopped and were leaning against the polished mahogany wood rail, other passengers also admiring the view. Both of them were in a reflective mood, saying little and feeling very contented.

"Isn't this wonderful," Jean said, putting her arm around Jack's waist, snuggling in close.

Before he could reply, something made the ex-policeman turn around and he found himself confronted by a tall man in white ship's officer's uniform.

"Good evening, sir, ma'am. You have a very keen ear," he said to Jack. "I didn't mean to disturb you. My shoes have non-slip rubber soles and are very quiet. I'm Mike Donnelly, ship security officer. Welcome aboard."

Facing the man, Jack said, "Good evening. This is my wife Jean and I'm Jack Sterling." He began to extend his hand, but remembering the health notice, withdrew it quickly.

"I trust you folks are enjoying your cruise so far?"

"So far, so good. Nice ship."

"Yes, it's the newest in our fleet, launched two years ago. If you are interested in its statistics, our front office has pamphlets for our guests, about its size and operation. You might find it interesting. Have you cruised before?"

"Oh yes, this is our third time at sea."

"Where've you been?"

"One trip in the Eastern Caribbean with Carnival, and the other through the Panama Canal to Cartagena, back to Miami, with Holland America, about four years ago."

"Did work get in the way since then?"

"I suppose you could say that," replied Jack.

"May I ask what you do, sir?"

"Well, at the moment, nothing. I just retired, and Jean and I decided to take this trip. We like the idea of being on the open sea for a few days, with no stops."

"Yes, that's why this cruise was designed that way, to give a feeling of being at sea. It's also called *blue water sailing*. What did you retire from?"

"The Metropolitan Toronto Police Force, after 35 years of service."

"Interesting. You must have some stories to tell."

"Oh, yes. Enough to fill a book. Or two."

"Is there anything I can tell you or help you with?"

"Yes, there is one thing. Is it possible to do a tour of the ship?'

"Yes. That will be done after we leave La Palma and head out into the Atlantic. You'll get a news bulletin about it. Just to let you know, there is a charge, I'm afraid. Well, nice talking to you. I'll probably see you around. Enjoy the rest of your evening."

"Thanks, Mr. Donnelly. By the way, what do the weather charts look like for the remainder of our time at sea?"

"Happy to say, generally calm and warm. That's why we do these voyages in May. Good night, sir, ma'am," he said, tipping his cap.

After a grand dinner and a stroll through the *Marine Arcade*, where the shops were located, and past the noisy and crowded casino at one end, they walked up the three flights of stairs to their stateroom, ready for a good night's rest. As was their habit, both of them read before turning off the light.

Jean said, "There's some interesting things in this book, hon."

"Uh hmm," he mumbled.

"Some *really* interesting stuff…."

Her words got through to him. She was reading *Fifty Shades of Grey*. Looking at her, he said, "Oh, right, sweetheart," placed a book-mark in his novel and set it aside.

◆ ◇ ◆

Both women had had a very pleasant day, settling down into ship's routine, nosing around the various decks—"Checking stuff out," as Rebecca Gessner had said. They strolled through the shopping area on deck 3, noting the high-end name brands of some of the merchandise.

They parted company at two, Mrs G. going for a rest and Hannah to the promenade deck to take in some sun and read.

At 7 o'clock, Hannah met Mrs. Gessner on the forward promenade. They chatted in the warm evening sun for a few minutes and Mrs. G. could tell that Hannah was a little anxious to leave. She was going to a pop concert in the *Aries Theater*, which had a small stage, for small music productions—very cosy.

Rebecca Gessner had a dinner reservation for 7:30 p.m. alone, but at a table with other guests. The dining room was quite full this evening and two other couples joined her at the six-person table. From the conversation, she could tell they knew each other and felt a bit uncomfortable. The woman sitting next to her realized this after a few minutes had passed and no one had joined her, and she started to include her in the conversation. Rebecca felt obligated to say something about her 'status' and told them she was a widow. She heard the usual regrets but was used to that sentiment now.

After dinner was finished, her new acquaintances asked if she would like to join them in the popular *Polo Lounge*. A new, rising young American classical jazz singer named Tello Williams was performing.

Rebecca said, "Tello. What an unusual name. I haven't heard that before. Where's she from?"

"She's from a small town in southern Idaho, Pocatello. Her mother, Tanya Williams, was an opera singer and sang at the Met. Tello's voice is somewhat similar to that of Diana Krall, the noted Canadian jazz singer, if you know of her."

Rebecca nodded. "I do."

"The difference is that Tello does not play the piano while she performs. She's appeared in concert at the Lincoln Center, so, we're lucky to have her on this trip. Please join us. If you like jazz, you'll love her voice."

She did and was glad she went.

SUNDAY, MAY 18
Cadiz and Seville, Spain

Jack Sterling got up at six o'clock, quietly. After dressing in casual tan slacks and matching shirt and doing his ablutions, he left, going up to the track deck for a twenty-minute fast walk. The rising sun glowed in a clear sky, portending another warm day. The ship was due to dock at the Port of Cadiz at eight this morning. Along this stretch of coastline, the shore looked empty.

When he got back to his stateroom, Jean was up and ready to go for breakfast, taking along her large shoulder bag.

They had decided to take the tour to Seville today, and tomorrow, hang out around the small town of Cadiz, doing a walking tour. During breakfast, they noted the dark blue hull and white superstructure of a Holland America ship tied up ahead of them. Dozens of coaches were lined up on the dock, which was teeming with people.

When they stepped ashore, they found their bus number among about ten similar coaches. Showing their tickets, they climbed aboard. The bus was full by the time it pulled away, heading in a general northerly direction for the one-and-a-half-hour ride to the old, sprawling city. Sitting across from them was the woman and her young companion—her daughter?—they had talked to on the dock in Barcelona, saying, "Hello, nice to see you again."

Their female tour guide, Esmeralda—"Essie, for short," she said—gave the passengers the customary greeting, "*Buenos dias, mi amigos, bienvenido a Cadiz*." Continuing, she said, "Make yourselves comfortable.

We have about 115 kilometers or 70 miles to travel to ancient Seville, along the A4 main highway, about one and a half hours from here. When we do get into the city and start our tour, Manuel, our experienced driver, will hand each one of you a hearing device and explain how to wear it. We find this is a good system, to ensure that no one misses what I have to say while we are walking. This way, you don't have to crowd around me so much and we can avoid the problem of stragglers....

..."I will say a few words about this part of Spain, called Andalusia. Except for some factories in Seville, most of this area is agricultural. The land is relatively flat and has a typical Mediterranean climate, which allows for the mass growing of fruit, such as oranges, olives, grapes, as well as sugarcane and even tobacco and cotton. You will also see—you can't miss them—hundreds of huge hothouses producing mostly berries and vegetables: strawberries, raspberries, tomatoes, lettuce, etcetera. Much of these crops are shipped to other parts of Europe and is a big business for the local economy. As you can guess too, all of my country is a tourist destination. We are proud of that. Spain is also a very romantic place, so to the women, watch out for the *hombres*, the men. It is their habit to kiss the back of your hand, so don't be offended, please...."

A few of the female passengers smiled at the prospect, while others had already nodded off.

At the first stop, the guide cautioned, "Another thing to mention: personal security. Unfortunately, even Seville has its pickpockets, so please be aware of your surroundings. Carry shoulder bags across your shoulders, holding on to the strap. With the men, don't put your wallets in your back pocket, and keep some money separate. Side pockets are better and may I recommend you buy clothes with velcro fasteners for extra safety. It is not necessary to bring your passports on these day trips; one thing less to lose. Alright, go and enjoy your walk."

The first stop was the magnificent Cathedral of Seville where Christopher Columbus is buried. The third largest church in the world, its construction started in 1401 and finished 127 years later. Inside it was fantastically ornate, with gold being the predominant finish. The huge, stained glass curved windows were outstanding for the color, variety and complexity of the glassware, giving a warm glow to the interior.

Late in the afternoon, leaving the tour bus dockside, the Sterlings said goodbye to Essie, thanked her for a most informative and interesting tour, and slipped a ten dollar bill into her hand and another for Manuel the driver.

Jean said to her husband, "You know, all of this stuff is a bit overwhelming, isn't it? I mean, what is it with Spain and its huge, old and brand new architecture, pushing the limits it seems on style and scale. Seems to me, Jack, we have a lot to learn about our world. Can we live long enough to see much of it?"

"You're right. We have a lot of catching up to do."

The pair from Miami climbed the gangway right behind them, chatting easily about the sights and sensations experienced.

♦ ◇ ♦

After dinner at seven in the main dining room, buffet style, the Sterlings took a walk around the deck as it was getting dark. Inside again, they stopped to listen to Renée Richelieu, a French-Canadian pianist from Montreal, play a mix of lively jazz, R&B and New Age music on the Steinway in the Lounge. They danced on the small round floor with a few others, while the silver ball above their head filled the ceiling with moving, sparkling, diamond light. Taking his wife's left hand and kissing the back, Jack said, *"Buenas tardes, señora. Qué hermosa."*

Jean whispered in his ear, "I know the first part means 'good evening'—but what does *'qué hermosa'* mean?"

"It means, 'You are beautiful.' I saw it on a billboard in Seville today, advertising lingerie, which reminded me of you. I hope you are not offended, *señora*?"

Jean smiled and replied, "I am not in the least offended, *señor*," giving him a long, warm kiss on his neck, and dancing close.

♦ ◊ ♦

Mrs. Gessner and Hannah had enjoyed their day in Seville. The weather and temperature had been pleasant. In the city center, its ancientness was very evident, from thousand-years-old stone buildings, cobblestone streets, church spires everywhere. Yet they could not help notice, in eye-jarring comparison, more recent structures with names like McDonalds, Subway, KFC and Burger King, all garishly prominent and out of place.

"No escape from them wherever we go," Rebecca Gessner lamented as they walked up the gangway. "Well, at least now we can enjoy a good meal aboard ship in relatively decent surroundings. You know, if cruise ships ever bring these fast food places on board, it's the last cruise I take."

It was seven o'clock and they were getting hungry. "Where would you like to go, Hannah?"

"Why don't we try the *Captain's Lounge*? It has table service, in a nice room with ocean views and live piano music. The way we are docked, if we get a table on the right hand—starboard—side of the ship, we should get a nice view of the sunset out over the Atlantic. Would you like to go to the casino after?"

Rebecca Gessner nodded in the affirmative.

As they departed the gangway onto the dock, both women read the following notice on the dockside bulletin board:

SHIP DEPARTURE TODAY at 6 P.M. – 1800 HRS

Please remember that you must be back on board
no later than 5:30 P.M.

Thank you. Have a wonderful day.

The smell of the Atlantic Ocean was quite strong, pushed ashore by a steady westerly breeze. It was 8 a.m., another cloudless day and their last day in sunny Spain.

Over breakfast, Rebecca Gessner and Hannah had read brochures about the place. They were going to experience Cadiz, the oldest inhabited city and port in Spain and the longest inhabited town in southwestern Europe, going back to the days of the Phoenicians, over three thousand years ago. "No wonder," said Mrs. G., "given its location and a natural, protected harbor."

"Well, let's get walking, Hannah. I'm anxious to see the place."

They strolled along the outer edge of the peninsular, most of the way next to the ocean, breathing in its slightly pungent aroma. As they walked along and into the town, they found many of the streets were very narrow and some of them still cobblestoned, with no sidewalks.

Houses and other buildings dated back centuries. Much of the city was made up of a number of small plazas where most of the shops and restaurants were. As they walked, they noticed the first public place they came to, near the end of the peninsular, was the Museum of Cadiz. The two women spent a fascinating two hours there, looking at artifacts going back several millennia. Each exhibit represented the different eras of the life of this ancient city.

By 12:30, they were hungry. Hannah spotted a fairly new restaurant at the end of the dock area called Balandro's. It was clean, with white linen tablecloths and silver place settings. Looking at the menu, Mrs. Gessner spotted a dish called *Tortillitas de Camarones*—shrimp pancake. "Hmm, this sounds good," and she ordered it with a side salad and local bread and butter. Hannah was persuaded to do the same, but preceded it with a bowl of *pescado de sopa*—fish soup.

After a first bite, Mrs G. exclaimed, "Oh my God, Hannah, this is delicious!" When Hannah's was served, she immediately agreed, "We've got to get the recipe for this. Maybe we can have Maria make it when we get home."

Calling the waiter, she asked to speak to the chef who obligingly wrote it out for her, indicating the cooking time should be about 5 minutes each side, or until golden brown.

"Thank you so much. Would you please sign your name?"

"Jes, I will be 'appy to," he said, writing on a menu:

Gozar! Alejandro Casaolo, Master Chef, Balandro's, Cadiz.

"I think I could spend a few days here, it's so relaxing," said Mrs. G. gaily. "Another place to add to the list, to visit before I die."

♦   ◊   ♦

Aboard ship, the security section was dealing with a complaint of the loss, or possible theft, of a bracelet consisting of three strands of freshwater cultured pearls. A female passenger said she had removed it in one of the public restrooms on deck 7 to wash her hands. She got talking to a cleaner and walked out without them. Returning a few minutes later, she could not find them, and the cleaner had left. She reported the loss in person to the purser's office. They were valued at one thousand dollars. She was visibly upset, saying the pearls were a wedding anniversary gift from her husband this year. She'd rather not replace them.

Mike Donnelly was advised and sent one of his female officers to check the washroom, going through the trash bin, checking the stalls and floor. In her check, she noted that the trash can had been emptied. She checked the purser's office to see if the bracelet had been turned in, but response was negative. She went looking for the cleaner but could not find her on that deck. Next, she called Mike by cell and reported her findings.

Mike mulled over the matter in his head: 'There's one of three possibilities; the cleaner still has them and is going to turn them in at the end of her shift, or she's not going to report her find, or a passenger entered the washroom after the cleaner had left, saw them and took them—or, maybe a fourth possibility, that the passenger has not returned them in yet. It's only been a matter of about thirty minutes. Let's deal immediately with the first two possibilities…' Calling her supervisor, he asked her to find the cleaner and report back.

Three minutes later, the cleaner called. "Mr. Donnelly, it's Sophie Lindemann, cleaning staff, deck seven. My phone battery has run down. Before you ask, yes, I have the pearls with me. While I was cleaning, there was a passenger there. She left. I went to wipe off the counter again and noticed paper towels left and on picking them up, saw the pearl strands underneath. I went out to look for her but she was not around. As I was almost finished my shift, I decided to wait to take them to the purser's office. Am I in trouble, sir?"

Technically she was, because the rules clearly stated a found item should be turned in right away, but Mike sensed an honest intention.

"Just to remind you, Sophie, the policy is to take any found item to the purser's office *immediately*. Would you do that now, please, and I will call the passenger. I expect she will be relieved and thankful you found them. I'll tell your supervisor that you are not in any trouble with security. Thanks."

Naturally the passenger was extremely grateful. Another satisfied customer, and more importantly, an honest crew member. Made Mike feel good. 'With no other major complaints, it's shaping up to be a good trip,' he thought. 'I just hope we don't have to leave anybody behind when we leave the Canaries.' The ship did, two years ago, on its maiden voyage. Two people missed the boat in Arrecife, in spite of waiting an extra fifteen minutes for them. They had to take a small inter-island flight to the western end of the islands, La Palma, the next morning, to catch up. 'Good thing it didn't happen in La Palma,' he thought or they'd have had to fly back to Miami. Turns out they had been drinking in a local taverna and forgot the time.

♦   ◊   ♦

It was 8 p.m. and the ship, after two hours at sea from Cadiz, was traveling south-southwest at a speed of 19 knots, heading for the island of Lanzarote, the easternmost island in the Canary Group, due to arrive the day after tomorrow at 8 in the morning. Jack and Jean Sterling were standing near the bow, gazing into the distance. It was a clear evening with a bit of a breeze and good visibility, with the sun still above the horizon. They had spent the day relaxing, but had gone ashore for a walk into town and have lunch. On their way back to the ship, she said to Jack, "You know, honey, I've enjoyed our days in Spain. I like the country and the people. We'll have to come back."

In the near distance, off the starboard bow, in line astern, they could see three ships inbound to the Mediterranean. The first two were commercial—a freighter and container ship—and the third, a cruise ship, too far away to see which cruise line it was. On the port side was another container ship, heading west into the Atlantic. It appeared to be a bit closer. An interesting situation became apparent to Jack. The *Seascape* had to cut between these four ships to head south. Jack pointed this out to his wife, wondering if there was enough space for them to get through. "I thought I detected a slowing down of the outbound ship on our left, which I think means he's going to allow us to continue our course. Also, I haven't noticed a change of pitch with our engines, so we're continuing at the same speed."

"I wonder if there is a law about ship movements at sea?" asked Jean.

"Well, I should think so, otherwise there'd be chaos. There must be nautical conventions going back hundreds, if not thousands, of years. I would think their rules would allow giving the right-of-way to other ships as a courtesy. It all probably comes down to a matter of judgement, based on nearness to each other, weather and sea conditions and maybe even ship size. Undoubtedly some conversation goes on too, waving flags in the early days, and using radios now. That's an interesting question, sweetheart. Let me google it." He did and the information more or less confirmed his thoughts, except that, generally, he found that the ship on the left usually yielded position. It also depended upon location. Commercial shipping has to stay within *sea lanes*, which can vary in width apart, from 12 miles to very narrow channels close to shore.

"In our case," Jack said, "I'm guessing our ship is probably a bit closer to crossing the space between these ships. In any event, we're not slowing down. Hope that helps, honey?"

"Yes, thanks. Now, looking to our left, that's starboard, right?"

"Actually, it's the port side. Let me see, how can I help explain. The forward end of the ship, or bow, determines left and right sides. Here's a simple way of remembering which is port and which is starboard," Jack said. "The word *port* has four letters, the same as *left*. *Starboard* has more than four, as does the word *right*."

"Well, that's easy to remember. Okay, am I right in saying that the

land we see in the distance, on the *port side* of the ship," she emphasized, "is part of Morocco?"

"Yes, you are. You're getting good at your geography, Mrs. Sterling.
Want to go to dinner now?"

♦   ◊   ♦

Tonight the casino was packed and very noisy, with the slot machines
creating an almost deafening babble of noise from the many different
tunes they played, topped with the clanging of shrill bells announcing
the next winner, accompanied, of course, with intermittent human
screaming. 'Thank God, they do not allow smoking,' thought Jean
Sterling as she gamely played on, pressing the *play* button and losing
again, the twenty dollars she had started with dwindling now toward
the last dollar—four, 25-cent plays. Her shoulders were beginning to
ache and she was happy to finish. 'I'll go find Jack and see how he's
doing.'

She rose from her well-padded seat, only to have it occupied immediately by a very plump young woman, anxious to plug in her cash
card and begin playing, certain that Jean's string of loses would help
her own odds

When Jean found Jack, she asked, "How you doing? Better than
I did, I hope!"

"Jeez, that didn't take you long, sweetheart. Need some more
cash? I'm about even."

"No. I'll watch you play for a bit."

Jack liked the twenty-five cent poker machines. He felt that at
least a player had a little bit of control over his destiny, by having to
make decisions about which cards to get rid of before he pressed
the *select* button and got his new card. Not like those stupid machines—*one-armed bandits* most people called them, with good reason—where the barrels just rolled around without a win most of the
time it seemed. At one point, he was up forty-two dollars from the

twenty he had deposited. He'd thought about going to a gaming table to play actual poker, but they all seemed crowded this evening. The minimum bet was five dollars a play, and he could easily go through a hundred in no time. 'Better not,' he thought. 'We've got much more time to play aboard this ship. Once we are out to sea past the Canary Islands, I may be looking for something to occupy my time.'

TUESDAY, MAY 19, and
WEDNESDAY, MAY 20
At sea

At midnight, the ship was 110 nautical miles south of Cadiz, on a southwesterly course to the eastern Canaries. This was to be a full day at sea. The travel time from Cadiz would be 37 hours, arriving at 0700 on May 21.

A full day like this at sea early in the cruise tended to allow people to get organized and to attend a host of functions put together by the cruise director. The casino opened from 11 a.m. to midnight. The two swimming pools and hot tubs were fairly crowded and the various eating establishments busy. Deck games were popular. Guests were getting more acquainted with the ship's various decks, locations of dining rooms, cafes, ice cream and pizza stands, bars, the two theaters, purser's office, shopping, the two promenade decks and, not the least important, hunting for toilets. Generally it took a couple of days to accomplish all this.

Captain John Stuart took the opportunity in the morning to meet with his heads of departments, other than bridge and engineering staff. These would include the hotel manager and subordinate supervisors of housekeeping, food & beverage, the cruise director and the senior doctor. Captain Stuart knew it wasn't necessary to remind them, but nonetheless he reinforced in everyone's mind the need for absolute cleanliness aboard ship. With so many people in close contact, a viral outbreak could take hold rapidly—with the potential for sickness and even deaths, not to mention significant impact to WCL's image and profitability. "Our goal is for everyone, passengers and crew, to arrive in Miami alive and healthy," he emphasized.

He liked to hold what he called *informal–formal* gatherings, in his cabin office. Each person gave a brief account of their department's state of affairs, including reference to any problems, needs, suggestions and so on. Mike Donnelly, as chief of security, was always present. All of them knew their jobs well and the captain required little clarification. The heads could tell their new boss was a fair-minded but no-nonsense individual. All felt respect for the man; they knew of his navy background and that they would be allowed to run their departments without undue interference—provided they did their jobs.

Captain Stuart was advised in the late afternoon about two passengers, independent of each other, with a case of diarrhea which could possibly arise from food eaten ashore, or perhaps, a first indication of Norovirus or similar. He asked Dr. William Kent to do a thorough examination of the two people and to kindly ask if they wouldn't mind staying in their staterooms for a full day, just to be sure. Another examination would be done in 24 hours. Medical staff were prepared for this eventuality, and both the cleaning and hotel personnel were asked to maintain the utmost cleanliness. He reminded them that although there hadn't been such an outbreak on any World Cruise Lines ships, he didn't want his watch to be the first.

The rest of his day was occupied with *walking the ship* matters— on the bridge, in the engine room, a walk around a couple of the decks—mainly for two reasons: to be seen and to answer questions, and to eyeball that his *team*, as he liked to call the ship's company, were carrying out their duties. Apart from the niggling little worry in his head about the two sick people, he felt quite confident that things were going well.

◆   ◇   ◆

"Here's the tour sheet for tomorrow for Lanzarotte, sweetheart. Seems like we have three choices: walk around the city center, do a bus tour of the city and other nearby areas, or a tour around the whole island. We dock a 7 a.m. and leave at 5. I'll read the descriptions out to you," said Jack. From the three choices, they selected the walk-about, on their own, with a stop for lunch.

After dinner in the main dining room this evening, they elected to return to their stateroom, talked to Avery via skype, and watched a bit of TV—they turned off CNN after watching a bit about the latest Middle East crisis. Finally they settled on an old re-run of the 1939 movie, *The Third Man*, starring Orson Welles, in grainy black and white. It was quiet in the passageway: no kids running up and down, shrieking and crying. Not a bit like their last trip in the Caribbean.

"And we haven't been interrupted by a phone call about a murder or some other gruesome business," Jean noted happily. "I'm so glad you have retired. Someone else can look after Toronto's crimes now."

WEDNESDAY, MAY 21
Arrecife, Canary Islands

The *Seascape* docked in the capital city, Arrecife on the island of Lanzarote, right on time at seven. No other cruise ships were there. Although it would be leaving at 5 p.m. this evening, not that many people seemed to want to go ashore. Over an early breakfast, the Sterlings read about this island which was almost nine hundred kilometres south of Spain, but still owned by that country, and just 125 kilometers from the coast of northwest Africa.

With a population of about fifty-five thousand, the town only dates back to the 1400s when it was colonized and became a re-provisioning point for the Spanish navy and commercial sailing ships, very active at that time, exploring their way south and west across the Atlantic. A variety of the Spanish language is now spoken but hard to decipher by mainland Spaniards. Apart from tourism, agriculture was the only other major means of livelihood although now there is an increasing number of so-called *'long-stay'* people, mostly more wealthy retirees from eastern Europe, here to escape the brutal winters. They too helped the local economy.

It was typical Canary Islands weather: brilliant sunshine with brisk westerly winds coming in off the Atlantic. Not cold, but enough for people to carry a light jacket. The Sterlings had elected to take a walk through the small town, along with others, to browse the market and have lunch. A coach service was provided for the short distance there.

The promenade, called Avenue La Marina, was very pleasant. Lots of open-air eating places and small shops and stalls.

"Probably more expensive than in town," said Jean as she and Jack breathed in the fresh ocean air. Surprisingly little humidity. At one of the stalls, selling Canary Islands manufactured summer clothing—colorful cotton shirts, shorts, hats, scarves—they met up with the two women who'd been on the Seville tour with them.

Rebecca Gessner smiled graciously. "Hello again, nice to see you."

"Taking a stroll like us, I see," said Jack. "Very pleasant out here. Enjoying the cruise?"

"Very much so, one of the best I've been on. Look, we're going for lunch a bit later. Do you care to join Hannah and me?"

"That would be nice," replied Jean.

They walked together for an hour, along the harbor front and a few of the city center streets. At noon, Mrs. G. spotted the *La Puntilla restaurante*. It seemed clean and had a deck facing the water, the wooden tables covered with big, bright, sun umbrellas. Not crowded.

"What do you think?" she asked.

"Seems quite good," replied Jean. "Let's try it."

The menu said *la comidilla* and underneath the title, in brackets, *Light meal and talk. Enjoy!* They chatted while eating a variety of fish and vegetable soups with fresh baked bread and buns, and patties of salty butter, followed by slices of Spanish flan, all served with heavy-duty coffee in demitasse cups, thick cream and brown sugar provided if required.

They talked about the cruise so far, how enjoyable it had been, and looking forward to some lazy time as Jack put it, crossing the Atlantic.

The chat was lightweight, polite, with no one really getting into personal matters, least of all, Jack. Jean Sterling had been a bit slow in agreeing to have lunch together, knowing how Jack felt about sharing information with strangers, but also feeling that they had to be charitable with people, especially with fellow cruisers. Jack, she knew, could handle himself if the conversation got too personal—especially if asked about his work. And, of course, he was no longer a cop. He could just say 'retired civil servant.'

But Hannah and her employer did not pry and, in fact, Jack thought the two women were very likable and friendly. He enjoyed his lunch with them as the three women talked about their purchases, the weather and coming activities aboard the *Seascape*. Hannah reminded him of Avery with her young person confidence.

They parted after their meal and Jean and Jack continued walking south along the promenade until they came to a golden yellow beach called Playa Reducto (*short beach* in English). Removing their sandals, they walked along it, holding hands, the fine, granular sand comfortably warm beneath their feet, Jean's large brimmed sun hat flapping in the breeze. "This is so peaceful here, Jack."

They sat on the low rock wall and watched seagulls circling over the sparkling ocean and a few small sail boats gliding along. Even though they knew the coast of Morocco and Western Sahara was 'out there', the land was too far away to be seen. Nevertheless Jean was conjuring up scenes in her mind of endless tracts of wavy sand dunes, camel trains and casbahs. "I want to see that before I get too old," she said. "Now that you are retired, we can travel more. Certainly that new job will give you lots of time off if you insist."

"Want to walk back to the ship, or get the coach?" asked Jack.

"Let's walk," Jean said with a laugh. "With all the fine meals on board and on shore, the exercise'll do us good."

◆ ◇ ◆

Back aboard ship by 4 p.m., Hannah found a pamphlet on her bed-cover from the ship's spa, the *OceanSpa Treatment Center*. She read the details describing the aromatherapy. It involved a variety of essential oils like camomile, lavender, sage, rose, rosemary, eucalyptus, and others. Apparently when the oils are applied to the skin and absorbed, and also smelled by the nostrils, all connected to the brain, this triggers the limbic system, which influences the body's nervous systems and hormone levels. The different oils have effect on heart rate, blood pressure and breathing, while the hand massage treatment is very relaxing, enhancing these reactions. 'Interesting. I didn't know that.' Hannah had paid for one previous spa experience in Miami and enjoyed it.

"What do you think about having an aromatherapy treatment, Mrs. G.?" she asked over the ship's phone system. "You've had them before, I suppose?"

"Yes. Sounds great, Hannah. Do we need to make an appointment?"

"I'll make one now and let you know."

Two hours later, after the treatment they sat in the luxurious spa lounge, sipping cold lemonade and feeling thoroughly refreshed, inside and out.

"What strikes your fancy for this evening?" asked Hannah.

"What's our choices?"

"Well, lots actually." She picked up a daily activities sheet from the coffee table. "Okay. There's a musical review in the *Seascape Theatre*. I think it's music from the sixties and seventies era. A jazz quartet in the *Star Lounge*, a five-string group doing classical stuff in the *King Arthur Room*, and, for something really exciting, bingo in the upper cafe at eight, or the cruise director's usual evening quiz game in the *Polo Lounge*. Of course, if you'd like to spend some money, the casino opens after we get out to sea. Need to think about it?"

"Let me sit here and relax for a bit."

"Would you excuse me now, please? I'd like to go and skype Mom and Dad—see how they are. Be back soon."

Later, standing on the deck in the warm sunshine, the two women watched Lanzarote Island disappear behind them. Hannah had just returned from her skype session.

"Everything okay at home?"

Hannah said her parents were both fine, and send their regards.

"That's nice of them. How does a nice dinner in the *Blue Sea* dining room sound, Hannah?"

"Yes, I'd like that."

"Alright, let's meet there at 7:30. Afterwards I think I'll pay a visit to the casino. See if I can get lucky. I take it you want to go to the jazz review?"

♦ ◇ ♦

Captain John Stuart was on the bridge when the ship undocked and left Arrecife Harbor at 1700 hours, no one missing the boat. 'One more stop and I don't have to worry about that,' he thought to himself. So far, he was happy with the ship's on-time schedules, his crew, and so far again, lack of vexing problems. Dr. Kent had confirmed his diagnosis that it was the big 'D' that had upset the two passengers, not the big 'N', which was good to know.

The next stop at Santa Cruz de la Palma on the westernmost island of the Canaries, was only a little more than two hundred nautical miles by cutting through the channel between here and Fuerteventura Island just to the south. It was a 12-hour sail. After tomorrow evening, he'd have nine clear days of sailing to Fort Lauderdale. This should enable him to continue writing his memoirs about the Royal Navy, at which he'd now begun crafting the Falklands War chapter. As far as he knew, no other British naval officer had penned what that experience was like. Besides being cathartic, he felt as though he owed it to the memory of those who lost their lives, in what he considered an unnecessary conflict, and would dedicate his book to them.

He planned to stay on the bridge until they cleared the straight between the two islands. Like many big-ship captains today, he couldn't help but think occasionally of the recent fate of the Italian cruise ship *Costa Concordia* on the Italian coast, and its captain, Francesco Shettino. Best to take extra care sailing near shore.

He took stock of himself for a minute, reflecting about his life as it was now. He had a very responsible command of a large, new ship, with a lot of people to care for, good pay, and respect for his position. At 55, he did not feel his age—rather, not much different from when he was forty or so. He was fit and kept himself that way, and a nice bonus on this cruise, his lovely wife was with him. Really, what more could a man ask for? Life was good. The first officer noted the slight smile on John's face, thought he knew what that meant, but said nothing.

◆ ◇ ◆

In a similar vein, Mike Donnelly, in his office in the security section— having successfully boarded all his 'clients', as he often referred to the passengers, once again—was feeling good about himself. It reflected well on him and helped solidify his position in the WCL's security system. Moira had made a comment to him a long time ago, about assuming command of a ship, and he had dismissed that as wishful thinking on her part; just being nice to him. But she did sow that seed in his mind, inadvertently or on purpose, and that is what he was also reflecting on. Did he want to continue with security work until retirement, good as it was, or try to rise further in the ranks, so to speak, and, who knows, make it to the master's position? He knew that would require a lot of work, study, practice, and not the least, to be given the opportunity to advance by the Company. At this moment, it seemed like an uphill battle that he was not sure he wanted to take on, or indeed, could even achieve.

Thinking back to when he'd first joined World Cruise Lines as a lowly, junior security officer, he had done well for himself, and ought to be satisfied. And he was, but only to a point. 'Human beings, we are never satisfied,' he mused with a smile. His phone rang and broke his line of thought. Tucking it back into his mind, he picked up the handset phone and answered, "Security Section, Mike Donnelly."

"Mister Donnelly, it's Karl Goertz, deck eleven patrol. Was there an announcement after we got underway, about the casino not being open this evening? A passenger just asked, and I did not hear it, although I could have been busy."

"Let me check with Steve Marks. I'll call you back."

The cruise director said that he had called the purser's office as the ship got underway to ask them to announce the casino would be closed. By now, most passengers likely understood about the 12-mile gambling limit, and in the case of this sailing to La Palma, the ship would steam in a direct line, almost all of it inside that limit. Steve too had been busy and had not heard the announcement.

A check with the purser's office revealed that it had not been done.

"For some reason, we were swamped with people at the counter and telephone calls and overlooked that message. Sorry about that. We'll do it right away," said the desk clerk.

Mike asked the clerk to tell people why, that they were sailing within the 12-mile limit of Spanish territory, and that the casino would re-open tomorrow evening.

Mike called Karl back to tell him: "Just goes to show people can't wait to lose their money. They'll have to wait until we clear La Palma. Everything else okay, Karl?"

"Yeah, boss. Not a lot of people on this deck right now. Must be eating."

♦   ◇   ♦

The Sterlings had reserved places at a dinner table for eight, although there had been the option to eat by themselves. The other couples were from Ludwigshafen in Germany, Christchurch in New Zealand, and Austin, Texas, all retired. The German couple spoke fluent English. Quite a mixture of accents though. It seemed to Jack that they were a compatible group in spite of their geographical separation.

For ship's guests, tonight was the first dress-up night. That meant for the men, black tie or business suit and tie, with white shirt if possible, and if men had them, black patent leather shoes. The notice placed in each stateroom included two extra words for the men: *proper grooming*.

Jack said, "What do you think that means, hon? Do they refer to shaving, or to making sure your zipper is pulled up?"

Jean chuckled. "You missed out *clean fingernails*. No, I think it just means *no stubble*. If you shave, shave; if you have a beard, that's okay. I'll check you out before we leave. I would not go out with a scruffy dude."

For the ladies naturally, it meant a formal dress with jewelry. In Jean's case, a pale blue just-on-the-shoulder creation.

"I don't like to be without *some* support" she told Jack, to which he replied, "Well, I can see why, love."

A medium-length pearl necklace and matching earrings finished her appearance, and she carried a pearls-on-silver lamé clutch purse. Though her jewelry was likely not in the same value range as Mrs. G. from Miami Beach, Jean still kept whatever she wasn't wearing in the small combination-lock safe in her cabin.

They were a handsome couple.

Formal dinner was in the *Grande Dining Room*, with a string quartet playing classical stuff. Jean and Jack generally enjoyed this kind of table arrangement. It was interesting to hear where people were from and about their backgrounds. Jack never said he was retired from a police force, but that he was a former bureaucrat, and if pressed, doing statistical work. When he said that, people would respond with a bored *'Oh'*, and quickly moved on.

After dinner, guests made their way to the *Seascape Grande Theatre* at the aft end of the ship for an eight o'clock concert by the ship's orchestra, all professionally trained musicians. The guest maestro, Francesco Scallini from Florence, had been trained in Vienna, and at one time, had conducted the VSO. This evening's repertoire of music included some European classical from the nineteenth century:

Mozart, Bach and Guiseppe Verdi—often referred to as 'Joe Green' by the stand-up comics on TV—and from the twentieth century, works by Verdi and Pucinni. The music from *Aida* was especially well-liked. On a lighter vein, music by George Gershwin was also performed.

After the concert was over at ten, Jean and Jack went up to the top deck for some air, a quick stroll around, taking in the smell of the warm ocean breeze as the ship moved along under the bright light from the third-quarter moon. They finished the evening at the little bistro coffee shop with a mug of hot chocolate, small slices of apple pie and Neapolitan ice cream, which Jack thought quite appropriate to finish off their evening. They'd be up early tomorrow to do a tour of La Palma.

THURSDAY, MAY 22
Santa Cruz de la Palma

The *Seascape* tied up at the only dock, close to the center of town, promptly at 7 o'clock, one of two ships in port, the second being a Spanish Navy destroyer escort. Captain Stuart thanked and said goodbye to the pilot. He was pleased to note the bustle of activity near his ship. That indicated that re-supply materiel—fuel (for the long voyage), water, fresh food—were ready to be taken aboard, starting at 0800, after many of the passengers had departed for tours on the awaiting motor coaches. He liked it when things were organized. Later in the morning, he intended to pay his respects to the captain of the navy ship, something he liked to do in ports whenever time permitted. The Spanish Navy had an especially good reputation for hospitality. After all, they'd been at it for centuries, he thought. Tactfully, he wouldn't mention the defeat of the Spanish Armada in 1588.

Another warm, bright, sunny day. 'Good for my passengers,' most of whom were taking advantage of walking on land for the last time, for a few days.

Satisfied that all seemed to be going well, he left the bridge and returned to his cabin. Susan was having a coffee at the small dining table and reading the latest world news, transmitted to the ship in early morning by head office, printed in the purser's office and distributed in clear plastic boxes in public areas. One item that was omitted was the news of a cruise ship, of another company, having its generators quit in the middle of the Caribbean. That meant no air conditioning, no functioning toilets, cold food and having to be towed back to Miami.

"God, Susan, hope that never happens to me!"

He'd learned about this breakdown from his private line source.

She said, "It'll be nice when we get underway this evening. I'm looking forward to a more relaxing time for you and for me."

"Yeah, would be good. This is the first time you've crossed the Atlantic with me, sweetheart." He didn't tell her about the low pressure system building up about a thousand kilometres to the west, bringing the possibility of a bit of stormy weather. But, with luck, it would veer to the south and pass them by.

♦   ◊   ♦

"Good morning, folks. Steve Marks talking to you again. World Cruise Lines welcomes you to the island of San Miguel de la Palma, the westernmost of the Canary group of islands. That huge chunk of rock that you see on the port side this morning is the remains of a collapsed volcano, called a *caldera*, almost eight thousand feet high as it stands now. That's roughly 2400 metres. It occupies a lot of ground on this small island. It's not been active for some time, and our captain assures me it won't erupt today. Your tour guides will tell you much more. "

It was 7:30 a.m. and most passengers had finished or were having breakfast.

Continuing, Steve announced, "Those of you leaving for shore trips by bus should be prepared to disembark shortly. As usual, go to the theatre with your tickets. This stay here in La Palma is a short one. We will be departing promptly at 5 p.m. If you are taking a walking tour, please keep that time in mind. Also note, this is the last piece of land that you will be walking on for the next 9 days. This evening, we head out into the Atlantic Ocean. I'll talk to you later today. Have fun and take care."

♦ ◇ ♦

The tour bus was almost full: 50 passengers.

"Good morning, everyone. Welcome to my bus and your tour of the island of San Miguel de la Palma. My name is Renata Alvares— 'Rene' for short—and driving us today, we have the best driver in all of the Canaries: Benedito Costas or call him 'Ben.' We shall take a quick drive around town and then head out around the outer ring road, called the Island Road.

"Anyone know why these islands are called the Canaries? No? Good. The early settlers to these islands were thought to be from the Cro-Magnon era, based on skeletal findings, the pre-cursor to Modern Man. In their physical form, they were believed to have had blond or yellowy hair, hence the name *Canarios*, Spanish for the yellow Atlantic canaries. Since none of these people were around more recently, I'd like to know how they know that! But I digress. Obviously, we all speak Spanish, of course, but with our isolated position relative to Spain, we naturally speak with a different accent. Mainland people have a hard time understanding us, so we try to speak more formally with them. They tend to give us that 'long-lost cousin' look when they reply.

"This archipelago consists of seven islands, spread out over 270 miles from east to west, with, it may surprise you to know, a combined population today of a little over two million, with Las Palmas, here, the largest city. The mean average daily hours of sunshine is ten, and temperature is seventy Fahrenheit…."

♦ ◇ ♦

In the security office aboard ship, the large wall clock read 10:30 and most of Mike's day shift staff were enjoying their coffee break in the staff cafeteria. Things had gone well with the debarking passengers on their day trips, in two different departure times. An automatic passenger count indicated that almost all had gone ashore, as Mike Donnelly expected they would. He had instructed his officers to re-mind passengers of the *Seascape*'s departure time today, to reinforce the sign at the bottom of the gangway.

The ship's company appreciated the absence of passengers, as the ship was quiet for a change, and there were less demands on their ser-vices. They wouldn't get another such break until Miami. When he'd finished his routine paper work, Mike took the opportunity to call Moira, who was on the same time zone, Greenwich Mean Time, also referred to as the Western European Time Zone. She was in her office at work and although she said it was okay to talk for a while, he didn't like to do that. "Just checking up on you, Mrs. Donnelly."

"I suppose you'll be wantin' to hear me say *I love you*, Mr. Donnelly. Well, 'tis true. I do and I'm missin' your presence here. Yes, the boys are fine. Sean got an 'A' on his math test, so he did. I'll tell them you called when I get home. Bring something home for the lads, will you?"

After he hung up, for a few moments he felt lonely. 'This sailor'ing business is hard on a man at times,' he thought. 'Not the best fit with fathering and being a husband…'

◆ ◇ ◆

Everyone was back aboard ship by 4:15 p.m. Clearly *no one* wanted to miss the boat… a bit of a relief for the captain and the chief of secu-rity. If a poll had been taken of these passengers asking two questions: 'Have you ever crossed an ocean before?' and 'What do you think about that?'—most would have replied 'no' to the first and 'I look forward to the experience' to the second, with, maybe, the proviso, 'Hoping we don't hit rough seas.'

At exactly two minutes to five, the gangway was pulled back into the ship's hull and the huge steel door closed. At five o'clock, the ship's horn sounded and the signal 'let go fore and aft' given from the bridge. This was done smartly by the shore crew. Imperceptibly at first, the huge vessel started inching its way out, parallel from the dock.

The railing along the upper deck's starboard side was crowded with people, and many others were out on their cabin verandahs, all wanting to get a look at their departure from the island and the last piece of land for a while, as the ship glided out past the jetty and did a slow turn to port into deep water. The pilot left the ship after twenty minutes out, climbing down into a small launch that whisked him back to port to await the next incoming ship.

Seascape headed north to clear the top end of the island, before turning west into the Atlantic. Shortly after they were underway, the ship gave a distinct shudder. People on deck began looking at each other, one person asking if that was an earthquake they had felt. After all, the Caldera de Taburiente loomed large in the near distance.

Hannah Goldman and Rebecca Gessner were sitting on Mrs. G.'s expansive balcony, watching La Palma gradually fade off into the distance.

"Well, Hannah, I very much enjoyed today. Our tour guide was a very personable woman, with a good sense of humor and very informative. Although she did tend to use a lot of flowery language in her descriptions. Part of a tour guide's stock-in-trade maybe. Apart from Barcelona and Cadiz, I have enjoyed being here the most. I think I could easily stay for a week or more at that little town we stopped at for lunch—what was its name again?"

"Los Ariadne, I believe," replied Hannah.

"Yes. I really enjoyed our walk on the volcanic beach in our bare feet. The black sand felt very comfortable and the breeze quite bearable. The problem with these shore tours is that they're so darn brief and don't give enough time to take in all that you should see and hear. They try to cram in too much… But not to complain. I'm glad we got off the ship to do that. Do you mind if I sit here alone for a while? I need to do some thinking. Meet you for dinner at seven, okay?"

Hannah knew she wanted to think about her husband and re-member him, and respectfully left Mrs. G. to her thoughts.

♦ ◇ ♦

Tonight, few were on deck, except for the die-hard fitness buffs, some running around the track, and others doing brisk walks. The wind had picked up and it was too cool to sit around or go into the pools.

Activity below decks this evening consisted of several choices. An hour of bingo in the buffet dining room which could seat 300 people comfortably. Cards were one dollar each or five for four dollars. In the three small entertainment lounges, one could take in the string quartet for classical stuff, or a male jazz singer behind a piano, or a female singer accompanied by piano, trumpet and clarinet, doing current popular songs.

The shopping mall on deck four was crowded, including the *Olde English Inn* pub, boasting top British beer, such as John Smith's, various English stouts, India Pale Ale and something called Black Sheep Ale—from Yorkshire—very popular. Plus Guinness, of course. The center of the evening's activities though, was the *Casino*: jammed with people, with some waiting patiently behind a sitting player for the person to leave. It had opened promptly after the ship had been at sea for two hours.

Jack and Jean Sterling, after a buffet dinner, decided to 'walk the ship' and eventually wound up at the dastardly gambling den, as she called it.

Jack felt like playing, but one look at his wife's face suggested it might be better not to, not tonight. Both of them had done a fair amount of walking today on a tour, and, without a word necessary between them, took the elevator to their deck to turn in for the night. As they walked down the passageway to their stateroom, they passed a cabin door with a sign on it that said *Egg Hunting*. After passing by, Jean said,"What does that mean?"

Jack said, "I'll tell you when we get into bed."

It took another second or two before Jean said, "Oh, I get it."

◆   ◇   ◆

In his Navy commander days, John Stuart had been schooled in *walking the ship,'* an ancient British Navy tradition. This evening, he was on the bridge to begin his usual evening-at-sea ritual. It was 2300 hours. The officer of the watch signaled him over.

"Just to let you know, sir, we have a low pressure system ahead of us, approximately one thousand kilometres distant, bearing east-northeast. Intensity is 990 millibars, wind velocity 40 knots. With our present speed of 18.3 knots, we can expect, if it continues this direction, that the leading edge will meet us in approximately 18 hours—1700 hours tomorrow."

"Thanks, Mister Moresby. Noted. Let me know of changes, please."

Weather updates, via satellite, from U.S. National Weather Service, were constant. The situation would only become worrisome if the LPS increased in intensity and speed, and maintained its current direction. At this latitude, twenty-eight degrees north, it was not common for tropical systems to be quite this far north, and it may well swing off to the south. 'I certainly hope so,' John said to himself.

Crossing the Atlantic was never a predictable exercise in navigation.

The ship, and its human cargo, were slowly beginning to settle into 'life at sea' routine.

Hannah Goldman decided to be lazy and treat herself to breakfast in her cabin. When it arrived—fresh-squeezed orange juice, medium boiled egg, two slices of whole wheat toast, marmalade and a carafe of coffee—she settled down at the white plastic table and chair on her verandah, with the daily newsletter delivered with the meal, and her laptop. 'Really,' she mused, 'do I really want another job? This sure beats going to an office!'

She had called Mrs. G. who was doing the same thing. They agreed to meet at noon on the eleventh deck for a stroll. The sun was well up in the eastern sky and she could feel its warmth. She removed her bathrobe to absorb the rays on her bare arms and shoulders. From her south-facing position on the port side of the ship, she could see a low line of clouds in the far distance, just above the horizon. 'Hmm, hope that's not bad weather we're heading for.'

Hannah didn't care for being on a ship that moved around a lot beneath her. In the information sheet left in her cabin, she'd read that this vessel had stabilizers that were supposed to prevent excessive rolling. Checking the term out on *google*, she found that under the waterline were a set of fins, gyroscopically controlled, to counter the kind of movement caused by high wave activity and winds. They were supposed to lessen the effects of seasickness. She hoped so. No telling what kind of weather lay ahead. She decided she would not point that out to Mrs. Gessner when she met her for a late lunch. Best not to worry about what Fate might bring.

♦ ◊ ♦

At 7 p.m., a uniformed maid knocked on the double doors to *Crown Suite 7001* and called out, "Housekeeping." She waited fifteen seconds and did that again. A few more seconds elapsed and the door was opened three inches, showing an older woman's face.

The eyes regarded her for two or three seconds before the woman opened one of the doors and said, "I'm sorry, I was at the far end of the suite and didn't hear you knock at first," letting in the young woman. "You're here to do my suite for me, I suppose. Is—what's her name—Teresa, off tonight?" she asked.

"She's sick and I'm filling in for her, ma'am," the maid replied. "My name is Vessie," she added, touching her name tag that read *Vesna G.*

Her duty was to do any tidying up, wash dishes, empty several waste baskets, remove and replace soiled towels, replace toilet paper rolls, turn down the bed covers, leave two small cubes of Cadbury's chocolates on the pillows and, finally, make an animal out of the fresh towels and face cloths and place it on the bed cover. She decided on a tortoise and finished it by placing two black dots for eyes at the end of its short towel neck. All of this took her just over fifteen minutes.

While engaged in these activities, she noted the occupant was getting ready to go out. Her evening dress was laid out at the bottom of the huge bed and beside it, her jewelry. Vessie couldn't believe her eyes. The diamond necklace, with a large ruby pendant, was at least twenty inches long. Next to it was a soft, grey cloth jewelry bag with the Tiffany Company logo and name embossed on the side. No doubt there were more treasures in the bag.

Mrs. Gessner saw the maid eyeing the jewelry and removed the necklace and bag to the bathroom where she was applying her makeup.

'My God!' the young woman thought. 'What could that be worth? Well, she must have *lots* of money—this suite must cost an arm and a leg. Probably more than I make in a year.' For the rest of the evening, she could think of nothing else. 'That necklace is simply to *die for.*'

♦   ◊   ♦

After a lazy day, enjoying being at sea, no land in sight, no screaming kids, the Sterlings watched a glowing red sunset while they enjoyed a buffet dinner. The afternoon weather had been somewhat stormy, but nothing unsettling. They went for a promenade walk and then up to the *Lido* to watch an evening movie on the big screen, just as it got dark. It was a new George Clooney film, *Gravity*, released earlier this year, co-starring Sandra Bullock. He was Jean's most favorite actor, and Jack appreciated Sandra's perky character.

"Enjoying the cruise so far, Jack?"

"Very much so, honey. Nice to be able to relax like this. Nothing much to do. No housekeeping, no meals to cook. As an Australian police inspector I met at the Canadian Police College would say, *'No worries, mate.'*"

♦   ◊   ♦

Soon after 9:00 p.m., when she was off duty, Vessie met her male friend in the staff dining room on deck two for a late meal and told him about the jewelry.

"How much do you think it's worth?" he asked.

"Don't know. Lots. It's a Tiffany necklace. Tens of thousands, I should think."

"Gotta be if she can pay over thirty grand for her room. What I could do with that money! Rich bitch would hardly miss it if it was gone…."

SATURDAY, MAY 24
At sea

Yesterday, during the day, human activity aboard ship was minimal. People were just 'vegetating'. The storm from the west had sideswiped the ship as it passed by yesterday afternoon, producing a bit of slow rolling motion, with stiff breezes and cloudy skies, so that people had to bend forward a little when walking. No one sat outside. Pools were empty. Many spent much of the day resting, or reading magazines and books in the library, or playing chess and other games, or browsing in the *Arcade*. The casino did good business. Some took the opportunity to connect with relatives by skype, phones or email. The *Seascape* had traveled 439 nautical miles further west across the Atlantic in 24 hours.

Today was quite different; cloudless skies, little wind and a steady ship. The upper decks were active, most of the deck chairs and chaise lounges occupied, many tabletops had tall glasses with little colored paper umbrellas stuck in the liquid, the swimming pools were filled with splashing people while others were playing deck shuffleboard or chess, with three feet tall pieces. A noisy, happy group, enjoying their lives at sea.

At 12 noon, Steve Marks' voice sounded on the PA system. "Good afternoon, ladies and gentlemen, a gorgeous day. I hope you are enjoying yourselves. According to our weather people, the next six days should be like this one." He was standing on the pool deck amid some of the passengers. "I have a couple of things to remind you about.

First, it's bingo night! The jackpot so far is unclaimed, and now sits at $2,500 dollars. Starts at eight in the upper lounge.

"Next, a reminder about our musical event happening this evening. In the *Starlight Theater*, a shorter rendition of none other than the critically acclaimed Broadway musical, *Cabaret*! It's the kind of show that, if you've seen it before, you'd love to go again, and here's your opportunity. There are two presentations—first at 7:30 p.m. and the second at 10. As always, seats are first come, first served. I'll have another announcement in a day or two about our final stage show on the thirty-first.

"Finally, just another gentle reminder, folks, about your health. Use the hand cleaners often, and if you have to, sneeze carefully! Thanks for your attention. By the way, if anyone needs to see me, I'm available in the library lounge for a couple of hours in the afternoons, from two to four. I have a desk with my name on it—Steve Marks. Do come say hello."

◆ ◇ ◆

The presentation of *Cabaret* had been reduced in scale and scope to fit the ship's stage and a one-hour time limit. While the *Starlight Theatre* could seat about 1,000 people per show, many guests, arriving less than ten minutes before show time, were turned away. They'd have to see the later show.

The Sterlings had thought about the show's likely popularity and decided to arrive when the doors were opened at 6:45. The best seats were in the center section, halfway back, and that's where they were sitting. Both had seen the 1972 movie, starring Liza Minnelli and Joel Grey, but not the stage version and were really looking forward to a different experience. The production company was from Los Angeles, with professional singers and dancers.

The music was to be provided by the ship's resident orchestra, but, unusually, none of the introductory music was played before the curtain went up. Jean remarked on this and Jack said, "It's probably for dramatic effect, I would think."

The lights dimmed and went out. The theater became very quiet. There was a feeling of anticipation in the air.

Just as the curtain was rising, the first few bars of the opening number, *Wilkommen*, blasted into the theater from the orchestra pit, as the female singer-dancers appeared, doing a Can-Can dance. Behind them, the set showed the inside of the Kit Kat Klub in Berlin, circa. 1931, with small, round, beer tables occupied by men, a few wearing the red, white and black Nazi swastika armband on their jackets. Sitting at one of the tables was the male lead, Clifford Bradshaw, a young American writer. The first song finished with the chorus girls in line, in a slow tap dance, repeating "*Wilkommen, bienvenue, welcome!*"

The actress playing the lead role as Sally Bowles even looked and sang a bit like Liza Minnelli in the movie, especially the theme song, *Come to the Cabaret*. It was as much as anyone in the audience could do, not to break out in song and join in. The show was a hit, the whole audience giving a standing ovation to the cast, spread out in line across the stage, taking several bows. On their way out of the theater, everyone was humming or singing the songs.

Jean said to her husband, "Let's parade around this deck for a while, in our nice clothes, Jack. We're lookin' good."

"Jean Sterling, you're a bit of a show-off. You should have been in show business," replied Jack, as he took her arm and began to promenade, "Feelin' good, too!"

It was a bone lazy day for the Sterlings. "What day is it today, Jack? I'm already losing track of time," asked Jean as they got up.

"I think it's a Sunday, May 25."

After a leisurely breakfast, they did a fast walk round the deck track, followed by a swim and a hot tub soak, which made them feel good, and healthy. Jean found two chaise lounge chairs, and Jack walked down to deck 5 to the purser's office and picked up a copy of the news sheet, called the *Seascape Daily News*. On the wall behind the long front desk were 6 clocks showing the current times in major world cities, and on a large LED screen, the ship's current position at sea, in latitude and longitude, miles traveled today, and miles from final destination. For the Europeans, the distances were also shown in kilometres.

Back on deck, Jack covered himself with a high index sun tan lotion, put on his Toronto Blue Jays baseball cap, sunglasses, sat down and stretched out on the deck chair to read the *News*. Jean was wearing a wide-brimmed floppy sun hat and sunglasses. She was halfway through reading *Fifty Shades of Grey* by the British author E.L. James. She could be heard occasionally muttering, or saying 'Oh, my God!' to the amusement of Jack.

"Really getting into that story, eh, hon?"

"It leaves little to the imagination. Not sure I need to read the second and third volumes. Wonder if Avery has read this?"

"I'm not sure I want to ask her. By the way, I see in today's shipboard bulletin that there is a ship's tour tomorrow and Tuesday—three hours each day—from bottom to top except the engine room area. Sounds interesting. Mind if I go? It's a hundred and fifty."

In the afternoon, Jack spent a couple of hours in the casino, while Jean browsed the shops in the arcade, looking for something for her daughter. When they met later in the *Bistro*, they compared spending notes. She had spent just over one hundred dollars on clothing, and he had spent exactly one hundred dollars—on nothing....

♦ ◇ ♦

It was 6:30 p.m., and the *Imperial Dining Room*, classy by any world standard, was busy. Still beautiful weather. Hannah Goldman had decided to go to a five-piece violin recital in the *Music Room*, while Mrs. Gessner, dressed up for dinner, arrived in the dining room just after seven, to find most of the eight-person tables almost full. Taking a seat with six other guests, she said, "Hello" and introduced herself.

Abe Shuster found himself in the same situation. Spotting one vacant seat at a table, he politely asked if anyone else was expected. No one was, so he sat down and introduced himself. Looking at Rebecca Gessner, he asked if she was with the other guests and she said, "No, I'm traveling alone. And you?"

"Yes. Me too. I'm sorry, what did you say your name was?"

"Rebecca Gessner."

"Once again, Abe Shuster. Enjoying the cruise so far?" he asked, noticing the gold band and diamond engagement ring on her left hand.

"Yes, I find it very relaxing, especially now that we are at sea. Those shore trips are fine and interesting, but a bit tiring, don't you think?"

"Yes, yes. I agree. And it's nice to get away from the bustle of Miami." He also noticed the expensive jewelry she was wearing around her neck, glittering under the overhead chandelier.

"Oh, I'm from that area, up the coast a bit at Palm Beach," Mrs. G. replied softly.

"How about that. I live in Coral Way. I noticed you here yesterday evening, with a younger woman. Your daughter?"

"Oh no, that's my assistant, Hannah. She's at the jazz thing this evening. That's not really my kind of music."

"I take it you've cruised before?"

"Yes, a few times, but not on this crossing. You?"

"Likewise. This is my fourth cruise. It's a nice ship. It's been a few years since my last one. My wife, Esther, she died five years ago and I've been busy with my business since."

"Oh, I'm sorry to hear that. My husband passed about that time too."

Abe Shuster thoroughly enjoyed dinner with his new-found companion. He found her very personable and quite good looking. While desert was being served, he said, "If I may ask, Mrs. Gessner—"

"—Please, call me Rebecca."

"Rebecca. Are you doing anything after dinner?"

"No, not much. I usually like to go for a stroll on the upper deck if it's not too chilly."

"Would you mind if I accompany you? I like to walk too. Good for the digestion."

When they were finished their dinner and stroll, he got up the nerve to ask her if he could escort her back to her cabin. When he arrived at *Crown Suite 7001*, he realized he had chosen the wrong noun. *7001* was hardly a cabin.

"Thank you, Rebecca, for a very pleasant evening. So, two o'clock for lunch then?"

"Yes. I'd like that. Give me a call beforehand. You know my suite number. Thank you for a nice evening too, Abe. Goodnight."

◆　◇　◆

"Ship security," answered the female operator. The time was 9:55 p.m.

"Hello, this is John Clements, the evening casino manager. Can you send a couple of your people here, right away? We've had an assault."

"Do you need a male and female officer, or two males?"

"There's a woman involved, so I guess a man and a woman would be better."

"Okay. Hold on a minute while I dispatch them, then I'll get more details." Back on line, she said, "Okay, John, two security officers attending and Mr. Donnelly is also on his way. What happened?"

"We've had a fight. Four people, two males and two females. From what I can make out, at least initially, is that one of the men bumped into the female partner of the other guy and swore at her after he spilled his drink on his clothes. The other guy took offense and the fight was on, with lots of shouting and swearing between them. One of the women was knocked down in the melee and banged her head, causing a small cut. She's being escorted to the infirmary to have the wound sutured. Casino staff have separated the two combatants, but they're still both very agitated. You can hear the shouting still."

Ultimately the incident required four male officers to intervene and safely remove the two somewhat inebriated men from the casino to the security office. Both were told that unless they calmed down, they'd be placed in the ship's brig overnight. As well, there would be the possibility that they would be barred from sailing with World Cruise Lines again, and that one of them could face an assault charge. In any event, the matter would have to be reported to the FBI in Miami.

They were escorted back to their cabins, much subdued and a bit chagrinned, and told to remain there for the rest of the night. They were also advised that if they left, security would know by monitoring the CCTV cameras. The injured woman would be returned to her stateroom after treatment.

Mike Donnelly would see the two individuals tomorrow morning at eight to check their attitudes and meet with Captain Stuart after, to check on what else, if anything, he wished to be done. Obviously the ship could not turn back to La Palma to eject the two miscreants. Hopefully that was the first and last problem on this trip, Mike thought to himself, finishing off the report.

♦   ◇   ♦

"How was your evening, Mrs. G.?" asked Hannah as she entered the suite for a quick visit, before retiring to her cabin. It was just after ten.

"I had an absolutely wonderful time except for when we walked through the casino. I'll tell you about that incident in a minute. Hannah, *I met a very charming man!* —at my table," she replied, telling Hannah about the meeting over dinner. "And he's from the old part of the city, Coral Way."

"That's nice. Tell me more."

"Well, his name's Abe Shuster. You just missed him by the way. He saw me to the suite—a real gentleman. He's about my age, a widower, his wife having died about five years ago, and has one son, who now runs his business, the biggest GM dealership in the city, Miami GM. He still remains active, kind of overseeing the operation."

"Well, I am pleased for you. Maybe I'll meet him tomorrow?"

"Yes. We are meeting for a light lunch on the pool deck at 2 o'clock. Would you like to join us?"

"Thank you. I might drop by and say hello. What happened in the casino? Was Abe—Mr. Shuster—with you?" and Mrs G. told her about witnessing the fight.

On her way down to her cabin, Hannah thought to herself, 'Well, how about that. I'll have to check this guy out. Is he genuine, or a gold-digger? At least he's Jewish.'

She'd do some online research this evening. 'Miami GM has a huge presence, so maybe this guy is super rich too.'

MONDAY, MAY 26
At sea

M ike Donnelly had discussed the case of the rowdies from the evening before with his staff. He had re-interviewed the culprits earlier this morning, in the security office. This morning the two men were very subdued and apologetic, and obviously a fair bit intimidated by the threat of their actions being reported to the FBI. Mike let that hang over them. When he met with the captain later, he explained they were very apologetic and he did not expect anything but the best of behavior from now on.

No report to the FBI needed, agreed Captain Stuart, just to remain on the ship's daily log. "Let's hope we're trouble-free for the remainder of the cruise."

♦　◇　♦

"Good morning, ladies and gentlemen. Your cruise director, Steve Marks, again. Another beautiful day for us all. I have a few updates for you. These are in today's daily news sheet. You will notice an announcement about our next and final theatrical presentation for this cruise. It's called *North Atlantic* and will be staged one night only, May thirty-first. More information to follow.

"Today in the *Polo Lounge* at ten-thirty, an interesting talk about the operation of this cruise ship. What moves it—the engine room—and how we sail, or navigate. Once again, that's ten-thirty in the *Polo Lounge*. Enjoy yourselves."

◆   ◇   ◆

Finishing their breakfast at nine-thirty, the two women went for a brisk walk around the pool deck a couple of times and found two empty deck chairs together, near the salt-water pool. They'd catch a few rays, then move into the shade. Hannah carried a satchel from which she produced her 13-inch MacBookPro laptop, and with her boss's okay, started tapping away, while Mrs. G. glanced at ship's bulletin newsletter. It had a bit of world news, U.S. news and, of more interest to her, the stock market quotes from last Friday.

Hannah, meantime, had almost finished her discreet investigation of Abraham Joseph Shuster. She was now reviewing the financial standing of Miami GM and confirming the status of his residential property: registered in his name, with no mortgage. Approximate market value: three million. 'Hmm, unless he has ulterior motives, sounds like he's genuine,' she concluded. 'Would be nice for Mrs. G. to have a little spice in her life. We'll see how it goes....'

Sometime later, Rebecca Gessner interrupted their conversation to say, a little excitedly, "Speaking of the man, there he is," pointing at the person on the other side of the pool. "Shall we say hello?" she asked Hannah.

"Sure, why not?"

Leaving their towels on their chairs, they walked across. After a few minutes of conversation, Hannah was convinced he did not pose a threat to Mrs. G. She would monitor from a distance however.

Abe asked if they would like to join him for lunch later. Mrs. G. said that would be nice, while Hannah graciously declined. She said that, after calling her parents, she'd spend the rest of the day by herself reading, unless Mrs. G. called her.

♦ ◊ ♦

Mike Donnelly kept the two combatants in suspense until four o'clock before letting them know of his decision. In the late afternoon, he did a walk-around of the decks—his *law and order patrol,* as he referred to it. At times, he had to admit that he felt a bit like the captain walking the ship. 'Hmm, I wonder if one day that could be me with four bars,' he thought to himself. 'Anyway, hope there are no more problems.'

The passengers seemed to be settling down for the long haul. He spotted the retired Canadian police officer, sitting on deck with his wife. Mike thought about saying hello to them again, but they were in conversation, and he did not want to interrupt.

♦ ◊ ♦

Day three at sea found most everyone had gained their sea legs, now obvious from the lack of staggering from side to side. People were anticipating the slow roll of the deck. The warm sun and cool air kept many passengers top side, and all the deck chairs were occupied. For most people, it just felt good to be lazy.

Rebecca Gessner had had a great day, spending much of it with Abe Shuster, and an even nicer evening. First, an early dinner in the *Grande Dining Room,* and then on to the *Lido Club* for some energetic dancing. She found she thoroughly enjoyed Abe's company.

By 9:30, she felt a bit tired and he escorted her to her suite, reluctantly saying good night to her, outside.

"See you tomorrow?" he asked, hopefully.

She nodded and said she would call. He reached for her hand and kissed the back of it elegantly, smiled, turned and walked to the elevator. It was now 9:45.

After showering, Rebecca toweled-off and used the blow drier on her hair. She dressed in her blue silk nightie, brushed her teeth, and opened the door to go to her bedroom, looking forward to continuing her almost finished new book, *The Scarlet Sentinels*. It was a story about the Canadian Mounties—which she could hardly put down—given to her by her friend, Mrs. Becky Schultz, who had recently returned from a trip to Vancouver. Reading typically helped her to fall asleep. She wouldn't have that opportunity.

♦ ◊ ♦

The man was dressed in black pants and a continental style, short, cutaway, white waiter's jacket. He carried a tray on the upturned flat of his left hand, held up next to his head, while he knocked on one of the double doors to *Crown Suite 7001*. It was just after 10 p.m. After a few seconds, he knocked again, more firmly. He was wearing white gloves. No response.

'Good,' he thought. 'Still out.' He inserted a pass-key card into the metal slot, withdrew it quickly and pushed open the door, walking in. He expected to be in there for only a couple of minutes or so.

The vast suite appeared empty, but he still called, "Room Service."

No response. As he made his way across the rug, the phone rang. It startled him. He stood still and let it ring, five times, until the ringing stopped. 'Place is definitely empty,' he thought.

As he advanced into the bedroom, the first thing he saw was the diamond necklace and earrings Vessie had told him about, lying on top of the white, brocaded bedspread. 'Bingo!' he silently exclaimed. Picking them up, he stuffed them into the small side pocket of this waiter's jacket. Spotting the Tiffany cloth bag, he was putting it into his trouser pocket, when he heard a woman's loud voice—.

As Rebecca Gessner left the bathroom, turning to enter her bedroom, she stopped in her tracks. There was a man dressed in what looked like either a cleaner's or waiter's uniform, standing by her bed. Very surprised, she said in a loud, demanding voice, "Who are you?! *What are you doing here?!*"

Her sudden appearance startled him and before he could reply, she quickly walked toward him, noticing part of a chain of diamonds hanging out of the small side pocket of the white jacket. Taking a fleeting glance at her bedcover, she noticed one thing that was obviously missing—her necklace!

She rushed at the man, knocking him on her bed, screaming furiously, "Give me my necklace back!"

The man reached out to the serving tray he'd laid on the bedspread, knocked the metal cover off, pushed the teapot aside and picked up a short-bladed, serrated knife. She was punching and slapping him on the face, and shouting.

Blocking her barrage with one arm, he managed to sit up and then stand up, pushing her hard onto the bed. She fell on her back, partly across the mattress, her legs over the edge, and head resting briefly on one of the six pillows. By now, she was in full-volume screaming mode, ear-piercing sounds of *"Help! Thief! Somebody HELP ME!"*

'Jesus!' thought the man. 'I've got to shut her up or I'll get caught.'

Raising his left arm, he was about to bring the knife down when she reach up with her right hand and grabbed the blade. Pulling his hand and knife back forcibly, he then swung his arm down and plunged the blade fully into the left side of her neck, cutting the carotid artery. Then, with some effort, he pulled the blade around her throat to the right ear. In doing this, his hand slipped down the knife handle a bit, cutting the outer side of his palm, through the glove.

Under the bright light of the elaborate chandelier, a look of shear terror was locked in her eyes, a sight that would haunt him the rest of his life. Except for a combat situation back home during the war, this was the closest he'd ever been to someone he knew he'd killed. She'd stopped screaming and the only sound in the now almost quiet bedroom was her rasping efforts at trying to breathe, while the dark-red venous blood spurted from the jagged gap in her neck. Her body shuddered for a few more seconds, then all muscles released. Blood had sprayed onto the pillow. With the edge of the mattress depressed by her weight, a voluminous quantity of dark red blood flowed quickly alongside her buttocks and onto the carpet where the man was standing. He was out of breath and surprised at what he'd just done.

Willing himself out of the shock, the man realized he had to get out of the suite as quickly as possible, without leaving evidence in the suite or being obvious out in the passageway. He noted some blood on the palm of his left glove. 'Hers or mine? I need to clean up.'

Carrying the knife, he went quickly into the bathroom. In the mirror, he saw a spattering of blood on the front of his jacket and white tuxedo shirt. Taking off the gloves, he discovered a small cut on the outer side of the palm on his left hand. 'How the Hell did *that* happen?'

Turning on the faucet, he rinsed the blood off the knife, splashed his hands under the water and dried them and his sweaty face with the folded paper towels on the counter, throwing them in the waste bin. The cut still slowly leaked blood, so he wrapped his palm in a face cloth.

'Alright,' he said to himself, 'how do I hide the blood on my shirt? I know—take the jacket off, reverse it, put it on again and turn the lapels outwards to the front.'

While he did that, seeing the toilet bowl reminded him that he urgently needed a pee, so he quickly relieved himself.

Carrying the gloves, he returned to the bedroom, taking one quick glance at the dead woman, her hands up at her neck. He shuddered, then replaced the knife on the serving tray and put the white gloves under the tray cover. Glancing around, he noticed red footprints on the rug! Shrugging, he thought, 'Nothing I can do about that now. I gotta get outta here *fast*.'

Just as he was about to step through the door into the passageway, he reminded himself, 'Oh yeah, hold the tray up in my right hand.'

As he got off the elevator at his cabin deck, he bent down and placed the meal tray on the floor. Somebody'll take it away and it'll be cleaned, he knew. Any evidence would be washed away.

Lying in his single bed in the darkened cabin, he groped for his watch on the small side table and moved the luminous dial close to his face. *0600*. He'd last checked at 4 o'clock. No sleep in between. In fact, he'd hardly slept during the night. His mind was reliving the events of the previous evening.

He'd seen death and dying in his young life, but this was different. He wondered if it all wasn't just a bad dream, a throwback to his youth in his home country of Croatia.

Sitting up, he put on the sidetable lamp. As his eyes moved around the small, two-bed room, he saw the dining table with an empty glass and a liquor bottle beside it, remembering the three or four stiff undiluted drinks he'd had on his return, around ten-thirty. He thought they'd help him sleep, but it didn't work. He remembered replaying, over and over in his mind, what happened—what he did.

'Why am I upset? I've killed before.' When he reflected on that though, he believed he'd only killed when his life had been under threat, from rifles or machine guns, at a distance. And he wasn't certain any of his shots had actually killed someone.

Sitting on the side of his bed, head bent forward, he ran his hands through his hair, thinking, 'Shit! Shit! *SHIT!* What am I going to tell Vessie?'

She was back on day shift, after a couple of evening spells relieving someone. That was when she'd seen the jewelry.

He next thought of the necklace and opened the small drawer in the side table and took it out, laying it on the top. He had flushed the small, Tiffany cloth bag down the toilet earlier. Even in the reduced light of the 60-watt bulb, the necklace's many diamonds and rubies gleamed, almost mesmerizing. 'Was it all worth it?' he wondered. 'Better be.'

He was lucky to be assigned a room by himself. He didn't like to share and when he had to, he tried to get a different shift for work, day or evening. He was on days for this cruise, having to be 'on-deck' literally, at 0700 hours to 1500, as a ship's cleaner.

Decks were always the first to be done, as the pools and deck games were often in use until late evening, and sometimes left in a bit of a mess. Decks had to be scrubbed and hosed down, furniture, deck-rails, handrails and glass surfaces cleaned with a strong detergent to ward off the dreaded norovirus that seemed to afflict some cruise ships. Shaking hands among crew members and among passengers was strongly discouraged to try to keep the virus at bay. Cleaning was taken seriously, and supervisors, wearing white gloves, would sometimes follow cleaners to check their work. The pools were continuously 'dipped' for water samples. For Rad, cleaning wasn't a strenuous job but very boring. It was paid work though—and there were the tips to share in at the end of the cruise.

'Alright, let's get myself sorted out. Not a lot of time. First, hide the necklace, but where? If they search the cabin now, they'll probably find it. Hide it on the ship somewhere? Two possible things wrong with that idea. First, what if someone sees me hiding it? Second, it could be found by a crew member doing inspections or cleaning.'

Pondering this for a minute, he decided to put the jewelry in a sock and carry it in his pocket, in his uniform, or in his civvy pants. 'That way, as unlikely as it is, if my room is searched, they won't find it and maybe they won't search me. I'll have to give that a bit more thinking. There aren't no real police on a cruise ship anyway.'

He'd already discarded his waiter's uniform, having changed in his cabin after he'd returned from the suite, placing the pants and the bloody, white jacket in one plastic bag, and the shirt and serving gloves in another, putting them in two separate waste bins nearby on the crew deck. That reminded him about the one-inch-long cut on his hand. It wasn't deep and he had covered it with a handkerchief before lying down. He did not have a band-aid. By now, the cut had dried. 'Must get a piece of tape from one of the ship's first aid kits and cover it up.'

He remembered leaving the serving tray, tea pot and chinaware in the elevator on the way down. No cameras in there.

'Okay, a quick call to Vess before she leaves.' It was early but he had to tell her.

With the minimum of conversation, Rad made arrangements to go to her cabin when he got off work. He did not want to discuss anything over the phone.

♦   ◊   ♦

Marie Fortunato got off the elevator at aft-deck 7, pushing her cleaning cart to the large double doors of *Crown Suite 7001*, straight ahead of her. It was 8:35 a.m. and her first stop of the morning. She had been cleaning cabins, of all sizes, passenger and crew accommodation alike, with WCL for the past 3 years. For the most part, she enjoyed her work and found most passengers treated her well. Tips were generally good, although it had been her experience that people in the smaller rooms tipped her better than those in the bigger staterooms, or the 3 big opulent suites. Strange how people with money were so cheap. 'I guess that's one way of staying wealthy, keeping your money.' She didn't like the slobs either, as her friends called them: people leaving their dirty clothes and wet towels on the floor, food on the plates, the TV on, and toilets un-flushed. But this lady in *7001*, the lone occupant, was the opposite; her place was always clean and tidy and she was very polite to her, almost friendly. Marie was expecting a nice gratuity for once.

She noticed there was no *RESTING* card in the door slot. That meant that the suite was still occupied or the occupant had left, forgetting to put out the *SERVICE REQUIRED* sign.

It was breakfast time. Many guests had vacated their cabins by now, though because the ship was at sea, the lady could be having a late breakfast. As a cleaner, the rule was, knock and wait for a response, twice, and then use her pass-card to enter, standing just inside the door and calling out, "Housekeeping."

Hearing no reply, she entered and pulled her cart into the huge foyer area and left the door open by means of a small, rubber chock: another rule. From here, she could go right, into the bedroom; straight, into the large living room; or left, into a lounge, library, TV room and then into a kitchen area. Behind all of this ran an outside verandah the whole width of the ship. It would take her an hour to clean the place. Her first room would be the bedroom.

Reaching down to the cart's bottom shelf, she removed her cleaning cloths, disinfectant soap and spray polish. The order of cleaning was: make the bed, dust all the furniture and apply polish, wash down the bathroom, toilet and shower, replace the towels and toilet paper, do the marble floor and clean the glass and mirrors. Next, the kitchen and sitting room, and the lounge, followed lastly by vacuuming all the rug-covered area, finishing up at the door.

While she was taking cleaning items off the cart, out of the corner of her eye, she noticed two or three red marks on the tiled floor of the foyer, to her right. Standing up, she noted more, a bit smudgier, and then, taking a pace forward, saw more red, footprint-like marks on the pale blue carpet in the entrance to the bedroom. At first, her brain wouldn't register what they were, until she took four paces into the bedroom, avoiding the marks. Then she saw, and knew.

As she raised her eyes and looked over toward the bed, she saw a pool of reddish goop on the rug beside it and a nighty-clad body on the edge of the bed nearest her. She tried to scream but was momentarily paralyzed.

"*Oh! My God!*" she finally blurted out, putting her hands up to her face, as if to blot out the vision.

After a moment or two, recovering herself, she backed out of the bedroom and saw the white slim-line telephone on the ebony table beside the doors. Picking it up, she pressed the number for the ship's operator, who responded, "Front desk. May I help you?"

Marie hadn't thought about what to say.

The operator repeated, "May I help you?"

"*Yes, it's me!*" Marie finally shouted. "I'm in *Suite 7001*. Someone's been hurt. I think the person may be *dead!*"

After getting the cleaner's name and why she was in the suite, the operator told her to calm down, wait where she was and that she would call her supervisor.

As a result of the frantic call, the supervisor of housekeeping operations, Ellen Sokolofsky, arrived in three minutes. Her first job was to calm Marie down. The woman had taken a chair and placed it beside the doors to sit and wait. She refused to re-enter the bedroom when asked.

The supervisor went in alone and could be heard to gasp at what she saw. Coming out, she said, "I'm going to call the hotel manager, Marie. I'm afraid you'll have to stay."

Using her cell phone, Ellen made the call.

♦ ◇ ♦

The hotel manager has a large responsibility aboard a cruise ship, part of the four main operations: the bridge and deck (which includes security), engine room, technical and hotel. This last designation has by far the largest number of crew and includes catering (food preparation), kitchen, wait staff, ship and cabin cleaning, and entertainment. Managing this operation was an exhausting task and required a high degree of organization, stamina, patience and long, continuous days at work. Today, however, was not typical.

Now that the death had been officially reported to him, Hotel Manager Fritz Hauptmann thought it prudent to call the chief of security before leaving his office in the administrative area. He asked Mike to meet him at the suite asap, explaining that there may have been a sudden death of the female passenger there.

Mike Donnelly quickly checked the passenger list for that suite, noting only one occupant registered, a Mrs. Rebecca Gessner, from Miami, probably American.

With another security officer, he arrived at the suite six minutes later, meeting Hauptmann and the two women standing just inside the doors.

He entered the bedroom, being careful where he stepped. He stopped short of the bed and looked, observing a late-middle-aged female, dressed in a bloody, pale blue nightgown, lying on her back in a pool of blood, with, from where he could see, her throat cut. He'd never seen a murder victim before and was taken aback by the brutality of what he saw. There was no doubt in his mind she was dead.

"Jesus, just what we need!" he lamented half under his breath.

"Captain's gonna be unhappy," Mike said to the security officer. "Guess I'd better let him know now."

He called the bridge with the details as he saw them.

He was right. The captain swore. "Call Dr. Kent, Mike, and have him attend right away, please. Get back to me as soon as you can. I'd like you here when I call the Head Office. And, Mike… do everything you can to keep this quiet from the crew and passengers."

Mike made the call, asking the physician to attend as soon as possible, which he promised to do.

Returning to the suite's foyer, Mike asked both women for an account of their activity, and told them to make notes about that as soon as possible, telling them not to discuss this with *anyone*, he emphasized.

He asked Marie to take off her shoes and show him the soles.

Seeing what looked like blood on the bottoms, he told her he would need them and would get her another pair before long, asking her supervisor to arrange that.

Before leaving, Fritz Hauptmann asked Mike why he was keeping her shoes and not those of the supervisor and his. Mike explained that the housekeeper was first to find the body. Unlikely as it seems, he said that made her a possible suspect and her shoes, or more particularly the blood on the soles, could be evidence. Seeing that Fritz and Ellen arrived *after* Marie made her call, they were very unlikely suspects, he said, with a slight smile.

'Gees, where did I get that idea from?' Mike asked himself. 'Good thing I watch police shows on the telly, because this goes *way* beyond my training.'

♦ ◊ ♦

In the suite, absent the female staff, Dr. Kent remarked to Mike about the bloody mess as he examined the body, both men careful to not to step in the rubbery blood patch on the rug beside the bed. Mike asked if he could officially determine the cause of death—which seemed somewhat obvious—and time of death, without moving the body just now. The doctor inserted a thermometer into the victim's rectum, "Which may be the warmest part of the body, to check her temperature," he told the officer.

He then asked Mike to check the room temperature, which felt a little warm. With the initial result of this test for rigor mortis, he estimated that death occurred yesterday evening, without giving an exact time, making a note of this on his pad. "I need to come back and do a more thorough examination, probably should work through a full rape kit procedure. I'll check a few items and call you with any results of this preliminary examination, Mike."

Rather than use the ship's communication, Mike thought it better to report the details to the captain in person. It was a five-minute walk from the aft of the ship to the bridge, and he needed those few minutes to compose his thoughts and create his next course of action. He had asked the security officer to wait in the suite, near the doors and to touch nothing.

On the way, he remembered something that may prove useful for the investigation. He recalled speaking to a retired Canadian cop on deck, at the start of the cruise. 'What was his name? Something to do with *silver*, I think. I'll have a quick look at the passenger list, searching for Toronto home addresses, before I speak with the captain.'

◆   ◇   ◆

On the bridge, turning to his OOW—officer of the watch—Captain John Stuart said, "Confirm current position, Mister Erickson."

The second officer said, "Aye, aye, sir," and checking the AIS (automatic information system ship tracking device), called out, "Time, 0918 hours; course, west by northwest; position, 27 degrees, 37 minutes north; 30 degrees, 48 minutes west; speed 18.30 knots; 1390 nautical miles west of La Palma."

Jotting the information down, John confirmed by repeating it. "I'll be in my quarters speaking with Head Office. Mr. Donnelly will be with me. You have the Con, Mr. Erickson."

"I have the Con, sir!" he replied. Duly recorded in the ship's log book.

In his cabin's spacious office area, John, Mike and the staff captain took their seats and quickly reviewed the incident. "A couple of questions before I make the call. So, Mike, we've had a female passenger killed in *Crown Suite 7001* and death confirmed by Dr. Kent?"

"Yes, sir. He tentatively put the time of death at yesterday evening, possibly between 9 p.m. and midnight. Woman's throat was cut; a real gory mess in the bedroom area. She was found by Marie Fortunato, housekeeping staff, around eight-thirty this morning. Victim's name is Mrs. Rebecca Gessner, from Miami, traveling alone as far as we know.

She's the only person registered to the suite. I have one of my people guarding the suite."

"Alright, thanks, Mike."

Picking up his satellite phone, he called World Cruise Lines Head Office in Miami and asked to be connected with the vice-president of operations at his home, adding that he had an urgent situation to report. It was 0710 hours now in Miami. After apologizing to the VP for disturbing him, John reported the murder and gave the ship's position as of five minutes ago, clarifying that he was en route to Miami.

Fred Swanson said, "So, you're well beyond La Palma now. I don't have a map in front of me, but I think your position puts the ship well out into the Atlantic, almost a point of no return in this case, it seems to me."

"Yes, you're right, sir. We're about a third of the way between La Palma and Miami: 1400 NM from the Canaries. My preference, of course, would be to continue, but this person is a U.S. citizen, so I believe it's a matter for the FBI to decide, and I don't know what their view would be."

Fred Swanson said he would make a call to the CEO and one of them would contact the FBI. He would await directions and call back via skype.

Mike Donnelly signaled to the captain before he hung up.

"Excuse me, Mr. Swanson, could you hold for a minute?" John put the phone on mute.

"Yes, what is it, Mike?"

Mike told him about the retired Canadian police office on board and wondered if he could be of assistance?

John nodded and un-muted the phone.

"Fred, I'll let you have a word with my S.O., Mike Donnelly."

The security officer told the VP about meeting the just-retired senior police officer from the Toronto police department, and that "maybe he could assist us, since the FBI won't be able to get here. His name is Jack Sterling and he was their chief of detectives."

"Okay, Mike, leave it with me. I'll let you know. Why don't you round him up and sound him out. If he agrees, tell him it would be pending approval from the FBI, of course. Get back to you and your boss soon."

♦   ◊   ♦

The Miami office of the Federal Bureau of Investigation office was on Northwest Second Avenue, in North Miami Beach. It was now 7:40 a.m. Eastern Standard Time. The switchboard phone rang and Janetta Wilson answered.

The voice said, "This is World Cruise Lines calling from downtown. May I speak to the officer in charge, please, on an urgent matter?"

"I'm sorry, sir, the SAC is not in at the moment. It's a bit early, but I can transfer you to our senior agent, Clive Lundgren, if you'd like."

"That'll be fine, thanks."

When the call was answered, he said, "This is Andrew Hollinger, the CEO of World Cruise Lines in town. We currently have a ship at sea, MV *Seascape*, in mid-Atlantic, en route Miami, due here in six days. The master of the ship reports the murder of a passenger, a woman. As our passenger is of American birth, we are aware of the crime reporting procedure."

"Alright, Mr. Hollinger, a few basic questions. When did this happen?"

"As far as we can tell, in the evening, yesterday, May 27, an estimate by our senior doctor, William Kent, who examined the body this morning."

"How do your crew know this was a murder?"

"Well, in this case, it is apparently quite obvious. Her throat was cut while she was in bed and the scene, in her suite, does not lend itself to any other conclusion, according to our head of security onboard."

"Do you have the victim's name?"

"Yes, it's Rebecca Gessner, age 65, of the Miami area. U.S. citizen."

"Alright. She's definitely our responsibility then. What's your ship's present position?"

"Approximately two thousand, two hundred miles east of Miami. I can give you her exact co-ordinates if you like?"

"No, that's okay. Send that and all other pertinent info to me by fax or email. What was *Seascape*'s last port of call?"

"La Palma, the far western island of the Canaries group, leaving there at 1700 hours local time, May 22. The ship is now approximately 1400 miles west," giving the distance in land measurement for the agent. "At her present rate of speed —18.3 knots, or about 21 miles per hour—that should take her just under five days to arrive in Miami for the scheduled time of 0800 hours, June second.

"Mr. Lundgren, our next cruise departure is at 1800 hours, the same day. Keeping to that schedule would certainly suit us in terms of ship turnaround. Save a lot of inconvenience for our departing and arriving passengers. Save us a bundle of money, too."

"Yes, I understand. We'll keep that in mind. And it's too far for you to turn back?"

"Yes, I'd say so."

"Where's your ship registered?"

"The British Virgin Islands."

"Have you advised them yet?"

"Yes, we just did. They merely acknowledged the call, without further discussion. I thought it important to call you next since the murdered woman is, or rather was, an American citizen and our next port is Miami."

"Okay. We'll give the embassy or consulate a call and discuss. I take it your security section onboard is now involved and standing by for instructions?"

"Yes, our senior officer in charge entered the suite with the doctor at shortly after 0900 hours today, ship's time, which I believe is 2 hours ahead of us, Eastern Standard Time, in Miami. The body remains in the suite, which is now locked and under guard."

"I take it your ship is still on the same course."

"Yes. I've given instructions to the captain to continue on his present heading," replied the CEO.

"Can you give me his name and how I can reach him?"

"You can use the ship-to-shore line or regular land-line long distance method. I'll email you the name and appropriate numbers to call in a minute."

"Mr. Hollinger, we would like to be able to put agents aboard, but from your current position, I don't think that's possible. We have what we call 'away teams' to get agents to crime scenes, but you are too far out to sea in this case."

"Yes, I thought that would be so. There is something else I should let you know. My security officer discovered the presence of a recently retired Canadian police officer on this cruise, formerly a senior detective with the Toronto, Canada, police department. Could you use his services and expertise to assist our security section, I wonder? They have no experience in this kind of crime."

"Well, let me have his name then and I'll get back to you. I'll have to check with my SAC."

"Yes, I understand. His name is Jack Sterling."

"Is that with an I-R or E-R?"

"E-R, I've got it written down as," replied Andrew Hollinger.

"Good. I'll check with the agent-in-charge and get back to you as soon as possible. Let me have your number, please. Meantime, perhaps you could arrange to have Mr. Sterling brought to the bridge and standby. Fill him in on the details and obviously, ask him if he'd be willing to assist if requested."

"Yes, I understand that he's on his way there."

♦ ◇ ♦

Five minutes later, after receiving details via email from Andrew Hollinger, Clive Lundgren asked his Ops Center operator to get the telephone number for the Toronto City Police. He'd make the call himself, he said.

"Toronto Police, may I help you?" asked the male voice. "Yes, my name is Clive Lundgren and I am a senior agent with the FBI office, Miami. I'd like to speak to the senior officer on duty, please."

"Just a moment, sir."

"This is Superintendent Wall."

"Superintendent, my name is Clive Lundgren, FBI, Miami. I take it you are the senior officer on duty."

"Yes, I am. For the Night Watch. We change shifts at 0800 hours. How can I help you?"

"I have a quick question for you, followed by an explanation. Did you have a detective Jack Sterling on your staff? He's recently retired, I believe."

"Yes, we certainly did. He was our C of Ds, Chief of the Detective Division, who retired effective March 31st, this year. Is he in trouble already!?" Wall said with a laugh.

"Good heavens, *no!*" replied Lundgren quickly, chuckling. "I'm actually confirming his employment with your department, as we need his assistance. Here's the story. A cruise ship, with World Cruise Lines, now at sea in mid-Atlantic, reported the murder of a U.S. citizen aboard. Ship's crew discovered Mr. Sterling was on this cruise and would like to use his services to help with the investigation, and we concur. Cruise ships do have security people on board but they are not police officers and have no expertise in such matters. It goes without saying, I suppose, that Sterling has a great deal of investigative experience?"

"Yes, I served with him about ten years and can personally vouch for him. He was top notch at his job—probably attended dozens of murders before becoming chief. A murder at sea would be his first though, to my knowledge. I know he'd be willing to assist. If you talk to him, give him my regards, please. I'll tell Chief Constable Forsythe when he comes in. He'll be tickled to hear this."

◆ ◇ ◆

Thirty minutes later, Fred Swanson called the *Seascape* via skype. "Hello, John. I've discussed the issue with the CEO. He confirms that you are to stay on the same course for now. I'm waiting for the senior FBI agent in charge of their day watch to phone back again. I guess it's their call as to what you need to do. Meanwhile we have the well-being of around 1150 passengers to consider. I fully realize the situation you are in. What are you going to do with respect to letting people onboard know what's happened? Don't want them to feel threatened."

"No. I'll talk to the communications officer and draft a low key, somewhat vague statement. There's a bit of time yet, and I want to get an investigation under way and get the body out of that suite first. I'll get things started here with Mike Donnelly, and wait to talk to the FBI. That okay? Oh, and I'll talk to Mr. Jack Sterling, the Canadian detective."

"Sounds good. By the way, if this man agrees to help and gets the nod to do so from the Feds, get him to the bridge for a discussion. Or if he's amenable to it, why not ask him to your cabin for tea and a confidential talk when you find him? Oh, one other thing. We have officially notified the government of the British Virgin Islands about the situation, okay? All they asked for is updated reports."

◆ ◇ ◆

"Attention, passengers. Attention, passengers. Would Mr. Jack Sterling please report to the administration office on deck three? Mr. Jack Sterling to administration on deck three. Thank you."

"I guess that's me, honey. Wonder what they want? Did we lose anything?" Jack asked Jean as he got up from his dining room chair where they'd had a late breakfast. As was his habit, he checked his watch, noting the Atlantic Ocean time: 10:27 a.m. He said he'd be right back. He was not.

"What can I help you with, sir?" asked the uniformed woman at the counter.

"I'm Jack Sterling. I was paged to report here."

"Just a minute, please," she said.

A woman with two gold bars on her shoulders appeared and said to Jack, "I'm Susan Chambers, the ship's purser. I've been asked by the captain to bring you to the bridge, if that is convenient for you now?"

"Yes, sure. What's up?" he asked.

"Well, I'm sorry, I don't know myself," she replied, "but I've been asked to take you to see the Captain," she repeated as she motioned him to follow her.

They took the elevator to the bridge deck and entered its broad expanse, stretching from port to starboard. A man dressed in white, wearing 4 gold bars, walked over and introduced himself.

"I'm John Stuart, Captain of the *Seascape*. Good of you to come, Mr. Sterling.

Thank you, Susan," he said to the purser. "I'll take it from here."

Pointing to four leather-covered bucket seats, set back from the long console, he directed Jack to take a seat, asking him if he'd like a refreshment. "Coffee, tea, juice, water?"

Jack said, "Thanks, coffee would be good. Excuse my appearance, sir." He was wearing an orange shirt, with green banana leaves, short white shorts and large, ugly leather sandals. "Dressed like this I feel like I just walked off the set of *Hawaii 5-0*."

"You're appropriately dressed on this ship, Mr. Sterling."

"Please, call me Jack."

Captain Stuart was direct. "You are probably not aware, Jack, that there's been a murder committed aboard ship?"

Without waiting for a response, he continued, "It apparently happened last night. A woman was knifed to death—her throat cut—in her cabin, and the body was not discovered until sometime after eight o'clock this morning. Our senior physician has been there and pronounced death, and the officer in charge of ship's security has locked the suite and posted a guard. Because this passenger is an American citizen, such an event is to be investigated by the FBI, although the ship is registered in the British Virgin Islands. This matter has been reported to the Virgin Island authorities and, of course, due to our position at sea now, neither of these entities have the ability to get someone to the ship, even if they wanted to. So, I'm coming to the reason I've asked for your presence here—you may have guessed that by now?"

"Yes," replied Jack, "I think I can," and allowed himself a brief smile.

"You may want to know how you were identified as being a retired police officer?"

"Hmm, let me think. Yes, on our second evening at sea, my wife and I were on deck leaning at a railing when one of your officers spoke with us," said Jack. "In the brief conversation, I mentioned that I'd just retired from police work in Toronto, and told him our names."

"In the circumstance, it's fortunate that you did, for us at least. That's why I've been asked if you will speak to the FBI in Miami."

A nod from Jack.

"Good, I've also got my staff captain who is my second-in-command, and my chief security officer on their way here. Let's wait until they arrive if you don't mind and then go into my office. What kind of police work were you involved in?"

"I was a detective," replied Jack, "retiring as chief of detectives for the Toronto Police Service."

A steward approached with a carafe of coffee on a silver tray with a variety of biscuits.

"Please, help yourself."

As Jack did that, the two officers arrived on the bridge and were introduced with nodded heads, not offering their hands.

Security Officer Mike Donnelly said, "I've had the pleasure before, sir, if you'll recall?"

"Yes. Little did we know we'd meet again in such circumstances," replied Jack.

They walked down the corridor to the captain's quarters.

"Okay, gentlemen, if we can continue," said the captain, looking at his S.O. "I'd like you to fill in Mr. Sterling with a few brief details, so that he has an understanding of the situation before he talks to the Miami FBI people."

Mike did, repeating essentially what the captain had said, adding that the TOD—time of death—could only be guessed at, as Dr. Kent had said, partly because of the room temperature, which was quite warm the next morning, and that he was not an expert at this kind of thing.

Mike had taken a few preliminary photos with a smart phone at the scene. These he shared with the Canadian, assuring him the room was still under guard.

"Any questions, Jack?"

"No, other than asking the obvious. Any suspects yet?"

"No," replied the S.O.

"Alright, I think I'm ready to speak with the FBI, and in the meantime, could you send one of your security people to find my wife, Jean—I left her in the main dining room—and tell her briefly about the reason for my call to the purser's office? Say that I'll get back to her at my first opportunity, although that may be some time yet, knowing what I think I'm going to be doing. She's wearing a pink and white striped blouse and pale blue shorts."

The captain asked Mike to take care of that and to inform Jack when she had been notified. "You can tell her the reason is a sudden death and that at the moment, the matter is being treated in a most confidential way. You might also apologize on my behalf for any in-convenience caused."

◆   ◇   ◆

"Federal Bureau of Investigation, Washington, DC. May I help you?"

"Yes, it's Clive Lundgren, with the Miami office. Can you patch me through to the Assistant Director, please, if it's not too early."

"I'm sorry, sir, Mr. Johnstone is currently in Paris giving a lecture to the Interpol people. Will the Director be okay?"

Clive laughed. "I guess he'll have to be."

"Hello, Clive, Richard Hastings here. What's up in Miami today?"

"Well, this is somewhat of an unusual call, sir. Earlier this morning, we took a call from the CEO of World Cruise Lines, out of Miami, reporting the murder of a female passenger, a Mrs. Rebecca Gessner, age 65, resident of the North Miami area. The ship is now well out into the Atlantic, 5 or 6 days to go to get here. We cannot get anyone to the ship. The flag state, British Virgin Islands, has indicated no in-terest in investigating.

"There's two things that arise out of this situation. One is, do we let the ship continue to Miami? It's last port of call is now over three days behind it. I'm reviewing the options on this. The second is po-tentially problematic. I'll explain. While the ship has security officers on board, apparently none of them have peace officer status, and very little training, and with at least 5 days to port, this puts an investiga-tion like this into real jeopardy. However, as luck would have it, we've been advised of the presence on the ship of none other than the recently retired Chief of Detectives from the Metropolitan Toronto Police Department as a passenger. I've confirmed his credentials with a call to Toronto. My suggestion is that we use his services to lead the investigation, remembering that he's an alien with no police authority either. We can discuss that issue with the prosecutor later. Better the investigation be done properly while it's fresh than not at all for five more days.

"I'll be in constant touch with this man via phone and skype, and can coach him along if and as needed. I'll ask him to submit photos of the scene, take statements, gather any evidence, as soon as he can, provided of course I get your permission, sir."

"Alright, Clive, I approve your request. You may have to be diplomatic with the ship's captain and the security officer. Be interesting to see how the Canadian handles this murder investigation. No suspects at the moment?"

"No, sir."

"Alright, let me know what happens, please."

◆ ◇ ◆

The ship's incoming calls line rang at the bridge console and was answered by the staff captain. He called Captain Stuart over and said it was the FBI, Miami, asking for him. Agent Clive Lundgren explained his agency's priority in conducting the investigation, stating that he would be using the investigative experience of the Canadian police officer, who, Clive would prefer, will lead the investigation, on instructions from the FBI Director in DC. He'd appreciate the captain's consideration and assistance, and, would he advise his security officer of this, please?

"Of course, Mr. Lundgren. I'd be glad to cooperate fully and I know that my S.O. will too. My head office has told me that you've been informed of our situation, and we have awaiting your call. I have with me, Mr. Sterling and my senior Security Officer, Mike Donnelly, and Dr. William Kent, my chief physician. Would you like to speak to them now?"

"Yes. Just one thing before I do. I believe you've been given instructions to continue to Miami?"

"That's right. Makes sense to me.

"It goes without saying, but I'd like to make the point anyway. This situation you are in is a rather unusual one. There are very few murders at sea involving U.S. citizens and rarely do we find one that is unreachable for our agents. What I'm going to say next is more for the ship's officers, rather than Jack Sterling, who will be very familiar with investigative process and procedures.

"Gentlemen, this matter concerns the death of an American citizen. Our agency has to rely on your personnel to conduct this investigation, according to a set of rules, or protocols. In general, these are done in order to ensure the proper collection of evidence, to try to establish the identity of the perpetrator, and in the process, to ensure that his or her rights are not violated under U.S. law, even if that individual is not a U.S. citizen. The point being, of course, that the person may be tried in the United States. Failure to comply with these procedures may well result in the matter not going to trial, or, if it does, to be dismissed."

"Yes, I fully understand that. I think I'll have to rely on the experience of Mr. Sterling. Who would you like to speak to next?"

"If you'd put Mike Donnelly on the line first. Thanks, Captain."

"Mike Donnelly."

"Clive Lundgren. May I call you Mike? Can you briefly tell me what you've got and what you've done so far?"

Mike brought the agent up to date, telling him about how and when the body was found, that he and a ship's doctor went to the scene, the doctor pronouncing death and giving an approximate time as the previous evening, and that the suite was under guard. He added that they had discovered the murdered woman had a young female traveling companion, but that she has her own cabin. "We'll eventually take a statement from her."

"Okay. Is she a suspect?"

"Don't know yet. We'll get to her a bit later in the day. I guess we are fortunate that no suspects can escape, unless they go overboard."

"Alright. Who else has been in the suite?"

"The housekeeper's immediate supervisor, the hotel manager, Dr. Kent, one guard and myself."

"Any sign the door had been forced open?'

"No, the lock appeared intact."

"If that's the case, you'd need a key card to enter, right? Or the occupant may have opened it?" asked Lundgren.

"Yes. We thought about that and, of course, it suggests that the culprit may have been a crew member, although the card could have been stolen."

"So far, Mike, you've done well. Okay. Got a pen handy? Here's what I'd like you to do. You and the doctor help Jack Sterling put an investigative-forensic kit together, as best you can. I'll talk to him in a minute about that. Hope you don't mind that we've asked Jack to lead the investigation?"

"No, not at all. I wouldn't know what to do anyway."

"Good. One other thing. Your ship has Closed Circuit TV. Do the cameras cover the hallways or whatever you call them?"

"Yes. I'm already working on that aspect. I've got one of my officers checking the video from the time period in question, the evening before. There is a camera near the doors to the suite, covering much of the passageway so we may get lucky."

"Okay. Good. Do you have the capability of transmitting the footage to our office?"

"We do. The latest technology, in fact, called Global Maritime Distress and Safety Systems or GMDSS, which is normally used to help our medical staff perform emergency surgery. I'll need your electronic monitoring systems information."

"Okay. I'll email it to your bridge asap. Also, Mike, does the ship have what we call a holding cell, just in case you *do* get lucky and find the perpetrator?"

"Yes, it's called the *brig*."

"Oh, one other important thing. Can you send me the names of all passengers and crew, for an indices check?"

"Actually, I can get that emailed to you directly from our head office."

"Alright, Mike. Feel free to call me back if you need anything. Can I speak to Doctor Kent now?"

"Dr. William Kent."

"Hello, Doctor. Clive Lundgren. I know you've been to the scene, conducted your examination and pronounced death, with an approximate time. I need you to return for a second exam. This time verbalizing what you see and do, on camera, please. Use a recorder for the audio—even a cell phone—so that is clear to transcribe. If this matter goes to trial, it's great evidence to have. Please use a rape kit and turn the evidence over to Mike Donnelly, writing each step down in your notes. As an MD, I know you're familiar with the four causes of human death. We have to consider each of those when investigating sudden deaths. Even with a throat cutting, there's always a possibility of suicide. You're certain this looks like a murder to you?"

"Yes, I'm almost certain. During my hospital internship, I worked in an emergency ward and saw several throat slashings. Of course, your forensic pathologist will be more conclusive."

"Great. Thanks for your help. Oh, by the way, do you have cold storage facilities?"

"Yes. We have a small morgue on a lower deck, well separated from food storage as you can imagine, set aside for the occasional deceased person while at sea. With thousands aboard and many elderly, it is not unknown for a heart attack to claim someone. I've never attended a murder at sea before though."

"Good. Any questions for me?"

William Kent said, "No," and was asked to hand the phone to Jack Sterling.

"Jack Sterling speaking."

"I'm Clive Lundgren, Miami FBI. May I call you Jack?"

"Yes, if I can call you Clive?"

"Deal. Before I say anything, I take it you've agreed to assist?"

"Yes. Just to let you know that of all the murders I've investigated, this is the first one for me at sea; a novel experience it's going to be. I take it you have some remarks for me and some instructions?"

"Yes, and as you might have guessed, I've confirmed your previous employment with Toronto. I talked with Superintendent Wall. He sends you his regards."

"Thanks. He served under me for seven years. Did he make any derogatory remarks?"

"No, *au contraire.* Before I called him I did not know your position when you retired. He said you were in charge of five hundred detectives. Whew, that's a lot of people. How many officers on strength with your entire city department?"

"Just over fifty-four hundred. It's the third largest police force in Canada, after the Ontario Provincial Police and the largest, the Royal Canadian Mounted Police, whom we refer to as the 'Feds'—somewhat like your agency, I guess, except they also do regular municipal and provincial police patrols in many parts of the country."

"Yes, I've done business with the RCMP. Good organization. During your service, you've seen a lot of mayhem then. So much the better for us.

"Anyway, here's the anomaly we face. We have an American-owned vessel, owners residing in the U.S.A., but registered for operational and business reasons in another country—the British Virgin Islands—manned overwhelmingly by a non-American crew, in the middle of the Atlantic Ocean, that is owned by no one. The deceased is American and the perpetrator could be any nationality. As a law enforcement agency, this creates a mix of legal, ethical and operational problems for us in which to operate.

"To continue," said Clive, "the first point is regarding the seeming lack of legal authority for you and the ship's S.O. to conduct a police-type investigation. He's not a sworn peace officer as you may know, and you are an alien in our wonderful immigration parlance, with no jurisdiction—with all due respect, Jack. I'm not an expert in matters like this. After all, we rarely get calls of this nature. But let me try to explain further. From where you did your police service in Canada, you are probably unaware of a piece of American federal legislation called the *Cruise Vessel Security and Safety at Sea Act*—or *CVSSA* for short—passed by our Congress in 2010. It's been designed specifically for American-owned commercial shipping and deals almost exclusively with ship safety: fires, collisions, pollution, piracy and security, the so-called 'big ticket items' for these ships. It is important to note that this act was written from an American perspective. While it covers the responsibilities of ship security officers quite well concerning those major events, what it does *not do,* in our view, is go far enough to designate these people as peace officers, thereby giving them the power to arrest, search, seize evidence and to use the Miranda caution, for our cases at least, when faced with criminal activity aboard ship that might wind up in an American court. To repeat, that kind of action cannot take place outside the 12-mile limit. More on that point in a minute.

"This cruise line is registered offshore in an independent nation, British Virgin Islands—BVI—and secondly, most of the cruise ship's security personnel, are *not* U.S. citizens. So, trying to create peace officer status may be *ultra vires,* that is, beyond the legal authority of anyone to do that.

"And, anticipating your question: yes, our agency has contacted the BVI about this matter. I believe World Cruise Lines has also done that. Their response was, 'Thanks for letting us know.' I take that response to mean that's as far as they will go. Now, you may ask, 'Why is *Seascape* registered with a foreign country?' The answer is mainly twofold: to reduce ship operating costs and to avoid some of the rules and regulations of the ship owner's country.

"It seems to me that unless international law can be changed to create police officer status for security personnel aboard cruise ships, or failing that, if they wish to appoint at least one person, the chief of security, say—regardless of nationality—this *lack of authority*, to use that phrase, will continue. The *CVSSA*, however, does offer some small degree of law enforcement training—typically two weeks—most of which deals with ship safety aspects, which in reality, of course, is the major concern, but there is only eight hours of investigative training.

"This training is delivered by our agency, though I have to say, it does little to help with investigating serious criminal activity aboard ship, like murder, rape and so on. I can only say 'Thank God' these types of offenses rarely happen, which also means, of course, that security people get little chance to practice doing investigations. I've advised the captain that I'd like you to assume control of the investigation and for people to take instructions from you, and he and the Company head office have agreed. Okay?"

"Yes, that's fine," said Jack.

"I'd like to spend a few minutes briefing you in the matter of seagoing legislation, and the lack thereof. The first is about safety of life at sea, called *SOLAS*, an international convention adopted by the International Maritime Organization (IMO) in 1980, and two years later, the *Law Of the Sea Convention* (UNCLOS) was concluded by the United Nations in Geneva. The first comes under the direction of the IMO, headquartered in London, England. What I have to say next is important to the outcome of this investigation. These treaties govern the operation of merchant vessels, including cruise ships, on the high seas. They focus on ship construction, equipment, operation and safety, rules of the road, pollution, piracy and, to a lesser extent, crime at sea. Of course, the rules are only binding on states that have signed on. The United States is *not* a member of *UNCLOS* but, strangely, is a signatory to SOLAS. There are over 170 members of this convention.

"A treaty is nothing more really than a bunch of mutually agreed upon set of rules governing seagoing matters by member states. I don't think I have to tell you that this form of 'law' is not at all the same as legislation governing a country's land-based laws which people have to obey, or face the possibility of arrest, or some form of penalty. Members of a treaty *'agree to obey'* those rules and take effective action if they are disobeyed, but the glue to bind them together and commit them to action, it seems to me, is weak, at least in respect to criminal matters. Not all member states take action when there is a necessity as is the current situation with the British Virgin Islands and this ship. You see the problem we face?"

Jack answered in the affirmative.

"The words *high seas* in the *Law Of the Sea Convention* cover the areas of the world's oceans over which no state has jurisdiction, the so-called open waters or high seas or more colloquially, *no man's land*. Anyway, the UN's main focus is the safety of ships, physical, mechanical and human, but with added emphasis today on piracy. It also includes rules governing navigation and pollution prevention. The *Law Of the Sea Convention* mentions the safety of passengers but does not really define what is meant by that, unless it's meant to fall under the whole rubric of passenger safety which would obviously include criminal matters. The convention states that flag states have criminal jurisdiction over that vessel. That's all well and good but the problem lies in the fact that such countries are often small and located in remote parts of the world, giving them little capability to effectively conduct or guide on-board investigations and, as I said, often little desire to do so. In many or most cases, they are in the ship registration business strictly for the money."

"Okay, we're following you so far, Clive," said Jack. "Please keep going."

"Now, if I could conclude with one more piece of sea stuff to add to the mix, so that you get the complete picture of what controls international shipping, I'll refer you again to the *CVSSA*. I'd like to read these two significant paragraphs from it, in part, to show why it is so different from the two conventions. Its enforcement is the responsibility of three American federal agencies: the FBI, the U.S. Coast Guard and Homeland Security.

"Section two, sub-section seven states: 'Except for United States flagged vessels, or foreign flagged vessels operating in an area subject to the direct jurisdiction of the United States, there are no federal statutes that explicitly require cruise lines to report alleged crimes to U.S. government officials.' What that means here, is beyond the twelve-mile offshore limit. I take that to mean involving U.S. citizens as well. Now, sub-section ten is also interesting. Goes to the heart of what you are about to do now, Jack. It reads: 'It can be difficult for professional cruise investigators'—whoever *THEY* are; my words— 'to immediately secure an alleged crime scene on a cruise vessel, recover evidence of an onboard offense, and identify and interview witnesses to the alleged crime.'

"In my view, no truer words were written. What is also significantly missing in that sentence is 'identify the perpetrator.' It seems to me, that what the language needs to be clearer about, with *UNCLOS, SOLAS* and *CVSSA,* is how to effectively conduct on-board criminal investigations, together with necessary equipment, by people who are properly trained, with authority to act as investigators. Frankly, I don't know how that can be achieved."

The agent took a long deep breath.

"Hmm," Jack replied. "All of what you've told me is a lot of detail, and a bit confusing, but, in the short term at least, should not prevent me from helping out. I understand that the captain, or master, of the ship is fully responsible for taking action with whatever takes place aboard. In this case, of course, he's already set that in motion through his security team."

"Yes. That's the obvious start to this process. To reiterate, it's good to have you aboard to help us out. Of course, it remains to be seen what the eventual outcome might be, if you identify a culprit. See what you've got yourself mixed up in!"

"Yeah, you're right. Anyway, thanks for telling us all this. I had no idea that this situation existed. Why didn't you tell me about this before I accepted, Clive? I might have turned you down!"

"No, I don't think so. You regard this as a challenge to your abilities, I suspect. No offense intended but the security officer has had very little training in doing criminal investigations, nor does he have the equipment to do so, just rudimentary stuff. The last thing to mention is to have a court of competent jurisdiction try these matters. Should we—you, in this case—get lucky and make an arrest, the matter would be referred to a Federal Court in the United States. In our case at hand, that could well result in a long legal argument. I'm damned if I know what would happen to a suspect who is not an American citizen.

"Anyway, Jack, that's our problem, not yours. The FBI, of course, has an obligation to carry out as thorough an investigation as possible where an American citizen is concerned, so, I'm going to have to rely on you and the S.O. to do the best you can, in the circumstances. To have no investigation done, or only a rudimentary one, would probably result in the perpetrator 'getting away with murder.' In your absence we could try from here to guide the security people through the investigation procedures—talking to witnesses, suspects, collecting and preserving evidence, etcetera—but that would be difficult to say the least. Given that you are there, and with your experience, is a much better solution for us. You good with that, Jack?"

"Yes, quite okay, Clive. I have one question about how the FBI requires to be advised about crime at sea, as it involves U.S. citizens. Is your agency covered by statute for that purpose?"

"Yes, but only under the *Cruise Vessel Security and Safety at Sea Act* and, as I said, within the territorial limits of the U.S.A. where U.S. citizens are involved. The flag state, in this case, appears it is not going to act. I hope all of this is understandable?"

"I think so. I'll have to dwell on it. As you point out though, it doesn't really concern me."

"Now, we will have to deal with our U.S. Attorney if you do manage to find the culprit. I'm not 100% sure though, in these circumstances, that charges can be laid even if we have a smoking gun case. If it doesn't work and the person in this case walks away free, that may be enough to make the UN re-think its maritime responsibilities under the *Law Of the Sea* and cover that seeming oversight by incorporating suitable language, through that *Convention*, to set up some kind of legal investigative unit, with those powers. Another thought too: could Interpol's mandate be expanded or changed somehow to include performing this kind of work? There is a rule under their strategic priorities mandate that 'authorizes the deployment of teams specialized in incident response,' whatever that means. Seems to me though, that Interpol exists more for organized crime, and not what I call regular types of crime. That's just a guess on my part. It does not help us now though. Unfortunately, it sometimes takes an event like this to make things right, so to speak. With the world's political situation as it is, a most difficult task."

"I fully understand, Clive. I promise you I'll do my part. Of course, you may be worrying unnecessarily. I may not find my man, or woman…."

"I've had dealings with Canadian police before. Very professional people. So, I've asked Mike to help you put together some investigative aids. You, he and the doctor will have to do the best you can with whatever you can scrape together. Are you going to use the ship's camera?"

"Mike will. I have a brand new Blackberry Z10 smartphone, as one of two retirement gifts from my staff. It has a built-in camera and flash for taking excellent, 8-megapixel photos. The photos are date-and-time stamped and can even be geo-referenced for location. My daughter Avery has instructed me in the phone's use, so I should be good to go."

"What was the other retirement gift, if I may ask?"

"A large bottle of one-hundred-years-old Irish Delamain Extra Cognac. I'll keep a mouthful for you when you next get to Toronto."

"Thanks, Jack. I look forward to that. So, I take it you've formulated some kind of plan to get going?"

"Yes. Just a reminder. I have not been to the scene yet, and I am aware of the golden hour principle. The sooner we get to work on the crime scene, the better. My first task is to cobble together some evidence-gathering materials, and do a plan, or a sequence of action, for when we get to the suite. This ship will have a rape kit—or at least the materials to assemble one—and I'll ask the doctor to use it and get him to examine the body in my presence, and to give us an initial opinion if there had been sexual activity. He's never done a murder scene before. I need him to tell me the probable cause of death, even though it's apparently really evident in this case, and for him to make detailed notes. I understand the scene is a mess and it's going to take some time to examine it, do our forensic stuff, etcetera, and, I imagine we need to get the body to the cooler asap.

"As well, I'll turn over all exhibits to Mike Donnelly, making sure our respective notes reflect the chain of custody. He has secure lockers in the security office. When we've concluded our examination of the scene, we'll remove the evidence we collect and then lock and seal the suite to await your forensic staff, which I expect you will try to put aboard by helicopter when we are closer to Miami. Okay with that?"

"Sure, sounds good."

"It's a very large suite I'm told, some two thousand square feet. When I get there, I'm going to try to use skype first to do a panoramic view of the scene to give you an idea. If you are not available, could you have one of your agents on standby? By the time we get organized and walk to the suite, it might be another hour or so."

"Yes, okay. I'll have Agent Ralph Harkins ready here. He's done a number of murder investigations. By the way, has this incident been made public aboard ship?"

"That I don't know. Here's Mike Donnelly. Maybe he can tell you."

Mike told the agent that it had not. "The captain is thinking about putting a brief announcement in the daily news sheet distributed to each cabin, categorizing it as an unfortunate sudden death, which of course is true, at least for the time being. Hard to keep something like this completely under wraps though," he finished.

"Thanks. One last request. Would you send us the names of ship's personnel who are now witnesses, with their DOB, addresses, nationality, etcetera. We'll run their names through the system. You never know, right? Now back to Jack, please."

"Sterling."

"Jack, having you aboard on this cruise is a bit of serendipity for us. With all due respect for security personnel on cruise vessels, they seldom have murders to deal with, and it would seem, fewer bodies since most would go overboard. Let me know what I can do from here, Jack. I take it your wife is with you?"

"Yes, Jean is. Not to worry, she's used to me being not being around for long periods of time when duty calls."

"Yeah, I understand. That's law enforcement for you. Talk to you soon."

♦   ◊   ♦

Meanwhile, Jean Sterling was by now, getting a bit concerned. It had been over an hour since her husband had departed and she wondered what on Earth would keep him so long, without letting her know what it was about. 'Was something wrong at home?' she wondered. 'Dammit, I'm going to check at the purser's office'—which she did.

The purser said, "I'm sorry, Mrs. Sterling, I only know that our security officer asked your husband to accompany him to the bridge. I'll try calling if you like?"

The outcome of the call was that Jean was escorted to the top of the ship and talked to her husband, relieved to learn that this summons did not concern their family. After telling her briefly about the murder, Jack said, "Listen, darling, I hope you don't mind what I'm about to do. The FBI asked me to help out, and I don't think I really have any other choice, do you?"

"No, of course not, but what a coincidence! Are you ever going to give up doing whodunits?" she laughed. "Hope you at least get a chance to come to bed tonight, instead of another of the all-nighters you used to pull."

Jack introduced her to Mike Donnelly, saying she may remember him greeting them near the start of the voyage.

Mike said, "Mrs. Sterling, I'll arrange for a personal bridge tour in a day or two. We're sorry we did not find you earlier to tell you. Meantime, if you need anything, please give me a call," giving her his business card before she left.

Jack asked Mike Donnelly if they could use his Ops Center office for a discussion on strategy with the doctor, and from there, go to the infirmary to put together the items needed for the investigation. Mike told him the space would be his to use.

While Mike was arranging that, there was a call from Hannah Goldman, asking, in a tremulous voice, about what happened to her companion—"There is a guard at her door who won't tell me what's going on, and won't let me in, and her phone isn't responding. He said you were the only person who could explain. Is she okay? What's happening?"

Mike had to think about his reply a few seconds, not wanting to answer her question right now. "Look," he said, "how about I call you back later this morning or early afternoon and we can meet and talk. I will explain then. Please don't worry."

The doctor, Jack and Mike sat in Mike's office.

Jack said, "I need to review briefly what needs to be done at the crime site. There is a protocol for gathering evidence that needs to be followed. It goes like this. With every item you seize, you need to place it in a separate container of some kind—a box or bag or bottle—labeling it with a sequential number, the date, time, location found, brief description, and your name. Maybe make a note of being briefed on procedure in your notes now if you would. I'll look after the photographs. I will try *not* to handle any evidence. The more

people handling exhibits, the more problem with the chain of custody and therefore in getting them admitted as evidence when it goes
to trial. Okay with that?"

Mike said, "Yes. As well, may I suggest you use one of our tablets
to show and transmit the crime scene. The screen is quite a bit larger
than your phone as you know. Also, we have to complete a ship's
form, called an Incident Account, to be given to the captain. He'll
send a c.c. to Head Office with a copy to the FBI."

"Good suggestion, Mike. Okay with this, Doc?"

Dr. Kent nodded, "Your approach sounds logical to me."

♦   ◊   ♦

At the ship's clinic, a nurse put together all the medical equipment
needed, placing them in two boxes. Surgery room clothing was put
in three bags. The non-surgery items needed were collected from the
security office and the pharmacy. Dr. Kent called the officer in charge
of cold storage, advising him of the arrival in the afternoon, of a deceased person for the morgue. He reminded him to place a sign on
the morgue door: *No admittance without permission of Officer i/c Security
Section*, who would deliver the body and take charge of the key.

When Jack got to the clinic, he was pleased to find all the items
he needed had been found and were present.

"Well done," he told the nurse, "and thanks for your efforts."

Turning to the doctor, he mentioned the eventual need for a gurney, but, upon reflection, decided they did not really want to wheel it
through the ship with passengers about. "Suggestions?"

Dr. Kent said, "We have just the transportation for this kind of
event. It's a gurney of sorts, but looks like an extra-long, two-shelf
delivery trolley, long enough to fit a body on the bottom. We place
the body in a SUB—that's an acronym for Special Use Box—suit-
ably covered, on the lower shelf, and carry pots and pans or cleaning

equipment, on the upper shelf, to disguise its purpose. The only times we've had to use it was for natural-cause deaths."

"Well, you've had some practice. Good," said Jack. "Okay. I think we can get ready to go. Doctor Kent, I'd like us to wear surgeon's gowns, trousers, masks, hats, shoe covers and latex gloves in the suite. To avoid stares and unnecessary worry from passengers and crew, let's carry them and put them on just inside the suite door. Before we move farther forward into the suite, I'll scan around the area and decide where we walk. This precaution may seem a bit *CSI*-like, but don't forget, the movie people copied these procedures from police investigation methods. I'll be taking pictures as we proceed. When we reach the bed and the deceased, what I'd like you to do, Doc, is examine the body again, paying attention to the neck wound, measuring it, telling me the cause of death—for the record—and do another estimation of the TOD. As well, use the rape kit procedure. I take it you are familiar with all this?" A nod from the doctor. "We need to collect blood samples, on and around the bed and any other place deemed necessary. I'd also like you to do a fingernail scrape. You've already been to the scene. Is there anything in particular I should know?"

"Well, I'm not sure—after all, I've never been to a murder scene before—but I wonder why this woman was alone in such a large suite. Was she traveling alone, and if so, who would want to kill her and why? And how did the person get in, unless it was someone she knew, or it was a staff member?"

"Good observation, Doc. Apparently she had a traveling companion who is staying in a separate cabin. We have a lot to find out."

Mike Donnelly had returned with three sheets of paper, one for each of them. The list identified these items, each marked as *'collected'*.

Rape Kit

Petri dishes with covers

Test tubes – vials, stoppers

Scissors – two

Several combs − new, in package

Exacto knife

Glass/plastic, liquid containers/covers

Thermometer - digital

Cotton swabs

Alcohol rubs

Q-tips & tongue depressors

Talcum powder or Corn starch

Latex Gloves − box

Stick-on labels − 2 or more packs

Scotch tape − 3/4 inch

Plastic bags − various

Paper bags − 2 doz. 9x6

1 doz. cardboard boxes − various, flattened, plus wide tape

Pill containers − new, with lids − 2 doz.

Elastic bands − 40

Tweezers − 2

12-inch ruler, steel, inches & centimeters

15-foot (5 metre) retractable tape measure, metal

Magnifying glass

Flashlight

Marker pens

Sketch pad − or 12x8 Bond paper

Envelopes − manila & white, 50+

Note books − spiral-bound, 3

Tie-on tags − 30

Body bag

Surgeons gowns, pants, caps, shoe covers, face masks

To both men, Jack said, "Are we missing anything?"

They both said the list looked okay.

"Let's each take a new notebook now and we can go to the clinic and pick up the rest of the equipment. Can you bring along two security officers? By the way, how is your staff member doing with the CCTV review?"

"Still looking and organizing the images. She'll let me know what the camera shows before long, I would think. Tell me, Jack, what do you need the talcum powder and combs for?"

"You'll see, Mike. Before we go, gents, a word about making notes. We've each got a note book and I need you to make notes as we move around the scene, especially with respect to any evidence that you deal with. These form the basis for formal reports—one for you, Mike, one for you, Doc, and one for the FBI which will form a guide to the prosecutor's case in court if it gets that far. As well, if you are called as a witness, you may be asked to produce your notes, and you may also ask the judge for permission to read from them, if needed. Defense counsel will get a look too. So you can imagine how important they are.

"Also, just let me remind you of the protocol involved in collecting evidence at a crime scene. It comes under the heading called *chain of custody*. It's a methodology that works to ensure that every piece of evidence, of any kind, passes through the possession of as few people as possible, until it is presented in court at trial. Everyone who has access to that evidence in the investigation will likely be called to the stand to say what part he or she played on its way from the crime scene, to the courtroom. Defense counsel will look for any break in that chain of custody and, if there is one, it's highly probable that item may not be admitted into evidence. If that happens, the case could be dismissed. Enough said, I think."

On their way to the aft end of the ship and *Suite 7001*, Mike took the opportunity to point out the locations of some of the cameras. He said they cover most of the decks, and are monitored 24/7 from the

Ops Center where there is a wall of monitors watched by one of his staff. Everything is digital and recorded to a secure, solid-state storage device. As the men approached the end of the passageway at the aft end of deck 7, Mike pointed to the only camera monitoring that end—on their left side as they were now facing the rear of the ship. Nautically, on the starboard side.

"We don't operate the cameras in a clandestine manner—people know they are there. As much as anything, they're for passenger safety and comfort. For example, it helps us with noisy people, running in passageways, drunks, crude behavior and coincidentally, to keep an eye on our service people going about their work. Just as importantly, while monitoring the decks exposed to the open air, we keep a closer eye on the public areas, especially the pools, railings and stairways. One last but very important thing the cameras are there for, is to monitor emergency situations such as burst pipes and flooding, fire, and personal accidents. You can see how useful they are and indeed, necessary."

"Yes, very much so. In this case, let's hope we can identify the murderer. Okay, having said that then," replied Jack, "we can considerably reduce the amount of time spent to examine and isolate the time frame our culprit appears on screen. We know when housekeeping entered the suite in the evening—it was about 8:45 p.m., wasn't it?"

Mike nodded.

"I understand your door locks have the ability to record the entry times, so let's start reviewing the film from just before that time, okay?"

"That's already being done, Jack."

"Yes, of course, what am I thinking? Sorry, Mike. You know your ship."

◆ ◇ ◆

In the Security Operations Center, Sheila Turner, the officer reviewing the CCTV footage covering the aft area of deck 7, enters the time of 8:40 p.m., as asked, so as not to miss the housekeeper entering. Fast-forwarding the film, she observes the female crew member knocking on the door at 8:45, and then entering, using her pass-card, leaving the room twenty minutes later. Again, she forwards the film until she sees more human activity but it was people walking by. Almost thirty minutes later by the CCTV time stamp, she observes a man and woman stop at the door. After two minutes of conversation, the man leaves toward the elevator and the woman enters the suite. The officer notes the screen footage and time for each event.

Sheila now advances the footage further until she sees what looks to be a waiter, carrying a serving tray, appear from the top of the stairs, walk to the double doors and knock. Though she can't be positive, from the person's build and posture, it appears reasonable to assume this is a male. His head is not visible to the camera, as the tray is held high up and obscures the view. Waiting a few seconds, he knocks again but the door is not opened. Using a pass-card, the man enters. Time: 10:10 p.m.

He leaves seven minutes later, the tray now in his right hand, again shielding his face. 'That's a long time to deliver food,' Sheila muses. 'Must have been chatting.'

He entered the elevator, presumably on the way back to the kitchen.

Sheila re-winds the film back to 10:04 and starts viewing forward again, past 10:10 and continues to 11:45 hours, stopping three times, seeing passengers walk by the suite doors, probably returning to their rooms in the same area. Except for the waiter, no one entered or left the suite in this time interval.

◆　◇　◆

Thinking a bit, she theorized that because the time of death was estimated by Dr. Kent to be in mid to late evening, based on what she had just viewed: that the waiter, as the only person other than the woman passenger to enter the suite in this time frame, should have called about finding a body. That did not happen, so, *ipso facto*—a phrase she had read recently in the detective novel she was half-way through—it's got to mean that the murderer *must* be the waiter!

Sheila knew there was still footage to review for the rest of the night and early morning up until the cleaner's arrival before her observation could be conclusive. She sat and agonized a minute or so about whether or not to call her boss immediately. She didn't want to appear too 'Sherlock Holmesy' as she said to her roommate later, nor did she want to delay giving him the information. The latter won out.

Mike Donnelly answered his cell phone and listened to an excited voice. "What time was this, Sheila?"

She told him what she had seen from the CCTV camera, including the time, and what she thought it might mean, in respect to a possible suspect.

"Thanks. Good observation, Sheila. Okay, I'd like you to print off stills from the CCTV—the man and woman outside the door talking, him going to the elevator, when the woman entered, and the waiter entering and leaving. And make a duplicate of the entire video of that time period, so I can send it to the FBI in Miami. Well done and thanks for letting me know. Not sure how long we'll be. I'll check in on you when we are done here in the suite."

Turning to Jack, he told him what his assistant had said. "We apparently have our killer on tape, a waiter. The images are black and white and a bit grainy for reproduction, but likely quite useful. This would give us an exact time of death. In this case, between 10:10 and 10:17 p.m. Sheila believes she's solved our murder for us. Looks like this may be coming together, Jack."

"Let's hope she has. I can get back to my vacation! Now let's look at the crime scene first."

♦   ◊   ♦

The five of them stood just inside the doors of the suite, the trolley with all the investigative aids pushed to one side. Jack noted the time—11:05—and said, "God, this place is huge. This is what I call *First Class Passage*. It's about the size of my home in Toronto. Are there other cabins like this?"

"Yes," replied Mike, "this is one of three suites like this. It's 2,000 square feet stretching across the beam of the ship. You may have noticed in your brochure. They are called *crown suites*. One is unoccupied on this trip. If you like I'll show you and your wife around the vacant one before we get to Miami. Doubt she'll want to see this one."

As they gowned up—paper pants, medical gowns, shoe covers, hair nets, masks and gloves—Mike commented that this was the first time he'd dressed up like a doctor going into surgery. He dismissed the guard already on duty and asked the two officers he'd brought with him to sit down in the nearest chairs by the only exit door, and wait. They were not required to dress up. He'd need them later to wheel the trolley down to the cold storage area.

Jack said, "First thing. Let's lay out all the investigative aids on the two shelves of the trolley."

"Kind of like we do in surgery," said Dr. Kent.

"As we slowly proceed into the suite, I'd like you to follow me as I take pictures of the scene. Have your notebooks handy. A reminder, Mike, you'll have to be the designated 'evidence man,' taking charge of any item that has to be removed, after it has been identified. Just put it all on the trolley. Mark each item with a number, and identify them in that order in your notebook, as we discussed. Okay with that?"

Both of them nodded.

Jack scanned the rooms and floor area with the ship's tablet, capturing video and speaking as he moved slowly forward, noting the barely discernible bloody footprints on the pale blue rug, slowly increasing in visibility as they went forward. At the white marbled-floor dining area, which divided the combined drawing room, living room and library to the right, and the large bedroom to the left, the dark-red shoe prints were now prominent. Mike left the trolley here.

The glass-topped dining table had on it, beside a huge bowl of fresh flowers, a small china plate with a knife and fork neatly placed together, with a few crumbs. No blood on the knife.

A large bone china mug had a residue of a dark brown stain on its inside. Bending down over the table, Jack sniffed and declared that it smelled like hot chocolate. "We'll bag this stuff later. Let's enter the bedroom, the scene of the crime. Wait until I've had a look and taken a few shots."

Stepping to his extreme left to avoid the bloody mess on the floor, he looked intently at the corpse on the bed and exclaimed to Mike, "My God, I know this woman! We met on the dock, waiting behind Jean and I, to board the ship. We spoke briefly and she had a young woman with her. We did a tour with her too and had lunch in, uh, what was the name of the island?—*Lan-* something."

"Lanzarote," said Mike.

"Yes. Couple of nice people. I wonder what happened?"

Regaining his composure, he started taking photos with his phone's camera, at one point leaning over to get some close-ups, especially of the knife wound. He noted the body was close to the edge of the massive bed, thinking that's not where someone would normally sleep. Her blood had pooled under her head, shoulders and back, and some had run onto the carpet. She had no bed clothes covering her, plainly showing her pale blue nightie at its full length. He also noted that her clenched right hand was covered in blood, but not the left.

"Dr. Kent, notice her closed right hand has blood on it, whereas her left hand does not. Would you please pry it open."

Dr. Kent opened the hand, part way, and found a gash across the palm, about three inches long. "Looks like it may be a defensive wound," he suggested, "maybe to ward off the knife by grabbing at it."

"Yes, I suspect you're right," said Jack, taking a couple of shots of the cut. "Now, I know you did an initial rape test when you were here with Mike but I'd like you to do another one, so we can show a coroner and maybe a jury, that this was done. Speak as you are conducting this exam, and I'd like you to measure the wound to the neck, that is, the full length, and the width at its widest and note that. Check the rigor mortis again, and body temperature. Also, note the pillow and the pattern of the outward blood spatter or spray, to the left side of the head. Can you to make a comment about that and the nature of the wound?"

"Let me look and I'll do that now if you like."

After a careful examination, he said, "With regard to the cut, it was obviously made by a sharp instrument, probably a knife, possibly with a serrated blade because it is a bit ragged at the edge. I believe the cut was started high up on the deceased's left side of her neck, cutting the carotid artery and going in deep, then being dragged around the throat, above the laryngeal prominence or Adam's Apple as it is commonly known, and finishing on her right side, but not as far up, or as far back. Without the results of an autopsy, for now I'd say the wound became shallower as the knife was dragged around the throat, from her left to right side. To me, that suggests a left-handed person made the cut with a dragging motion. Mike, would you pass me the measuring tape, please?"

The S.O. took the tape from the top shelf of the trolley, which had been rolled to the foot of the bed, and handed it to the doctor.

Bending the tape around the neck, Dr. Kent pronounced, "The length of the cut is seven-and-three-quarter inches, or nineteen-point-five centimetres, and at the widest part gaping open to one inch or two-and-a-half centimeters, gradually reducing in width. The blood spray on the pillow would come from the jugular suddenly being severed, with blood pressure spewing it out. Have you got pictures?"

A nod from Jack.

William Kent continued, "With respect to condition of the body, it is quite stiff, in full rigor, with no noticeable difference since I was last here. As you're most likely aware, Mr. Sterling, given your past employment, full rigor mortis sets in, in twelve to eighteen hours, always dependent upon location of the body and the ambient air temperature. This later condition is called *algor mortis*. Obviously, blood loss has been considerable which could possibly affect the onset of rigor too.

"Mike, would you mind checking the room temperature on the wall control? This would be the ambient temperature."

Mike did and read out, "Seventy-two degrees."

Placing a thermometer into the woman's rectum, the doctor checked the interior body temperature. Reading the result from the glass tube, he said, "Internally, the body is at sixty-one degrees Fahrenheit. I'm declaring the cause of death was by means of a cut around the throat leading to extreme exsanguination. With these factors present, I'm going to take an estimate of the time of death—approximately late in the evening, yesterday, Monday, May 26. Between nine and midnight."

As the physician gathered samples of pubic and head hair, skin scrapings, swabs inside and around the genitals and rectum, scrapings under the fingernails, blood and inside-cheek DNA, etc. and the victim's clothing, he stored each item of evidence in appropriately-labelled rape kit packages. Sterling watched him use two clean combs from the trolley, one to comb the victim's scalp hair and the other, her pubic hair. Hairs found on the combs were bagged and would be tested for foreign hair. As well, using tweezers, the doctor removed fifty or so pubic and scalp hair samples, and placed them in separate envelopes. He also took the magnifying glass and looked for loose hairs around the body. All he spotted were placed in separate containers.

Jack asked if he could determine whether or not the victim had had sexual intercourse sometime close to her death.

"I can't definitively say but think it's unlikely, from my initial examination. There is no bruising or tearing, and no semen obviously present. As you know, Jack, the autopsy and lab results will determine that more definitively. I note she is wearing a wedding ring and what could be an engagement ring with a very large diamond, on her left ring finger. Makes me wonder what the motive was for this death—such as theft of her jewelry. Likely whoever killed her could not get the rings off easily if they tried, due to what appears to be the onset of arthritis in her knuckles. I can't remove them now without instruments, so will leave them on the corpse."

"Yeah, good point. Takes time to hack off fingers too."

That thought made Jack look up at the bedroom wardrobe unit, situated to one side of the bed, and where a security box would be located. "Mike, can you see if the safety box door is open?"

"Let me get a bit closer. Yes, it is. It appears to be empty."

"Okay, let's get a photo of that. She may have put valuables in her purse, or suitcase, or dresser, etcetera. Let's check for these items before we leave, and with her companion as well. This woman must have been quite rich and would have brought some valuable jewelry along to wear at the formal attire events."

At the entrance to the suite, there was a knock on the door. One of the security people opened it and said, "Yes, may I help you?" to a young woman.

A bit surprised, she said, "I'm sorry to bother you. My name is Hannah Goldman. I'm Mrs. Gessner's traveling companion. I was here earlier this morning, as we'd arranged, to go to breakfast, but there was no answer. I really would like to know what is going on, please—how she is."

"Just a moment, ma'am. Please wait in the hall."

Turning, the officer called out, "Mr. Donnelly, there's someone at the door."

Mike went quickly to the entrance. The guard said, "This lady, Ms. Goldman, is asking about the…"—he was about to say 'victim' but quickly substituted the word "occupant."

Mike, still clad in his full evidence-collecting clothing, stepped out into the passageway and said, "Um, Ms. Goldman—"

Before he could continue, Hannah anxiously interrupted, "Please, I need to know what's happening. I am her traveling companion and friend. I work for her. Is she sick? Are you a doctor?"

She had presumed he was in medical garb, gowned to prevent spread of infection. Mike didn't correct her misconception.

"Ms. Goldman, thank you for your concern. If you'd bear with me a little longer, I promise I'll call you. Please go back to your cabin and I will call you shortly. Do you have a cell phone?" He took her number. "Please try to be patient."

"Who was that?" asked Dr. Kent.

"A woman friend of the deceased," replied Mike. "Possibly the young woman Sheila identified as knocking on this door at 0815 today." Turning to Jack, he said that he'd told her they would speak to her a bit later.

Jack said, "Did she give you her name?"

"Yes. Hannah Goldman."

"That's right. I forgot. That's the deceased's companion. We'll give her a call as soon as we can. Need to ask her about any valuables Mrs. Gessner may have carried with her."

"Do you think we could turn down the heat a bit, Jack? It seems a bit warm in here. Is there any point in leaving it on?"

Jack said that was a good idea. To the doctor, he asked if he was finished with his examination of the body. If so, would he be good enough to take some extra samples of blood, from the body and the bed, sealing them and putting a completed label on each sample.

Now that the doctor had taken fingernail scrapings from both hands, Jack asked him to put a paper bag over each hand and seal them with tape. "Let me know when you're done. Hope you don't have too many patients waiting in your clinic. We have a lot to do."

While the doctor was completing his examination and ensuring his notes were thorough, Jack and Mike knelt down on the rug and began to examine several footprints, taking photos and measuring the size, first placing the metal 12-inch ruler beside one of them, to show

scale. The measuring tape was used to size the length of the shoe im-
prints, certainly big enough for men's shoes. There was no discernible
pattern from the sole on the tight-weave carpet material. Jack asked
Mike to tighten his cotton slip-ons and place his covered shoe alongside. He noted a difference in length of about one inch, Mike's being
longer. "What size are your shoes?"

"Size eleven."

"So, what do you think? Size nine and a half, or ten?"

A nod from Mike.

Jack asked if crew shoes were issued.

Mike said, "Yes. They're plain rubber soles, non-slip, for use on
open decks. Most of the crew are issued with plain-soled shoes. A
good hint for us I would think?"

"I'll keep that in mind," Jack replied, making a note.

Jack did a small drawing in his note book, showing the number,
location, measurements between them and direction the shoes pointed, in this case, away from the bed. He used a pair of tweezers to pull a
bunch of blood-covered fibers from the rug, bagged them, put a note
in his book and gave the evidence to Mike. Mike applied a label with
a sequential code number, recorded a description of the item in his
list of evidence, and placed it on the cart.

"Can you reach the flashlight for me? I'm going to look around
the bedroom at the furniture and anything else that may hold fingerprints. I might get lucky and find one or two that I can possibly lift."

"How can you do that? We don't have a fingerprint lifting kit."

"That's where the talcum powder comes in handy. If I find a sample, I'll show you. Anyway, I think you may be asking yourself why I'd
need a light to look for prints. Aren't they almost invisible? Yes, they
are, but if you hold the light so that the beam is pointing at a surface
at an acute angle, they show up quite well. Just hope I find some. I
need to have the lights off in here for a moment, Doctor."

Jack looked at the security box in the clothes cabinet. However,
the metal top and one side that were accessible had a rough, finely

grated gunmetal finish and the small door had close, vertical and horizontal lines, both surfaces unsuitable to retain fingerprints. Almost missing it, lying flat on the bottom of the box, Jack found a United States passport in the victim's name, that Mike had missed on his search earlier this morning.

Shining the light along the polished countertop of the dark rosewood armoire, he spotted a fingerprint, near the edge. "Mike, I've found one. Have a look. Looks like it might be suitable. I haven't done this for a long time as you can imagine. Detectives nowadays rely on the forensic people to do this."

Taking the small tin of talcum, he very lightly shook a sprinkle over the print, the tiny holes in the lid preventing excessive powder from spilling out, from about six inches above. He next took a three-inch strip of three-quarter-inch wide clear adhesive tape, gently blew the excess powder off the latent print and then very carefully, slowly, lowered the tape onto the print area. Using the left edge of his right thumb, he pressed it very lightly along the tape, twice.

"Okay, let's see if this works," he said, more to himself than Mike, who was intently watching the procedure. Using a fingernail, he pried up one end of the tape, teasing up just enough so that he could get a grip, and very slowly, gradually, pulled the tape off. Holding the tape up at both ends, he turned toward some light and held it out in front of him. "Have a look, Mike. See the lines?"

"Yeah, I do. That's neat. Did you learn to do this in training?"

"No. I picked it up while watching one of our Ident people use it, before the days of forensic sections. When you do this kind of work over a period of time, you develop a clinical eye for details. When I finished my basic police training at the Ontario Police College and reported to my police inspector, he said that I was 'no goddam use to him until I had five years of service.' I was offended by that remark—after all, I'd been trained I told myself, ready to go out and 'clean up crime in my community.' Of course, he was right. I had a lot of learn. Anyway, back to the present...

"I can see a few ridge lines, but I'm not sure there's enough. The fingerprint readers, and the automatic machines, will probably need more than this in order to conclusively make a match. I'm going to take a photo to see if what I have will be visible. Same with any more I find, and we'll send them to the FBI. The ridges shown here appear to be large enough to be from a male. Women's prints are generally finer. I don't know if you know, Mike, but police forces in North America and elsewhere have access now to a system called the International Automatic Fingerprint Identification System or IAFIS. It's incomparably faster than the snail's pace when humans examined prints, one at a time, using magnifying glasses. If a computer hit is made now, it still takes two human beings though, to confirm the unique origin of the fingerprint for trial purposes."

"Yes, we heard about that in our eight-hour-long investigators course," Mike said holding up both hands using the quote sign. "First time for me being involved in something like this. Interesting."

"While I continue, how about you give the doctor a hand if he needs it? I'll call you if I find any evidence that needs to be bagged and recorded. When he's finished, I think we can remove the body. Not going to be a nice experience, I'm afraid. Also, would you mind checking the number of dining table place settings—how many, then check the number of sharp knives. Is one missing? Don't handle them. We'll wrap them and take them as an exhibit, or pieces of evidence, for later examination. Oh, while I think of it, check her suitcases and dresser drawers. See if there's anything we need to look at. I think we can leave stuff like that in the cabin—*suite*," he corrected himself. "It'll be under lock and key for the rest of the trip. FBI forensics team will want to have a look."

Jack did a quick flashlight sweep of the suite, mainly of tabletops and furniture, the piano and coffee table in the lounge room, kitchen cupboard doors, then moving into the bedroom-sized bathroom. The lights were too bright and he put them out. On the dark grey countertop, at one end, he spotted a decent looking print, which, under the light of his flashlight, looked small and fine enough to be female. He toyed with the idea of not bothering to lift the print, thinking that it was probably that of Mrs. Gessner or a cleaner, but said to himself, 'Well, you never know,' and did a lift. Quite clear this time. As he was doing this activity, he wondered how many sets of elimination fingerprints would have to be taken in Miami if they hadn't found a suspect by then. All the staff who had any possible connection to the case by being involved, and of course, himself.

After checking the number of place settings—six—and that each piece, including the six serrated-edged steak knives, was present, none with blood on them, Mike placed them carefully in a cardboard container, marking the contents on the lid. This evidence indicated to Jack that an outside knife had probably been used, possibly from a food tray, or belonging to the culprit, or, just maybe, he'd used one of the suite knives and washed it off after. Thinking about this for a few seconds, he discounted that idea, knowing that it would take time, and that the individual was probably in an agitated state, wanting to leave. The cutlery had to be seized as possible evidence though, if only to eliminate them.

When he put the lights on again, he looked at the toilet bowl and noticed the yellow color of the water. The seat was down. In front of the bowl, on the floor, were two very faint red smudges on the white marble; possibly footprints he thought. A *man* stood here to have a pee. Typically, he did not lift the seat, and less typically, did not flush. Jack took a couple of pictures at different angles and from the top, looking into the bowl. 'Okay, I'll have to get some liquid samples.' Examining the seat, he noted what looked like dried splashes of what could be urine. 'Hmm, how can I collect that? I don't want to scrape it off, nor do I want to dilute it by removing it with a swab. Okay, have the seat removed and take it as a piece of evidence.'

He asked Mike to arrange for that, sending one of the guards for some basic tools. He suspected that urine, at least in a healthy person, was quite sterile, meaning that no DNA material would be there, but

there was still a possibility that a urine sample could be linked somehow to an individual. He just was not sure about urine diluted with
water. Of course, he could be wrong and the stuff in the bowl was
from the victim. 'Have to make a note of that and remind the FBI
people to get a sample if possible, at the autopsy.'

Going to the evidence trolley, he took two vials and asked Mike
to fill them with samples from the toilet bowl, seal and label them.
Mike asked if the samples would be DNA tested. Jack said that they
would, but may not yield definitive evidence.

He turned his attention to the sink. At first glance under the
bright bathroom lighting, it looked clean enough. As he was about to
turn away, he noted a spot of red on the white ceramic basin, at the
top back, immediately under the hot water handle, close to the main
stem. Blood? If so, whose? The culprit's? Stood to reason. It had dried,
so, getting the box cutter knife from the evidence box, and extending
the blade, he swiped the blade with an alcohol swab, and let the blade
dry for a few seconds to be totally sterile. Then he carefully peeled the
dried blood off the surface, placing the tiny sample in a test tube and
made a note. He stood thinking for a minute about his find. Knowing
that the victim's hand had been cut, could the culprit's also have been
cut in the struggle for control? Possibly, even likely. Be good if it was.
'This'll have to wait though until we get to Miami. Must remember
to ask Clive to let me know back home, if this was the case.'

Jack turned off the lights again in the bathroom and used his
flashlight for one more look for prints. The sink counter had too
many water stains to reveal anything. Shining the light on the chrome
tap handle, the top of which was flat, he detected a small set of ridge
lines; again, not a full set. Could be from a hand palm. He managed to
get what was there onto the scotch tape. Better than nothing. Looking
in the waste bin, he removed three crumpled sheets of paper hand-
towels, with pale smears of blood. More evidence? He bagged them.

While Dr. Kent was finishing up with his samples and making
notes, Mike scoured the suite for jewelry, and found none. 'Seems to

me,' he thought, 'that a woman of means would have some with her. She could have brought along cheap costume jewelry'—which he couldn't find anyway—'but, given where she was staying on the ship, that was probably unlikely. She'd have the Real McCoy stuff. Have to check with her companion.'

He reported his observations to Jack.

Looking around, Mike saw a gold-colored leather handbag on the night table beside the bed—opened, he noted. He was about to pick it up by its sides but caught himself. 'No, leave it in place and take a photo.' Taking his pen, he pried the bag open a bit more and looked inside. He could see a gold-colored wallet, with the snap closed. 'Better take this with us,' removing it carefully with his gloved hand. Beside the handbag was a notepad provided for guests. Four numbers were written on it in pencil: *6018*, possibly a cabin number. Using his cell, Mike called the purser's office and was told that cabin 6018 was registered to an Abraham Shuster from Florida. While he was talking to the purser, she told him that Sheila Turner from his office wanted to speak with him again. He'd call her.

Mike next made a check of the verandah deck, across the back of the suite. The doors were locked from the inside and did not show any signs of forced-entry.

Jack stood in the dining room, which allowed a look into each of the living areas: the bathroom, to one side, bedroom straight ahead, and the recreation room as he called the combination TV, library and music room, on the other side. Eyeing each room slowly to see if he'd overlooked checking anything and thought, 'Was there something I've missed? Can't think of anything. I'll get Mike to have a look from this spot too.' Jack used to perform this two-person double-check when he was a street detective. 'Two pairs of eyes are better than one. And two brains,' he mused. Looking at his watch, he was surprised the time read 2:47 p.m. They'd been in the suite for over three and a half hours.

In the bedroom again, he asked Mike and the doctor if they were finished. "Take a final look. Doc, I'd appreciate it if you would get me a copy of your typed notes in due course. You'll take care of the rape kit and other evidence you gathered. If you could refrigerate it, please, that would be best. Locked up, with no one to get access to it. Thanks.

"Mike will have to make up a file folder for the whole investigation. In that respect, Mike, would you check with the ship's engineer to see if there is a scale diagram—some form of blueprint—of the layout of this suite? It would help greatly for referencing locations for presenting evidence in court if this matter goes to trial. We can show on it the furniture layout, the position of the body, blood splatter and pooling on the carpet, footprint smears and so on. Okay. We need to move the victim out now. Let's get her loaded. I think the three of us can manage that.

"First, let's see if we can wrap the bed sheet around her. Might be a bit difficult given her position. I don't think it will matter if we remove the sheet from the room. Lay out the body bag next to her, then we'll lift her in. Mike, put a tag on her toe, with full name, date of birth and nationality, followed by date of death—May 27. You can get the personal info from her ship registration card. Sorry, you know that. I don't know about you, but I'm getting rather peckish. Before we eat though, let's go down to the laundry room and let them know to be on the lookout for any bloody clothes, towels, and so on that may have been discarded by the perpetrator."

It took the three of them considerable effort to lift the corpse, Dr. Kent gently holding the woman's head. It was quite awkward, her nightie stuck to her back and covered in congealing, dark red blood. With the bag zipped up and sealed with a metal clip, the body was placed in the SUB box, also brought to the bed, then carefully lifted onto the lower shelf of the trolley and covered with a fresh grey sheet. The pillow and its stained white case were also bagged. The boxes with the exhibits and the investigation kit were put on the top. Jack asked one of the security officers to remain. Mike told him he'd be relieved in due course and to let nobody in. In the foyer, the three of them removed their investigative clothing. Mike announced their time of exit from the suite as 3:16 p.m., and wrote this in his notebook.

On their way down the service elevator and to the morgue, they passed no one. Too nice a day out for many guests to be inside the ship.

Mike said to Jack, "Why don't you go to my office? I'll call ahead and have someone bring you some lunch. I'll make sure Mrs. Gessner is safely tucked away and then go to the laundry room to see if anything bloody has come through. Shouldn't be long—back soon."

"Okay, Mike. Take the camera with you and—if they've already found anything suspicious—get photos of the clothes, laid out, and the bin they were found in, and a shot of the hallway—sorry, passageway—where they were found. Of course the names and statements from whichever staff member discovered the item, time, etc. I'll wait for you in your office, then we'll see Sheila regarding the CCTV results. Thanks."

◆ ◇ ◆

Thirty minutes earlier—3:45 p.m.

Hannah Goldman, sitting in her cabin, had worked herself into a state of complete angst, thinking the worst of the situation, fearing her mistress had caught some horrible infection and died. What other explanation for the garbed people in her suite and guard at the door? As far as she was aware, the woman was healthy. She exercised almost every day at home and had no major health problems. Hannah knew that some people die unexpectedly, but could not believe this was the case. The thought of her being murdered somehow did not enter her mind.

She'd been told that she would be contacted by security but that had been *when*? How many hours ago? She'd been asked to stay in her cabin, but simply could not sit still any longer. She left and went for a walk on the promenade deck for twenty minutes trying to clear her brain and figure out what should be done. Nothing made sense.

Back in her room, she checked her daily diary, found the cabin number for Mrs. G.'s new-found male friend, Abe Shuster, and tapped in the number on her cabin phone. It rang four times and she was about to hang up when it was answered. "Hello, Abe speaking, is that you, Rebecca?"

"No, it's me, Hannah Goldman," she replied. Before he could go on, Hannah blurted out, "Something's happened to Mrs. Gessner! I went to her suite this morning, only to be turned away by one of the ship's security officers, with no explanation—."

"—Sorry, Hannah, to interrupt, but do you mean she called you this morning?"

"No, no. Sorry. We arranged to meet today. It's been almost six hours now and I still don't know and I'm so worried! She's not answering her phone and there are medical people in her suite and it is quarantined with a guard at the door. It must be very serious. You saw her yesterday evening, Mr. Shuster. How was she then?"

"She was fine. As you know, we went to the mid-cruise captain's dinner, and then for a few dances at the *Lido Room*. I walked her to her suite and left her there at around quarter to ten or so."

"Yes, I knew about that dinner. She told me she was going with you."

"We ate the same food, and I'm fine, so it's probably not food poisoning. What do you want to do, Hannah? Can you come to my cabin?"

"Yes, I'll come right away. You are in 6018, right? That's on the same deck as my cabin."

"On second thoughts, how about the *Promenade Lounge*? Don't want you to come down with something, just in case I've got germs too. Okay? Say in five minutes?"

♦ ◇ ♦

In Mike's office, Jack sat and ate his late lunch: roast beef on rye bread, with a slice of cheddar cheese topped with long, kosher-style pickles and a mug of strong, black coffee. His blood sugar level restored, the detective reviewed his notes and began to put together a short list of next steps. He'd told Sheila they'd wait for Mike to look at the video.

When Mike returned, they discussed their next moves while he too had a sandwich. It was now close to 4 o'clock.

"What time will it be now in Miami, Mike? Sailing across six time zones it gets a bit confusing."

He checked his hand-held, did a quick calculation regarding the ship's current position, and told him it was a few minutes before 2 p.m. in Florida—there was two hours difference.

"That's good," Jack stated. "It'll give us some time to see the videos and review before we make a call. I've made a few brief to-do notes—not in any special order. I'll read them out to you; see what you think, anything to add and so on. I'd like to do this call by skype. Can we do that in your office?" and received a nodded *yes*.

"Alright. Examination of crime scene. What Dr. Kent and you and I observed and what we each did there. A list of the evidence collected and what you and the doctor are taking charge of. The only items I took were the two fingerprints and the blood sample from the bathroom sink, which I did in your presence and formally turned over to you, each of us making a note of that. Oh. Yes. Another thing: the drawing of the shoe tracks too. Speaking of the bathroom, where will you store the toilet seat lid?"

"Not to worry, I've got a secure locker for that."

"Next on my list is the results of our CCTV review. Let's have a quick look at the waiter's image and get the photo. I'll tell the agent about that, and we can transmit it to him. And we need to do some short first interviews. You have an interview room I take it, Mike?

"Yes, I'll let you have a look when we're done with the CCTV stuff."

"Good. We need to speak to Hannah Goldman and Abe Shuster

to begin with, then with staff members. The housekeeping woman who turned down the bed last evening, the cleaning maid who found the body this morning, her supervisor, the hotel manager who was also in the suite, the two cleaning staff supervisors, morning and evening, and, I suppose, your staff member, Sheila, who is checking the CCTV film footage. Anyone else?"

"Well, me too, I suppose." replied Mike. "I also went to the suite."

"Okay, you up for this? Do you want to do the talking in the interviews or leave it to me?"

"I defer to your expertise and experience, Detective Sterling," Mike said, with a smile. He'd reflected coming back from the morgue how surprisingly good he felt about being involved in this matter. It was a challenge for him and way out of his usual routine duties, but much less stressful with the Canadian detective overseeing the evidence-gathering, than it would otherwise have been. 'Maybe I missed my calling?' he thought. 'I'll tell Moira.'

◆ ◇ ◆

In the Ops Center control room at 4:10 p.m., Mike and Jack sat on either side of Sheila, watching the screen. A maid entered *Grande Suite 7001* at 8:28 and left about fifteen minutes later. At the 9:40 mark, they watched a man and a woman, both seniors, stop at the door. Only the woman entered.

"That's the victim," said Jack. "Mrs. Rebecca Gessner, clearly identifiable."

Her male companion walked to, and entered, the elevator. The elevator door closes.

Sheila advanced the footage at 16X speed, slowing to show the occasional passenger pass through the camera's field of view. The next person to come to the suite door is a waiter, seen appearing from the top of the stairs, and walking to the doors with a serving tray held up by the flat of his left hand. His face is hidden by the items on the tray. After knocking, he uses a card to enter. Time code: 10:09 p.m. Forwarding the film a little, they watched the waiter leave—seven minutes later on the time stamp—and go to the elevator and disappear, not clear whether up or down.

"We need the maid's name and to talk to her. Can you get that info, Sheila, before we leave, please?" asked Jack. "Would you roll both clips back to 8:28—to confirm the entries and exits. When you get to the waiter, stop."

Looking at him in the shot, Jack asked Mike if he noticed anything.

Mike looked hard. "Yes. He has an entry pass-card. I'm sure they are not issued to regular table wait staff; just to room servers."

"That could mean then, that he may have borrowed the card, which means, there's a possible accomplice, or he stole it. Make a note, Mike, to check that out. Now, Sheila, please roll the video forward until he reappears on screen, leaving the suite, and freeze it. Good. Note he's carrying the tray up high with his *right* hand. That blocks his face from the camera to his right now. Can we get an approximate height, do you think, judging from the door frame?"

"Not sure," said Mike. "Let me think about that. Maybe same height as me—six feet. There's only one camera at that end of the passageway, on the starboard or right side of the ship. He is facing toward the bow as he exits. That means the waiter's face is hidden entering and leaving. Sorry, I don't think I needed to explain that. Just thinking out loud."

"Don't be sorry, that's a good observation, Mike. Anyway, it's too bad you don't have two cameras there, one on either side of the doorway entrance. This should tell us a couple of things. First, he's more than likely to be a crew member and, that he probably scoped out this aspect of surveillance, which, when I think about it, tells me he'd planned this and knew something of value was in this particular suite. If not, how would he know which suite, if any, to attempt to rob? Did someone tell him—a cleaner or attendant perhaps? An accomplice might very well explain his pass-card. Or he was simply 'fishing'? There's two other things to note. He's not wearing his white gloves coming out, and we did not find any in the suite, so that must mean he carried them out. Under the tray lid perhaps? And, why not wear them? Did he have them on when he killed the woman and they became bloody? Also, look at his raised right arm. Notice where his watch band is: on his right arm. He wears it loose, and, I believe, is most likely left-handed. The band looks like it's made of chrome, silver or steel, but the face is too indistinct to tell the make or style. Anyway, look at where you and I wear our watches—on the left wrist, where I think most right-handed people wear theirs. While I think of it, Sheila, can you do a photo enlargement of the watch for me?"

"That's good, Jack," said Mike. "Kind of confirms the left-handed cut across the throat theory. Gives us a couple of things to look for. As well, when I think about it, all food orders delivered to guests are recorded: date, time, room number, type of food, and the waiter's name. Shouldn't be too difficult to find this guy," he said, with optimism. "—If he's an actual waiter."

"You may be right. Let's hope so. Good point about the food order, Mike. Let's get the morning and afternoon wait staff shift supervisors in here soon, to take a look at the pictures. Remind them, *not a word to anyone!*"

◆   ◇   ◆

Ralph Harkins, in the FBI office in Miami, appeared on screen, the Hollywood image of an agent: dark suit, pale blue shirt with matching tie, well groomed, with a bit of a Texas accent, age: around forty-five.

He said, "Howdy, folks, good to see you. As we say in the United States now, *'Whassup?'*"

It was 2:35 in Miami.

Mike replied, "Hello, Ralph. I'm Mike Donnelly, the Chief of Security. I have with me retired Chief Superintendent of Detectives

Jack Sterling, formerly with the Metro Toronto Police Department. I take it you can see us okay?"

"Yes, good to see you two. Jack, thanks for offering to help."

Mike continued. "You know roughly what the situation is here. Do you want a recap now?"

"Sure, that'd help."

"Alright. I'll let Jack do the talking."

"Ralph, some of this information you already have: name of the deceased, age, address, date of murder, photos of the scene, etcetera.

"Mike and I have just returned from the suite, where we spent over three hours examining the place and the body, with our ship's head physician, Dr. William Kent. Note that this is a very large living quarters, two thousand square feet, divided into three main living areas and the foyer entrance. The palm of the woman's right hand was cut, likely indicating a struggle over the knife, a defensive wound. That, plus the way the neck was sliced open, strongly suggests the culprit is left-handed.

The body has been examined, tagged and removed to our morgue, under lock and key. We collected and numbered many pieces of evidence, including fingerprints. We've just finished looking at our CCTV footage and found what we strongly believe is our suspect, a waiter or someone posing as one. We're sending you a couple of pictures, and they are quite revealing, as I will explain in a minute. We noted that the maid entered the suite at about 8:30 p.m. and came out fifteen minutes later. Clearly not the killer since the victim didn't arrive until later, but she could be a suspect, as an accomplice."

"Thanks, Jack. Sounds like you guys have been busy. With regard to the photos of the waiter, we'll examine them and keep them handy, in the event that you manage to identify the suspect. And hopefully we can find some comparison points from the fingerprints you collected." Looking at the detective on his screen, Ralph said, "Well, Jack, what else can you tell me? Your general thoughts?"

"There's a few things to comment on, not necessarily in order.

First, as a matter of pure coincidence, my wife Jean and I had lunch with the deceased a few days ago. I guess that makes me a possible suspect too. Maybe I should recuse myself!"

"You are kidding, of course...."

Jack smiled and nodded. "To continue. I think you know that we lack two things: full forensic equipment and a forensic investigator. That's the principal reason why we've left the crime scene as it is, with the main exception, of course, of removing the body—oh, and the toilet lid. You can see that we gowned up before we started. We have seized a large number of exhibits: blood, hair, body samples, including urine from the toilet bowl and the seat, fingernail scrapings, a blood dropping from the bathroom, and all the kitchen knives. We've done a sketch of bloody foot prints, pulled carpet fibers, and we'll get a printed plan of the suite from the ship's engineering department.

"By the way, that list of investigative items we made up and sent to you, came in handy. It is amazing to me what we found available on this ship, almost a full forensic kit."

"Yes, I showed it to our SAC, Clive Lundgren," said Ralph. "He was impressed."

"I went over everything as best I could looking for prints, and found two, one quite good though probably a woman's and the other larger showing four ridge lines, possibly male. You have pictures of them via email attachment. They're not the best, lifting them with talc powder and scotch tape. I can see four ridge lines on one. Hopefully, the IAFIS fingerprint system may be able to point to someone aboard, with a name. That may have to wait, of course, until I can hand them over physically. What I don't know of course—can only guess—is, what did he do with the gloves while in the suite? Did he wear them all the time so as not to leave any prints? If he wore them in the attack, with all the splatter, one or both gloves would have blood on them. Was one of the gloves cut in the quick struggle? He clearly did remove them before he left the suite, as noted in the exit photo. We found no gloves in the suite in our search, so he probably put them under the tray lid to carry them away. If he did get cut, I hope your forensics will be able to get a blood match with the bathroom evidence—if we can identify a suspect. And before I forget, the suite is securely locked up. Mike Donnelly doesn't have the staff to post a guard 24/7. Hope that's okay with you?"

"Thank you, Jack. That's a very comprehensive report. Seems things are coming together. Hope all your work is not for nothing. We do have a shrinking window of opportunity for investigating as the ship continues to Miami and will discharge passengers and crew."

Continuing, Jack said, "Yes, that does make this murder investigation somewhat unique. Let me comment on the usage of the rape kit by Dr. Kent. When he first entered the suite with Mike Donnelly, after the killing was discovered, he took some samples, but only collected evidence vaginally. When I was there, he followed the full procedure, examining the victim vaginally, rectally and orally. Hair samples—the complete drill. I've made sure the samples were placed in proper receptacles, and labelled accurately. With respect to rape/murder victims, as you know, it's a difficult proposition for the prosecutor to prove, unequivocally at trial, that sex was forced or consensual. The victim is dead. Up to the judge and/or jury, in considering the nature of the evidence, to determine. In Canada, if the judge finds rape was committed in the commission of the killing, that finding can affect the punishment—life in prison. As I understand it in the U.S.A., in some States, murder plus rape can trigger a death penalty."

"Yes," replied Ralph, "that's the case here in Florida, but this offense would be under Title 18, a federal offense, where the punishment could also be the death penalty."

"You know, Ralph, this could be a crime of 'unintended consequences'. By that, I mean, I'm not sure she was killed premeditatedly. The killer may have disguised himself, with the intention only of stealing jewelry and other valuables. It's certainly a possibility. And, if you're wondering why he did not throw her body overboard—"

"—You certainly are anticipating my thoughts, Jack," interrupted Ralph.

"Yes, I raised that idea with Mike," Jack continued, "and he explained that the design of the suite precluded any outside access to either side of the ship for disposal—the steel superstructure wraps around at the stern, this end. The full-length balconies, or verandahs as they are called, slope down at an angle to the lower decks, so that a body dumped from deck 7 would land on the protruding verandah of deck 6 below it, and so on. I don't think he would take a body out through the suite door. It's facing the center of the ship and leads to the passageways, left and right. Besides, he was probably in a hurry to leave.

"I think our next steps will be to interview two persons of interest to test the veracity in what they saw and know. One is Mrs. Gessner's companion as she refers to herself, a Ms. Hannah Goldman. She has her own cabin. The other is a recently-met 'friend' of Mrs. Gessner's, one Abraham Shuster. I think you've run a National Crime Index check on them both?"

"Yeah, NCIS was negative and our in-house indices as well."

"By the way, Ralph, has Mrs. Gessner's NOK been advised?"

"Don't know that. I'll check, let you know. I need to send an agent around to her house anyway, see what we can learn from doing a search there."

♦ ◊ ♦

Emilio Cardozo, working in the waste management facility in the bowels of the ship, was sorting through plastic bags gathered from all the public waste bins placed around the ship. Not a great job, but as his supervisor said in his first training session, a necessary one, as much of the waste could be recycled. Even with huge fans going, there was a distinctly unpleasant odor in the vast room. A pile of bags was on a metal bench beside him. In front, an array of bins. Each piece of trash had a designated place to go. Opening a bag, he pulled out clothing: a waiter's white jacket, shirt and black slacks. 'Why are they in the garbage, rather than the laundry?' Emilio wondered.

He was about to toss them onto a tray for transport to the laundry, when he noticed a red stain on the white, inside-out jacket and the shirt front. Looking at it closer, he was not sure if it was a red wine spill—no, a bit too dark for that and would be just a stain, not gummed up like this was. Tomato ketchup? No smell. Paint? Not thick enough, and no fumes. Blood? Yeah. Possibly congealed blood. He called for his supervisor to have a look. While he was waiting, he found the bloodied gloves in the next collection bag.

After his examination of these items, the supervisor too thought it was blood and suspicious. "Okay, better turn this over to the security people."

He called Mike Donnelly to tell him, and ask him what they should do.

Mike's phone rang. He excused himself from the discussion and moved to a corner. "Donnelly here."

"Mr. Donnelly, it's Reggie Furtado, waste management room supervisor. Sorry to bother you. One of my sorters found some clothing—a waiter's uniform with what may be blood on it. There's black pants, a white dickey jacket and shirt, and a pair of white serving gloves. There's what looks like congealed blood on the jacket, which was turned inside-out, and on the gloves and shirt. They were found in two general waste containers picked up in a passageway on deck three. Staff uniforms normally would be sent to the laundry when soiled, not put in the waste. This seems fishy. Want me to send the stuff to your office?"

"No, thanks, Reggie, I'll come and get it. Keep it all in your custody and attach the name of your person who found it, on the bag. I'll be down soon and will need to take a statement from both you and the person who found the clothes. Excellent work. Thanks for the call."

"… No, we don't have an obvious motive for the killing," Jack was saying to the agent when Mike stepped back into the room. "More than likely a robbery, or an attempt that went wrong, but we've not determined anything is actually missing yet because we don't have an inventory of valuables to check against. We hope to establish that with Ms. Goldman." As he was saying this, Mike waved his hand at Jack, off screen.

"Excuse me, Ralph. Yes, Mike?"

"Sorry to interrupt. We got a call from the sorting room in waste management. One of their workers found a waiter's uniform with what they think is blood on it. They're holding it for us."

"You heard that, Ralph? Another piece of the puzzle maybe. We'll go down shortly and get it and let you know what we've got, in due course. Again, be nice to get a blood match."

"Yes, we could use some luck. So, after you've spoken to Ms Goldman, what next?"

"I think we'll take 'clarification' statements from the ship staff involved. The cleaning woman who found the deceased in the morning, her supervisor, the hotel manager and the housekeeping woman from yesterday evening. Dr. Kent is writing a statement as to his involvement, declaring death; his examination of the body, and details about the care of the exhibits he took. I will forward all this info to you when we've finished."

"Sounds good. How about a brief 'one-liner' or two from the security people you had attending at the suite. Just to say they were there, but did not enter the accommodations beyond the entrance foyer?"

"Good point. If there is anything significant resulting from my talk with Ms. Goldman, I'll let you know. Talk to you soon. By the way, what time are you off duty?"

"Well, unlike you were, Jack, I'm not unionized, so I literally don't know from day to day, but usually six-ish, which I guess would make around 8 p.m. your time. So long for now." And the screen went blank.

"Okay, Mike, let's you and I go look at that uniform, and then we'll get Ms. Goldman in for a talk. She must be really agitated by now. Just give me a minute to call Jean." Looking at the office clock, he noted the current time—five o'clock.

♦ ◇ ♦

In the vast and humid waste management facility on deck one, Jack took the black pants, white jacket, shirt and gloves from the plastic bag, and laid them out on the metal counter. The pants had no belt and appeared to have blood splatter on them. He asked Mike if, with issued clothing like men's pants, a belt is included. Mike was fairly certain they were, as he had been.

Turning to the jacket, Jack noted it was turned inside-out, and that the large blood stain was on the 'inside' which was really the outside.

"See this, Mike? Why is it inside-out? Did he take it off, leaving it that way, or was it deliberate, before he left the suite, to hide the blood in case he encountered anyone? Examining the gloves, the palm of the left one had much more blood than the right, and a small cut on the outer edge. There is some blood *inside* that glove too. Let's look at the CCTV pictures again to see if the waiter's left hand is bloody or bandaged. I did not notice anything and I'm assuming you didn't either? Anyway, we'll take a photos here of these garments and you can take them. Would you get the names of the finder and the supervisor for the record, and a statement to the effect that they found them, and at what time?"

"Jeez, Jack. I almost forgot. Employees' jackets and pants have their employee number stenciled in black on the inside label. They use indelible dye for that. It's done for identification and cleaning purposes. Let's check the jacket."

Mike found the number, the worse for wear but still readable. "I'd say that is *0396*," showing it to Jack, who confirmed that and took a photo. "Hmm. Interesting. Could this be our man? I'll call personnel and get his name!"

A moment later, he reported that the uniform had been issued to Henri DuBois, designated a waiter, currently assigned to the *Lido Deck Restaurant*. Cross-referencing to his personal data revealed he was a French citizen from Marseille.

"Working now or not, Mike?" asked Jack.

A minute or two later, they knew. The man was on late shift.

"Okay," Jack said, "we'll get to him in a while. I'll let Ralph know right away via text message so he can run a background check. Let's get Goldman and Shuster in next."

It was now 5:30 p.m.

♦ ◇ ♦

One hour later

"Mr. Shuster. Ms. Goldman, hello again, nice to see you. Sorry this has taken so long. Thanks for coming to see us. My name is Jack Sterling and this is Mike Donnelly, the senior security officer on the *Seascape*, and the other lady present is Ms. Moreno of the security staff. You and I have, of course, already met, Ms. Goldman. I wonder, sir, if you wouldn't mind waiting in the purser's office while we talk first with Ms. Goldman? Shouldn't be too long. Thanks."

Abe Shuster was escorted to the outer office.

"Ms. Goldman, do you mind if I call you Hannah?"

She nodded her head.

"I'm not one for formalities. You can imagine my concern when I learned this matter concerned Mrs. Gessner, especially after our last meeting. I can see that you are upset and I apologize for not meeting with you sooner, but Mr. Donnelly and I have been quite busy doing our work on this situation. You must be wondering what I'm doing here. Just to let you know, I'm a retired police officer helping out in this investigation. Before I continue, I take it you don't know what happened to Mrs. Gessner?"

Hannah nodded, obviously trying to hold back tears. "She's dead, isn't she? Was it her heart?"

Jack and Mike exchanged quick glances. In the two or three seconds it took for him to respond, Jack decided he was certain Hannah really did not know the cause of death. 'Okay, how do I say this to her?' Reflecting on the times when, as a police officer, he had to give notifications of a death to relatives, he wanted to choose words to soften the impact. 'How do you say 'she had her throat ripped open' in a nice way?' he asked himself.

"Hannah, I'm very sorry to say Mrs. Gessner was killed sometime last night. We are working very hard to try to find the perpetrator."

Hannah burst into tears, her shoulders shaking. "*Oh no!* Why? She was the nicest person! *How did she die?*"

Mike got up and put his hand gently on her shoulder as she sobbed, offering a box of tissues.

"She was stabbed," replied Jack. "She was a brave woman, as she tried to repel her attacker."

"Oh no. *Oh no. Oh no,*" Hannah kept repeating as she slumped forward and convulsed into sobs.

"We're very sorry," Jack said gently after a minute. "Please tell us when you last saw her. It might be important to help find the culprit."

After a few moments, Hannah wiped her eyes, composed herself and said, "I saw her early in the evening with Mr. Shuster. I was going to a recital at seven. When I got back to my cabin, around 10 p.m., I called her, but there was no answer. I guessed she was still out, or perhaps, sleeping... *Who would DO this?!*"

Allowing the young woman to settle down a bit, Jack said, "We don't yet know why she was attacked. Can I ask you, confidentially, about your relationship with Mrs. Gessner?"

She told Jack that she had been in Mrs. G.'s employ for the past year as her private secretary and assistant, and now her travel companion. There was also a maid who lived in Mrs. G.'s residence.

"What you know about Mr. Shuster? Did they know each other before, or did he meet Mrs. Gessner on this ship? If so, I'd like to establish when and how they met and were you present when this meeting happened?"

"No. She told me that she met him at a dinner table with several other passengers, a couple of evenings ago. That would be the day we left La Palma, I think. Rebecca—Mrs. Gessner—and he seemed to hit it off. They've seen each other two or three times and she seemed quite happy. He seemed like a nice guy, well mannered. As Mrs. Gessner's secretary, I also look after her work, including finances. She's quite wealthy so I'm always suspicious of men she meets from time to time. There's always a possibility they may be gold-diggers. Anyway, Mr. Shuster owns a big auto dealership downtown, in Miami, so I ran a credit check on the company. It's been in business for over forty years, with young Mr. Shuster taking over from his father about twenty years ago. Credit rating is excellent. He too is Jewish and attends the big synagogue in Hallandale. Mr. Shuster went there only occasionally and it's obvious they never met. I don't know what else to say."

"Thank you, Hannah. I'd like you to treat this information confidentially, please. Did Mrs. Gessner carry anything of value with her—money, jewelry, perhaps?"

"Yes. Not much cash and I have one of her credit cards. We use that when we're out together, paying hotel bills, limousines and so on. The jewelry she had was *very* expensive, a Tiffany diamond and ruby necklace and matching earrings, especially. *Oh no!* Is it missing?"

Again, Jack and Mike exchanged quick glances. Jack thought, 'I guess I have to tell her.'

"Well, we're not sure, because until now, we did not know about the jewelry. I can tell you her lock box was found open. Did she use it for safe storage?"

"Oh, yes. She loved that necklace and the earrings. It was a for-tieth wedding anniversary present from her husband. I don't know if you know, but Mr. Gessner died five years ago."

"What did she keep the necklace in?"

"A grey cloth Tiffany bag, with the earrings."

"By the way, did she wear them to the captain's dinner?"

"Yes."

"Was Mr. Shuster with you then?"

"Yes." Getting the import of the question, she exclaimed, "Oh no! You don't think *he* did it, do you? Are we both suspects!?"

"Well, I wouldn't put it quite that way. At the moment, we have no suspects. We're just fact collecting. Again, what I would like you *not* to do, please, is discuss what we have talked about with anyone. At least for the time being. Can you do that for me?"

A nod 'yes'.

"Alright, Hannah, I won't keep you much longer. What I need is a detailed description of the necklace and earrings."

"Yes, I can give you a general one, but Mrs. Gessner has pro-fessionally-taken photos of them at home, you know, for insurance purposes. All of Mrs. G.'s valuables are well insured, of course—Mrs. G. was the majority shareholder of a large insurance company. After I leave here, I'm going to call Maria, her housemaid, tell her what hap-pened—she will be so shocked and sad. I'll ask her to fax the photos somehow to the ship, if you'd like. "

"Thank you, but no, I don't think the maid needs to do that. An FBI person will be going to the house, to speak to the maid—what's her full name? Will she be able to show the photos and insurance de-scriptions to the agent?"

"Maria Gonzales. And, yes, she knows where all the files are kept in Mrs. G.'s office. The address is 8060, South Ocean Boulevard, in Palm Beach."

As Jack was writing that down, he said he would inform the FBI office in Miami and ask the visiting agent to pick up the photos and insurance papers and send them to the ship. "They'll be very useful to us to identify them, if we should find them. Do you know what they are valued at for the insurance?"

"Yes, one quarter of a million dollars." Jack suppressed a whistle. "Alright, thank you for seeing us. I'll get back to you tomorrow. Take care, please. Oh, one other thing before you leave, Hannah. Do you know who her next of kin is?"

"Yes, that would be Ronald Abramowicz, her brother, in Los Angeles."

"Do you know if he is her executor?"

"No, I'm sorry. She has no other relative, so I'm assuming he might be."

When she left the room, Jack said, "Well, Mike, we didn't find a jewelry bag in the suite, so we can assume the necklace was in it when taken. Also, did you note what she said about calling Mrs. G. sometime around 10 p.m. and got no answer. That tends to confirm about when the dirty deed was done. We need to tell Ralph about this right away, and get his agents to pick up the photos and the insurance papers, and to send us a copy when he has them. I'll make the call after our next interview. Would you ask Mr. Shuster to join us here, please?"

♦ ◇ ♦

Hannah Goldman immediately called her mother in Miami. She tried to control her feelings, but burst into tears when the phone was answered.

Mrs. Goldman, now extremely concerned, said, "What is it, dear? Please tell me. Are you okay?"

"Oh, Mom, Mrs. Gessner is dead!"

"Oh, my God! How, what happened, when?"

Hannah told her about the interview with the ship security people that she had just left. "Mom, I have to try to find out more. I don't know who could have done it but her jewelry is missing. I was thinking of calling her brother in LA but maybe I should hold off a bit. Somebody has to notify the next of kin. What do you think?"

"Alright, dear, you know best. If you want me to call him, I'll do that for you."

"No, it's okay, I'll call him soon. Actually I promised the detective I wouldn't tell anyone just yet, and I've just told you! Oh, this is all so terrible. I had to tell *someone*. I don't know what I'm going to do now until we get to Miami."

"May her memory be a blessing, Hannah. This is sad news."

♦ ◊ ♦

"Mr. Shuster. Sorry to keep you waiting so long," said Mike as he and Jack stood up when Abe entered the room. "This shouldn't take too much time. Have a seat. Before we continue, I'd like to record our conversation, please. It's just a routine procedure," pointing to the tape recorder on the table. "I'm Mike Donnelly, the senior security officer and this is Jack Sterling, who is assisting me. First of all, we have some very unpleasant news. I'm sorry to inform you, about Mrs. Rebecca Gessner. Unfortunately, she was killed in her suite sometime yesterday evening Her throat was cut."

Jack had told him to use those exact words to observe the man's reaction. Jack closely watched his face and body for tell-tale signs of knowledge and/or guilt. In their discussion later about Shuster, they agreed that the reaction was one of genuine shock.

In his reply, Abe said, "Oh, my God! Hannah—Ms. Goldman—told me that something was wrong, she couldn't get into the suite to check on Mrs. Gessner because there was a security office at the door." He bowed his head, and said to himself, *"Baruch dayan emet."*

Continuing after a moment of silence, Mike said, "As you know, we have an obligation to find out what happened and who did this. I understand you are, were, a new friend, having met her on this cruise, so, if you don't mind, a few facts to begin with, please: your full name, date of birth, where you live, working or retired, etcetera."

Abe gave them this information, saying that he was semi-retired from the auto sales business—not mentioning ownership of a dealership. He lived in North Palm Beach and was a widower.

Picking up on that point, Jack said, "Excuse me, Mr. Shuster, I'm sorry to hear that. What was the cause?"

"She died of cancer five years ago."

Mike got the message that Jack would like to continue. Jack said, "Can you tell me how you came to know Mrs. Gessner?"

"Yes, certainly. We met at dinner about four days ago. She was sitting at an eight-person table with one vacant chair and I asked if I could join them. All the other tables were occupied."

"I take it you've seen Mrs. Gessner since that occasion?"

"Oh, yes. Rebecca and I seemed to 'hit it off' as the expression goes and we've met each day since. She's a wonderful woman—" he said, choking up.

"Take your time, sir."

"I'm sorry. It's going to take time before this sinks in. I have to refer to her in the past tense now. *Who would do this? Why?*"

'Maybe that's a question I should ask you,' Jack thought, and he did. "Do you have any ideas, Mr. Shuster?"

"Gracious, no!" Abe replied. Realizing he may be under suspicion, he asked the question, "Do you think I—*did this?*"

"Mr. Shuster. May I call you Abe?"

Abe nodded.

"No, my colleague and I have no reason to believe that at this moment. You do understand that we are just beginning our investigation and we have a number of people to talk to. We just have to ask everyone these kinds of questions. We try very hard not to conduct interviews with pre-conceived ideas. Just one quick, final question, a personal one if you don't mind."

Again, Abe nodded.

"Have you visited Mrs. Gessner in her suite?"

"No, I haven't."

"So if fingerprints are taken, we will not find your prints in her suite?"

"That's guaranteed. I never went into her suite. We were still getting to know each other, and it was all very respectable. She was a wonderful lady."

"When did you last see her?"

"Last evening. I walked her to her suite, around nine-thirty or so, I believe, and said goodnight there—outside her door."

"Alright, Abe. Thank you very much for coming in. I'll have to ask you to keep this matter to yourself. You understand?"

After Abe Shuster left—looking very despondent—Mike asked, "What do you think, Jack?"

"On the surface, you'd think that he might be a good suspect, given that he's only just met Mrs. Gessner, noticing the jewelry she was probably wearing. The CCTV pictures show him, apparently, saying goodnight outside the suite and him leaving, at the time he stated, and before that waiter got there around ten-ish. Abe's physique is somewhat similar though, to that of the waiter, but probably shorter.

"No sign of Mrs. Gessner wearing the necklace in the CCTV footage, although it could have been hidden by her dress. So, for the moment, we have to give him the benefit of the doubt. Your opinion, Mike?"

"I got the sense that he's innocent too. We'll see. How about taking a break until 9 a.m. tomorrow—okay to meet then?"

"Sure. I've got a date tonight with my wife. Goodnight, Mike."

◆ ◇ ◆

Back in his room at eight, after a late supper with Jean, Jack showered and changed. It would be another early morning for him tomorrow.

"So, Mister Sterling, are you any closer to solving the murder?"

"No, nothing solid. The suspect in the waiter photos hasn't been identified and the fill-in cabin attendant isn't strong as a suspect. We did find some bloody clothes in the laundry but they're useless to the investigation without blood tests being done: comparison blood type and DNA, and we don't have that equipment on board. We found out which waiter they belong to and we'll talk to him tomorrow. It was quite surprising of course to find the victim was Mrs. Gessner. I'm not sure that's ever happened to me in all the murders I worked on— knowing the victim beforehand. Almost makes it personal, doesn't it? I'd like to get it wrapped up before the Feds get here."

"Why do I have a feeling you will, Jack Sterling?"

"Thank's for your confidence, sweetheart. Let's hope you're right. Mind if I turn in now? It's been a strenuous and somewhat emotional day."

"Sure. I'll give you a back rub to relax."

At 0630, Jack Sterling's alarm went off underneath his pillow. He always carried a small alarm clock when traveling. Sometimes hotels missed their wake-up call and they'd had some near-misses with airplane connections. As well, he didn't want the room phone to ring and wake up Jean. He quietly used the bathroom, got dressed, picked up his Apple laptop in its case, together with his notes and carefully closed the cabin door, making sure the *RESTING* card was stuck in the outside slot.

On his return to his cabin yesterday evening, Jean showed him the copy of the daily newsletter left by the cabin steward. On the back page, framed within black lines, was a small notice.

NOTICE

It is with regret that we announce the passing of one of our guests sometime during the late evening hours, Monday, May 26. We cannot release any further particulars of the individual, pending notification of next-of-kin. The cause of death is under investigation by ship's security and medical staff, and will have to be confirmed when the ship arrives in Miami.

John Stuart, Captain

Tuesday, May 27

♦   ◇   ♦

Back again early in the security office Operations Center, Jack and Mike sat around the oblong wooden table, covered in various paperwork, the result of their previous day's activities. Jack mentioned the death notice item to Mike and asked what he thought about it.

"Well, I think our director of communication services did a good job. It's appropriately vague for the time being. Quite neutral, leaving no cause for alarm in the village," as Mike sometimes called the ship. "Let's just hope the real cause doesn't get out. If it does, the atmosphere aboard will change, don't you think?"

"Yep, could do."

They'd do a quick review of the day's work ahead of them. They had a number of people to talk to first, followed by investigative work resulting from those conversations.

"Mike, I've noticed a variety of nationalities crewing this ship. Where are they all from?"

"It's a motley crew, Jack. They're largely Filipino and Oriental, with a smaller number of Caucasians, mostly European—you can tell where 'Oim' from," he emphasized, "and a smattering of citizens from the U.S.A, Canada, Australia and New Zealand. Skipper, of course, is Scottish. As an Irishman, I try to overlook that. Anyway, a United Nations of people. They all get along quite well too—a happy ship." Thinking for a minute, Mike added, "Well, not so happy today, I suppose."

"Interesting. Yesterday must have been a very different day for you. Not part of your normal routine. What do your regular duties entail anyway?"

"I guess you could call them 'general security.' That includes walking the ship, keeping an eye on things and people, taking the pulse as we call it. Looking for potential problems: noisy kids, running in the passageways, drunks, druggies…." Seeing Jack raise his eyebrows at that, Mike continued, "Yeah, we do get a few aboard on some trips. A big part of our duties though, is embarking and disembarking passengers. There's the occasional fight, marital disputes, petty thefts, lost and found stuff, sometimes nude swimming late at night. A few people, mostly women it seems, like to walk down the passageways in their underwear at night, or in the nude. Some of them definitely should not be uncovered."

"How do you handle things like that?"

"We send out a male or female security officer, depending on the gender, with a dressing gown, escort them back to their cabin and call them in for a talk the next morning. Don't get me wrong. It's not an epidemic. Makes for an interesting time for us though. A ship is a bit like a small town, only really confined. To give you an example, two trips ago, we had ten or so men and women in their early twenties, who were here to party hard."

"What do you do when that happens?"

"With that rowdy bunch, I sized up the situation, decided it could get ugly, so I got the permission of the first officer to bring along a few of my beefiest male officers to discreetly stand by while I strongly indicated to these people that I'd like them to break up the party and go to their cabins for the night, and had my crew members follow them. Next morning, when they were sober, I interviewed all of them separately, and told them that a repeat of this behavior would result in them being locked up and put ashore at the next port of call and we'd notify the FBI in Miami. One of them, still a bit under the influence, said, 'Big deal. We get off in Miami anyway.' So I said, 'Yes, you do, but if we called the Feds, you'd be met on the dock and taken away. You'd also be placed on most cruise lines' *No Cruise List*.' End of problem, but we do have their names on record at the Head Office, and may refuse them passage on WCL again."

"Sounds like you, especially, are on the go all the time. Alright, let's make a list of activities for today and call Ralph Harkins or Clive Lundgren with what we know and plan to do. Also confirm they have run a criminal name check on our latest person of interest, Henri

DuBois, and ran the name past the Sûreté, the French National Police. Wonder if his fingerprints are on file anywhere? Can they confirm his DOB, physical description, land address for me?"

One of the secretarial staff in the purser's office had typed and printed their respective notes, and witness statements while they were absent for their evening meal and had forwarded them to Agent Harkins at Jack's request.

They now arranged this paperwork into five piles: the CCTV photos, photocopies of notes, etcetera from their activities in the suite, list of evidence seized, copies of the statements taken so far, and the results of the FBI criminal checks.

"Not much to go on, Mike. With regard to the bloody uniform, we'll have Mr. DuBois in first thing for a discussion. Let's call Miami first and review with them what we've done."

"Where we are, Jack? Are we anywhere, or nowhere?"

"Good question, Mike. I'm always optimistic though. I'd sure like to wrap this up tomorrow. You know, this detective business is one where you have to have equal amounts of blood and optimism in your body. Lots of little grey cells would also help."

◆   ◇   ◆

"World Cruise Lines. May I help you?"

"Yes, please. My name is Clive Lundgren, FBI office, Miami. May I speak to your CEO, Mr. Hollinger?"

"Yes, sir, I'll put you through." The call was logged in at 0815 hours.

"Andrew, here. Hello, Clive. Can I help you?

"Yes, Andrew, a few things to discuss. I would imagine you are as much up to date as I am with the situation on the *Seascape*. As I now understand it, the in-suite examination has been completed, the body removed to your morgue and the suite locked. Apparently your CCTV system has identified a waiter as a potential suspect and your S.O. and the Canadian police officer are pursuing that aspect. As well, you're still on course for Miami. What we'd very much like you to do is have your ship do a slight diversion and stop just offshore near King's Wharf, Bermuda, to pick up our *Away Team* people—four agents—so they can have the opportunity over the two days left at sea to do the forensics stuff, and to liaise with the Canadian detective. That would mean a very slight change in direction. We've checked and there's no need for you to dock. Their Pilotage Authority has said they'd be glad to take our team out to the twelve-mile limit for the transfer while underway. We've figured that the *Seascape* could arrive to pick up the team about midnight or so. As I said, that would give them two days aboard ship—May 31 and June 1—to do the forensics and other stuff that may need to be cleared up, for the ship's regularly scheduled morning arrival at 0800 hours, June 2. One other thing to consider. By doing this at that hour, there'll be few if any of your passengers up and about, and you won't lose time, and incur the expense of having to dock in Bermuda. Are you okay with this arrangement?"

"Yes, depending, of course, on weather conditions. It would certainly suit our cruise schedule. Very considerate of you to minimize disruption. I'll have to check with my Ops Center people, have them work out the slight change of direction and verify the ship's speed to meet this time frame. Let me call you back as soon as I can, Clive."

♦　◇　♦

"Jean. Hi, honey," said Jack on his cell. "Listen, just checking to see how you are. Didn't want to wake you up earlier."

"No, you didn't. How's it going, sweetheart?" his wife asked. "Do we have any suspects yet?"

"Well, yes, technically about 1600 of them."

"You mean all of us aboard ship? So you're going to question me too?"

"Of course, sweetheart. It would be remiss of me not to. I'll question you later this evening. I'll use my special spousal police caution."

"Oh, the one that goes, 'I have the right to say anything sexy to you?' That the one? Well, I ain't saying nothing to you, copper," she replied, in her best James Cagney accent.

Jack laughed. "You know that one by heart."

"So I take it you'll be away most of the day then?"

"Yes. We have a lot of witnesses to be interviewed, and physical investigation to do. It's looking a bit complicated, I'm afraid."

"Why's that?" his wife asked.

"Well, for a couple of major reasons. One, as I think you already know, is to do with me. As a Canadian passenger, I have no authority. I cannot be deputized, so, in reality, I'm helping out—at the request of the FBI.

Secondly, the chief security officer has no official police officer authority either, but he does act under the direction of the captain. I'm not at all certain how this would play out in an American criminal court, but Mike and I will do as thorough an investigation as we can. If we do find a strong suspect, he can be held in the ship's brig—a prison cell, if you like. As well, if that happens, I can expect to be delayed in Miami to review the investigation with the FBI."

"Can you tell me specifically how Mrs. Gessner died now? You didn't yesterday."

"I suppose I can and you must tell no one at risk of jeopardizing the investigation, and alarming the passengers. Her throat was slashed."

"Oh, how awful. The poor woman. What a terrible thing to do!"

"Yeah. Reminds me of a phrase I heard as a young constable: 'There's a line between Good and Evil, no wider than a razor's edge.' A very fitting metaphor for this case, don't you think? The in-suite investigation took us over three-and-a-half hours. As I told you, the place was a mess. Blood everywhere. The ship is going to have to at least replace all the carpet, yards of it, and the bed. I'll be away for most of the day but I'll try not to be late. Heard from Avery?"

"Yes. This morning, about an hour ago. She asked if you were with me. Of course, I said, 'No' and she said, 'What's he doing?' and I said, 'One guess?' She replied, 'Oh, Mom, tell me,' so I said, 'The Chief Superintendent is back on the job.' There was a few seconds of silence while it sunk in, and she said, 'You mean he's being a policeman again!?' So I told her that you were helping the ship's security people. All she said was, 'Good God! Can't he stay away from it? Why the Hell did he retire!'"

"I'll call her later today, time permitting and explain," said Jack. "Sorry, I've got to get back. Lots to do. I'm not sure I can meet you for dinner, Jean. If I don't, you've heard this before: 'Don't wait up for me.'"

After hanging up, Jack said, "What time is it in Miami now, Mike?"

"Ship's time is 0910. Through the night, we've traveled about 200 land miles, but we're still two hours ahead of Eastern Standard: 0710. By the way, we've got a reply from the Feds about DuBois. They confirm the information he gave us, and that the French police have no record against that name, with that date of birth. Also, the FBI has sent someone to Mrs. Gessner's house."

"Good. Who's first on the interview list?"

"We've got the waiter whose uniform was reported missing: Henry [instead of *Henri* as Jack had pronounced it] DuBois. By the way, it was his pass-card that was used that night. Second, I have the waste management manager, Reggie Furtado, standing by. Why do you want to see him again, Jack?"

"Just for an official statement. He'll be on the witness list because of his inadvertent involvement—as will other crew members, including you and me. Have you written down the activities of your security personnel—those who went to the suite, your Ops Center people, etc.? Both of us can talk to the supervisor of waiters and Ms. Marie—what's her last name?"

"Fortunato," replied Mike.

"—who found the deceased. I've been thinking of calling in the female housekeeper who prepped the room before Mrs. Gessner returned from the dinner that night. Just to see if she can add anything of value."

"I'll get you the name, Jack, and arrange for that."

♦   ◇   ♦

When Henri DuBois entered the office, the first thing that Jack noted was his physique—his similarity to that depicted in the suspect waiter's photos but a bit heavier. He had a monk-style haircut, bald with a three-inch fringe of hair and a thick mustache. The mustache could not be compared, of course, because the waiter's face in the CCTV photos was hidden from view.

'Unless this guy is an accomplice, looks like I'll have to rule him out. See what he has to say,' Jack thought. 'I'll try a bit of my Canadian French on him. I'm a little bit rusty but I'm sure he'll understand. Helps to be friendly with people when questioning them, rather than being judgmental.'

"*Alors, bonjour, monsieur DuBois. Comment ça va, aujourd'hui?*"

"*Ça va bien, merci.*"

"*Vous êtes français?*"

"*Oui, bien sûr. Je suis né à Marseille.*"

"*Bon. Je m'appelle Jack Sterling et c'est mon ami, Michael Donnelly. Nous sommes associés à la sécurité de la vaisseux. Nous avons quelque questions à-propos de votre uniforme. Mais, vous devez m'excuser. Ma niveau, c'est-à-dire, ma compétence dans la langue française n'est pas bon. Veuillez me permettre de continuer en anglais?*"

"*Mais oui, certainement. Je comprend l'anglais.* I understand English fluently, of course. That's what most guests speak."

"Good. Thank you. When you depart the ship at the end of your tour of duty, where to you go? Back to France?"

"Non. During the summer tour season, when I mostly work, I 'ave a small apartment in the Miami area."

"Would you mind giving me the address please, just for record purposes?"

"*Oui*. It is apartment 301, 9811 West Broward Boulevard, in Fort Lauderdale."

"Are you married?"

"*Oui*."

"How long have you been a server with World Cruise Lines?"

"*Trois années*. Sorry, three years."

"I understand from your supervisor, that you could not find your uniform yesterday afternoon, when you reported for duty. Did you lend it to anyone?"

"*Non*."

"Where do you normally keep it?"

"I 'ave a—'ow you say?—a 'peg' which to 'ang it upon, in the shange room."

"Is your name on or above that peg?"

"*Mais oui, au dessus*—above. Can you tell me why I am 'ere?"

"Yes," replied Jack, "it's part of an investigation we are doing. I'm sorry, I cannot give you any information right now. What shift did you work yesterday? I presume it was in the morning?"

"Yes. From 7 a.m. to 3 p.m. I am changing to ze afternoon shift today."

"Can you tell me anything about your uniform?"

"Yes. Actually it is missing from two days ago. I told my supervisor, and got another one."

"Do you deliver meals to passenger suites?"

"No, *monsieur*. I work in the restaurant only."

"Alright. *Merci beaucoup*."

By prior arrangement, Mike had posted a guard outside the small interview office door with a one-way glass window. If Jack gave a signal, the guard, who could see in, was to knock on the door and say there was a message for him. Jack made that happen. He asked to be excused for a minute, and he and Mike left the room.

"How do you read the man, Mike?"

"Well, in my very limited experience, I think he is being honest. You?"

"I'm inclined to think he is, but there is still some doubt. I've met some convincing liars in my time. What if he loaned someone the uniform? Someone who is not a waiter, but a male friend say. I understand there are no female servers. A steward perhaps? Someone who has access to the cabins. I was thinking that I'd show DuBois the CCTV photo of our suspect to see if he could recognize the individual, but now I'm not so sure, based on what I've just said. I'll be prudent and not do that, for now. At least he has no police record in France, and I take it none in the States?"

"That's right."

"That doesn't mean he has not committed a criminal act, in this case, by being an accomplice. He may have been lucky in the past and just got away with it. Check and see who he is sharing his cabin with. As well, we need to get in there for a look."

"If you don't mind me saying so, Jack, you seem a bit cynical."

"Spending thirty-five years in the police trenches tends to make you that way, unfortunately, but sometimes, it pays to be that way. Alright, Mike, think of anything I've missed asking him?"

"Not at this time. Let him go?"

"No. Ask him to wait here. Get him a drink of water or coffee, and let's get his supervisor in for one or two quick questions. As well, get the name of his cabin partner and what he does, please."

"Sure. By the way, your French was good. Where did you learn it and do you use it a lot in Toronto?"

"Learned it in school, twelve grades. Not much use for it in my job though. Toronto is a long way from *la belle province de Québec*."

♦　◇　♦

The morning waiters' supervisor added little or nothing to the enquiries, saying that Henri did his job efficiently, was never late, and seemed to be liked by his co-workers. As far as he could remember, no uniforms had been stolen previously, and he was a bit puzzled by this happening. He was shown the CCTV photo of the suspect and said that he did not recognize him from this shot. He did note the man was wearing white gloves and remarked that was unusual. He too, was cautioned about saying anything, and was gently reminded by Mike about security of pass-cards. While they were talking to the supervisor, Mike was given the name of the other man sharing the cabin with DuBois, a Marc Brevault, a kitchen worker, currently on shift.

"Alright, Mike. The next step will be to search DuBois and Brevault's cabin. We don't have the legal right to do that, only by permission, and of course, it's shared by someone, but I believe the captain has that kind of authority, provided he is convinced of the necessity. Let's call him and explain. Before we search DuBois and Brevault's room, would you go to his partner's work site and take a quick look at him—see if he resembles our suspect waiter. Remember the watch, shoe size and possibly being left-handed. Meanwhile, I'll contact the captain for the equivalent of a search warrant, okay?"

◆   ◇   ◆

Captain John Stuart gave verbal permission and said that he would follow that up with a written order transmitted to the security office. Jack wondered aloud with John what he would say to Henri about the search. The waiter would immediately become concerned and ask why.

"Guess we could use 'We're looking for something and it's just routine. Probably nothing to do with you.' We'll have Henri present during the search."

Jack grabbed a coffee while waiting for Mike to return from the galley.

In ten minutes, the S.O. was back. "No, his partner is definitely not the man on CCTV. Older, wears glasses, much shorter, and his watch, with a black leather band, is on his left wrist."

"Thanks. We might talk to him later. Let's check the cabin now to be sure."

When Henri was asked about searching his room, he nodded his head in agreement and was given a copy of the captain's order to search. A fifteen-minute search of the fairly small quarters turned up nothing. Henri was thanked for his cooperation, told that he need not be concerned about anything, and asked to not discuss the matter with anyone.

Jack said, "Best we find Mr. Brevault and have our talk with him. He's probably French."

He was not. He was from Belgium and spoke good English. It was a brief interview, both investigators satisfied with his answers and manner.

◆ ◇ ◆

Back in Mike's office, Jack said, "Right. Can we get Marie Fortunato in next, followed by Isabella de la Reyes, the evening housekeeper? We're making steady progress on our list."

Ms. Fortunato, from Lisbon, Portugal, was nervous. She explained what she saw when she entered the suite. It was obvious from her voice that she was reluctant to replay her experience.

"I understand how you feel," said Jack. "Take your time, please."

She described how she first noted red, almost brown, foot marks on the rug which became more distinct when she entered the bedroom. As her eyes travelled from them to the bed, she saw the pool of blood on the floor first, and then the body. "Can you say how far away from the body you were?" asked Jack.

"Not far, maybe a few feet. Same like I am from you now."

"What did you see exactly?"

"A woman—it looked like Mrs. Gessner, and," she paused, obviously finding it difficult to pronounce the words, "and her throat was cut open!" She shuddered a bit.

"Did you go any closer?"

"No! I think I screamed. I went to the phone near the door and called my supervisor and waited. After she arrived, I wanted to leave but she asked me to stay, and then this gentleman," pointing to Mike, "came in and asked me to stay longer. I didn't touch nothing."

As she left, Jack reminded her to remain silent about the matter and she nodded her head, obviously relieved to be allowed to go.

Ms. de la Reyes had a hunch why she'd been called to the security office. She had seen the notice about the death of a woman, then she'd seen that *Crown Suite 7001* was crossed off her housekeeping schedule, and wondered if that was who had died. She seemed genuinely sad when Jack confirmed her suspicions.

"May Jesus bless her soul," said the housekeeper, crossing herself in the Catholic manner. "She seemed like a kind woman. She will be in Heaven with our Lord now."

From her answers during the short interview, Ms. de la Reyes was ruled out as a suspect including the possibility that she 'aided and abetted' the male suspect.

♦ ◊ ♦

Jasmin Rhinehart said to her fellow agent, Jim Walker, who was driving, "Should be coming up shortly."

Agent Walker read out the house number they were passing on South Ocean Boulevard, in Palm Beach, "*8022.* These houses are well spaced out along this street," he said. After another seventy five yards: "Here it is, *8060.* Bit of a misnomer to call this place a house. This is huge."

They pulled the agency car into the white gravel, palm-tree-lined, U-shaped driveway, and stopped under the portico of the Spanish-style mansion.

The doorbell chime, mimicking London's Big Ben clock, was answered by an Hispanic-looking, mid-forties woman who said, "Jes, may I 'elp you?"

After introducing themselves by name and showing their FBI identity cards, the pair were shown into a large, ornately furnished, Spanish-styled living room and offered a seat. Maria gave her name in full and asked if they would like refreshment— coffee, tea, soft drink?—which the two agents politely declined.

Jasmin said, "Ms. Gonzales, we are sorry to trouble you and won't take much of your time. We are sorry for your loss of Mrs. Gessner—which is why we are here."

"Thank you. Jes, Ms. Goldman, she call me jesterday to tell me. I am—'ow you say—'eartbroken. She was a good woman," Maria said, with a catch in her throat.

"Yes. We understand that she took her Tiffany necklace and earrings on her cruise. Hannah Goldman has reported her jewelry missing. Apparently there are photos here at the house and an insurance policy covering the value. Ms. Goldman said the documents are in the filing cabinet in the office. Would you mind showing us where that would be, please?"

The documentation was produced and Jim wrote out a receipt, saying they needed to take the folder to their office to be copied and transmitted to the cruise ship. Everything would be returned tomorrow.

On their way back to the office, Jasmin said, "Well, those diamonds are a motive for murder if ever there was one."

Her partner agreed.

♦ ◊ ♦

Jack answered his Blackberry. It was the purser's office: Susan Chambers herself on the phone.

"Mr. Sterling, I've just received some photos of jewelry from the FBI and other papers. Would you like them delivered to you in your cabin or in the security office?"

In Mike's office, Jack opened the envelope and both of them looked at the Tiffany jewelry, in color. The resolution was excellent. Without the necessity of looking at the accompanying insurance papers, it was obvious they were top-of-the-line quality, and why the insurance valuation was $250,000 dollars.

"Wow!" said Mike, "no wonder she could afford to be staying in a crown suite."

"Well, someone on this ship is sitting on a small fortune. Question is: *who?* and, *where's* the loot stashed? As they say on TV, 'stay tuned, folks, as this show breaks to a commercial.' That said, now we've got less than an hour to solve this, Mike."

It took a couple of seconds for the penny to drop.

♦ ◊ ♦

Teresa Montoya lived in Barcelona. She'd worked as a housekeeper for WCL for two years, and had made this cruise run to Miami four times. She enjoyed her work and felt lucky to have the job, which she did conscientiously. She was therefore a bit apprehensive when asked by her supervisor to report to the ship security office. "Am I in trouble? Have I done something wrong?" she asked her boss.

"Don't know. I hope not."

So, it was a nervous woman who was ushered into the interview room in front of two men, one in officer's uniform and the other in civilian clothing, and a female staff member.

"Ms. Montoya," said the guy in white after introducing himself and Jack, "Please take a seat. We won't keep you long."

And he didn't.

She was told about the death and that the suite was now closed until the end of the cruise. Asked if she worked the same shift and if she noticed anything unusual during the last nine days of servicing the room, she said, 'Yes' to the first part of the question and 'No' to the second, adding that she had missed one evening duty as she was not feeling well.

"When was that and do you know who took your place?"

"It was five nights ago, I believe, and Vessie took my place. Sorry, I don't know her last name. You'll have to ask my supervisor."

She was thanked and cautioned about discussing the matter.

"Well, that was of no help," said Mike.

"No, I didn't expect anything; just covering the bases."

"Do you want to see this Vessie? Is there any point?"

"Probably not. Let me think about that, Mike."

◆   ◇   ◆

Jack Sterling, Mike Donnelly and Agent Ralph Harkins looked at each other across the Atlantic via the marvel of skype. It was 10:30 ship's time, in mid-ocean. The discussion covered the activity that had taken place so far today.

"We have another woman to go through the motions with, a relief housekeeper named Vesna Gorenko," Jack spelled out the name, "who turned down the bed in the suite two evenings previous. The regular maid was off sick and we've verified that with the ship's Infirmary. I'm hesitant to talk to her relief, as she was two days removed from the murder. I will if you would like, Ralph?"

"Yeah, why not. You know this could be a loner who did this, but please cast as wide a net as possible."

"Yes, I've certainly considered him being a loner, but how did he—we're fairly sure it was a male—know about this spectacular jewelry? This offense likely was not committed on spec; too much coincidence that a quarter of a million stash was awaiting in this suite.

Seems to me that was a motive for the killing. The doctor has pretty well ruled out sex. Mike had his security staff painstakingly review all the CCTV tapes to see if the same individual entered the suite at some time earlier, say on a fishing trip, knowing that the passenger had to be rich to afford such surroundings. Nothing showed up. Some routine traffic in the halls but no one entering the suite. By deduction, it seems to me that there's more than likely an accomplice—most probably a female, I should think—who had the right to enter, but we can't make a clear connection, certainly not with the female crew members we've interviewed so far.

"We all know that women can kill, but what gets in the way of that theory is the on-tape presence of the male entering the suite late in the evening, with, purportedly, a meal, but no trace of a meal order could be found. Also, as we're pretty sure, he's not on the wait staff."

"So, the two men in the picture at the moment, um…."

"Abe Shuster and Henri DuBois," said Jack, helping with the names.

"They are not solid suspects?" Ralph asked.

"No. Neither of them show that kind of aura. Both right-handed, wrong shoe sizes, body shape not closely matching, etc. They're not off my radar yet though, Ralph."

"Alright, with regard to the crew members, there's something like 452 aboard."

Mike said, "Yes, I think that's right," before Jack could respond.

"Do you know how many are male?"

"The ratio is about 60:40, sixty percent being male, so that means around 270 men."

"A lot of potential suspects. Okay, Mike, this may sound like a tall order, but is it possible for you to set up a surveillance on one or more of the women, say two today and two tomorrow? See where they go, who they contact?" asked Ralph.

"Well, since we're at sea, and there's less for my section to do, I suppose I could try to do that. There's only twelve on security staff in total though. What do you think, Jack?"

Jack felt a little uncomfortable about being put in the middle of this request and said, in a non-committal way, "Well, I imagine you could. We'd have to figure out how to do that in the narrow confines of the ship. Mike and I can discuss and try to set something up. To be frank, Ralph, given the ship's configuration, it will be difficult, trying to be surreptitious. Anything else?"

"No. Sounds like you don't need the FBI! I believe you know we're thinking of meeting with the ship, just off Bermuda, but that's not confirmed yet. When will you talk to the Vessa woman?"

"Sometime today," replied Jack, not correcting him on the name.

"Okay, Mike, any suggestions in how to go about our spy mission? You know your ship," said Ralph.

Putting his right elbow on the table, his right forefinger and thumb supporting his chin, Mike said, "Hmm, this is gonna take some thinking and planning. The three crew women suspects live in three different crew cabins on one-and-a-half decks. There are fewer CCTV cameras in crew areas. I don't know about how to keep an eye on the passenger, Ms. Goldman. I'd have to dress my people in civilian clothing of some kind, and they'd have to move around the passageways so as not to be conspicuous. I'd have to get them in here for some procedural instructions before we let them go. Maybe Jack can help with that with all his experience with stakeouts. Let me run this past the staff captain for approval. See how it works. I'll get back to you."

"Oh, by the way, Ralph,' asked Jack, "I suppose the copy of the male fingerprint I sent was insufficient for a match? It wasn't a great photo."

"Yes, unfortunately, Jack," said Ralph. "Only four points for comparison. Good try on your part though. You know, one of the redeeming aspects of identifying a suspect aboard ship is that he cannot leave, especially when in the middle of a large ocean. Would be nice if you got lucky and were able to identify the killer and hold him, or her, for us. If you can't, when the ship reaches Miami, the individual may well be able to slip through our hands and disappear, making our job that much more difficult as you know. Anyway, time will tell. Anything further, Jack?"

"No, I don't think so. Talk to you later, Ralph."

♦ ◊ ♦

The staff captain was skeptical about doing such a thing, wondering how personal surveillance could be accomplished discretely and with any degree of usefulness that couldn't be achieved using the CCTV.

His series of questions to Mike included: 'How many people at one time would be used for this? Would they act in pairs or singly? Would they be stationary or move around? How would they be dressed? Given the lack of space in the passageways, how and where could they situate themselves in order to be inconspicuous? How long would their shift be? How would they follow their targets? Would the shifts be required 24/7? Mightn't other crew members recognize some of the security staff and be suspicious of their activities? What about the targets themselves, if they knew they were being followed?"

Mike had no reasonable answers for most of them and wished that Jack was with him to give his views. Having had this discourse with the staff, it was obvious how difficult the surveillance would be to put into operation.

"Leave it with me, Mike, and I'll have a word with the captain. He should be aware of what the FBI wants us to do. Get back to you soon."

♦ ◊ ♦

Captain Stuart said, "I've never had to do this before. You, Robert?"

"No, sir," replied the staff captain.

"It seems to me we have three choices. One: turn the FBI's request down with a full explanation, of course. Two: try to accede to the request and do the best we can. In this respect, I'd appreciate any suggestions from Mr. Sterling. Or three: try to reduce the time spent by putting our people in place, say, an hour before their target goes on shift, and when they go off shift. Our people are not trained in using subterfuge. I don't much like doing this."

The end result was a tentative approval from the captain. In his cabin, he told Jack and Mike he'd approve the operation for one day and see how it went, based on his third alternative. "Get it up and running as soon as you've reviewed the details and we'll review how it's going this time tomorrow."

Back in Mike's security section office, Jack said, "So, how do you think we can do this spying thing? How many people can you spare, Mike?"

"Well, we've got five people to follow, so that means five of my staff. Seems to me to be a waste of time to do this really, for the people we've already interviewed. I think we agree that none of them appear to fit the bill as strong suspects. To me, it would be a bit like the dog chasing its tail, but, I am here to serve my master, and so I guess we should have a *stab* at doing it, using that *bon mot* appropriately in this situation. Frankly, Jack, I'm not sure how to go about it."

"I think one of the first things to make sure of is that whoever in your section you pick to do the job, doesn't know any of the three women staff we've talked to so far. A second is how to dress them. Not in security uniform, nor I should think, in civilian dress, especially if they have to spend some time down on the crew deck. How about an office uniform of some kind, say one from the purser's office and have them carry some papers or a folder? If you do that, you'll need to instruct your purser about confidentiality. Each of these people will carry a cell phone for direct contact with you?"

Mike nodded.

"As for Ms. Goldman, whoever follows her should, I think, wear civilian summer clothing. I guess the same should apply to Abe Shuster. Do you know who you want to do this job?"

"Yes, but we definitely have to get them in for some specific directions. Can you help me out by giving them guidelines to follow, Jack?"

"Alright, Mike, let's get the WCLSIU underway—that's the name of our new creation: World Cruise Lines Special Investigation Unit," responding to his quizzical look. "Like it?"

Mike smiled and said it made him feel a bit better.

While Mike was making his arrangements, Jack sent a message to Miami, asking the FBI to do a national and international name check on Vesna Maria Gorenko, DOB January 28, 1974, residing in the Miami area. He'd need to see her next, just to get the formalities out of the way and to comply with the agent's request.

He also used some of the time to review what he and Mike had done over the last day and a half, and to try to formulate in his mind what next he could do. 'We haven't got very far and time is running out to identify the culprit before reaching Miami.' He couldn't help but think that there had to be more than one person involved, knowing in his bones that this was not a random bit of quarter-million-dollar luck the fake waiter had when he entered the suite. He had to have been tipped off. But by whom? The finger of suspicion pointed back to all those who had been in the suite, likely the cleaning staff, at least on the day of the murder and maybe before. His long-honed instincts told him though, that they were all 'weak' suspects. 'I just hope I can get my man—or woman—before we leave the ship.'

♦ ◊ ♦

They met at 2 o'clock at the *Seaview Cafe* on deck 8, forward. It was Day Two after the murder. There were a number of tables vacant, the lunch hour largely over with. Susan Stuart saw Jean leaning over the rail on the port side, recognizing her from the clothing description

Jean had given: white shorts and pale blue, sleeveless tank top, and wearing a white, peaked sun visor. Coming up behind her, she said, "Hello, you must be Jean Sterling?" As Jean turned around, she added, "I'm Susan Stuart."

"Nice to meet you," replied Jean, neither holding out their hands.

The meeting was at her husband's suggestion. He'd said to her, "Would you mind having lunch with Jack Sterling's wife, Jean? I don't imagine she knows many people, probably none, and she'll be alone much of the time while Jack is occupied with this murder."

"Be glad to," she'd told him, and called Jean to arrange the lunch.

Jean said, "This is very considerate of you, Mrs. Stuart." Pointing to a table, she asked if it was okay.

"Please, call me Susan," who nodded her head toward the table.

Lunch consisted of shrimp cocktail on a bed of young lettuce, with chopped zucchini and tomatoes, seafood dressing and bread sticks, followed with a toasted, rye bread Montreal ham sandwich, with a side of hot Coleman's mustard, long slices of Polish pickles, and Red Rose tea—the latter at Jean's suggestion. They chatted amiably, as though they'd known each other for some time. Jean thought her companion about the same age, perhaps three or four years younger. She noted the waiter was particularly solicitous and attentive.

The women compared personal notes, telling each other about their husband's careers, their own backgrounds and their families. Susan was the author of a book about cruising, entitled *High Seas Travel*, an interesting explanation of how a large vessel, like the one they were on, is prepared for sea, its operation, stocking of food—called *victuals* and bought in enormous quantities—and many other facts of general interest. "Would you like a copy, Jean?' she asked.

"Thank you, I'd love one. Will you sign it for me?"

"I'll have it delivered to your stateroom."

After the two women had eaten, and finished with their generalities, Jean raised the issue of the murder. "That's a shocking thing to happen aboard ship. I imagine your husband must be quite concerned about this situation?"

"Yes. Well, this is a first for him. It's very fortunate that your husband is aboard to lend a professional hand to us. Our security officer has no such experience in criminal investigation."

"Jack hasn't told me much. I understand the need for confidentiality, especially after spending thirty years living with a cop," Jean laughed. "From what little he has said, it seems to me there could be more than one person involved—a conspiracy, perhaps?"

"Well, from what John has revealed to me, that's not definitely been established," replied Susan, "but I think you could be right. Time, with luck, will tell, although there's less than five full days left before we reach Miami."

"I have to say that, while Jack is my husband and I'm definitely biased, he's very good at what he does. But as you may be aware, he's hampered by the lack of authority and a full-scale detective and forensics team."

"Not to worry," said Susan, "having met Jack, I know he will do his best. If you don't mind a question or two, Jean, are you both from Toronto and how did you meet?"

"Yes, we are, although we lived far apart. Metropolitan Toronto, with a current population of around 5 million, is spread out a bit like Los Angeles and he lived on the other side of the city. I was an elementary school teacher and like most schools, ours invited people from different organizations and professions, mostly public in nature, to give talks to the kids. Of course, we always had police officers appear for talks on safety matters, bikes and traffic, etcetera, and one day, this tall, handsome young constable arrived, looking dashing in his dress uniform and white shoulder lanyard. For me, it was game over as a single woman. We were married a year later, both in our late twenties. How about you?"

"You know, my story is somewhat similar to yours. As you can tell, I'm English, born and raised in Dartmouth on the south coast.

There's a large Royal Naval College there, including an officer train-ing academy. At the time, I worked in a large insurance company office, and occasionally, several of the secretarial staff would go the monthly dances on the RN Base. That's where I met *my* dashing man, in his white dress uniform. At the time, he had six months left to graduation. We were married just after he received his commission and posting—aboard a warship. Bad timing, for he set sail six months after, on a very long voyage to the Falkland Islands. I was worried silly. I take it you know about that conflict, Jean?"

"Yes, I do. And you're right, what parallel stories we have. Both our men in uniform. So, how did he wind up to be the captain of a large cruise ship?"

"Well, after serving twenty-five years, he was thinking about pull-ing the pin, as they say in the armed forces. He was in command of his own ship and could have served another ten years but like many men reaching a mid-life crisis, was looking around for something dif-ferent, a change of scene. A job opportunity as a bridge watch offi-cer with World Cruise Lines was advertised in the monthly *Maritime Newsletter*. He thought that work would be interesting and may lead to being in command of his own cruise ship. He eventually wrote his captain's exam and was appointed a ship's master, as the title is known. That was five years ago and here we are: all at sea, so to speak."

"What an interesting life you must have had so far, Susan."

"Yes, except for many lonely stretches, he being at sea, I wouldn't change anything. Look, Jean, I wonder if you'll excuse me. I have to get back to my office—in our quarters—to make a couple of long distance calls and, due to the time zone differences, well, you know."

"Yes, of course. Susan, it's strange how people are brought togeth-er, sometimes by happy occasions and sometimes by tragic ones—in our case, a murder, but whatever it is, I'm glad we met and had this opportunity to talk."

"Me too," replied Susan. "Look, how would you and Jack like to have dinner with me and the ship's master—but not mine?" she said with a smile and wagging her finger. "I'll call, okay?"

♦ ◇ ♦

Rad got off work just after 3 p.m. and went directly to his cabin on deck two. He was tired, having not slept much last night and from getting up early today for his shift of ship cleaning. The first thing he did was to open his cabin's steel lock box and pull out the jewelry for a look. He took it to the porthole to examine it better it in the natural light. He had no experience with diamonds and rubies but could tell, from the reflected light they emitted, that they must be real and of first class quality. 'God, these must be worth a whole lot of money!' he thought to himself. 'Alright, I've got to see and tell Vessie about this and maybe figure out how we can hide them until we leave the ship. I'll call her now.'

He changed clothes, freshened up a bit, and re-combed and sprayed his hair. Just as he was about to leave, he put the diamonds in his pants pocket. He felt a bit nervous.

♦ ◇ ♦

Her cabin phone rang. It was 3:35 p.m. Picking it up, she said, "Hello, this is Vessie."

"Hi, it's Rad. Glad you're in. Can I see you now?"

"Yes, sure." Putting the phone down, she thought his voice sounded a little nervous.

Opening the door a few minutes later, she let him in, noticing he was a bit agitated. They hugged briefly.

Speaking in her native Croatian language, she said, "Is everything okay? Your call sounded a little bit urgent."

"Yeah, I'm okay. Did you read the death notice on the crew bulletin board?"

"Yes, I did. It was the woman in *7001*, wasn't it?"

He nodded without looking at her.

"Did you have to kill her!?"

"I didn't want to get caught. No choice if I really wanted those jewels. You know what they say: 'No witnesses, no case.'"

Vessie had been working on this ship for the past three years and knew about the CCTV cameras and the fact they were monitored. At one time, she was friendly with a girl who worked ship security. "Didn't you think about the cameras, Rad?"

"I'm not dumb, you know. I sat down and thought out what I was going to do. Three days ago, in the early evening, I took a walk to the end of the 7th deck passageway where the big suite is, checking for camera positions. There's only one at that end, on the starboard side, pointing across the width of the ship to the end of the passageway on the port side. All that is outside the suite is the elevator and the stairway going up and down. No cabins in between like there is further down. The double doors into the suite are at mid-ship."

"Well, wouldn't you be seen by the camera?"

"Yes, you're right but only from one side and my back."

"I don't understand. Isn't that enough?"

"Well, I figured it out," and told her how he'd used the serving tray to hide his face, entering and leaving. "I also wore gloves while I was in the suite, so no fingerprints and threw them out after."

"Where did you get the key card?"

"Got lucky. I checked several pockets of the waiter's jackets hanging up in the change room, and found one. He must serve cabins to have a card. Don't worry, it's not around. I cut it into small pieces and put it in two public garbage baskets. And I took another fellow's uniform that was my size."

She was afraid to ask. "Tell me what happened."

"At first, I thought she was out. After I knocked hard a couple of times, I went in. I've never been in a crown suite before. It was huge, and seemed empty. I started to look around and noticed the necklace and a pair of earrings laying on the bed cover. I put them quickly in my pocket and was about to leave when a woman came out of a side room—the bathroom as I found out. Thing is, I didn't hear no sounds even after I said, 'Room Service.' She must have been taking a shower and the door to the bathroom was closed. She was wearing her nightie.

"She said, 'What're you doing here? I didn't order anything. Please leave. Get out!'—something like that. She rushed at me and knocked me onto the bed. I pushed her off, took a knife off the tray and shoved her down on the bed. We struggled a bit—she surprised me with her strength. She was screaming real loud. I got one knee on her chest and we grappled with the knife. Then I managed to stick it in one side of her neck and pull it around her throat. After a minute, she stopped struggling and lay still, with lots of blood pouring out of her all over the place."

Vessie put her hand over her mouth, feeling like she was going to be sick.

Continuing, Rad said, "You know, I remember one night when our unit was on night patrols. We were ambushed by the Serbs and I got into a hand-to-hand fight with one of the women partisans. Got my face badly scratched and I could feel her going for my eyes. I have to hand it to her, she died fighting me. That incident came back to me in a flash and I didn't want a repeat with this woman. Couldn't afford to go to work badly scratched up, could I? You know, I've never killed anyone this way and was surprised at all the blood that spurted out. In a few seconds, it was flowing out of her neck, over her pillow case, her nightie and eventually onto the floor. She made horrible gurgling noises, her body shaking and I got off her quickly. Cut my hand in the struggle," he said, showing her the cut.

"Then I needed a pee real bad and walked into the bathroom. Took the gloves off and washed my hands. After I finished, I looked at myself in the big wall mirror and saw lots of blood on the lapels of the serving jacket. 'Shit!, I can't leave like this,' I thought, so I took it off and turned it inside out and put it on again, which made some of the blood go onto my shirt. At least it was hidden when I left.

"After I washed my hands again and cleaned the sink basin, I did my jacket up, re-combed my hair and checked myself in the mirror again. Looked okay, even though my heart was pounding. Taking my gloves, I went back into the bedroom and the phone rang! The ringing scared me a bit. I couldn't answer it, so I let it ring until it went silent. My first thought was, 'Someone's calling, maybe to check up on her. I'd better get out.'

"Putting the gloves on the tray, under the dish cover, I did one last look around, noticing a few bloody footprint smears on the rug. Couldn't help it, and, nothing I could do. At the door, I listened for any noise, opened it slightly to hear a bit better and take a peek. Before I left, I put my tray on my right hand, held it up to the right side of my face—blocking the camera—and left. I took the elevator down to our deck, leaving the tray and dishes on the elevator floor after removing the gloves. I knew a staff member would pick it up."

While Rad was telling Vessie what he did, she was forming a few questions in her mind and trying to digest what had happened. She thought she really had no choice but to help him now. When he was finished, she asked, "How did you know when to go to the suite? I mean, weren't you taking a chance the woman and whoever she was traveling with would be there?"

"Yeah. I thought about that. If anyone was there, I'd just excuse myself and say, 'Sorry, wrong room' and turn away. When I entered, I called out but got no reply. I'd only been in the room a minute or two when the woman appeared, from the bathroom. The rest you know."

"Alright, one other point. When you left the suite, you were not wearing the gloves, and the way you were carrying the tray meant that you'd leave your fingerprints on the bottom."

"That's right." He thought for a few seconds and said, "Okay, I think it'll be alright. Whoever took the tray from the elevator would return it to the kitchen where it would be washed."

"Did you touch anything while you were in the suite, with your bare hands?"

Going through his actions in his mind, he replied, "I'm not sure. I took the gloves off in the bedroom, because the left one was quite bloody. After I washed my hands and changed my jacket around, I washed the bathroom sink bowl—there was a bit of blood showing. Then I went back to the bedroom like I just said."

"One idea," said Vessie. "Did you turn the tap off with your bare hands?"

Thinking, he said, "Damn! Yes, I did!"

"You could have left some blood. Well, maybe you don't have to worry. The security people on the ship are not trained cops. They probably don't have the equipment to take fingerprints or blood anyway. Probably nothing to worry about," she said again. "One other thing though. This is a terrible thing to ask, but why didn't you just push the woman overboard? You would not have had to kill her in the suite and leave a mess."

"She was a real fighter for an old lady, so it would have meant killing her or knocking her unconscious before I could have tossed her body anyway. I couldn't throw her out from the verandah because these suites are on a slant and each higher deck one sticks out a few feet less than the one below it," he said, demonstrating with his two outstretched hands, one on top of the other like two decks, to illustrate, "so a body wouldn't fall into the water, instead it would go into a lower deck. I clean these areas so I know. And at both ends, the ship's superstructure goes around, preventing access to the sides of the ship, so I couldn't push her overboard that way.

"It all happened so fast, I didn't have time to think much. It was only 10 o'clock and there would still be people out and about, so I couldn't take the body into the hall and throw it over a side railing.

"If I'd left my arrival till a bit later, I think very few people would order a meal then and I may have run into a security patrol, and they might do some checking. I don't think I had much choice, Ves. I didn't plan for her to be there and to have to kill her."

"So, I take it you have the necklace and earrings?"

"Yeah, they're in my pants pocket right now," he said proudly, getting his sock out and taking the jewelry out to show her.

Looking at the diamonds sparkle in the cabin light, she said, "Let me hold them for a minute." She first held them in her hands, noticing they felt heavy, and then held the necklace around her neck, looking in the small wall mirror next to the TV. She looked more closely at the stones and told Rad that her first guess at the cost was too low. They were worth much more than ten thousand. She felt some reluctance as she gave them back.

"As you know, I'm alone on this trip, but I don't feel good about leaving them in my room," said Rad. "Suppose it's searched?"

"Well, someone would have to suspect you, and that does not appear to be the case. You've put security off by wearing a waiter's uniform and there's no means of identifying you, is there?"

"No, I don't think so. Do you think you can hide them?"

"Alright, Rad. Keep them for now. I'll do some thinking about what to do. We also have to get it off the ship somehow to go through Customs." It was the 'end of tour' for both of them. "God, I feel terrible about this."

He left her, feeling a bit more relaxed. She was a bright woman and he felt lucky to have her as a friend.

◆　◇　◆

At 3:30 p.m., Jack was back in the security office, making notes, when Mike entered. "How are the sleuths doing?" Jack asked.

"A bit early to say," said Mike. "I decided to use my female staff—less conspicuous than men I think for this job—and have them distributed alone. They are to report by cell each hour and make notes of where their respective target goes and the time frames. They will have to move around a bit. Standing or walking in one location for any length of time would look suspicious, don't you think?" Mike asked, looking to Jack for affirmation of what he'd done.

"Yes, you're right. We'll make a cop out of you yet."

"I have to say that I'm not quite sure what they are to look for. 'Anything innocuous' seems a bit unclear. I said, 'just make note of where they go, who they contact, noting the description, how long they stay or visit, and try to overhear, if possible, anything that's said'."

"Yeah, I agree, Mike. I'm doubtful it will produce anything useful, but, as I've said before, 'you just never know.' So, let's talk to the last person on our list and get that out of the way: Ms. Vesna aka Vessie Gorenko. I take it she's off duty now?"

"Yes, I believe she is. I'll check and get her here."

"Before you do that, Mike, check with her supervisor, in person if you don't mind, as to what part of the ship she cleans and when, what she's like, also, if she has a boyfriend—I mean on the ship, of course. Remind her about confidentiality. Then we'll see Ms. Gorenko, I guess, the sooner the better to check that off our list. Thanks."

♦   ◊   ♦

The FBI check on Vesna Gorenko came back moments later. Jack read the transmission and looked at the accompanying photograph— of a much younger woman—and noted several things about her record check. She was born in Croatia, originally part of Yugoslavia, in 1974, making her 39 years old now. No dependents on admission to the United States as a refugee at the Port of Miami on June 17, 1995. Her name did not show on U.S. Criminal Indices. Mike ran off a copy for the ship's file.

♦   ◊   ♦

Radovan Rudman and Vesna Gorenko had met in Miami, through the auspices of the Croatian Society of America, Miami Club, in late 1995. They had not known each other in Croatia. Both had applied for refugee status that month, which was later granted. They had been referred to the Croatian Society by the U.S. Immigration and Naturalization Service, for help in getting settled somewhere and to find work. Once their refugee status was approved, they could then apply for Green Cards for work purposes. In April of 2002, both were granted U.S. citizenship. For almost two decades, they had remained acquaintances and later friends, but never lovers.

◆ ◇ ◆

Gino Scarpini looked for and found his second-in-charge of room services, a French woman named Michelle, who ran the cleaning services on decks 5, 6 and 7.

"Can I ask you about Vessie, one of your cleaners?"

"Sure. She's assigned to Deck 7. Why, Gino?"

"Well, security has asked me to check. The chief of security didn't say, but I believe he's looking into the death of that passenger in *Crown Suite 7001*. My guess is they are checking on all crew who had access to the suite. Did she?"

"Yes. Teresa Montoya, the usual cleaner reported sick, so I assigned Vessie in her place, just for one night, let me see, about five or six nights ago, I believe. Is she in trouble?"

"Well, I really don't know, but I guess they want to talk to everyone who may have been in there. What kind of a woman is she? Reliable, do a good job?"

"Yes, she is and is courteous to people. She has an accent, Eastern European of some kind."

"Where does she bunk down?"

"She's in cabin *A-311* on Deck 2. She's off duty now."

"Alright, Michelle, thanks. Check your roster and give me the exact date and shift time. I've been asked by security to tell you to keep this strictly to ourselves, okay?"

The information was given to Mike, who asked Gino to find the woman and ask her to report to the security office. No need to escort her.

♦   ◇   ♦

The interview room, off to one side of the main security office, was a bit of a misnomer. It wasn't much bigger than a cubby hole, with one small, one-way glass window. The sparse furniture consisted of an oblong metal table with a microphone, and four chairs, three of them on wheels with cushions, the other on legs with no cushion. Nothing on the walls but a clock which read 05:05.

Mike, in his white security uniform, and Jack in his civvies, were inside the bullpen, as Mike liked to call the main office area of the security section. When Vessie arrived, she was shown to the room, innocuously labelled *Waiting Room*, and was offered the wheel-less chair. She had to wait 15 minutes until Jack, Mike and Sheila Turner knocked and entered.

Mike said, "Hello, Ms. Gorenko. Thanks for coming now. Sorry for the wait."

She was standing, in deference to his rank.

"Will you please be seated," he said, pointing to the no-cushion chair, where she had been sitting.

After Vessie sat, the two men took a chair on either side of the table close to her, and Sheila stood near the door.

Vessie glanced at the other man and at the red folder in his hands.

"This gentleman is Mr. Jack Sterling who works with our security staff and Sheila is also with ship security."

Jack said, 'Hello, Ms. Gorenko."

"We shouldn't keep you long," said Mike. "This is just a routine talk with several people like you, who have had access to *Crown Suite*

7001 in the past six days. As with the other people, we would like to record what is said, for accuracy and for writing up our notes later. I'll start off by asking if you are aware of the death of the occupant of that suite, a Mrs. Gessner, three nights ago?"

Jack pulled the folder to him and opened it. "Take your time. No need to be nervous," he said.

Vessie didn't answer for a second or two, then simply said, "Yes."

"How did you know about this?" asked Mike.

Again, a hesitant response. "I read about it on the crew bulletin board," she replied, glancing from Mike to Jack.

"I understand you were assigned to prepare her suite for bedtime a few evenings ago. The regular housekeeper was off sick?"

"Yes, I took Teresa's place."

"What date was that?"

'Let me think. Um, May 24, I believe."

"Was the lady in the suite when you arrived?"

"Yes."

"And what time was that?"

"I'm not sure. Just before 10 o'clock, I think. Maybe earlier, around 9:30. I don't remember exactly."

"So you told her you had changed with her regular housekeeper?"

Vessie nodded.

"I'm sorry, you have to reply with words to the question, please," said Mike, gesturing to the recorder.

"Sorry. Yes."

"Tell me what you did, please."

"I went about doing my job, preparing her room for bedtime while she got undressed in the bathroom. It looked like she had been out. Her jacket and purse was on the bed."

"Did you notice anything else in particular?

She hesitated a second or two before saying, "No."

"How long did you spend in the suite?"

"Not long. Less than ten minutes, I think. She told me to leave the bed and that the bathroom was okay."

"Have you been back since?"

"No."

Looking at Jack, Mike asked if he had anything to ask.

"Yes, just a few things." Looking at the woman, Jack said, "Alright, Vesna. As with the other employees we've talked to, we'd like to verify some basic facts about you. As a crew member, you know that the Company has to do a background check when you apply for a position on the ship?" Jack questioned, and Vessie nodded. "I'll just go down my list and check some information off with you."

When she verified her tombstone data—date and place of birth, current address in the Miami area—he made a mental note, later converted to a written one on his notepad, of her place of birth: Croatia.

Jack wasn't sure of the dates of the Croatia-Bosnia conflict, but wondered if she was old enough to remember, or to have been involved, being that she was now 39. 'I'll google that later,' he resolved. As she was leaving, he reminded her of the confidentiality of this matter, and noted a sheen of perspiration on her upper lip.

After she'd left, Jack and Mike sat for a few minutes, discussing the interview. "What did you think of her, Mike?"

Mike paused for a few seconds to consider this response. "On the surface, she seemed okay. A bit economical with the truth, I think, and a tad nervous maybe. Perhaps that comes from making her wait a bit. Her English is quite good. She's been in America for almost twenty years now. Wonder why no man or kids in her life?"

"I think a bit more follow-up would be warranted. I'll tell you why. You remember, Mike, during your short investigation course that you had to take, your instructor telling you about people's body language when being questioned? Things like fidgeting, stammering, swallowing from dry mouths, sometimes a thickening of speech, perspiring, quick glances around, crossing and uncrossing legs, wiping the palms of hands on slacks or a dress and so on?"

Mike nodded.

"Ms. Gorenko did not show *all* those nervous symptoms but I think she was seriously trying to control her behavior, almost as if she'd been through this routine before. As you may have noted, she looked quite worried and she was a bit hesitant in replying to a couple of very routine questions. So, I'm thinking we need to do a bit more work on her. I'm going to talk to Ralph about getting more of her background if possible. Ask him to check with the American USINS, and with the Croatian police authorities for one and Interpol for another. Secondly, let's get one of your surveillance staff checking her and maybe find out who she hangs out with in her off-duty time. You can, I think, pull off your officers checking on the two ship's staff, and I think, on Ms. Goldman and Abe Shuster. Meantime, I'm going to do some checking on the Balkan conflict—you know, the Serbian-Croatian war in the early 1990s. Ms. Gorenko would have been in her late teens around this time and maybe in the military. Both sides used females as soldiers, I believe. While I think of it, I'll ask the FBI to check with the U.S. Embassy people in Zagreb, for any information about her, including a check of military records. War can certainly harden people, being exposed to so much violence and cruelty. In this business, Mike, the more you know about someone's background the better, for interview purposes."

"Mr. Sterling, if I may make an observation," stated Sheila somewhat shyly, "I wondered why Vesna didn't ask *how* Mrs. Gessner died. That bulletin board notice only stated that a passenger died, and didn't explain if it was an accident or illness—or a murder. If it was possibly a contagious illness, like a N-virus we are all being so careful about, wouldn't someone be worried about being infected themselves from being in the same room?"

"Yes, thanks for pointing that out, Sheila. Good observation," said Jack. "Another reason to include her in the surveillance."

◆ ◇ ◆

Ralph Harkins said, "Alright, Jack, we'll do some more digging. A check with the INS people may be useful. Let's see: our enquiry with our Embassy in Croatia will have to be routed through the State Department in DC. We can ask for it to be expedited, but it will not be quick, as it's way after working hours in that part of Europe. We'll let them know your situation. How's it going otherwise?"

The time was 5:30 p.m.

Jack replied, "Just so-so. Mike Donnelly has his people out on surveillance, but so far, nothing worthwhile." He had told the FBI agent that his interview with Vesna hardly made her a solid lead. "I've pulled off the watch on the two passengers, Goldman and Shuster, and put one on our Croatian cleaner, primarily to see who she associates with when off duty. So, for the time being, not much to do. Of the total of about 270 male crew members aboard, we can eliminate at least half of those, by virtue of the shifts they work, and I'm thinking probably eliminating watch keeping and maybe the engine room crews, although I am keeping an open mind on that."

"This must be a switch for you, Jack. No cruise ships in Toronto?"

Jack laughed and said, "No, although there is a huge lake—Ontario—washing up against the city, and sometimes washing up a body or two. This case is an interesting one, and after some hesitation about your offer of *free work*," he emphasized, "I'm glad I'm able to lend a hand, although to what end, remains to be seen."

"There's one thing I forgot to tell you about yesterday during our discussion over *Law Of the Sea* matters. It's about the CLIA—Cruise Lines International Association—formed to represent their interests. This includes such matters a 'fostering a safe, secure and healthy cruise ship environment' as their website proclaims. In reading through the description of 'security matters', it appears that the focus, in criminal matters at least, is on violations of American law which, as far as I can determine, only applies within the twelve-mile coastal limit. I understand this comes under the umbrella of the *Cruise Vessel Security and Safety at Sea Act*—CVSSA."

"Yes, I'm somewhat familiar with that *Act now,* from reading it online yesterday."

"My conclusion is that no country's laws apply on the High Seas. I alluded to this in our previous discussion over the *UNCLOS* treaty."

"And I thought Canadian criminal law was complex enough. If there's nothing else, we'll get back to you soon, and thanks."

♦ ◊ ♦

Mike Donnelly had given his second-in-charge, Paul Manson, the responsibility of looking after the surveillance team, now reduced to three suspects. The two alternating female security officers, dressed in nondescript purser's office tunics, had met for a quick bite to eat at change-over time and agreed how boring the job was.

So far, they'd spent four hours of two shifts each, with nothing to report. The Gorenko woman had gone to work, finished her shift, then gone for a meal in the crew dining room. She'd shared a table with two male crew, both in cleaner's outfits. Both were about the same build and appearance. A quick stroll by the table had produced nothing notable and they were not able to read the name tags. The security person hung around and watched them leave, the two males together. She wondered if they were gay. The subject went to her cabin and was still there, as of fifteen minutes ago.

One said to the other, "I'm wondering if we're wasting our time in this case?"

"You could be right. Oh well, what else do we have to do now?"

"See you in two hours," said her partner.

♦ ◊ ♦

Radovan Rudman was nervous. Vessie had called to tell him about her interview with security people. While the questions were inoffensive enough, she felt very uncomfortable in the men's presence.

She did not mention knowing Rad, and had asked why she was being interviewed. She was told it was because she had been in the woman's suite, and all those who had been in there over the last few days were being questioned. She didn't feel, however, that she was under suspicion, at least at this time. "We need to talk and do something about the jewels," she said. "I have an idea."

"Okay, Ves, how about I come over now? Let's discuss what we can do, okay?" She agreed and he went to her cabin. He knew there was no CCTV camera in the immediate area and when he knocked on her door, he took care to check that there was no other staff member in that part of the passageway—that he could see.

Vessie had already looked around her cabin for somewhere to hide the jewelry. She was very glad she had no roommate on this trip. There didn't seem to be a really secure place to put them. If the room was searched thoroughly, they'd likely be found. Looking in her bathroom cabinet just above the sink, she saw her several jars and tubes of cosmetics. The largest one was a round, white plastic, 400-gram jar of Nivea Cream. Staring at it for a minute, the germ of an idea formed in her head. 'I'll tell Rad about it and see what he thinks.'

At the knock on her door, she looked through the peephole and saw Rad, noticing his head quickly swivel to the left and right. When she opened it, he stepped quickly inside and closed it. They hugged for a minute.

"So," he asked, "how are you?"

"I'm okay. You?"

"A little bit nervous. I've got the jewelry with me."

"Sit down, Rad. I'll make some tea. Need anything to eat? I've got crackers."

"No, thanks, I'm not hungry."

She plugged in the small electric kettle and while it boiled, they talked. She told him about checking out her room and not being happy with what she found, or rather what she could not find, in terms of a hiding place. However, she did have an idea that might work. After a couple of minutes, with his mug of tea in hand, she said, "Come into the bathroom for a minute."

Opening the cabinet door, she pulled down a jar of cream and unscrewed and removed the top. There was less than a quarter of a jar of cream remaining. "You know the old saying, 'If you want to hide something, hide it in plain sight'?"

Rad nodded his head, understanding where she was going with this, and before she could go on, said, "If they search your cabin, won't they look inside the jar?"

"They might, but this is what I believe might work. Think about this for a minute. Suppose I buy *another* jar of the same cream. The top is sealed with some kind of tape. There's two things I have to do. One is to remove a bit more of the cream I have still left in this jar," she said, holding it in her hand, "leaving just enough for a few days of use. With my new jar of cream, I first remove *most* of it. Then I place the jewels carefully inside and replace as much of the cream as I can, shaking the jar to make it fill up all the space. You with me?"

He nodded.

"Okay. Hear me out about the remainder of my plan. It's probably something that a man would not think of," she smiled. "I'll fill it up close to the top of the jar, wiping any cream from around the inside rim. Then, for effect, I'll take a teaspoon and make a swirl on the top of the cream, so it looks like none has been used. In other words, unopened. To put on the finishing touch, I'll wrap the same piece of tape around the outside of the lid to really make it look like no cream has been used."

Before she could go on, he said, "What if the security people open it?"

"I thought about that too. That's why I'm going to keep the used jar in front of the new one," she said. "If they do look inside the first jar, it may be obvious why there is a second, unopened jar. If they go so far as to open the new one, hopefully they will see it's not been used, or disturbed. I guess that if they dig into the jar, then it's game over for us. What do you think, Rad?"

He said nothing for a second or two and Vessie thought he would shoot the idea down.

"Brilliant. Fucking brilliant. I would never have thought of that. Could just work during a search, *and* when we walk off the ship."

"Alright. I'll go buy another jar of cream now and let's do it, but let me see the diamonds one more time before we get them all messy." She took the necklace and two earrings from him and, holding the long necklace in her hands, held them up to her neck. "Absolutely gorgeous," she said, looking in the mirror.

◆　◇　◆

It was the third evening after the murder. The four of them were dressed up, Captain John Stuart in his full dress whites—worn more for the ship's guests than for his present company—all enjoying a seven o'clock dinner at the captain's table in the *Tuscany Room*. It was the poshest dining room aboard, finished with faux marble, fluted plaster Roman columns, with statues of naked men and women, also of plaster, recessed into backlit alcoves, and a pale blue and white, fresco-painted ceiling of angels, cherubs and foliage done in Baroque style. Jack wondered how many copies of these kinds of fresco paintings there were in Mediterranean Europe, still popular after 500 years.

The tuxedo-clad male waiters were all Italian it seemed, but spoke passable English with a delightful Italian accent. The large menu was inset into a black leather folder and in Italian only. At the top of the page, it read *Speciale di sera*—evening special. For discussion purposes, Jack was next to the captain, and Jean next to Susan.

Châteaubriand, cooked to order, and baked Alaska salmon were the two dishes on offer, accompanied with small, whole, boiled potatoes covered in béarnaise sauce, young asparagus tips, lightly sautéed mushrooms and baby carrots topped with a sprig of parsley, all washed down with a bottle of 2001 Châteaux Red, from Cabernet Franc grapes from France's Loire Valley—captain's choice. This was followed by a selection of trifle, chocolate-striped vanilla ice cream on sliced mango, cherry-topped custard pie, or *pomo al forno*—baked apple with *caramella* topping.

"You've got to stop feeding us like this, John!" said Jean, rubbing her tummy.

Smiling, John Stuart stood up and said, "Well, seeing that we are all from Commonwealth countries, it's appropriate to toast Her Majesty." Raising his glass, he said, "The Queen"—to which the others, also now standing, replied, "The Queen, God Bless Her," and drank some French wine.

The dinner conversation became one of sharing information about their respective backgrounds. Jack said, "Jean tells me you served in the Royal Navy and were in the Falklands conflict. That was a tragic and unnecessary affair it seems to me. However, from what I read about it at the time, I agreed with Prime Minister Thatcher's decision to take action."

"Yes, that's a fair observation," replied John. "Being in the Navy, we could not express a public opinion, of course, but to a man and woman aboard ship, certainly my ship, there was full agreement. We had to 'do our duty'. The Army and Navy lost 255 soldiers and sailors, a high price for success in this instance for such a short campaign. The Argentines paid even more dearly than we did. All so unnecessary, as you say. The Argentine should have known they couldn't bully John Bull. But enough of that, Jack. I imagine your thirty-five years of police service saw a lot of action too, both good and bad?"

Jack really did not want to discuss his police career. He'd had enough of crime and brutality, but he was the captain's guest, so thought it politic to commiserate a bit. He briefly touched on gang wars and the collateral damage that occurred from street gun battles and innocent victims, even children, getting shot. Another very dangerous activity was attending to domestic violence incidents. Over the years, several police officers had been injured, and a few killed. "Humans are the cruelest of animals in the world, diabolically clever in ways of killing each other," finished Jack.

"No argument there," replied John. "Why don't we move to something much more pleasant," he said, after catching his wife's raised eyebrow and meaning.

Jean said to Susan, "You know about our daughter, Avery. Can we take it that you have a family?"

"Oh yes, we have a son and daughter. Jeffrey is thirty and Juliet, just turned twenty-seven. Jeff is a barrister with a firm in Edinburgh and Julie is still in university, St. Andrews at Fife, by the way the oldest in Scotland, founded in 1410. She's in her last year, doing post-grad studies in medicine. Don't know quite where she hopes to find employment yet."

"You must be proud of them both. As parents, we all wonder what our kids will grow up to be. Sometimes it's the luck of the draw, life's circumstances, that determines that path, don't you think?" Jack asked rhetorically.

Picking up the Château, John asked, "Refill for everyone?" and started pouring into four glasses, finishing the bottle. As he was doing so, his cell phone chimed.

"Excuse me." He sat and listened for twenty seconds and then announced, "I'm sorry, I asked not to be disturbed, but I have to go the bridge. We've received a ship in distress signal and I need more details. Hopefully, I'll be back soon but don't wait on that eventuality," and got up and left. He did not return.

The table talk continued amiably with Jack trying to maintain an interest, but his mind wandered and he wondered about the ship in distress. What kind of trouble? How far away was it? Hell of a place to happen, in the mid-Atlantic. Would our ship have to respond? If so, that would make us late in arriving in Miami, not that that really mattered to his and Jean's schedule.

If people are in trouble, you go to help them. Jack knew that events often happen in threes. 'What's next for this ship?' he wondered. 'Oh well, at least we'll have some interesting stories to tell.'

Two hours later, he and Jean were in the casino—the *Royale*—and Jack was getting ready to sit down at a maximum bet, one-hundred-dollar poker table, ready to lose a hundred dollars he told himself, but not all at once. Jean was nearby, trying her luck at a 25-cent one-arm bandit.

Jack had chosen a table with four players and was just about to sit down when his Blackberry rang.

"Hello, Jack. Hope I'm not interrupting anything?" It was Captain Stuart.

"No, I was just about to sit down in the casino and lose a hundred bucks. You may have saved me from that. Any news?"

"Yes. First, sorry to have left you and Jean so abruptly at dinner, but, duty called. Thought you would appreciate an update on a few matters. The ship in question, a bulk carrier of Norwegian registry, had a loss of power. Engines stopped. Seagoing protocol calls for the Master to declare an emergency, in case he can't re-start. His engineer is still looking at the problem and they've said they're okay for the time being. He's a long way from our position and apparently there are two other ships closer, so one of them would render assistance if needed. We can continue on our merry old way.

"But one thing I should tell you, Jack, relative to the murder, is that we'll divert our course a bit in order to pick up an FBI team out of Miami. They'd be flying to Bermuda. Not confirmed yet, however, but likely. And, by the way, Mike Donnelly says he likes working with you. Says he's learning a lot. Tongue in cheek, he said he's a little bit worried that you may take over his position! I think he regrets not going to a police force for a career."

"Thanks, John. He'd have made a good cop, I think. You do have a good security officer right now, and I do want to explore retirement, so his job is safe as far as I'm concerned. See you tomorrow. Goodnight."

◆ ◇ ◆

On his way to the bridge for a final check of the ship's state before retiring, Captain Stuart's cell rang again. "Captain Stuart."

"Hello, John, sorry to bother you. It's Andrew Hollinger. I've checked with our Ops Center and would now like to confirm the slight change in course for you. You're going to pick up the FBIs Away Team, as they call it, off the south tip of Bermuda, King's Wharf, just outside the 12-mile limit. Inmarsat [International Maritime Satellite Organization, which tracks the exact location of ships at sea] puts your position now at 34 degrees, 14 minutes North, 38 degrees, 20 minutes West. If you increase your present speed to 19.3 knots, with a slight change of direction, it should put you off the south coast of the island, at the 12-mile limit, at around one a.m. local time, May 31. That's seventy-three hours away at the new speed and the one-hour time change. I'll transmit your revised passage plan co-ordinates in a minute. This pickup will give the four FBI agents just under two days aboard to do their thing. You'll have to get Bermuda's pilotage authority direction for the precise pick-up point, and speed, as you approach the island. I'll include their ra-dio frequency for contact. This transfer should not affect your TOA at Port Everglades which is very good for us. Also, it's a good thing the rendezvous is taking place late at night. Hopefully, your passen-gers will all be in bed and the FBI's presence goes unnoticed. Okay with that, John?"

The captain acknowledged that he was. He, like the company president, did not want to delay his arrival at port, nor his departure the same day for the next trip.

"Before I leave you, any new developments in the investigation?"

"Not really. Ship security and the Canadian policeman are doing interviews and there is some physical evidence that they've picked up, but no one as yet is a solid suspect. When, and if, that happens, I'll let you know right away. If that's all, sir, I'll say goodnight."

The officer of the watch confirmed the math calculations and entered the new coordinates into the automatic pilot system computer. All duly noted in the ship's logbook. Bridge and engine room personnel were ordered not to discuss this change.

THURSDAY, MAY 29
At sea

Mike and Jack had an early breakfast in the buffet. Jack was starved, he said to his partner, and had a bowl of hot oatmeal with pieces of sliced banana and fresh strawberries covered in light cream. This was followed with two poached eggs, rashers of bacon, fried potatoes, whole wheat toast and two cups of strong coffee. He noted Mike eying his plateful of greasy food and, between mouthfuls, explained that this was *not* his usual breakfast fare, that he was just fortifying himself for the day ahead.

"Right," said Mike.

"Alright, let's see what Ms. Gorenko has to say."

In her second interview with Jack, she'd told him more about herself. Born in 1974 at home, in the Adriatic coastal village of Podstrana, near the city of Split, Croatia. In 1991, Croatia became a part of the former Yugoslavia, and the war of independence followed, for four years, against the Bosnians to the east. In order to defend itself and to achieve independence, Croatia had a conscription policy: everyone, men and women, in good health, on reaching the age of 18 years, was required to enlist in the militia. In January of 1992, after two months of basic training, most of it learning to shoot rifles, machine guns and mortars, her unit, a mix of men and women, was sent into action. The kind of military activity they found themselves engaged in was sporadic and deadly. She was shot in her right shoulder, leaving a nasty three-inch scar which she has always kept covered. It was not considered serious enough to be invalided out, a year before hostilities ceased. In the two years she served, she was witness to a lot of brutal killing. She'd had her fill of death.

When she returned home, the country was in a depression, and there was no work. Life was boring and dull. She told her mother and father she wanted to emigrate, at least to Germany or Italy, and maybe eventually, America. After a year, they reluctantly let her go and she made her way across to the Italian coastal town of Bari in the south, on the other side of the Adriatic, to a refugee camp. To her surprise, she found it a mix of Bosnian and Croat people and, equally surprising, they were living peacefully together. It made her wonder why in Hell the war had taken place. 'Leaders are so stupid and cruel,' she thought.

She spent a year in the camp. Finding places for displaced people to go was difficult, and the administration process slow, largely due to overwhelming numbers. One day, she was told to pack and be ready to go to Rome.

She asked, "Why Rome?" but there was no explanation. 'Well, that would be a more exciting place to go at least,' she decided.

The camp on the outskirts of the eternal city was much smaller, well organized and she received an issue of new clothing—castoffs but nevertheless, much more fashionable—and it was here she made an application to go to the United States, crossing her fingers as she filled the form in and not being completely truthful, especially about her military experience. America had agreed to help out the United Nations by taking a quota of civilians.

The United States Immigration and Naturalization Service made every attempt at weeding out unacceptable people. The military on both sides in the conflict had played dirty by international standards—accusations of 'ethnic cleansing' were frequently made. If there was a hint of wartime criminal activity, refugees would be summarily refused entry and returned to Croatia/Bosnia or to jail if Interpol had a warrant out for their arrest for such activity. The benefit of the doubt was given to most applicants, Vessie included. Ten weeks later, she watched from her window seat as American Airlines flight 203 approached the City of Miami International Airport under a clear-blue sunny sky. The date was June 17, 1995, two days after her twenty-first birthday. She was excited and apprehensive.

After her 'confirmation of admission to the U.S.A.', she was released from the so-called 'immigration quarters', a nice name for 'detention center', and was put in the care of the Serbian-Croatian Club where they sent her to live with a Croatian family, under their care and direction for a period of six months. The family were a great help in orienting her to the American way of life, and she soon began to feel at ease and reminded herself how lucky she was to be here. She got a menial job cleaning up and washing floors in a McDonald's restaurant, at minimum wage. Travel restrictions were imposed—i.e. not leaving the greater Miami area for that time. She was required to report monthly to the USINS office. A temporary employment card was issued, good for six months.

In her interaction with other immigrants, she later got work at the downtown Hilton Hotel, as a maid, but in good working conditions and more money. Two years later, someone directed her to an ad in the *Miami Herald* paper, for work aboard a cruise ship with World Cruise Lines, as a housekeeper, an even better job with slightly more pay plus good tips. She'd been with the company ever since.

♦   ◇   ♦

As a result of what he'd learned and his observations, Jack had a much stronger sense that she may be involved. While she had been in the victim's quarters, albeit well before the murder, she may very well have seen the jewelry. Yesterday afternoon, the female security officer reported that she had observed a male enter Vesna Gorenko's cabin at 1600 hours. He was dressed in civilian clothing. She was a bit too far away when he left and lost him when she tried to follow. He'd been in the woman's cabin for just under half an hour. From her vantage point just down the passageway though, she thought he could match the CCTV photo of the suspect. Good news. Maybe. What this meant was that somehow, the surveillance of her cabin had to be continued. Jack needed the identification of this individual and his cabin location. He had the feeling that this guy may well be 'their man'.

Discussing this with Mike, they agreed to two of the female security staff to alternate two-hour shifts, keeping a very discreet watch on Vessie's cabin. If the man visited again and left, he was to be followed as closely as possible to his destination. Better to risk giving away the surveillance than letting him get away unidentified.

Jack had followed Mike's suggestion that Vessie be allowed to continue her normal shift the next day—today—to eliminate possible gossip about her being absent from work and having to arrange for someone to take her place. Her work times alternated between mornings and evenings. Her supervisor was to have her to report to the security office this morning, before going to work at three o'clock.

♦   ◊   ♦

When interviewing people, suspects more than witnesses, Jack often made it a habit to delve into their pasts. Most people like to talk about themselves, feeling less threatened or intimidated, so he'd let them, rambling on if he felt their conversation might reveal 'something'. Contained in that seemingly harmless narrative were often bits of information that might be telling or suspicious. It helped to have a good memory when listening, so that he could intervene to clarify something said. Replaying the tape later gave him time to consider the ramifications of the language used, and tone of voice—'truthful or not?'

Truthful statements seldom vary; the truth is the truth, and the sequence of events stated is generally imprinted on the brain, able to

be recalled fairly accurately, even some time later. Untruthful statements require one to remember exactly what was said, in the original
rendition, when asked later. It is often difficult to remember the lies
told and in what order. Of course, what assists the police, in talking to suspects or 'persons of interest', sometimes to a large extent, is
the nature of the evidence collected, but not revealed. Interviewing
people can sometimes be a mental challenge. For most detectives, this
is an interesting and satisfactory part of the job. In the case of Ms.
Vesna Gorenko, he thought she was obfuscating a bit. Maybe related
to something that happened in Croatia.

When she was finished talking, Jack thought to himself, 'she's seen
enough violence and death in her early adult years. How has it affect-
ed her?', especially after she told him about being shot. While it was
a grazing wound, she knew that she had come close to being killed.
'Had that event inured her to violence? Was it enough for her to have
been involved in this murder?' Jack just wasn't sure. In following up
on her wartime experiences, he asked her if she had killed anyone.

She said she didn't know for sure. She certainly had shot at the
enemy, as did other soldiers alongside her and had seen people 'go
down' as she put it, but it was not possible to tell who, on her side,
was responsible.

'Okay,' Jack thought, 'she may very well have killed one or more
people.' "Did the killing bother you?" he asked.

"At first it did, but after, I didn't think much about it," was her
honest, but callous, reply. He reflected that, though the evidence did
not clearly identify Vesna as a suspect, her remarks indicated that she
may well have been capable of participating in an bungled robbery
and ensuing killing of Mrs. Gessner. He was reminded of one of
Shakespeare's lines: 'Something is rotten in the state of Denmark.'

"Well, Vesna," he continued, "you had a very interesting early life
in Croatia. Seems you were lucky when you were shot at, that it was
not worse. Thank you for sharing that information with me. I do
hope we find the person or persons responsible for Mrs. Gessner's

murder. If you can think of anything that might help our investigation, we will be very grateful. It will be better for everyone to wrap
this up quickly before the FBI takes over."

♦   ◇   ♦

Jack Sterling and Mike Donnelly had spent the morning reviewing
the case, going over the evidence collected and recorded, statements
taken, the various notes made by each of those directly involved, and
sorting out the photos and paperwork into some semblance of order or sequence. This activity would help them with two things: to
prepare the file for handing over to the FBI and, in this review to
notice something that they may have overlooked, that needed follow-
up. They still did not have their man or woman. Today, it was hoped
that the more intensive surveillance of Vesna Gorenko's cabin—she
was the only one left, the other people being no longer considered as
suspects—might reveal who he may be. The two security women, doing two hour shifts each, were monitoring the cabin. Mike Donnelly
reiterated that if the male was spotted leaving, he was to be followed
closely, with the security office being advised by cell phone immediately. It was vital to ascertain who he was and where he was living—
even if secrecy was compromised.

When they finished their review, Mike said to Jack, "You know,
this is like trying to put one of those giant jig-saw puzzles together.
So many pieces needing to fit in somewhere."

"Good analogy, Mike. Let's start looking for edge pieces—facts
we know for certain. Then we can see how the unknowns and may-
bes might fit within that."

♦   ◇   ♦

The weather for sailing ships of two hundred years ago was probably
the same as today, except the *Seascape* was not becalmed. The new

age of steamships allowed rapid progress over oceans. In fact, this one was moving due west at a quite respectable speed, now en route to Bermuda.

It was twelve noon. The nice weather continued: another cloudless sky, with the hot sun directly overhead. This was the fourth day after the discovery of Rebecca Gessner's body. Jack was taking a short break, having a quick lunch, on deck, with Jean. Looking up with his shades on, the sun reminded Jack of one of the verses from Samuel Taylor Coleridge's famous poem, *The Rime of the Ancient Mariner*, that he had to memorize in school, one verse in particular that described what he was looking at now:

All in a hot and copper sky,
The bloody Sun, at noon,
Right up above the mast did stand,
No bigger than the Moon.

The top deck was less than half occupied, it being lunch time. Jean was still reading her *Grey book*, as she called it. Jack had finished reading the ship's daily news sheet, catching up on condensed world news and sport scores. The stock markets had not yet opened at time of printing. Toronto's temperature was 70 Fahrenheit and partly cloudy—typical for this time of year. Of course, no mention in the paper of their next intended mid-Atlantic destination, just over a day away. Few people aboard—bridge crew, security, and the chief engineer excepted—knew where they were headed. The remainder of crew and the passengers would not be told. He was enjoying this short time off. After lunch, he and Jean would go for a brisk walk around the upper deck track, then he'd have to return to the security office. Lots more to do.

Jean raised her eyes from the book to take a break from reading and looked around the deck. Several lounge chairs were still occupied, no doubt by people who also didn't want to line up at the buffet. Her eye caught a member of the crew spraying and wiping railings. They seemed to do that frequently and she was glad about that. 'Help keep the dread virus at bay,' she thought.

The man doing the cleaning was Caucasian, tall and slender, dark hair, and good-looking, about 40-ish perhaps. 'I wonder what motivates people to work aboard cruise ships?' Their income was, she thought, quite good, with tips, and the working conditions were surely what most people would envy. Dropping her eyes back to the page, she began to read, but stopped after only reading a couple of sentences. Something about the individual. Looking at him again—he was a bit closer to her now—she wondered what made her do that. He was at a set of sliding glass doors and was reaching up, his back to her, using one hand to spray the washing fluid onto the glass, and then use the rubber blade in his other hand to clear the solution off. It seemed backward to how she'd do it, so maybe he was left-handed. Then she noted his right arm, now down at his side. He was wearing a watch with a metallic band, well down on his wrist, partly over the top of his hand. 'So, he's definitely left-handed,' she thought, remembering the ship photos she had been shown by Jack. 'Hmm, interesting. Could it be?'

Jack had fallen into a light snooze, dreaming of an albatross circling a cursed ship. He felt a hand on his left forearm and, opening his eyes, saw that it belonged to his wife. "Sorry to disturb you, Jack, but would you discretely take a look at that crew member washing the glass doors, just to your right a bit?"

Having just wakened, his state of mind was in neutral. He did as he was asked. It took him a few seconds to realize what Jean was looking at, and getting at, for he obviously saw the same. He looked at his wife and she looked at him for a couple of seconds or so, both coming to the realization that the guy they were looking at just now, could very well be the waiter in the CCTV photo!

Jack switched his brain to detective mode, which, after thirty years of marriage, his wife could almost see happen. "Hmm, that's a good observation, sweetheart. You should have been one of my detectives. Let me think about this for a moment. What to do? Three choices: walk up to the guy and talk to him? Walk by him and try to read his name tag? Or call Mike and ask him to send one of his staff for a look and a possible verbal check?"

Looking at Jean, he said, "How would you like to role-play a real detective for me?"

"You don't want me to talk to him, do you!?"

"No. Just walk close to him and see if you can read his name tag and get a clear look at his face, okay?"

"Alright." She rose from her chair and was about to walk away, when she said, "Oh, by the way, I don't come cheap, Jack Sterling."

"I already know that," he said with a grin.

On her return to Jack, she said, "Reporting as ordered, sir. The man's name is, first initial 'R', as in Romeo, surname Rudman or Radman. I couldn't quite make out the second letter. Height about 6 feet, weight 180 pounds, age roughly mid-thirties. Appearance and accent, Eastern European."

"You spoke to him?"

"Yes. I said, 'Hello, how are you today?' and he replied, 'Good, thank you, ma'am. Are you enjoying your day?' He was quite charming."

"So you can identify him if needed. You done good, detective Sterling. Thanks."

"What's next then?" she asked, pleased with herself.

"Well, first thing, I'll call Mike Donnelly and get him to check the man's name and cabin number. This guy must work the AM shift, and should be off around 3 p.m. That gives us some time to work out our next moves. I have a feeling this may be another long day, darling. Sorry, I've got to go."

"Leaving me alone with a murderer? I think I will adjourn to another deck."

◆ ◇ ◆

Just after 3 o'clock, Radovan Rudman walked to his work station area at the aft end of the ship and met his afternoon counterpart. This change of shift was euphemistically called the 'changing of the buckets' by the cleaning staff. He felt pretty good. No one from the security section had approached him, and he was reasonably sure that no one would. They had nothing to go on to link him to the death—he avoided using the word 'murder' in his thoughts, since it was more like an unfortunate accident she'd been there—and he looked forward to four days' time when he could walk off the boat, a free man. And a rich one. He didn't know how he would feel or react if Vessie was caught by the U.S. Customs. He'd face that if it came. He'd told her that he might not go to her cabin again for the duration of the cruise, just to be on the safe side. She understood and agreed.

◆ ◇ ◆

Mike Donnelly was engaged in more mundane tasks running the daily routine of the security section. The three women doing the surveillance work were back with the section, making less work for the others to do. His interest in the murder investigation had perked up again with the call from Jack about a new suspect. While waiting to meet his partner, he began his checks on the name he was given, starting with the personnel section office. The cleaner's service record card read:

> RUDMAN, Radovan Francêk, born 11 December 1974 in Split, Yugoslavia (now Croatia).
>
> Parents: both deceased. Arrived in the United States (Miami) in May, 1995, part of a group of political refugees that the U.S.A. had agreed to accept. He was eventually granted temporary Landed Immigrant status.

Residing in Miami in an apartment block at 424 East 23rd St., near the Hialeah Park racetrack.

Employed in his present position as deck-hand since 15 Jan 2011.

No listed next of kin. No complaints listed about his work ethic on his annual reports.

He would come off duty at 3 o'clock, Mike noted. Cabin number was *A371*, a small, double-bed quarters on deck 2. Only one occupant this trip.

'Good,' thought Mike, 'no complications with another employee. We'll need to look in his room sometime today—sooner the better.'

Mike began to make a short list of things to do next, in bullet form on his laptop, but decided to wait for Jack's return to the office before acting on them:

- advise the Captain of a new suspect,
- advise the FBI and ask what they require and request criminal record check,
- dig up the photograph taken for his ship pass-card,
- think about how he and Jack would handle this individual in the interview,
- decide what to do with the man if he showed strongly as the suspect—i.e., confine him to his cabin, or place in the brig, under guard.
- which would require the Captain's authorization, in written form,
- search his cabin—should also be authorized by the Captain in writing.

Thinking for another minute or two, he added:

- interview Rudman's immediate supervisor (before seeing the suspect),
- have one of my staff wait near his work station and follow him,
- check the suspect's hands for *cuts* during interview!
- should he be given the U.S. Miranda caution, and by whom?

'Gees,' he thought. "All this because the guy is left-handed? Hope this isn't a wild goose chase. Odd that he's from Croatia like Vesna. Or maybe that's not a coincidence....'

♦ ◇ ♦

Meanwhile, Sheila Turner, dressed in civilian attire—white running shoes, shorts, with striped top and sporting large sunglasses—was sitting in the shade near the back of the ship, upper deck, holding a magazine. It was 3:05 p.m. Her *quarry*—she liked to use security terms in her job—was due to check off here in a few minutes. She'd seen his crew ID photo on her iPhone half an hour ago when she was asked to follow him.

It was a relief to get out into the fresh air and sun, away from her main job of monitoring the bank of CCTV screens. She was pleased to know that it was her alertness with the video footage had been important, that her boss, Mike Donnelly, had told her that this guy Rudman was now a suspect. Make notes, he reminded her. Notice every detail.

The first four cleaning people, men and women, to arrive at the supervisor's position did not include her man. A couple of minutes later, she saw him, walking alone towards her. She opened her magazine and raised it to her face, hiding her cell phone behind the pages to compare his picture. 'Yep, that's Rudman,' she was convinced. After talking with his fellow cleaners for a couple of minutes, the man took the elevator down to deck 2 and went directly to his cabin, Sheila following. Although she was not that far from the security office, she nevertheless called Mike's number and reported in.

"Okay, Sheila, good work. Hang around somewhere if you can for the time being. Should get back to you soon."

Just as he said that, Jack Sterling came in, saying, "Hey, Mike, what's happening?"

He told Jack about Rudman, who was now in his cabin, and that

Sheila was standing guard nearby. "Also, while you've been munching on some of the ship's tasty food, I've made a short list of things I think need to be done," showing them on his laptop screen.

Jack read them quickly and agreed.

"I think the first thing to do is to advise our friends in Miami and have a discussion."

Mike hesitated a moment and said, "With all due respect Jack, can I suggest we tell Captain Stuart first?"

"Yeah, you're right, Mike. That's the proper protocol, for sure. You can do the honors."

When Mike returned, Jack asked him what response he got. "He asked if we were going to arrest him, but I told him I thought it a bit too early to make that decision yet. What do you think?"

"Sure. I think that's correct. In the meantime, let's get Rudman's supervisor in right away for a brief chat. Can you do that now, Mike?"

When he was off the phone, they discussed what they were going to say to, and ask, the FBI, so as to be on the same wavelength. Jack had a good idea about that, but ship protocol in this case was important in the scheme of things.

Francisco Donniletti, Rad Rudman's ship maintenance supervisor, had little to add about the man. He had known him for about a year, and found that he "does his job okay" and didn't miss his shifts.

He had seen him with a female crew member in his off hours but the supervisor did not know what kind of relationship it was. It wasn't his job to know anyway.

"Is he in trouble?" was his natural question. After all, why was security asking him these questions.

"So far, no," Jack understated. "We are just following up on some leads. Probably nothing."

Mike told Franciso he'd let him know if anything would affect Rudman's shift work.

♦ ◊ ♦

"Agent Harkins speaking."

"Call's for you, agent," the operator said, "from the *Seascape*, Mr. Sterling on line."

Log-in time (Miami)—1:10 p.m.

"Thanks, Janet," Ralph said and pressed the button on his desk telephone.

"Jack, how are you, my friend?"

"Well, thanks. Mike Donnelly has another phone stuck in his ear. I figure the time must be about one or so, your time, right?"

"Yeah, you're right and it's my lunch time. Good timing," he said with a chuckle. "Hi Mike, good to speak with you again. What's happening?"

"Some good news, we hope. We have a possible suspect. For the details, I'll refer you to my distinguished colleague, and add my two cents worth as we chat. Before we start, I believe you know we are bound for Bermuda with an ETA off the coast just after midnight on the thirty-first."

"Yes. Our team of four has been assembled, kitted up with their tools of the trade, ready to go. Try not to drop any of them in the water when your ship picks them up? FBI agents hate getting wet. They wear nice suits. So, Jack, don't keep me in suspense any longer. Tell me you've solved the murder and have a person in custody?"

"Would that we could, but let me put it this way. We now have a person of interest, at least, who, after we talk to him, may well turn into the suspect, or at least one of them. You can thank my wife Jean for being alert."

He told Ralph about her detective work on the upper deck earlier this afternoon—ship's time—getting a description and managing to read his name tag.

"He has the build and appearance similar to the waiter we saw enter the suite on the CCTV camera. Those pictures are taken in low light and not that good for details, but I feel we can make a good comparison. As you know, he's left-handed, and wears a watch on his right wrist with a metallic band. His full name is—ready to copy this down? Surname: RUDMAN, given 1: RADOVAN, given 2: FRANCÊK, with a circumflex over the E," he spelled out, giving him the place and date of birth. "Been in America since the year 1995, and has, you'll be pleased to know, American citizenship. He's been employed with World Cruise Lines for the past 3 years. His address is listed as 1930 East Fourth Street, apartment 302, in Miami. Okay so far?"

"Yes, great. That's very close to the race track. Not that far from our office. Good work. You've trained Jean well. How much does your wife charge for her services, Jack? If I can put it that way."

Jack chuckled. "*Nada*. She's glad to help, Ralph. We've made a list of follow-up things to do now. Mike, read them out, please. Oh, and of course, need I ask, an indices check on the man, similar to what you did with Gorenko. Captain Stuart has been advised."

"Sounds good, Jack. I've just relayed the info for a full check to my assistant. So, you know his cabin number and have one of Mike's staff waiting in case he leaves. Anything to add from his supervisor?"

"No."

"Alright. I take it, Jack, that your next steps will be to get him in for a chat and to search his cabin?"

"Yes. We're thinking that it may be prudent to get the captain to authorize the search, in writing. He has the authority, as I understand the *Law of the Sea*. Mike and I are going to review how we are going to handle the interview. With all due respect, with my experience, I should lead and have Mike step in when he feels it's appropriate, okay?"

"Sure, sounds good. Okay with you, Mike?"

"By all means. I have no experience dealing with serious crime at this altitude."

"Jack, how are you going to break the ice with him, initially and in the statement taking part?"

"Seeing that Mike is the senior security officer, I think he should tell the suspect why we want to talk to him. Play it down when we bring him to the office. To get him here, I thought Mike could have one of the front desk administration staff call him and ask him to report there first. I would just be introduced as a member of ship security. I don't know how you do your interviews—we're all a little bit different in this regard—but I like to have as much info as I can get about the person. Being friendly is generally the best approach to take, and to get the person to open up about himself. People like to do that I've found. Helps them to relax a bit. Agreed?"

"Yes, that's the typical approach we take. I defer to your experience."

"There's one thing. A bit of a conundrum I have, and maybe a rhetorical question for you. With neither Mike nor I technically be-ing police officers and with no arrest authority, at least that I can find, to use the American term, should we Mirandize Rudman before we get started? Personally, I think it would be on the safe side to do so, rather than not, although the rules in Canada, which I believe are similar to those in the U.S.A., do *not* require the police to give a for-mal caution if the individual is more like a person of interest. In other words, has not risen to the status of suspect in the mind of the police. If the matter does get to court and there is a *voir dire*, the prosecutor should be able to convince the court that every attempt was made to not trick the suspect into giving a statement, that his rights were fully stated to him and not abrogated, *regardless of who read the caution and did the questioning*," Jack emphasized. "Before you respond, another thought. In view of what I've just said, *does it matter* if the end result is the same: a caution given by a non-law enforcement person, or no caution given. In either of those conditions, would the statement be admitted at trial, or not?"

"Hmm, I don't think there's any consensus on the kind of situa-tion you're in, but, in the interest of your short time frame and need to do the interview, I'll give our Federal prosecutor a quick call and get right back to you as soon as I can. Hold your activity for now. I'll also have one of my legal staff do a quick on-line search and send you the reference if it applies. In retrospect, I should have anticipated this before now. Sorry, Jack. We certainly don't want to mess this up over a technicality we can avoid."

"No, that's okay, Ralph. I should have thought of that too. Okay, we'll hold on bringing him for now. Talk to you soon."

Turning to Mike, Jack said, "Let's go over our notes again, and your list, and settle on our approach."

◆　◇　◆

Forty-five minutes later, Jack answered Ralph's call.

"Okay, Jack, first, in response to your question about arrest and cautioning a person, if you haven't done so, check your in-box for these two references we found. Interesting but doesn't go far enough in your case, I think. The first is a rather long discourse dealing with the *Law of the Sea* and its jurisdiction over ships at sea, and more to do with territorial and ship emergency and other matters, than with individuals.

"The second is an actual case somewhat similar to yours, the only one we could find. Briefly, it concerns the murder of a woman, Muriel Barnett, a wealthy woman from San Francisco. Along with her male companion, she was on a cruise to Alaska from San Francisco in 1989. She was beaten to death in her expensive suite—with a champagne bottle!—just after leaving Victoria, British Columbia, on the return leg. A male suspect was found and he was taken ashore in San Francisco. The matter was investigated by the FBI, but because she was found to have been killed in Canadian waters, the Canadian government claimed jurisdiction. The result was that the suspect was returned to Canada, to Vancouver, and was subsequently convicted there. Seems to me, that with your case, we are charting new waters, no pun intended, with respect to murder at sea.

"As you'll see," he continued, "international law has given the right of any country that has a vessel flagged in its name, to assume jurisdiction over, in your case, the commission of a criminal offense by *any person*, he emphasized, so that means of course, of any nationality. I believe you already know that where the victim is a citizen of the United States, however, the FBI—under U.S. Law, Title 18, Section 7 of the *U.S. Code*, if you need the reference—has arguable jurisdiction to investigate, unless, of course, in the case of your ship, the British Virgin Islands, assert their authority, highly unlikely. If the victim was not an American citizen, and the State of Registration did not act, I'm damned if I know what would happen. In the case at hand on your ship, seeing that we are not able to reach it at sea, you and Mike are what we'd call the *pro tem* investigators for our agency, but, without police authority.

"The *Law Of the Sea* is silent on the question of powers of arrest, search and seizure of evidence, and giving cautions, so I'm advised that this matter then becomes a question of the ship's master's authority, under the *UNCLOS*. You don't have to worry about that. Your captain well knows his authority as it affects the safety of his crew and passengers."

"I take it that the matter depends on whether or not the ship's country of registration is a member of the *UNCLOS* Treaty?"

"Yes, I believe it does. I know what you're saying. What happens if a country isn't a signatory? I cannot answer that. Of course, it may be a moot point at the moment. Without checking, I'd guess that most, if not all cruise ship lines are domiciled in countries that signed on. Something to check, I suppose. Anyway, in view of this situation, our prosecutor suggests that if you need to do your police thing with the suspect—arrest, search his cabin and seize anything, that you write out the details and present them to the captain, with the request to authorize the arrest if that becomes necessary. Kind of like going to a judge to ask for a warrant. If he agrees, ask him to write something out, giving you, or rather Mike, as his subordinate, that authority. Perhaps you could compose that on the captain's behalf? You know what to write, Jack. Treat the investigation like you would a land-based one."

"Alright. Thanks for that. We'll get right to it. With what information we've got at the moment, I'm not sure we will caution him. I'll see how it plays out with his responses and attitude. While I don't have the authority to give a caution, Mike may well do, and I think it may then be given—depending on what he says, don't you think? Let the court sort it out later. We'll let you know what happened when we're done, if it's not too late at your location, Ralph. Okay?"

"Sure, I agree. Sounds good. Best of luck. Oh, one other thing. Have you heard any scuttlebutt from passengers about the death notice?"

"No, not a word. I suspect, the way it was worded, that people have forgotten by now. Good thing. Talk to you later."

♦ ◇ ♦

Turning to Mike, Jack said, "Okay, I'm going to write out some words explaining to the captain why we need an order from him to search Rudman's cabin, and if you don't mind taking it to him, ask him to read, and if he agrees, have him sign the order I'll typed up as well. I'll put the words down on a piece of Company letterhead to make it look more official. Make three copies. If it does eventually go to trial, courts like to see official-looking documents. Tell him I'm reviewing our approach with Rudman, and that we want to interview before we search his room. Doing it the other way around might shut him up. Come to think of it, it might be good for us to kill two birds with one stone and do the same for a look in Gorenko's cabin, after we search Rudman's. We'd have to have him in the cabin anyway, just make sure he doesn't contact her before we get to her place."

"Why do that, Jack? Couldn't we just say to her that we'd like to look in her cabin? If she didn't do the murder and doesn't have the jewelry, what does she have to hide? Knowing Rudman could just be coincidental."

"Yes, you could be right, Mike, but I have a feeling she may very well be complicit in this killing, *aiding and abetting*, or an *accessory* as it is sometimes referred to. In this case, tipping him off, holding or hiding the jewels, knowing they were stolen in the commission of a crime—murder. If we did just ask her to have a look and she refused, but we went ahead anyway—and even found the jewelry—that important piece of evidence, linking she and Rudman together, might well not be allowed into evidence at trial if the trial judge ruled it was illegally obtained, a major setback in trying to prove motive, and connection with each other. We've got to cross our T's and dot our I's to be on the safe side."

♦ ◊ ♦

While Jack and Mike read the emailed reference on state jurisdiction over its registered ships, and prepared their brief for the interview, they munched on toasted ham and cheese sandwiches and hot tea in a quiet corner of the staff dining room. Jack was anxious to get Rudman in for an interview.

Back in the security office thirty minutes later, Jack asked Mike to be prepared to read the Miranda caution card out to Rudman, and have him sign that he'd been advised of his rights, which would be audio taped. "I take it you have a copy of the card?"

Mike confirmed that he'd printed one off.

"How about a search of his cabin? When can we go ahead?"

Mike said, "The captain having the authority to order a search, the paperwork is done, and we can see him now. Anything else we need to discuss?"

"Probably, but can't think of anything pertinent for now," replied Jack, looking at Mike, who shook his head. "Alright, let's go see the Captain."

♦   ◇   ♦

With written permission to enter Rudman's cabin and now back in the security center, Mike asked one of the front desk staff to call Rudman and ask him to report there. No reason to be given. When he arrived, Mike would go to the front desk and bring him into the security office, and take him to the small interview room, already set up, tabletop cleared off with only the microphone in place. Ambience of the room and comfort was not a prerequisite for an interview with a suspected murderer. It was now 5:35....

♦   ◇   ♦

His cabin phone rang. After he'd answered, Rad listened as the woman said, "Could you please come to the front desk, sir? Mr. Donnelly would like to speak to you for a minute."

"What's it about?" Rad asked, his heart rate beginning to increase.

"I don't know, I'm afraid."

'Oh shit!'

He called Vessie right away and told her.

"Okay," she said, "you've got to go, but I think they're just fishing. I don't see how they've got anything on you to ask you questions. I mean, look at the trouble you went through to hide your identity. Just stay calm and answer questions vaguely—nothing specific. Have they been to your cabin for a look?"

"No."

"Alright. Good thing I've got the jewelry, eh? Call me when you get back. Good luck, Rad."

Rad arrived at the registration/passenger desk at 5:45 p.m.

Mike, dressed in a pale blue, open neck sports shirt and grey pants, came out to meet him and said, "Mr. Rudman, good of you to come. Would you come into our office. Shouldn't keep you long, I hope."

As he was escorted though the security office to the interview room, Rad noted a bank of CCTV screens on one wall, with an operator sitting at them. Fleetingly, he wondered if he'd done a sufficient check of the upper deck passageways to check on the presence of cameras. He felt reasonably sure he had.

Entering the small room, he was invited to sit in the chair that was offered him at a small table, upon which lay a red folder. There was another, older man present, dressed in a Hawaiian shirt and olive-colored dress pants who stood up and greeted him with a nod.

Mike and Jack had dressed casually so as to make the atmosphere less formal, intimidating.

Turning on the table microphone, Mike said, "I'm Mike Donnelly, chief of security and this gentleman is Mr. Jack Sterling, assisting our staff. I've turned on our recording machine as a matter of routine. We do this with everyone we talk to. Helps avoid errors in what's said. Are you okay? Comfortable, Mr. Rudman?"

He wasn't but nodded 'yes'. He'd let them do the talking, he decided. Be casual—nothing specific.

"May I skip the formalities and call you by your first name, Radovan?"

"Sure, it's Rad."

"Good. Thank you, Rad."

Jack wanted Mike to open the interview with a few questions, while he listened to the responses and watched his physical reaction.

"I have a bit of an Irish accent, so I hope you can understand me okay?"

"Yes, I can. Why am I here?"

"Well," Mike replied calmly, "you've probably heard about the death of an American female aboard ship a couple of days ago?"

"Yes."

"How or where did you hear about it, Rad?"

"Read it on the bulletin board in crew's quarters."

"Okay. It's the security section's job to look into the death and we have to talk to a few of the crew members, to possibly eliminate them as suspects."

"Am I a suspect!?"

"Not at the moment, but we do have a few questions to ask. Hope that's okay." It was not said as a question. Mike reached for the folder and extracted a piece of foolscap paper putting it on the table. "Now, you are here of your own free will?"

Radovan nodded his head.

"What I'd like you to do then is to sign this sheet of paper just above your name, which just says that you are here voluntarily. Can you do that for me? Please read it first."

Rad did and, taking the pen with his left hand from Mike, signed.

He did not notice the exchange of looks between he and Jack.

Mike continued, "Unfortunately, the woman was killed in her cabin four nights ago. Her jewelry was stolen. It's our job as ship security to look into the death. We have no police on board as you know," said Mike, "but the ship has security officers who act as police."

Jack noticed a very slight relaxation of posture in Rad when reminded of this. 'Good. He's thinking we're not trained and maybe he can handle us.'

Mike continued, "As you can understand, we have a number of people to interview who had some degree of contact, however small, with the woman."

"I didn't have no contact with her. Never met her. I'm a cleaner."

"We'll get around to that in a while. First, though, I'd like to know more about you. Our ship records show that you were born in Croatia in January, in 1974, in the city of Split, and on your application form you completed when you applied to work for World Cruise Lines, that you were conscripted—forced to join—your country's militia. How old were you then, Rad, and how long did you serve?"

"I was 18 and did my two years."

"Did you see active service?"

"I don't know what that means."

"Let me help him out, okay, Mike?" Jack interrupted and Mike nodded.

"The question means, were you involved in combat situations against the Serbs?"

"Yes, that's why we were forced to join the Army. There weren't enough regulars."

"I take it you were a foot soldier, infantry. Can you describe what kind of fighting you were involved in?"

"We were in firefights, as the Americans call it."

"Did this happen frequently and where? In towns, countryside?"

"Pretty much anywhere. We were always shot at first."

"I can take it then that you shot at a number of enemy soldiers. Do you know how many you may have killed or injured?"

"No, not really. Most of it was done at night and they were not close to us. I can't say," he said, wondering where they were going with this.

"Did you ever come across their wounded soldiers?"

Before he answered, he thought to himself, 'Okay, I think I know what he's getting at. Did we kill them off?' "Yes, sometimes. We helped the injured with first aid," he lied. He noticed the glance between the two men.

'They're trying to find out if I killed unarmed people. Maybe that's why they may suspect me. How did they come across my name?' He was trying to think of where he may have slipped up. The only quick answer he could think of at the moment was through the CCTV cameras. Maybe they got a partial look at his face. 'If they did, how did they match my face with my name?' He was beginning to feel warm in his clothing and his mouth was dry. He took a drink of water from his glass.

Mike's cell rang. He listened and said, "Okay, be right there. Will you excuse us for a minute, Rad?"

Rad nodded and both men left the room.

"Not being truthful, is he, Mike? Seems to me he's been through interrogation before, maybe a bit heavier than ours. Let's give him a couple of minutes. He's getting a bit warm. Time to bring up the Vesna connection."

Mike checked his phone: nothing had come back as yet regarding the FBI background check.

♦ ◇ ♦

In her cabin, Vessie had been thinking a great deal about the situation she was in. It was a heck of a predicament. Although the jewels were in a jar and invisible, she kept seeing them in her mind. The long necklace had been surprisingly heavy in her hand and she longed to put them on again for another look at all that glitter around her neck and cleavage. She also wondered, momentarily, if they were a bit heavy for the jar. 'Oh well, it's done.'

The thought of parting with them for money when they got home didn't sit well. 'What is it with women and diamonds?' she mused, remembering the song *Diamonds are a Girl's Best Friend*, made famous and sung so sexily by Marilyn Monroe in the movie, *Gentlemen Prefer Blondes*. Filmed on a cruise ship too. 'A bit ironic,' she thought.

As her emotions roiled, she was distressed that someone had died, and tried not to dwell on that. As well, there was the worry Rad had somehow botched the theft and may be caught. If the jewels were found in her cabin, could she get out of the situation by having some kind of excuse? The only thing she could think of was, 'Someone put them in there without me knowing'— a pretty weak statement when you think about it.

What would happen to her and Rad if they were caught? She put that thought out of her mind. Too much to think about. 'Where the hell is he? Should have called me back by now. I'll try calling.'

She did. No answer. 'Not the right time for him to be having dinner now,' she fretted, looking at her watch. 'What the Hell is going on?'

♦   ◇   ♦

The three of them were back in the interview room. Jack said to Rad, "Let's see, where were we?" as he looked at his notes to continue the interview. "Do you have a father, mother, brothers, sisters?"

"No brothers and sisters, and no parents, now."

"What happened to them?"

"They were both killed in the war—in 1991."

"I'm sorry to hear that. How did that happen?"

"They were killed during the shelling of our city by a Serbian Navy ship just off the coast, in August of that year. Our house"—he hesitated for a second or two, trying to find the right words—"was *broken down*."

"Demolished?" said Jack, offering the English language equivalent.

Radovan nodded, blinking his eyes rapidly.

"That's a terrible thing to happen. Once again, I'm sorry. You must have been very angry?"

Again, a nod.

"What made you leave your country?"

"I had no one left there and there was no work. The Militia were all let go when the war ended."

Rad told them how he eventually got to America, arriving in Miami in 1995, with many others applying as refugees. He had joined WCL in 2010, as a cleaner.

Rad was sitting at the table, leaning on his elbows with his hands clasped.

"Have you ever been in any trouble with American police, Rad?"

"No. Well, a couple of tickets, that's all."

"Okay. I notice you have a band-aid on the outer side of your left hand. Did you cut yourself? How did that happen and when?"

Rad shifted his left hand slightly to try to cover it up, and hesitated before replying. He'd been caught off guard and needed a moment to formulate a reply. "I cut it when I was peeling an apple with my pocket knife, couple days ago."

"Can you show me the knife, please?"

"It's in my room."

"Did you go to the medical center for treatment?"

"No. It's not that bad."

"Do you know a female crew member by the name of Vesna Gorenko?" asked Jack, looking directly into his eyes. If he denied it, Jack would tell him about being seen entering her cabin.

Once again, Rad was caught off guard. Hesitating, he looking up to the ceiling to his right, thinking to himself very quickly, 'They wouldn't ask that question if they knew I didn't.'

"Yes," he replied quietly.

"Can you tell me about that, please?"

"I met her in Miami almost twenty years ago. She's a refugee from Croatia like me and the Immigration people put lots of us under the care of a Serbian-Croatian Society to look after us and to try to help us find jobs and get settled down."

"Are you married to her or is she your girlfriend?" asked Jack.

"No, neither. We're just good friends."

"Did you know her in your country?"

"No, I was born in Split and she was born in a little village just outside the city, down the coast. We met first in Miami. She joined this cruise ship company before I did and helped me to get a job with them."

"So," Jack said, confirming the relationship again, "you're just good friends then?"

"Yes. She has a boyfriend in Miami."

"Are you married or living with someone?"

"No, I'm single."

"Well, you see, that's one of the reasons we're talking to you now. As you're aware—know—she, Vesna, is a crew member, like yourself, and a room attendant. She prepared the woman's suite two nights before she was killed, and, naturally, it's our responsibility to check that out. We do not know just who was involved in the murder and we are covering our bases, to use the American baseball term. When was the last time you saw her or visited her cabin, Rad?"

"Three days ago, I think," he quickly replied.

Again, a brief glance between the two interrogators.

"Was that the last time you saw her there?'

"Yes, it was."

"You're sure?"

"Yes, I'm sure."

"Rad, I'm going to show you a couple of photographs," said Jack, sliding them out of a manila envelope and laying them out in front of the man. "Look at them for a minute and tell me if you recognize the individual."

Rad's heart rate picked up immediately. He licked his lips. After a too-brief glance, he said, "No. He's a waiter and I do ship's cleaning. Not the same uniform." But he knew without a doubt the identity of the individual—'It's me! Thank God my face is hidden!'

Jack said, "Oh yes, one more question. Have you and Vesna discussed the murder of Mrs. Gessner?"

Again, thinking fast—'they can't know that, for sure'—he decided to be non-committal by replying, "She just asked me if I'd heard about it, and I told her only what I'd seen on the bulletin board."

"Alright, Rad. Thank you for your time. There is one other thing that we need to do. While Ms. Gorenko actually was in the woman's suite, even though it was two evenings before she was killed, there is always a slim possibility that she *may have* been involved somehow," he emphasized, "and for all we know, may have involved you, as unlikely as that may seem now, based on what you've said about being friends. What we'd next like to do, hopefully with your permission, is to have a look in your cabin for any evidence. We're doing the same with a couple of other people—just to be sure, you know?"

Rad suddenly sat upright in his chair. "What the Hell for?"

'Okay, careful what you say now,' Jack told himself. "Well, certainly for the jewelry that is missing, and any other evidence we may find. If there's nothing there, you've got nothing to worry about."

"I don't like you searching my cabin. I got nothing to hide but don't feel like I have to let you in."

"Well, we were hoping you'd co-operate but we do have a search order, signed by the captain—this is normal procedure. I'm going to give you a copy of that order now," sliding the sheet of paper to him, "and Mr. Donnelly and I will accompany you to your cabin, so you can be present during the search. Shouldn't take long, we expect. Do you have a cell phone?"

"Yes, but not with me. I leave it at home."

"If you'd just give us a minute," Jack said, and both he and Mike got up and left the room.

"Okay, Mike, he cannot be allowed to make a call to Vessie before we go to her cabin next, so he'll have to stay with us until that's done. When we get to his room, have him produce the pocket knife and bag it, then sit him down in a chair while we look. We don't need to make a note of what we've just said, as it's on record. He's decidedly unhappy with us but I'm not sure what that means. Maybe we'll get lucky. That was a curious response he made when I showed him the photos: 'He's a waiter and I do ship's cleaning.' Don't you think, if he was not involved, that he would *not* have said that, but merely say, 'No'?"

Mike said, "Yes, I think you're right. You know, that son of a bitch looks like the photo to me, even without the full view of his head. Also, he lied about when he saw the Gorenko woman."

"You may well be right about the photo, and he did lie. Why? While I think of it, Mike, let's get the cut glove from our exhibit locker. Have Rudman put the glove on to see if the cut in it matches the same spot on his hand."

"We'll do a kind of O.J. Simpson on him."

Mike's remark caused Jack to smile.

"Also, he's not wearing his watch, Mike. Wonder why?"

Mike opened the door. "You ready, Mr. Rudman? Let's go, please."

He nodded, looking angry, and the three of them left the office.

♦   ◊   ♦

In his cabin, Jack and Mike spent considerable time searching every nook and cranny looking for the jewelry, even removing a few ceiling panels, but, no luck. Checking his clothing for blood stains produced nothing, however, they did find his watch—a Timex with chrome-plated wristband, which Mike took custody of. His pocket knife was not found and Rad said he must have just lost it.

Standing outside, just out of earshot, Jack said he didn't believe Rad ever had one. "Well, the jewelry doesn't seem to be here, Mike. He may well have given them to Vesna. She's our next stop."

They had examined his work shoes—size elevens, as it turned out—and checked the soles carefully, with no signs of blood specks.

Mike said, "Not surprising, seeing that he gets them very wet washing down decks, and vacuuming a lot of passageway carpet. Should we take them, Jack?"

"I don't think they will yield anything. Take a photo and measure the size at least, for comparison. I'll check with Miami about that. We might as well go."

♦   ◊   ♦

Vessie was getting increasingly worried. She'd not heard back from Rad and had called him three times in the last two hours. What's keeping him so long? She checked her alarm clock on the bedside table—now 6:30 p.m. 'I'll just keep checking his room, I suppose,' she thought. 'God, what if they are questioning him now? I hope he hasn't confessed! If he has, he'd better not give me up and tell them where the jewelry is.'

On second thoughts, she did not think the latter possibility as likely, due to the passage of time. 'If security had questioned him and he'd confessed, they'd have been here by now.'

She sat down from her pacing and turned on the TV to try to calm herself. She wished she didn't feel this way—it was so unlike her. As she was switching channels, there was a loud knock on her door that made her jump. 'Rad? No, that's not his knock.'

Apprehensively, she went to the door and opened it. Her worst fears! Three people stood in front of her, the chief of security, a woman in uniform from his office and the older man, wearing civilian clothing.

"Ms. Gorenko?" asked the chief.

"Yes," said Vessie, her heart pounding.

"May we come in, please?"

"I guess so. What's this about?"

Entering her small cabin, Mike gave her a sheet of paper, and introduced the three of them. "We are conducting an investigation into the death of one of our passengers, a Mrs. Rebecca Gessner. Part of our responsibility is to check on all crew members who may have had contact with her just before she was killed. I may have told you before when we spoke to you that we'd be continuing to investigate."

Vessie nodded.

"That sheet of paper is an order, signed by Captain Stuart, allowing us to search your room." Pointing to Jack, Mike said, "You remember this gentleman on your first visit to my office?"

Again she nodded.

"We may be doing the same with others of the crew. Valuable pieces of jewelry were stolen at the time and that is what we are looking for. The woman accompanying us is Sheila Turner, of my staff. This is for protocol purposes. What we would like you to do, please, is to take a seat while we look around. It will be a rather thorough search and doesn't necessarily reflect any presumption of guilt or innocence. You understand what I've told you?"

Again, another nod.

"Alright, Sheila will give you a standard pat down."

While the female security officer did that, Jack and Mike began their search, the same as they had done in Rudman's. Every part of the cabin was checked—drawers pulled out and checked underneath, the mattress stripped and checked for evidence of cuts or tears in the fabric, pillows felt, the rug checked for signs of being pulled up and she was asked to unlock her safety box. Pots and pans, and food packages were opened, and the back of the flat screen TV removed.

Inside the bathroom, the toilet was checked, the shower cubicle drain—in case the necklace had somehow been suspended inside— and the underside of the sink. Her toiletry cabinet was examined by the female attendant. Vessie watched nervously as Sheila did this, especially when she picked up the first jar of Nivea cream, opened it and looked inside. Putting that aside, she picked up the jar behind, and noting the tape around the lid, removed the seal and unscrewed the top. Vessie found her mouth had gone very dry. After a quick glance inside the full jar, the woman replaced the lid and Vessie had to look away for a few seconds, to hide the overwhelming relief on her face.

'They didn't find the jewelry! THANK GOD!'

Jack looked at Mike and Sheila, and without saying anything, briefly turned the palms of his hands up in an 'anything else?' gesture. Getting no response from them, he thanked Vessie for her cooperation, apologized for the interruption of her evening, and they left her cabin.

As soon as the door closed, she pumped her right hand in the air and said to herself, quietly, 'Yes! It worked!'

She still did not know where Rad was and hadn't heard from him. 'I'll try one more call.'

No answer.

As the three investigators walked back to the security office, they expressed some degree of disappointment at the outcome. "I suppose we shouldn't be too hard on ourselves," said Jack. "This is a huge ship to hide a small item in."

Looking at his watch and noting the time—seven o'clock—he finished by saying, "Listen, I think we'd better give Ralph Harkins a call in Miami and fill him in before we knock off for the night. Then let's each review alone what we've done today and meet tomorrow at nine. Okay with you, both?"

Mike and Sheila indicated they were in agreement.

Sheila was very pleased at having been included in the search. Too bad she hadn't found the diamonds—that would have been so perfect.

♦ ◊ ♦

Jean Sterling was in her stateroom at seven o'clock in the evening, watching television, when her phone rang.

Her daughter said, "Hi Mom, how are you?"

"Well, thanks, Avery. You?"

"I'm good. Hope my call is convenient now. How's the chief superintendent doing. Made an arrest yet? Nabbed the villain?"

Jean laughed. "No, not yet. Sorry, your father's not here now. I'll tell him you called. So far, there's not a lot of evidence, but he's really working away and I don't get to see much of him. I've got to tell you, I did a bit of detective work for him today, and may have identified a likely suspect!"

Jean briefly described the event to Avery.

"Wow! Mom, good on you. Though I'm not surprised that some of Dad's skill has rubbed off on you after over thirty years of living together."

"Well, I wouldn't put it quite that way. He and Mike Donnelly, the chief of security, were going to interview the suspect today and then go and search his cabin. Jack's keeping the FBI in Miami up to date. Would be great if Jack manages to get a confession from the man. But, enough about us—what's happening in your life?"

♦　◇　♦

Back in his stateroom at seven-thirty, Jack found his wife watching an episode of the *Antiques Roadshow* about Qing Dynasty pottery, on the Public Broadcasting Service station. For Jack, not terribly scintillating stuff.

Jean looked up and said, "Shall I turn this off? It's a bit dreary. I'd like to hear how your day went. Did you get lucky?" She pressed a button on the remote and the screen went blank.

"I wish," he replied. He told her about the negative searches and she could tell he was disappointed. She knew Jack well enough to know that this was one case he'd really like to solve, and that he was frustrated.

While his reputation as a detective didn't matter so much now that he was no longer on active duty, she knew that his personal pride was being challenged.

She said, "I've got a read on you, my man, and I'm betting you'll *get your man*, to quote the Mounties."

"Thank you for your confidence in me, Jean. That's one of the reasons I love you—you've always been so supportive—but time is running out. Mike and I are not really much further ahead than we were a couple of days ago. And the FBI team will be here sometime early Saturday morning. Be nice to hand over the culprit—for Mike and me. In less than three days, we dock in Miami."

"So, your cleaner suspect had nothing to say?"

"No. I have a feeling he's been through interrogation before. He was conscripted for two years with the Croatian military, and was in combat situations—skirmishes to be more accurate. Short firefights. He's a tough-skinned, hard-nosed individual. Not inclined to respect authority, and I don't think we're going to get anything from him. Solid evidence will have to prevail if this goes to trial."

"Avery called not long ago. She's fine. Asked how you were do-ing—'nabbed the villain?'—was her question. I told her about my detective work today, and she was tickled with that. She has every confidence in you too, Jack. Have you eaten?"

"Yes, thanks. I had a late snack with Mike. Have you?"

"I had dinner at five-thirty. I was hungry and, obviously, didn't know when you'd be home. Hope you don't mind, love?"

"Of course not."

"Okay if I watch a little telly for a bit? I'm turning in early tonight."

"Yeah, me too. I have to be on deck early again. Listen to me, using nautical terms. Maybe I should get a job as a cruise ship security officer...."

Day 14 of the cruise dawned as it had for the previous thirteen, since leaving Barcelona: cloudless and warm, with a slight westerly breeze.

Speculation among the ship's passengers had long since fallen off as to how one of them had died, most assuming natural causes although there had been a wisp of a rumor that she may have been killed. Another rumor claimed it was food poisoning. Many of them said, "Poor thing, dying on a cruise," while others said something of the opposite, "If you gotta go, best way to do it."

Those relatively few crew members who'd had some connection with the investigation, had been told in no uncertain terms about the need for silence and strict confidentiality, on pain of dismissal if they were found to have leaked information. It was pointed out that it was in their long-term interest not to. "We don't want to scare away future passengers." So far, their silence had held.

Over a nice early breakfast, delivered to their room, Jean told her husband that she was being taken for a look at one of the luxury suites by the assistant manager of the hotel section, arranged by Susan Stuart, who would accompany her. There were three of those huge crown suites and one had not been booked for this cruise. She thought she'd go to the *Crystal Salon* later for a massage and have her hair styled.

"Have a great day, sweetheart," said Jack. We have a lot more to do, but I'll see if I can get time for lunch together. I'll call you later."

"Alright. Hope everything goes well. After dinner tonight, let's go dancing. There's a duet playing the piano and a trombone—calling themselves *Slight Jazz*—in the *Starlight Room*. I trust you'll be back for dinner?"

♦　◇　♦

Jack, Mike, and Sheila Turner met in the Ops Center interview room at nine-thirty. Overnight, a message from the FBI, Miami, labeled *confidential* had been received on the ship's secure line, for the attention of *Mr. Jack Sterling*. It was from the Croatian authorities via Diplomatic Services, and contained background information on Rudman. The data were essentially the same as that of Gorenko's: nothing outstanding. They confirmed his term of service in the Militia. No record of incidents lodged with the country's police force.

The small table was fully covered with notes, photos and interview tapes. Jack had asked that they start the review from the beginning of the investigation. "I guess essentially, what we're looking for is anything we may have overlooked, or didn't see. I think we all agree we have two *persons of interest*, at least, and maybe stronger than that. Why don't we start with the first report of the death by the cleaning woman, Ms. Fortunado. Sheila, would you mind making notes on the flip-chart, and we can tape the information to a wall."

They paid particular attention to the exhibits (items of evidence) seized, making sure they were all duly itemized in the order taken. In court proceedings, the prosecutor's job is made easier when the case is presented in chronological order, Jack told them.

They spent some time going over the events in the suite, identifying items seized that would require further technical and forensic examination, which of course, could only be done when turned over to the FBI and taken to their lab.

"Did we miss anything in the suites?" Jack asked. He realized he was dealing with people totally inexperienced in this kind of activity, but he nevertheless appreciated their input and observations. After all, he thought, 'even with all my experience, I can still overlook something.'

The three of them concluded that they had done all they could and taken the appropriate items of evidence from the scene. Jack asked Mike what would happen to the suite now. How long before it could be used again.

"I'm not sure, Jack. It may be fixed up during or after the next cruise. Repair people will come aboard when we dock in Miami and confirm what has to be done. The bed and rugs will need replacing, for sure. It is possible replacement materials will be put aboard in Miami plus a couple of tradesmen who will install during the upcoming cruise. That will mean one sailing out of use, unless of course, the decision is made to seal off the suite and wait until the off-season to do the repair work."

The next matter up for review were the various statements taken, by now amounting to seventeen witnesses, including a very brief one from Mrs. Jack Sterling. Each of them read each statement, agreeing that those taken from Ms. Gorenko and Rad Rudman contained some evasive answers, making them strong suspects. Mike Donnelly said something he didn't need to say, but felt compelled to voice: "If only we'd found the jewelry, that would sure help."

"Okay, next, the room searches. My question, a rhetorical one, is 'Did we do enough?' I've been on many of these and one can always second-guess whether or not you *looked everywhere*," Jack emphasized. "What do you think? Take a minute to review, in our mind's eye, what we did, or did not do."

Each of them did that. Neither Jack or Mike could think of anything, beyond maybe going back for a second look.

Sheila Turner took a few seconds longer, screwing up her eyes in concentration. 'What did I do in checking Vesna's cabin?' she asked herself. 'Checked her clothes, in the closet, drawers and luggage, her bathroom, her toilet, the wall cabinet and the toiletries, food containers…' visualizing what she did. 'No, I think—wait a minute, I looked into her two cream jars. One was unused, taped closed, and no cream had been used when I opened it. Both were Nivea Cream brand. Hmm.'

"What are you thinking, Sheila?" Jack asked, noting her hesitancy in replying.

She told him. "Now I'm wondering if I should have had a closer look at that unopened jar of face cream. It did look unused. Maybe I'm being paranoid."

"You may be, and that's good when doing security and police work. This kind of activity calls for a suspicious mind. It may sound trifling, Sheila, but let's check it out. When you think about it, not a bad place to hide something. And intuition or nagging thoughts—some call it their *gut feelings*—have led to vital discoveries in many, many criminal investigations.

"Alright, to be on the safe side, I think I'll ask the captain to sign another search order, just to do it right, then we'll have a look when Vesna gets off shift."

♦   ◊   ♦

At 11:40 a.m., the door to cabin *A311* was opened and Vessie stood there, surprise and fear starting to show in her eyes. The same three people who were here yesterday were back. They knew! Did Rad give her up!?

"You know who we are, Ms. Gorenko. We need to look in your cabin again."

Serving her the copy of the search order, Sheila went right to the bathroom cabinet. Opening the full, 500-millilitre jar of Nivea Cream, she showed Mike and Jack the inside. The cream appeared to be undisturbed.

"Go ahead, Sheila," Mike said.

Dipping her forefinger and middle finger deep into the cream, she felt something solid. Hooking both fingers around the object, she slowly pulled it out, some of the cream falling off. And there it was— the diamond necklace. Messy, but so good to see.

Taking a tablespoon from Vessie's cutlery drawer, Sheila scraped out the rest of the cream, putting it on a large plate, and found the two diamond earrings.

Jack and Mike did their best to hide their smiles.

Vessie sat on the edge of her bed and covered her face with her hands. She started to rock slowly forward and back.

With the sudden change of events, Jack had to do some fast thinking. 'Take photos—read the *caution* to her—take her into custody which might constitute an arrest?

While Sheila arranged the evidence on the table and Mike took several shots of it, with the cream still attached to the diamonds, and then with them rinsed off, laying the necklace out and the earrings, beside the colored photos they had brought along, to show the exact comparison. He also photographed the cream jar, outside and inside, to show capacity and that it was empty, and lastly, the cabinet, with the door open.

Jack said to Vessie, "Before I say anything to you, I'm going to ask the chief of security here, to read you your rights. It's called the *Miranda caution*." He thought it prudent that Mike should do that in his position as an employee of WCL, and of course, now, in light of finding the jewelry.

Tears had welled up in her eyes and were beginning to run down her cheeks. Mike Donnelly took his caution card out, looked at the woman, and said, "Please listen to this:

"Vesna Gorenko, you have the right to remain silent. Anything you say may be used against you. You have the right to an attorney, and if you cannot afford one, an attorney will be provided at no

cost, and to have that attorney present during questioning. Do you understand?"

Vessie nodded.

"I'm sorry," said Jack, "you have to verbally acknowledge that you heard it and understand, okay?"

"Yes," she mumbled.

"Alright, Vesna, I'm afraid you will have to come back to the security office, for the time being. You will likely be able to return to your quarters later on."

To Mike and Sheila, he said, "If you're ready, let's go."

"There's just one thing, Jack," said Sheila, on the way back to the office, out of Vessie's hearing. "It maybe worth a check, and that is, 'When was the unopened jar of cream purchased?' Was it bought just for this event? She had about a quarter of a jar left in the other one, and in my view, wouldn't need more for a while, depending of course how much she used daily. I could check the crew commissary and see if their sales records would give that information."

"Good thinking, Sheila. If you wouldn't mind, please."

◆   ◇   ◆

In Vessie's cabin, the wallphone rang several times. It went unanswered.

In his cabin, Rad, who'd been released earlier from the security office, hung up and thought, 'Okay, I suppose she's out somewhere. Wrong time to be eating. I can't go to her cabin, so I'll go for a walk and look for her. After one more try.'

The silence at her end of the line worried him a bit though. 'Three more days and we're home free… let's hope.'

◆   ◇   ◆

In another part of the ship, Jean Sterling was enjoying her afternoon. She was with Susan Stuart and Helga Gannschmidt, the assistant hotel manager, and was standing in *Crown Suite 6001*, one of three luxury suites on this ship.

"Wow!" said Jean, "this is big and beautiful."

"Before we go in any further, let me tell you a little about what you see," said Helga. "These rooms were designed by a company called LuxurySuite, in co-operation with the shipbuilder, Supermarine Designs Inc. of Copenhagen. It's obvious when you look, that World Cruise Lines spared no expense in planning and outfitting them. That's why there are only three. Most of the materials and furnishings are made in America by top-of-the-line suppliers. As we go around, I'll tell you about them."

Susan Stuart's phone rang and she said, "Sorry" and excused herself.

"First, we're standing in the entrance, called the *foyer*," continued Helga, speaking to Jean, "as it no doubt looks a bit like to the entrance to a small hotel. The white floor is Carrera marble, from Italy. It continues around into a bathroom to your right, one of two in the suite. Marble is pretty, easy to clean and no wear. You'll note the tall crystal vase on the round, glass tabletop, has no flowers. No one is in here on this cruise. When there is a guest, the flowers are replaced daily. They come from our cool flower room on deck one. Turn right and go into the spacious bathroom. The wash basin counter is made of light grey Scottish granite and has two marble basins. The mirrors are wrap-around so you can see yourself from any angle. The second bathroom is similar to this. The thick, white bathrobes are from Jacquard and, as you probably would have assumed, cruise ships equip the washrooms with bidets in their larger suites."

"I note there are two shower heads in the stall," said Jean. "Surely people are not in a hurry to shower while cruising?"

"No," Helga replied, "they're called *conjugal showers*. I can't think why two are needed though. And, we don't advertise them as *his-and-hers* any longer."

"Why on Earth not?" asked Jean.

"Well, think about it: it could be his-and-his, or hers-and-hers, these days, and we don't wish to offend anyone."

"Oh, right. Are you serious?"

Helga laughed. "Modern times," she said. "I say no more."

Susan re-joined them and said that it was one of her sons calling.

"Let's have a look at the *boudoir* next. I think the room deserves that name."

The king-size bed looked like a small landing field. By far the largest Jean had ever seen. The room was bright and airy, made more so by the huge, bowl-shaped, lighted crystal chandelier reflecting the light in a rainbow of colors.

"That's beautiful," Jean said, pointing at the light. There must have been hundreds of pieces, enclosed at the rim in a bright circle of brass.

"Should be. It's made of crystal, created by Palace Lighting out of Atlanta. They do some of the lighting in the Vegas casinos.

"The rug in this bedroom, made by the Walton Company in the United Kingdom, is deep pile and the shade is robin-egg blue—lovely color, don't you think? There's more to tell. All the wood furniture and wood accents are made of what's called Seritona cherry wood. In this case, grown in Georgia. Feel the bedsheets, Jean."

Jean did. "My, that's pure cotton. Beautifully made."

"If you're interested, the thread count, or TC, is 1500 per square inch," said Helga. "This linen gets washed separately from the rest as you can imagine."

Looking around, Jean said, "I like the large vanity mirror in the bathroom, surrounded by glamor lights. Must feel like you're getting ready to go on stage when you sit there."

"Alright. Two more rooms to show." Helga led the two women into the dining room, adjacent to the sitting room. Another, smaller chandelier hung over the glass-topped dining table. The chairs had the same wood finish as the bedroom furniture with padded, damask-covered seats. An empty crystal flower vase stood in the center. Helga told Jean that only the crown suites had their own dining room. Wealthy people liked to cater a dinner for their friends.

"Now I'll show what I think is the most beautiful room in the suite: the Lounge as we call it. In the olden days, it would be called the *Parlor*."

It was immediately obvious why Helga said that. At the far end was a wall of books and next to it was a Baldwin baby grand. Leather-covered lounge chairs and a chaise took care of the seating. The walls were covered with damask-style wallpaper, done in alternating strips of gold and red wine color, to match the wall-to-wall rug, an Axminster in a flower motif. One whole side of the room looked out onto the long veranda deck.

Jean said, "This is a lovely room. I could spend a lot of time in here."

She walked over to the piano and, looking at Helga, said, "I've never played a Baldwin before. May I?"

"By all means."

Raising the lid, she sat down and played a quick scale. She began with two Irving Berlin songs: *I Love a Piano* and *Say It with Music*, finishing with a classical piece by Robert Schumann, his lyrical *Traumerie*.

"Wow!" said Susan Stuart. "That was beautiful. Where did you learn to play?"

"Seeing that I live in Toronto, where else but at the Royal Conservatory of Music, during my formative years, up to age seventeen. I attained my grade seven level, but when I graduated high school I went on to university."

"Have you played professionally?"

"No. Just pretty much for myself and occasionally at parties."

"Well, I wish I'd known this before now," said Susan. "I'd have you playing in the *Grecian Lounge*! Well done."

Helga said, "Thank you for playing Schumann. With my German heritage, I grew up with the classics, of course. Well, the tour is finished, ladies. Time for a light lunch."

In the dining room, they were served with an appetizing selection of finger sandwiches: salmon, cream cheese, cucumber, etcetera, along with scones, topped with Cornish clotted cream and strawberry jam, and a pot of Darjeeling tea, all served on fine china by Aynsley, with a motif of tiny bluebell flowers around the rims of the cups and plates.

As they were leaving the suite, Jean expressed her thanks to her hosts and said, "So, this is the meaning of *first class passage*. I'll have to try it someday after Jack and I win a lottery."

♦　◇　♦

In Mike's modest office, the two of them discussed their approach to the *suspect*—now called that by Jack Sterling—and their follow-up steps.

While it was good to have the Gorenko woman in that capacity, they needed to *get* her male partner-in-crime, to close the case. Perhaps she would give him up? But one thing at a time.

"Before we talk to Ms. Gorenko, I'd very much like to verify, as far as possible, that those jewels came from the Gessner suite. The prosecutor will have to show they did. I think Ms. Goldman would be the ideal person to verify these exact jewelry items and place them in the suite. So, we'll do that first. If you could have someone find her, Mike, and bring her to the office as soon as possible, that would be good. If she seems uncomfortable or a bit scared, try to reassure her that she is an important witness. Okay?"

Mike made a call to Hannah's room, and asked a female officer to collect her. She had just returned from a late, light lunch, not feeling like eating, really.

Jack did some mental review while he was waiting. 'Did Vesna know about the murder plan beforehand? Was she complicit in it, and was she there when it happened? The latter was highly unlikely. No pictures of her entering and leaving the suite. If she told Rudman about the jewels, what was the condition of her mind at the time?

Was it just a passing remark? Something like: 'Wow! You should have seen the jewels this woman has.' Or was it somehow implied, or said, that she'd really like to have them, or even words like: 'I could kill for them'? At this moment, for Jack, the answer to those questions was a fifty-fifty split between Yes and No.

♦ ◊ ♦

Hannah put the phone down. She was still feeling very low and looked forward to when the ship docked and she could leave. She was not able to clearly visualize what would happen when she went to Mrs. Gessner's house to talk with Maria, or what she would do—or could do. No doubt Mrs. G.'s brother would arrive from Los Angeles, to take over her affairs. She had never met him.

'For that matter, what will I do now? Hell of a thing to happen. I wonder who did this? Will the jewels ever be found?'

The security people had just called, asking if she wouldn't mind going back to their office to *clear something up* as they put it. One of their staff was coming to collect her. She went into the bathroom, checked her hair, combed it a bit and sprayed, touched up her face and put on a light colored shade of lipstick. She looked a bit better, she thought, but didn't feel that way. Amazing how doing one's face could mask your feelings.

♦ ◊ ♦

"Hello, Hannah, how are you?" asked Jack as he and Mike stood up at one side of the small interview room.

"I'm alright, thanks. Just wondering why you want to see me again?"

"Well, first, good of you to come. Please take a seat at this table. You remember Mr. Mike Donnelly, of course?" he asked, as Mike, refraining from shaking her hand, directed her to a seat. "You might be surprised to know that we've recovered the diamond necklace."

"That's wonderful!" Hannah said—although her next thought was, 'poor Mrs. G. won't be able to wear them again. A shame. She loved them so much.' "Can you tell me how you found them, and where?"

"I'd like to, but because this is still an ongoing investigation, I'm a bit reluctant to provide any detail. You will no doubt find out in due course. What I need you to do is to confirm, if you can, whether or not they are the property of the late Mrs. Rebecca Gessner. You may know this already, but the FBI people in Miami—acting on your suggestion—have gone to the residence and retrieved pictures and the insurance forms, to help in the identification and to confirm their value. We'd like to go just a step further and have you look at them and confirm they belonged to her, and that she had them along on this cruise.

"So, here they are," he said, opening the cardboard exhibit box in which they had been placed, taking the necklace, earrings, colored photos and insurance sheet, and laying them on the desk top. "Please, pick them up if you wish."

In her service with Mrs. Rebecca Gessner, Hannah had not seen her best jewelry often, and every time she did, she couldn't help but think how beautiful they looked, sparkling in the light. Picking up the necklace carefully, as if the stones would break if she dropped it, she looked it over carefully for a minute.

Then Hannah pointed out to the detective, the neck clip, saying, "Mrs. Gessner didn't like the clip that it came with and had another one made at her jewelers in Miami."

Jack interrupted her by asking, "—Which jewelers was that?"

"It's called Feldmans, on Ocean Drive in South Beach. She also had the original silver thread wire replaced with a thin steel one—to prevent 'snatch and run' thefts. I was with her when she went to her jewelers to have it done, and that's the clip on this necklace with the jeweler's logo in miniature."

"Thank you very much. That's excellent recall. One more thing. Did you arrange for the insurance?"—showing her the paper.

"Yes, she asked me to take care of that. At the time, the necklace and earrings were valued by Feldmans at two-hundred-and-fifty thousand dollars. Can you tell me what will happen to the jewelry?"

"Well, I will have to turn it over to the FBI. It's *evidence* and has to be kept for presentation at a trial. When the case is over, it will be returned. In this case, I would suppose to her estate or her next of kin, unless," he thought for a moment, "she willed it to another person. Do you know that, Hannah?"

"No, I have no knowledge of what's in her will."

"Alright. I'll make a note to discuss the matter with the federal agents, when we turn these items over to them. Just a reminder about confidentiality, Ms. Goldman. If you can keep this matter to yourself?"

Hannah nodded a bit sheepishly, knowing she'd want to tell her mother immediately.

"Thanks for your time. Again, let me say that we are very sorry for your loss."

After she left, Jack said, "Well, that's a relief, now that the jewelry has been identified, and in such a thorough way."

In the meantime, Sheila had found out that on the day after the murder was discovered, only one jar of face cream, that size, had been sold, paid for in cash. The salesperson was not able to identify the buyer.

"Gives us an edge to work with, Mike. We need to speak with Vesna and then Rad, see if we can't wrap this up."

The woman was still in the waiting room, twiddling her thumbs.

"Give me a few minutes to think."

◆　◇　◆

Sipping a glass of iced tea, Jack wondered how best to go about talk-ing to the cleaner. She was now well beyond *person-of-interest* status, firmly into the *suspect* category, likely as an accomplice. One of two approaches. 'Tell her what we know, that she's not under arrest—but we'll have to re-caution her—and that her part in this matter, to us, is obvious, hoping she'll admit to what happened. If she wants to say nothing, tell her that because the jewelry was found in her cabin, this makes her a possible accessory to murder, at the discretion of the prosecutor, and that she could also very well be charged with posses-sion of stolen property over the value of ten thousand dollars, a felony offense. I'll have to explain what that entails, and that it could result in a long prison term.

'Of course, there is one other possibility. That she's innocent of complicity in the intent to steal the diamonds and the murder. That she may have reluctantly been coerced into helping Radovan out, af-ter the fact, by hiding the jewels.' His instinct told him the latter may well be her honest response but, it would not absolve her of the re-sponsibility to report the matter. Possession of stolen goods was kind of like being a 'little bit pregnant,' in the criminal sense. 'Okay, let's see what happens.'

"Mike, if you don't mind, let me do the talking, please. I'll ask you if you have anything to ask at the end, okay?"

Scooping up the necklace and earrings, he replaced the items in the box, and told Mike he was ready. "Let's bring her in for a friendly chat."

◆   ◇   ◆

In his long service as a detective with the Toronto police depart-ment, he had learned a great deal about facing and interviewing witnesses and suspects. It could sometimes be an advantage if they were nervous. Brains function a bit differently and the suspect's re-sponses tend to become muddled, argumentative, defensive or—only occasionally—making a complete and emotional confession, as in, "Yes, I did it! God forgive me!"

Defense counsel would sometimes make the argument that their client was somehow forced into that state—and made a false confession—by the language and body language used by the investigator. *Brow beating* and *intimidation* were the common expressions. A good detective would, with the degree and extent of evidence available, plus some information about the person in front of him, and other factors, be able to decide what approach to take and even the language to use. One useful approach, if possible, was to try to speak at the intellectual level of that person. The ideal, of course, was to foster honest responses to questions that would indicate guilt or innocence. Keeping an open mind was paramount.

Indeed, a detective's language and demeanor when giving evidence in court could indicate his degree of *fairness* in questioning people. After all, assisting in securing a conviction of the accused was part of a policeman's livelihood and his reputation was at stake. One look by Jack at Vesna Gorenko indicated her high degree of nervousness. 'Alright, go easy on her,' he thought.

Sitting alone, Vessie's mind had been racing, knowing she was in *very big troubles* as her parents might have said back home in Croatia. Because a person had died, she knew how serious a matter this was. 'What am I going to say? How can I explain why the jewelry was hidden in my cabin? Should I tell them all that I know, passing the blame on to Rad? I mean, I didn't know he was going to kill the woman! Should I just say nothing? They did tell me I didn't have to say anything. If I say nothing, am I implying that I know something? Oh Christ! Why did I have to tell Rad about the jewelry?!'

She found herself being directed back into the same bare, interview room.

When the three of them entered, Mike said to her, "Do you need anything? A drink, pen and paper?"

She nodded, and Sheila went for a glass of water. Vessie was looking decidedly unhappy.

"Ms. Gorenko, once again, sorry to keep you waiting. Hopefully we won't have to keep you much longer. Ms. Turner will stay because, as you know, protocol requires us to have a woman present during interviews of females. You remember Mr. Sterling, of course? Before we start, a couple of things. Just to let you know, the recording device on the table is on, and also that I will have to read you the caution again. Okay?"

Mike did that and Vessie acknowledged.

Jack went directly to the point. "I'd like to begin by reminding you about the jewelry we found hidden in your cabin. I must say that was a good place to hide it. We missed finding it on our first check of your room. Would you like to talk about that?"

'Here we go,' she thought. 'Should I say no, I don't want to say nothing, or tell them all I know?' Thinking about Rad, she said, "No, I don't want to say anything."

"Alright, if that's what you want."

He opened the lid of the box and took the jewelry out, laying it on the table. She took a glance and looked quickly away.

"Do you know the value of these diamonds?"

"No."

"Well, they are insured for two-hundred-and-fifty thousand dollars—American." When he said that, he noted a slight intake of breath by Vessie. A far higher value than she imagined, he suspected.

"That's a great deal of money," Jack continued. "We have confirmed that Mrs. Gessner—the woman who died—owned these items and they were in her cabin. You may not know this, but she has a companion traveling with her on this cruise and that woman has identified them for us. They were stolen and, as you know, found in your cabin, in one of your face cream jars. To us, that can only mean one thing: that you knew, at least, that they had been stolen. If that's the case, you can be charged for the criminal offense of *possession of stolen property over the value of ten thousand dollars,'* what is called, in America, a *felony* offense, which is serious. You could be facing time in prison. As well, with what we know and with the evidence we have collected, there is a possibility you were somehow involved in the death of this woman, which is an even more serious felony—with a far longer prison term, even a death sentence. Do you still wish to remain silent?"

Vessie bowed her head down. "Can I have a minute to think, please?" she asked in a whisper.

Jack didn't ordinarily allow that, but in her case he could tell she was wavering and thought it might be prudent to allow her some time. He said, "Okay."

Looking at Mike and Sheila, he shook his head slightly, indicating, 'Don't say anything.'

The room was quiet.

Vessie sat still, gazing at the tabletop, avoiding the diamonds, thinking. 'I do not want to go to prison. Rad never told me he would steal the jewelry. When I told him about it after I finished doing the evening check of that suite, I only made—what do the English call it—a *remark*, that the jewels were interesting to me. I made a big mistake when he came to me with the necklace, by agreeing to hide it, even though he told me he'd had to kill the woman. I can't believe that they found the jewels hidden in my bathroom. I can't dream that away. They've got me caught. Oh God! If only this hadn't happened!'

Raising her head, her watery eyes looked at Jack and he could see the sadness in them. The moment of admission had arrived.

He said nothing, just listened.

Vessie swallowed a couple of times, trying to find her voice. She told him essentially what she had just been thinking and finished by say, "I'm so sorry she died. If I hadn't told Rad about the jewelry, this would never have happened."

The change of atmosphere in the room was almost palpable. Jack had experienced this kind of feeling many times and, in a way, nearly always felt very satisfied: another case solved—well, almost. His efforts on behalf of a murder victim were vindicated. But this was only what cops called 'half a loaf'; the other part needing to be confirmed.

"Thank you, Ms. Gorenko. As you know, your statement has been recorded. We'll get that typed up and have you read and sign it before you go.

"I'll leave you in care of Sheila. If you need anything, bathroom, food and drink, she will help with that. By the way, do you have a cell phone with you on this voyage?"

Vessie said, "No."

Aside, he told Sheila not to allow Vessie to use an office phone, and to keep her in the office.

Out in the main security office, Mike said to Jack, "Well, I guess that admission goes a long way toward helping us when we talk to Rad, don't you think, Jack?"

"Only so far, unfortunately. He's the guy we believe 'did the dirty,' but in the absence of incriminating evidence, that may not lead to a charge of murder. We obviously need to have another go at him and use Vesna's evidence to help us. What we do not have yet, unfortunately, is conclusive forensic evidence, such as a blood match from the suite and maybe the glove, to convince him that we've really got him. That will have to wait until the FBI get our evidence to their lab. Anyway, this is what I'd like to do next. I think we can let Vesna continue with her duties until the ship docks. The FBI will want to re-interview her when they arrive aboard, but I don't see the point of detaining her on the ship. She has no place to go, except overboard, and I don't see her as a suicide risk. The Feds will no doubt take her into custody when we dock in Miami."

"Can't do that, Jack. The Company cannot permit someone who has admitted to possessing property stolen from a passenger to continue working in a position of trust—even if she hasn't been formally charged and appeared in court yet. Vesna won't be allowed alone into passengers' or crew members' quarters—ever again. But we can find other cleaning duties to keep her busy—in public areas, working always with another crew member—until we reach Miami."

"Okay, Mike, I understand what you are saying completely about Vesna. That's a generous solution you've come up with—some duties to allow her to keep her dignity somewhat, and her sanity over the next few days. Her world will be Hell when she gets to Miami.

"Now with respect to Mr. Radovan Rudman, we need to get him in for a talk, caution him, and when we're finished, lock him up—in your brig—for the remaining time we have at sea. We should keep him incommunicado, at least with Vesna, so he can't pressure her to recant her statement. I think that means, in a serious case like this is, that we have the concurrence and authorization of every action by Captain Stuart. I'd like it if you can see him in person, tell him about Vesna's admission of guilt, and get an order in writing authorizing Rudman's detention, and to do that right away. I can draft the wording. As soon as he is in our custody and isolated, we can let Vesna go. No communication between them, okay? I'll tell Sheila what we're doing. While you are talking with the captain, then getting Rudman, I'll get the glove from the evidence box and quickly review Rudman's first interview."

◆   ◇   ◆

Jack Sterling knew he had a tough-minded suspect in Radovan Rudman. In the Croatian militia, he'd been through guerrilla warfare, had been slightly wounded, and had almost certainly killed people. Jack read that people from his part of the world were known for being hardy and resourceful. He did not expect much, if any, cooperation—but he'd interviewed hardened individuals like this before, and mostly with success. It was just that he was now out of his home jurisdiction, in unknown waters, literally and figuratively, in this case. He was also dealing with a person with U.S. citizenship status, on the open sea, with no police authority, on a foreign registered vessel, on behalf of American authorities. 'How's that for a jurisdictional mess?' he thought. 'Seems to me I've stumbled across an extremely unusual law enforcement situation, and by extension, an unusual one for a prosecutor. I'd hate to see someone 'get away with murder' because of this. Be interesting to see how this turns out. Oh well, what the Hell. Nothing ventured, nothing gained.'

♦   ◊   ♦

While Mike was away, Jack called and spoke to Ralph Harkins in Miami, who expressed similar sentiments as the captain had about proceeding quickly. "No need to await the arrival of our team to interview Rudman. You know more about the matter than they do. See what you can do, Jack. Do get Mike to read the caution beforehand—that goes without saying. And Mike is the one to detain Rudman, if appropriate, as authorized by the captain. You have no official status to do so.

"By the way, that was good thinking on the part of your female officer—Sheila Turner—to find the stash. An absolutely critical piece of evidence. I concur about keeping Rudman in isolation for the duration. Good thinking again. Between my team and you and Mike, we may get lucky and put this thing to bed before docking in Miami. By the way, my team leader's name is Tom Bradley. Call me when you finish your interview, Jack."

Half an hour later, Mike returned with the necessary paperwork. He apologized for taking all this time, but said that the captain had been busy with ship business. He spent a few minutes with Mike, reviewing the *murder whodunnit* as he was calling it. "The captain was very pleased about the discovery of the jewelry and the result of our interview with Vesna Gorenko. He hopes for a similar success with the male crew member."

"You ready to see Rudman, Jack?"

"Yeah, I think so. Make the call to see if he's in his cabin. If he is, have Sheila walk Vesna back to her cabin. Not to say anything to Vesna about her friend. At the same time, have two of your male officers go to Rudman's cabin and bring him here. Have Sheila confirm that she's delivered Vesna to hers. Vesna can cool her heels there until you arrange some closely-supervised duties."

♦   ◇   ♦

On his way to the security office, Rudman tried to find out from the two escorts why he was being taken back. Their silence made him worried and agitated.

In the interview room, Rad said to Jack and Mike, "What the Hell am I doing here? I thought you were done with me! You looked in my room and found nothing."

Jack indicated to him to take a seat, but Rad tersely replied, "No, I don't want to sit. Just tell me what's going on."

"Rad—."

"—Don't call me Rad. My name is Radovan Rudman and I'm not answering any more questions."

"Okay, that's fine. Let me tell you that there have been some developments in this case that I'd like to discuss and hopefully, clear up. Before I do that, however, we need to read you a caution, it being recorded on the tape machine, so, please listen."

After saying who was present in the room, and the time and date, he had Mike read the card.

After Rad agreed that he understood the warning, Jack invited him to take a seat, doing so himself at the same time as Mike. Left as the only person standing, Rad shrugged and sat on the hard chair.

Jack said, "If there's anything you'd like to drink, let us know. I'm going to recap—go over again—what we talked about the last time we met." He reiterated the gist of that discussion and asked Rad if that was what he recollected, remembered, and Rad nodded his head.

"Sorry, Mr. Rudman, but when we ask you something, we need you to actually reply, for the tape recorder, okay?"

"Yes, I understand, but I'm not saying nothing."

"Alright, just to refresh your memory, you remember we showed you some CCTV photos, these ones?" Jack said, as he slid them across the desk in front of him, "of what looked like a waiter at the door to *Crown Suite 7001* and entering at around 10 p.m., on May 25, leaving about eight minutes later. You made the comment that it was not you as you are not a waiter on this ship, and have a different uniform."

Another nod.

"Yes or no, please."

"It wasn't me."

"Okay, I'll get back to that in a minute. First, I want to show you something." Without saying anything more, Jack opened the small cardboard box containing the jewelry, took the pieces out and laid them without comment on the table in front of the man, carefully watching his face.

Rad's eyes widened. Some of the color of his face drained. He stared at the them for two or three more seconds, thinking, 'Shit! How the Hell did they get these? Vessie had them hidden and they didn't find them when they looked! Did she tell them? If so, damn her to Hell! Wait 'til I see her.'

After taking a deep breath, he blurted, "I didn't take nothing! You told me I didn't have to speak and I'm not saying nothing else!"

Jack and Mike glanced at each other.

"Have you seen these before, Rad?" using his shortened Christian name again.

He shook his head.

"Is that 'no', Rad?"

"Yes. You told me I could have a lawyer. I want one now."

"Yes, we're required to inform you of that, but in practical terms, being that we are on a ship, at sea, that is not possible now. You'll have to wait until we get to Miami. What I'm going to do is continue to

talk to you, but ask no questions and you do not have to respond, unless you want to, understood?"

"Yeah, I understand," he growled.

"First, let's take a brief break. Need the bathroom?"

"Yes, I do."

Jack checked his watch: *15:16.* He took advantage of the break to
call Jean and tell her he may not be able to join her for dinner. "I'm
doing interviews and you know how long and unpredictable they can
be. I'll try to be back by six-thirty." He'd slipped her the news about
the recovery of the jewelry.

◆ ◇ ◆

On deck seven, deck attendants—called *DAs*, for short—Alvaro
Torres (Guadalajara, Mexico) and his Filipino friend, Danilo Tauli
(Lauzon, Philippines), were responsible for deck maintenance, including overhead lifeboats, fixing anything that broke, and re-painting.
They'd been together doing this kind of work for two years and knew
each other's capabilities and reliability. Although the work was often
mundane, it could sometimes be a challenge and dangerous.

Most of the lifeboats were covered with hard plastic or alumi-
num rooftops. They were also called *'tenders'* and, beside the lifesaving
function, were used to ferry passengers ashore at a port of call where
docking was not available. At ports where docking was available, crew
lifeboat drills were often carried out while in port for the day. The
tenders were located both sides of the ship, under the cover of deck
eight. It was just after three o'clock and after checking this last boat,
their shift would be finished.

Today, they were conducting function checks of the steel gravity
davits, used to raise and lower the boats. They used a tall A-ladder on
deck to reach the supporting arms above the boats. Checking meant
starting up the electric motors to allow the half-inch thick steel cable
to lower the boat a few inches and then raise it back into position.

Alvaro was standing on the deck at the control switch box and Danilo up the ladder checking the down and up movement of the cable around the roller. After it was lowered, Danilo called down, "Okay, Al, raise it up."

It didn't move and he thought his partner had not heard him. Leaning outward a bit, he called down again, when the boat suddenly began moving up. His long-sleeve shirt cuff caught in the roller.

Just as this happened, a small group of passengers approached along the deck, chatting and laughing, drowning out Dan's shout to, "Stop the motor!"

It did not stop.

Slowly, his left wrist was drawn into the roller. He screamed in agony. Al heard that cry and immediately cut the switch. But it was too late. Dan's wrist was mangled—pinch by the thin edge of the roller feed and nearly severed.

Mike answered his phone shortly after leaving the interview room for the bathroom break. "What!" he exclaimed, "when did this happen?"

Listening for a few seconds, he exclaimed, "Oh my God! So the guy's being taken to the medical clinic now? That's good. Where are you?" he asked his security officer. "Okay, I'm going to check on the man's condition first at the clinic, then I'll be right there at the tender area. Tape off the area so nothing is disturbed."

He signaled Jack that he needed to say something. Jack excused himself on the phone with his wife, and Mike very briefly said that a crewman had been badly injured and that he needed to go to the clinic first, and then to the scene of the accident. "Be back as soon as I can."

At the clinic, Mike found that the man was unconscious on an operating table. Dr. Kent was preparing to operate.

"Jesus, Doc, this is the fourth incident involving blood on this cruise."

"Yes, Mike," replied the doctor, "much more blood than usual on this trip. You've certainly managed to keep me busy. Excuse me."

The doctor had engaged a skype-like link-up to the Miami General Hospital. It allowed him to receive in-person instructions from an emergency ward surgeon. There was no option but to amputate Danilo Tauli's hand. It was hanging on by crushed bones and skin—not repairable, at least with his surgical equipment.

He told Mike later that he'd tied off the arteries, put a gauze cover over the stump and put spray freeze on it. That freezing would only last for an hour or so and would have to be repeated, he thought. The hand, wrapped in a gauze cover too, would be kept in an ice bucket, but not frozen. Time would be critical in terms of delaying tissue deterioration. There was a fairly narrow window of opportunity if an attempt was to be made at re-attaching the hand. It was certainly not an operation within the limited capabilities of the *Seascape*'s medical staff and facilities.

♦   ◇   ♦

Captain John Stuart had immediately contacted the Miami Head Office. He reiterated Doctor Kent's concern about getting the man to a treatment facility as soon as possible. Time was of the essence.

There was a slight possibility of the hand being saved, however. With late tonight being the pickup time to transfer the FBI agents to the ship, John wondered if arrangements could be made at this late date, to have their plane wait and transport the crew member back to Miami. If this could be done, Doctor Kent would send his senior nurse along. The Miami General Hospital would need to be alerted and an ambulance arranged from the airport.

The WCL operations manager said she would call the local FBI office and ask them, if possible, to make the arrangements, and would notify the ship immediately when confirmed.

An hour later, permission to transfer to the FBI plane was

confirmed. Doctor Kent in particular felt relieved, knowing his patient now had a significantly better chance of saving his hand. X-rays
of the arm and hand were sent ahead to Miami General via the ship
satellite transmission service.

When Mike was advised, he told Jack. "I suppose it's a damn good
thing we're stopping near King's Wharf tonight and able to do a fairly quick transfer. Thank God for that. What a day—and we're not
through with Mr. Rudman yet."

♦ ◊ ♦

In her cabin, Vessie paced up and down the confined space for a few
minutes, thinking. Until this cruise, her life had been relatively good.

She'd been able to put some money in the bank, aiming for enough
for a down payment on a small apartment. She had an American boyfriend, Ross, of British background, and he seemed amenable to the
idea of marriage and possibly one or two children. Given her age, she
knew that they'd both have to do something about that before long.
He had agreed to discuss the matter when she got back from this trip.
She'd have to give up her current job if she became a mother.

Now, she was not at all sure where she stood. 'Will I be charged
along with Rad? What will I tell Ross? I'd better call Rad and explain
to him before they drag him into the security office again.'

She called, three times in five minutes, but no answer.

'Maybe he's gone for something to eat. I'll try again later,' but she
had a bad feeling.

♦ ◊ ♦

It was now almost 5 o'clock. They were back in the interview room
after the delay while Mike dealt with the injured crew member matter. Sheila Turner was going to supervise gathering information—she
insisted in calling it 'evidence'—for the accident report.

Jack said to Rudman, "You okay, Rad?"

He nodded his head. He'd been sitting in the interview room alone for almost two hours, waiting with obvious irritation.

"Once again, sorry for the delay. A crew member badly injured his hand. Danilo Tauli—maybe you know him. Anyway, I hope you understand why we have to do this: talk to people. As we are responsible for ship security and safety, we have a duty to find out what happened and talk to everyone who may have had some connection, however little, to the case. I also remind you about the Miranda caution read to you earlier.

"What I'm going to do now is tell you a few things that we know. The diamond jewelry we showed you earlier are worth a lot of money, a quarter of a million dollars."

Rad's eyes blinked.

"That's a strong motive for killing someone. As well, it's our view that you knew that we had searched Ms. Vesna Gorenko's cabin and found nothing incriminating in there. When we went back the next day for another look, we found the necklace and earrings in a jar of hand cream.

"At the time, Ms. Gorenko said nothing to us. Also, you should know that someone has identified *you* from the video as the waiter entering the suite around 10 p.m. on that night. In looking at the CCTV images, we noticed the person dressed as a waiter was left-handed as we saw a watch on his right wrist in the photo of him leaving the suite. You are left-handed. You signed the Miranda caution with that hand."

Continuing, Jack said, "In trying to cover the side view of his face, the waiter held the tray up to his head on the left on entering the suite and on his right when he exited. A waiter's uniform was found in waste bins in the crew living area plus a pair of white gloves, believed to have been worn at that time. These items had blood stains on them, and there was a cut on the left side of the left glove. This is that glove," said Jack, taking it from a box and laying it on the table in front of Rad. "I note a small cut on the side of your left hand" —the band-aid having now been removed—"just around from the palm. As that hand is resting on the tabletop now, if you look at the cuts in the glove and on your hand, you can see the location seems to match. You also told us that you had cut your hand with your pocket knife. Seeing that you are left-handed, it seems to me that the cut should be on your right hand."

There was no answer.

"Would you put the glove on, please? If it doesn't quite match, then obviously you didn't wear that glove."

Rad took his hands off the table, and put them in his lap. He knew, of course, this was the glove he had worn and that the cut would match the cut on his hand. His forehead was beginning to perspire.

He swallowed and said, "I don't know nothing about the glove, so I don't need to put it on."

"Okay, Rad. We have to turn this over to the FBI anyway. If your blood and that of the victim is identified on the glove, and from the sink, where we found a drop, well, you see where you stand then."

Jack looked at Mike and asked if he had anything to say.

"Yes, one thing. When we talked to you the first time, you said— and were sure about this—that you last saw Vesna Gorenko *two* days ago," Mike emphasized, "but in fact you saw her *yesterday*. One of our security staff saw you enter her cabin. That was the day we searched and found nothing. Today, when we returned for another look and found the diamonds, you can see why we are now suspicious in your case."

While Mike was formulating these words, he was mindful of not inducing Rudman to say something. It was a statement, not a question.

There was no response.

He looked at Jack, who nodded and said, "Mr. Rudman, there's some things I need to tell you. Because the victim, Mrs. Rebecca Gessner, is an American citizen, the Federal Bureau of Investigation have jurisdiction—meaning *authority*—over this case. The ship security section, which we represent, has, in their absence, been obliged to conduct an investigation. The evidence we have now gathered and witnesses spoken to, strongly suggests that you are the person who committed this offense. In view of this, the FBI have asked that we place you under detention until we dock at Port Everglades terminal on June 2nd. Our captain has the legal authority to do that and has signed an *order of detention* to that effect. Here is a copy for you," said Jack, sliding it across the table. "Do you have anything further to say at this time?"

"Yeah. What does *order of detention* mean?"

"It means that you will be kept in custody, in the ship's brig, by yourself. The next people to talk to you will be the FBI. So, unless you want to talk to me any further, I'm going to ask two of our security officers to escort you back to your cabin, where you will pack up all your things and go with them to the brig."

Rudman sat still and silent, obviously thinking about his position.

'Should I say anything, or nothing? These people could be bullshitting me, trying to make me talk. I don't know what Vessie said and maybe I can get hold of her. Seems to me they don't have enough—what's the word?—*evidence*, against me, from what they've told me. I think I need to wait to talk to a lawyer.'

"No, I don't have nothing to say," he replied.

◆ ◇ ◆

The brig cabin was located one deck below the crew deck in a semi-isolated area on deck 1. While it was a bit fancier than a prison cell and in many respects similar to other crew cabins, there was no telephone, and no internet connection. However, unlike prison, Rudman did not have to line up for his meals, which would be catered from the galley, and he did have a television. He felt apprehensive about his position and that he could not make contact with Vessie. He wondered if she too was locked up. He badly needed to know what she had told the security people. He knew he would have to face the FBI at some time, and wondered how he was going to manage that. 'Say nothing, I guess, until I get a lawyer in Maimi.'

In thinking about his situation, the only thing that worried him was the blood they said they'd found on the bathroom sink and clothing. 'Was it mine or the woman's? If they do a DNA test and it matches mine, then I'm f--ked. All the rest of what they said, like being left-handed—that didn't seem like real proof. I was careful. I didn't leave nothing behind. Shit! If only they hadn't found the diamonds. I'm sure Vessie wouldn't have shown them. They just got lucky.'

He couldn't call her. '*Shit!*'

♦   ◊   ♦

The clock in the security office registered *5:50*. It had been another long day, especially for Mike Donnelly, who was usually up early and on duty at six. He'd never had to do the *'extra-curricular activities'* that he'd done on this trip, at least nothing like to this extent. He was glad of the experience though. He had another early duty tomorrow—greeting and briefing the FBI.

Jack Sterling had followed what he thought was protocol by first informing Captain Stuart about the arrest, or detention, of Rudman, asking him to inform his company headquarters, and they to advise the FBI. He would get a return call from the agency fairly quickly, he knew. He had done most of the directing of the investigation and much of the actual investigation.

Mike had learned a great deal and was thankful. Of course, this event had ruined the relaxing cruise Jack and his wife had anticipated, and Mike felt he should approach the captain and ask if it was appropriate to ask WCL headquarters for some monetary compensation—calling it an honorarium for his consulting services, perhaps. He had a notion that Jack would turn that down but at least an offer would show the Company's appreciation for his time and efforts.

♦ ◇ ♦

Jack called ahead at 6 o'clock and asked his wife to order something quick for dinner; he'd be on his way to the cabin shortly. It turned out to be a combination of Chinese foods, which he liked. They each had a rye whiskey and ginger ale to wash it down.

"Okay, now how was your day?" they both asked at the same time, and laughed.

Jean was anxious to know how things had gone. When he was finished his account, she asked him, based on the evidence gathered and statement made by Vesna Gorenko, what he thought of the chances for a conviction for both. "After all, you did find the jewels and you have her statement which seems to be a good one, enough to at least point the finger at—what's his name?—Rudman."

"Yes, you would think so, but there's three major stumbling blocks to that, a concern for the FBI. One is whether or not U.S. Federal Courts will or can, accept jurisdiction over the case. After all, the offense happened in the middle of the Atlantic Ocean. Defense counsel is going to vigorously argue that the case is without merit, *having no 'standing,'* meaning not triable in the United States. I think we discussed earlier that individual states in the U.S.A. have their own criminal law. That would not apply in this case. I'd like to be in court when that is argued."

"What's the second problem, Jack?"

"Something called *'probative value.'* Evidence which is sufficiently credible to prove something in court. I'm not sure yet whether we have enough.

"The third is the forensic examination of our evidence, especially the blood found in the bathroom and on the jacket and glove—is it his or the victim's or both. Hopefully it's both, and completes the circle of evidence—but that analysis can only happen after we get to Miami."

"Did Rudman admit to anything?"

"No, he refuses to talk. The evidence so far is largely circumstantial, and that's sometimes okay in court, provided that it's overwhelming, enough so that a reasonable person can conclude that the accused committed the offense. I'm not sure that the evidence we have could be called *overwhelming* in spite of the recovered diamonds as evidence. We don't have a direct link to Rudman yet, so let's hope the FBI forensic section get lucky with the blood analysis. If they do match, that puts him in that suite and he'd have some explaining to do. I think I've done all I can. After all, we are handicapped in doing a thorough investigation, like we would on land, with investigators, a pathologist and forensic examiners readily available. Does that all make sense to you?"

"Hmm, I see what you are saying. Be a damn shame if they get away with it, at least the murder. So, how was my day you ask? It was great. I spent two hours in absolute splendor this afternoon, in *Crown Suite 6001*, one of the three crown suites at the back of the ship. It's directly below the Gessner suite. Susan Stuart and the assistant hotel manager, Helga Gannschmidt, a delightful German woman, showed me around and told me about the furnishings, and we had a lunch served in the suite's posh dining room. Oh, and yes, I played a couple of tunes on the piano in the suite's lounge room. You must have been in the lounge in Mrs. Gessner's suite, so you'll appreciate just how nice it is. Probably identical. The word luxury doesn't begin to describe it. I don't suppose you really got a good look, with what you were busy doing and the awful bloody mess it was in. One day, when you win the lottery, I'll book one of those, and Avery can come along and stay in her own luxurious bedroom.

"So, Jack, are you ready to meet the Federal Bureau of Investigation people tomorrow? I can't remember but have you had dealings with them before?"

"Very rarely, at least rarely face-to-face. Most of my contact was email, phone or in writing, but still effective." Looking at his watch, he said, "Look, hon, I have to go back to the Ops Center to finish up with Mike and prepare for our meeting with the U.S. Feds early tomorrow morning. I don't think I should be too long and I'll try to get back so we can go dancing for a bit.

"If I'm not back by, say, 8 o'clock, why don't you go and listen to the string quartet in the *Polo Lounge* this evening. Very good musicians aboard this ship. Okay with you?"

Jean said, "Yes. Oh, before you go, don't commit yourself to anything for tomorrow evening. The musical *North Atlantic* is on and we simply *must* see that!"

Rising from his chair, Jack bent down and kissed her forehead. "See you later."

FRIDAY, MAY 30 and
SATURDAY, MAY 31
Island of Bermuda

The United States government Lear jet, two wheels slowly extending, wing flaps lowering and the twin engines whining as they were throttled back and changed pitch, was on approach to the runway at the L.F. Wade International Airport in the northeast part of the island of Bermuda. It was 9:40 p.m., an hour before the last permitted daily landing of aircraft. The four federal agents on board looked down at the bright lights of the capital city, Hamilton, in mid-island, not far from the airport.

At the terminal, they were welcomed by an inspector and constable of the Royal Bermuda Police Force and climbed aboard a seven-seater Range Rover SUV. Their suitcases and rigid-shell equipment cases were placed in a van to follow in convoy.

The senior officer told the group he was delivering them to the Bermuda Pilotage Authority dock at the very south end of the island, less than an hour's drive at this time of day. "You'll depart the dock at midnight. Expect about a sixty-minute trip. I take it you know the cruise ship's projected arrival time at the 12-mile limit is 0100 hours?"

The agent in charge nodded.

"Have any of you been here before?"

No one had.

"We have to go through the capital city, en route. You folks,"—he was going to say *gentlemen* but one of the agents was female and he quickly caught himself—"probably know this was formerly a British Crown colony, now officially a British Overseas Territory. It's still very English," which, as they approached the city, was apparent in the 1800s-era Victorian houses.

Rounding a large bay south of the city, called the Great Sound, they arrived at the Pilotage Station at the end of a spit of land called the King's Wharf. Nearing the dock, the inspector said, "I take it you know your flight is returning with an injured seaman from this ship. His hand was severed and that part is going with him. Hoping for a miracle re-attaching it, sounds like. When the pilot boat returns with the injured seaman, we'll rush him to the Lear jet for immediate take-off. We've arranged 'medical emergency' clearance to depart at night, due to the urgency of getting this man to Miami."

"That's good to hear—thanks for arranging that. The agency is glad to be able to help with our part. And thanks very much for the ride, inspector."

They were met and taken aboard by the skipper of the pilot boat. It was a small vessel, just enough room for its six passengers. Passing out fresh coffee and biscuits, the second mate told them they would be underway at midnight, pointing on a wall map where they would make the rendezvous.

"You'll probably be able to see the cruise ship when we round the Spit into open water. The seas are calm tonight and our boat should not bounce around too much. I don't suppose any of you have had this mid-sea boarding experience before?"

No one had.

"Let me tell you a bit about boarding. Cruise ships, unlike freight-ers which have long ladders to climb to the top deck, have an em-barkation platform, called the *break*, a few feet above the waterline. Our pilot matches the speed of the ship, approaches at an acute angle and nudges the side of the pilot boat alongside. To you, the vessel will seem enormous from sea level. The pilot radios the ship's bridge that the guests are ready to board and gets permission for them to do so.

"I will assist you onto the platform which has a side rail. Ship security people will be there to give you a hand. It should not be difficult at all tonight. We will hand up your bags. Don't worry, I haven't dropped one in the ocean yet," creating four relieved smiles with his guests. "Okay with that?" and got four nods of the head in return. "When you are aboard the *Seascape*, the injured crew member and his medical attendant will be transferred into our boat for the return trip. They will be brought to a police vehicle for the trip back to the airport, and on to Miami.

"Alright, when you've finished your snack, you're welcome to go on deck, in the well area only, please."

All four agents did so—partly because the cabin smelled strongly of diesel fumes, but more so, to breath in the sea air, to get a look at the cloudless night sky, the myriad of stars glittering like so many jewels above a full, May moon, a beautiful experience.

Once out of the bay and underway, they watched the brightly-lit cruise ship get larger and larger, eventually filling their vision with its enormity. The agents were enjoying their experience so far, though knowing they'd have just over two days on the ship to complete their assignment.

After the agents boarded the *Seascape* without incident, and the injured seaman and nurse transferred to the pilot boat, the order was given to the *Seascape's* helmsman to change course to "West-south-west, 248.2 degrees, speed 19.6 NM," en route for south Florida.

The timing of the ship's arrival at Port Everglades had been discussed between WCL headquarters, the FBI, and the captain. Its speed and distance to arrive at Bermuda, and from there to Miami, had been carefully calculated so as to put the ship 'port side' at its slated TOA (time of arrival) of 0800 hours on June second, thereby avoiding delays in debarkation and to allow the ship to provision and board the passengers for the next cruise. To accomplish this, they would have to kick the speed up a bit. The extra 1.3 knots added to the regular cruise speed would certainly boost the cost of fuel, but the Company was prepared to pay, as opposed to the much larger expenses of arriving late and having to cancel or delay the next cruise. A substantial amount of money was involved.

The agents were met by the staff captain and then taken by a steward to the dining room on deck 11 for something to eat. They would be meeting the security officer and the Canadian ex-police officer this morning in the Operations Center at nine o'clock. They'd be officially met by the captain a bit later. The agents were offered four empty passenger cabins for what remained of the night.

Jack's cabin phone rang. He glanced at the time on his watch. It read 8:15 a.m.

Mike Donnelly said, "Top o' the mornin', Jack. Hope you are feeling grand today."

"Top o' the morning to you too, my friend. Jean and I are both up and having breakfast in-cabin."

"Good. Hope you slept well. Ready to meet the Federal Bureau of Investigation people?" He liked rolling off their full title.

"Sure, Mike. Just to confirm, nine a.m. Exactly forty-five minutes from now by my watch."

"We passed through a time zone change overnight, Jack. Bermuda is one hour ahead of Miami. So it is now 0715 hours. I expect you'll be wanting to change your watch. Of course now you have an extra hour to enjoy breakfast with your good wife."

"Roger that," the detective responded with a chuckle.

"Jack, we'll meet in the interview room. It is a bit small for six people but should do."

"See you just before nine—ship's time."

♦ ◊ ♦

When the four agents arrived at the Security Operation Center, they were taken to just outside the meeting room, where introductions were made. Mike, in uniform, apologized for the tight space and the lead agent, Tom Bradley, said that would be quite okay.

To Jack, Mike seemed a bit overawed by the presence of the FBI. "Never happened on my watch before," the S.O. said later.

"Coffee for everyone?"

Nods all round and Mike ordered it.

When Tom put his hand out to shake, Jack realized he'd become accustomed to not touching people, but did so, a bit hesitantly, not wanting them to feel unwelcome, and understanding that the agents were not aware of the norovirus precautions aboard ship.

Jack asked how their trip to Bermuda was and especially what it was like to climb aboard such a huge ship from a comparatively tiny boat, at sea, at night.

"Actually, it was quite an experience, smooth water and under a full, very bright, Atlantic moon. Almost romantic," replied Tom. "Sorry to hear about your crew member," he said to Mike Donnelly. "Understand his hand had to be removed?"

"Yes. The doctor doesn't know if it's salvageable or not. Hope so. Good of your agency to help us out by getting him to Miami General as quickly as possible."

"Glad to. Hope the surgery goes well."

As full introductions were made, Tom Bradley explained that two of the team were here to do the forensics work and the third agent, Patricia Wilcox, was an investigator, like him. Taking their seats, Tom asked if Mike and Jack could first review the case verbally. He said to Jack, "I'd like to thank you for helping us out in this matter. Very good of you to interrupt your vacation. I hope your wife is an understand-ing person?"

Jack replied, "After thirty-plus years married to a cop, she's used to it although she did ask me if I could handle an investigation for the FBI—a bit facetiously. This has been a novel one for me and of course, out of my usual criminal habitat.

"As you see," he gestured, "our file is on the table, taking on some volume by now. I'll ask Mike to take you through how this started. When he's finished, he and I will cover our initial on-site investigation in the suite. You did see some of this activity when we skyped you. Please ask any questions as we proceed. When we're finished with this meeting, Mike and I would like to take you to the bridge to meet Captain Stuart, then to *Suite 7001* and then, if you'd like, to view the body of the deceased in the cold room. Your two forensic people, of course, can do their thing in whatever sequence they want. How's that sound?"

"That would be great, Jack. Thanks."

"Before I begin, there are some observations I'd like to reiterate about matters of jurisdiction. This case is far from ordinary. You may know what I'm going to say, given your location in Miami, where so many cruise lines make it a port of call or are headquartered. Perhaps you've had some dealings before concerning similar criminal matters, so you may be ahead of me." Jack quickly referred to the various elements of the laws of the sea, and the seeming lack of an appointed agency responsible for enforcement, except for the FBI and only involving U.S. citizens, and, the difficulty, as he saw it, in its application to this present case. "Consider that, in reality, none of what has happened, in my view, falls under American law, as it happened beyond the twelve-mile limit. As you know, the U.S. is not a party to the *UNCLOS* Treaty.

"This case is a murder of a United States citizen, committed aboard a foreign registered vessel, in the middle of the Atlantic, which no one owns, and investigated by a Canadian citizen with no police powers, assisted by someone who also has no police powers. Therefore, what we did—investigate this offense—may be, in law, of *'no force and effect'*, or a violation of someone's rights, therefore a *'nullity'*.

"I know the master of a ship has, among all his duties, the responsibility for maintaining law and order. It seems to me, though, that his authority arises from one of tradition over the centuries, rather than from legislation. So, how the captain goes about his duty is another thing altogether. Quite a tenuous position, given the understandable absence of what I'd call land-based authority—plus, of course, the lack of crew training and investigative equipment—we did what we did, and are now turning it all over to you."

"Well, Jack, this legal situation is something that has been in the back of my mind, and now that you've put it so succinctly, it's a discussion I will be having with our legal people and with the prosecutor. I believe though, that for the United States, this matter *is* covered under Title 18, of the *United States Code.* I think it's Section 7, but I'm not sure. Of course, the Statute is silent on how, and who, can conduct the investigation, but we're the Federal law enforcement authority for the United States, and, under U.S. Federal legislation, the *CVSSA*, which you mentioned, I believe we're covered. The defense counsel will likely argue that the investigation was conducted without authority and any evidence seized, not be admissible in court. Time will tell. But thanks for presenting this issue," said Tom. "It does bear thinking about. By the way, how did Mr. Rudman react when you told him we were coming to the ship?"

"He's apprehensive, I think, but I don't think he'll capitulate."

"Does he know who you are, Jack?"

"No. I just introduced myself as a member of ship's security. My Canadian accent didn't appear to give me away, since the crew is from numerous nations. Did I mention that I had the Miranda caution read to him by Mike, rather than myself? Police in Canada are required to read a caution to suspects, not just say it—as you can appreciate, this avoids arguments in court."

Mike, and Jack to a lesser extent, spent well over an hour in review with the agents, referring to documents, photographs and the list of evidence seized and what they and Dr. Kent did in the suite, cross-referencing to photos as he did this. He reiterated the regrettable lack of a police forensics kit.

"Seems to me, Jack, that you and Mike and the doctor did remarkably well with what you managed to put together," said Tom.

"It's too bad that the print you lifted did not show enough ridge lines for comparison purposes. Insufficient for the IAFIS system, as you know. Go on, please."

"I think we covered all our bases with respect to interviewing those people—crew that is—who had any connection to the case. Their statements are all together in the file, in order of interview. We got somewhat lucky with our CCTV camera coverage, catching what we're now certain is the culprit entering and leaving the suite, helping us as well to pinpoint the TOD. Dr. Kent was right on with his esti- mation. The photos don't give us good evidence in court, but do help with leads that we've been able to follow up on. I think you'll agree there's potentially some good evidence so far, though it's not over- whelming. If the blood spot and the urine in the bathroom, and the blood on the clothing, turn out to belong to Mister Rudman—and I believe they will—he'll certainly have some explaining to do. That should seal his fate, providing other aspects of the case are accepted by the court.

"Regarding the two suspects… What I'd like to do is wait for you to review the file and then compare notes, so to speak. See if you see things the way we do. Let's hope your forensic people get lucky with the blood and urine samples, and hair that we found. Rudman did ask for a lawyer and I don't think he'll change his mind when you talk to him. He's taking the all-or-nothing approach. Rudman is a pretty tough cookie. Spending time with the Croatian Militia in combat situations, and perhaps with the civilian authorities in that country, has made him very careful in his interaction with officialdom. There's nothing to show he was involved in any atrocities over there, but he does seem hardened. Through his lawyer, presuming this goes to trial, he'll likely make you fight to prove every bit of evidence."

"Yes, Jack. That's been my experience too. Helps keep us hon- est in our investigations. As an investigator, after you've done a very thorough job, it's not a nice feeling when someone walks out of court after beating you, and flips you the middle finger." Looking at the other three members of the team, Tom asked them if they had any questions or observations.

Patricia Wilcox said with a smile, "I'd sure like to get a look, and feel, of the necklace. Never held two-hundred-and-fifty-thousand dollars in silver and diamonds in my hands before."

Jack smiled and replied, "Consider it done, Patricia. Why don't we sign it over to you and you can enter it into evidence?" Looking at Tom, he said, "Would you or Patricia like to sign the paperwork as receiving the full list of exhibit items?"

Tom said he would delegate Patricia to do that later.

Jack said, "I take it you will re-interview Rudman and Gorenko? If so, do you want Mike and/or I to be present?"

"Yes, we'll need to speak to both of them. Um, let me think about that offer. I need to think about the value of your presence in terms of possible intimidation of the suspects, or conversely, the utility of having you present. Oh, by the way, we have copies of fingerprints for the two suspects, taken from their INS file when they entered the U.S. A little old now, but maybe still useable. We'll take both of theirs when we see them later."

"Very well," said Jack. "So, when you're all ready to speak with the suspects, Mike will bring them to you, separately. I'll hang out with my wife until you call. Use my cell phone number. Okay with that, Tom?"

Mike added, "Let me know when you're ready to see the boss."

As he was leaving the interview room, Jack asked Mike about someone taking care of their food needs during the agents' stay aboard ship.

"All looked after, my friend," Mike assured him. "Hospitality is our business. They have been issued *CruiseCards* like every other guest."

◆ ◇ ◆

At 0915 hours, Steve Marks came on the PA system with a review of daily activities for passengers. "Good morning, everyone. Another beautiful day at sea for you. As you read in yesterday's *News*, there is a special event in the *Starlight Theater* this evening. Our ship is hosting the very first production of a brand new musical called *North Atlantic*. Because of its length—one and a half hours—there is only one show, starting at 8 o'clock. I highly recommend you go."

"The *Seascape* has been selected by the Hollywood producers to 'try out' the show with a live audience. Consider this a way, way, way off-Broadway limited run of one night, out here on the Atlantic! In a way, this show is a counterpart to one of the best stage and movie shows ever: *South Pacific*. The cast, taken aboard in Barcelona, have been practicing daily behind locked theater doors. The set was designed and fabricated in Los Angeles and placed aboard ship in Fort Lauderdale before our latest return voyage to the Mediterranean. Those attending Opening Night will be given a special commemorative card to mark the occasion. Seats, of course, are not reserved."

In Mike's office today, Jack had told him that if he didn't attend the show, his life would not be worth living, as Jean had made clear.

"Sounds a bit like Moira. You'd better be there, Jack."

◆ ◇ ◆

At the same time, in the big theater, the cast and crew of *North Atlantic* was assembled.

The director said loudly, "Listen up, everyone. Quiet, please."

The stage gradually went silent.

"Thank you. I hope all of you enjoyed your day-off break yesterday? Today is *THE DAY*. One more shot at trying to achieve perfection. I'm going to get you to perform the whole show now, without stops. Treat this practice as your opening night performance, ladies and gentlemen. There'll be almost a thousand pairs of eyes on you tonight. Your future and mine, and that of the show hangs in the balance. Go for it. *Break a leg.*"

♦ ◇ ♦

The case review by the agents in the security office took a hour and twenty minutes. Tom Bradley paid particular attention to Rudman's recorded replies to questions asked, trying to gauge the mind-set of the man before the re-interview. He liked using a female agent to ask questions. Male suspects generally relate better—and reveal more—to women. He called Jack on his phone, asking him to meet again. Mike Donnelly was in the security office.

"Alright, Jack, you've done a neat job in putting this information together. We'll see what the two suspects have to say later. Let's go pay our respects to the captain, then we can go to the crime scene."

"Mr. Donnelly has made the arrangements."

♦ ◇ ♦

The six of them met Captain John Stuart on the bridge at eleven-thirty. The view was impressive, giving a sense of the vastness of the ocean and sky. The sea water sparkled like precision-cut diamonds in the noon sunlight. John seemed to be pleased with the FBI presence, and the update they gave him.

"Glad to have you aboard. It's good that you were able to get here. Your two days on the ship may make all the difference to the eventual outcome. You can imagine how much I, and the World Cruise Lines Company, are concerned."

"Certainly, Captain," replied agent Tom Bradley. "The incident is disconcerting for all parties. Thank God this kind of behavior is rare on cruise ships. My forensic team," he said, pointing to them, "know their work extremely well, and it's highly probable that we'll find some usable evidence. You'll eventually know if we do."

The meeting was brief. Over coffee and just-made donuts, they confirmed protocols for reporting to WCL Head Office, the FBI office in Miami (who were conducting preliminary briefings with the Federal attorney), and the BVI authorities.

"Alright, folks, thank you for putting me in the picture," said the captain. "I won't keep you. For lunch, may I suggest our buffet meal, a great choice of food. Please feel free to dress casually while aboard. If you need anything, Mike will be very happy to help. By the way, I'd appreciate it if all of you could have dinner with me tomorrow evening, say 7 p.m. It's our last night at sea. I look forward to seeing you then."

◆ ◊ ◆

Hannah Goldman and Abe Shuster were sitting at a table on the eleventh deck foredeck, under a large sun umbrella, out of the hot sun. Both were drinking lemonade from tall, slim glasses. They'd gone to an early lunch together, but just picked at their food. "You know, Abe, I can't wait to get off the ship now. There's no joy in being aboard. How do you feel?"

"A bit like you, I think. I've been through these feelings of losing someone special before. It's never easy. Just take things one day at a time. I only knew Rebecca a short time but her personality got to me. For me, that's two wonderful women who have left my life too soon."

Hannah reached across the table and put her right hand over his, not saying anything, but looking in his eyes. After a few seconds, she said, "You're a good man, Abe. Someday, maybe I'll meet someone for myself as kind as you are."

A tear rolled down his cheek. "So nice of you to say that. Can we remain friends?"

◆ ◊ ◆

"John Cooper from communications, Captain. This call is for you, sir—Ms. Judy Weiss at Miami General Hospital."

"Thanks, John… Captain Stuart here."

"Hello, Captain. My name is Judy Weiss, director of administration at MGH. This call is in relation to one of your crew, Danilo Tauli, who arrived here early today on a flight from Bermuda. Surgery has been completed and our chief microsurgery specialist, Dr. Charles Cates, and his team including plastic surgeons Drs. Ted Sharples and Mary McGhee, managed to re-attach the limb, after eight hours of complicated surgery. The prognosis is difficult to define right now, but Dr. Cates says blood flow has been restored and all major nerves, tendons and bones reconnected. As for future use, time will tell. The man will need extended long-term physiotherapy.

"The patient will be with us for about two weeks before he can be discharged to home care. He's an extremely lucky man. Good thing you had that jet at your disposal, or the outcome probably would not be the same. We will keep your head office here in Miami advised about a release date. It would be a great outcome if you could eventually get him back for work, Captain."

"Ms. Weiss, thank you so much for telling me this. Very good of you to call with such great news. Our ship will be in port early morning on June second and I will make an effort to visit him that day. Would you pass on my personal best wishes to Danilo, please, and thanks once again."

Calling the ship's front desk, he asked the clerk to page the chief of security and Dr. Kent. A happy announcement would be drafted to inform the crew.

♦   ◇   ♦

The four agents, escorted by Jack Sterling and Mike Donnelly, entered the luxurious suite. The two investigators stood just inside the double door, "to get an overview of the scene," said Tom Bradley. "No need for us to suit up."

The forensic people did, of course, and carried in their two Pelican cases of equipment to begin the examination.

Returning to the security office, agents Tom Bradley and Patricia Wilcox sat down and reviewed their next tasks with Jack and Mike. "That's a messy crime scene, gents. No wonder it took you over three hours to process. Lots to examine and much evidence to collect. Next thing on our agenda, I think, is to re-interview the two suspects. What do you think, Pat, talk to Gorenko first?"

"That works for me. Want me to do that alone or both of us?"

"I think both. Four ears and four eyes are better than two. We can feed off what each of us says and discuss her body language later if need be. Mike, would you be kind enough to bring her here? What we need to do is get into the conversation that she and Rudman had, in more depth. When we have Rudman here, I don't want to let him know what she said—only in general terms if need be—specifically about the finding of the diamonds. Jack, would you like to stay or stand down for an hour or two?"

"I'm uncertain what my presence would do, how it would affect the interview. I don't want it to inhibit her discussion, so I don't think it's necessary for me to stay. Call me when I can be useful."

♦ ◊ ♦

Jack called Jean to say he was free for an hour or so, but his wife did not answer—cabin or cell phone. It was 12:50. He went to the cabin and left a note on the bed in case she returned, then went up to the buffet counter, finding her there, having a shrimp sandwich and tea.

He told her he'd called her and when she checked her cell, it was off and she apologized.

"How'd it go?" she asked.

"Went well. Nice group of people including a good-looking

female agent—just like you see in the movies. I think they must pension female FBI agents off at age 40 or so in Hollywood's take on reality. Don't want no old folks. We reviewed the case, and I've left them to look at the file on their own, and to re-interview the two suspects. They're going to call me when they are done. Just one more brief meeting with them."

Over a sandwich and pot of tea for Jack, they discussed what their respective day's activities were likely to be. Jean told him that she'd had a call from Susan Stuart to remind about dinner tomorrow tonight with the captain and the FBI team, 7 o'clock. It would be their last night at sea.

Jack said he very much looked forward to that. "I think my tux will be suitable for the occasion, don't you?"

His cell phone rang. Before answering he gave her a quick kiss.

"See you later, sweetheart. Should be back in good time for some dinner and the show."

♦   ◇   ♦

Vessie Gorenko had called Rad's cabin several times, slowly realizing that he would not be answering—ever. He was probably in the ship's jail—she couldn't remember the other name it was called. She felt so insecure without him around. Their shared vision of being debt-free and each having money to spend, had disappeared. Not only that, they were both likely to go to jail for a long time.

She tried to keep those thoughts out of her mind, especially the possibility of Rad being sentenced to death. 'How did they do that in Florida?' she wondered. What she had said to the ship security people, she realized, could badly affect the outcome for him at the trial. She wished she hadn't said anything.

One more day at sea and they'd be back in Miami. She hated what possibly lay ahead. What was she going to tell her boyfriend? Would he dump her?

She began crying again, rolling in a fetal position on the narrow bed.

◆   ◇   ◆

Jack answered his phone. The screen showed 2:20.

"Hello, Jack. Tom here. We're finished with our file review, and concluded an initial interview with the two suspects. Tell you about that later. We're having lunch brought in to the security section instead of going to the buffet—for obvious reasons: our suits and ties. Care to join us?"

Jack declined, having eaten already.

"Regarding the suite, our two forensic people are finishing up. I think it would be prudent if we did a quick visit to de-brief them, then we'll have the room secured again until we get ashore. Our Miami team will likely want to do another examination of the suite while it is at the dock. I need to have a quick look at the body. Are you free to meet us back in Mike's office in say, thirty minutes?"

"Actually, I'll join you in a few minutes."

◆   ◇   ◆

Before the group left for the morgue, Tom Bradley asked Mike to transfer the various pieces of evidence and to sign the paperwork which had been typed up since their last meeting.

"Don't forget, Mike, I need your camera card, too, please. I'll return it to you later. For the tablet, your cell phone and Jack's too, we'll use a cable connection to our laptop to pull off the photos and video you took on those devices."

Mike Donnelly was reminded that these procedures and paperwork were necessary for the chain-of-custody rule. Mike would keep a copy of the transfer documents in the ship's file.

Tom said, "I like the way you did the paperwork, Jack. Your extensive police experience is very evident."

Jack expressed his thanks for the comment. "Well, you know, Tom, this is my first off-shore murder investigation, too, and hopefully my last. Let's hope the prosecutor feels a case can be made out of all this. After I've left the ship, I take it you will stay in touch and keep me posted on what's happening?"

"Absolutely. We'll likely have to subpoena you as a witness anyway. If that happens, I'll try to see you have plenty of notice, Jack, and we'll arrange comfortable accommodation while you are here."

◆   ◇   ◆

On the way down to deck one, to the morgue, Jack asked Tom how the interviews had gone with the two suspects.

"Gorenko pretty much repeated what she told you. She's in quite a state and in a way, I feel sorry for her. Like you, I don't think she imagined her remarks to Rudman would result in him killing the woman. If she had not agreed to hide the jewelry after being told about the murder, she wouldn't be in this mess and she knows that. Since she did make the wrong choice, she'll have to have her day in court, I'm afraid. I'm sure the prosecutor, if the case gets that far, will say something in her favor.

"As for Rudman, he's keeping his mouth shut. We reiterated what we had, or more precisely, you had, in the way of evidence against him. Let's just hope that forensics will be able to pin him down. He's not educated but neither is he dumb. I sense his Croatian military experience must have resolved in him not to talk to officials. Maybe something bad happened in his encounters with the Serbs that created this hardness of attitude. But, if you'll pardon the expression—I'm certain he's guilty as shit."

◆   ◇   ◆

It was damn chilly in the morgue corner of a vast cold storage area, so the two investigators and Jack did not hang around while the forensic agents did their examination of the late Rebecca Gessner's body. While the neck wound on the body was not pleasant to look at when it was fresh, it looked positively ghoulish under the bright, fluorescent lights.

"Hell of a way to die," noted Patricia.

Dr. Kent had been on hand to unlock the SUB from secure storage, and sign over the locker key and chain-of-custody of the corpse to an agent. After their scraping and measuring, the box and its macabre contents would be secured again, ready for a discreet removal at dockside.

From the coolers, the group went to the bridge. After a brief update to the captain, he confirmed they would be dining tomorrow evening in the *Savoy Dining Room*. There would be nine people present, including Mrs. Stuart.

◆ ◊ ◆

Tom Bradley, Patricia Wilcox and Jack Sterling returned to the Security Ops Center. Bradley said to Jack, "Can I ask you what your plans are for when we get to Miami? When do you fly home?"

"Well, we've got three days before we do that, on June fifth. We're going to rent a car and drive down through the Everglades and stay at Everglades City. Having said that, I'm wondering if you'd like me to go to your office?"

"If you and Jean could spare the time, yes. I'd like you to meet Clive Lundgren, our Special Agent in Charge, whom you've spoken to. He may have some questions. And, of course, if this matter goes to trial, you'll be an important witness for us. Where were you going to pick up your car, dockside or at the airport?"

"At the airport. Convenient drop-off for us when we catch our return flight."

"Okay, how about this? We'll take you to the rent-a-car company and then go to our office. One of the agents with me now can ride with you and provide directions. It is about a twenty-minute drive."

"Okay, Tom, we can do that. Where will Rudman and Gorenko be taken to?"

"They'll be held in the Miami Federal Correctional Center. Gorenko will likely make bail, but I shouldn't think Rudman will, given the nature of the offense, his background and his nationality, although he is a dual citizen now. He could be considered a risk for flight."

Jack said, "I suppose you have all the evidence together and a copy of the paperwork?"

Tom said, "Uh huh, all ready to go. Transportation for the two suspects arranged, in separate vehicles."

"Any idea who may prosecute this case for you, Tom?"

"No, not really. We have a short list of people though none obviously has tried a case like this. Whoever is appointed, you can bet we'll sit her or him down and have a heart-to-heart discussion. They're a pretty competent bunch though. I'll keep you informed if you'd like that?"

Jack said, "Yes, this is an unusual case, given its circumstances, and I'd like to know what eventually happens. Thanks, Tom. I'll leave you to continue your work."

◆   ◇   ◆

At 3:45 p.m., the four FBI agents, Jack and Mike met for the last time, to tie up any loose ends.

Jack said, "I take it you've thought about arresting these two people once we reach U.S. territorial waters?"

"Yes, we have. We'll do that early Tuesday morning."

"I know this is beyond my scope but I'm curious as to how this might pan out in the U.S. The thing is, Tom, I'm not sure how much impact our detainment of these two suspects—which was essentially an arrest—before your arrival aboard this ship, will have in your courts. I'm not sure if you know that in Canada, we have a *Criminal Code* that covers the whole of the country. A very useful instrument for law enforcement people country-wide. Anyway, there's a section which covers jurisdiction of a person. In a case like this, the *Code* clearly states that a superior court of criminal jurisdiction that has power to try what we call an *indictable offense*—a felony in America—is competent to try an accused, if that person is found, or arrested, or is in custody, within the territorial jurisdiction of that court. You must have similar legislation to that?"

"Yes, we do. Our federal courts system delegates powers of jurisdiction to individual States through the *Constitution*. It specifically gives them authority to conduct criminal trials for felony offenses where the offense crosses state and international boundaries. This case might be a bit of a stretch though. As you well know, Jack, we also have to prove our case in court 'beyond a reasonable doubt' for a conviction. I'll let you know in due course.

"If there's nothing else, folks, I think we can call it a day. Let me reiterate how much my team and I have appreciated all the work that you two have done. We lucked out in having you both on this ship. Anyway, unless I need to see you again, see you at the Captain's table tomorrow evening."

"Looking forward to that. Why don't you act like you're on a cruise tomorrow and take it easy for the day? And don't forget that ship's captains live by the clock," said Jack, tapping his watch.

"Alright. See you at seven sharp tomorrow then. I'll try not to call you. We're going to stay here for a while and complete the final touches for the file, for presentation to our senior agent when we get ashore."

While the agents worked on the documents, they talked. Patricia Wilcox said she was looking forward to dinner with the captain and his wife tomorrow.

Tom replied, "This is my first time on a cruise ship. Think I'll do one soon."

One of the forensic people said, "Nice break for us. Much of the work has been done already, especially with the rape kit evidence largely collected. The investigation was almost wrapped up."

"You know, I'm not sure any of us could have done any better than Mr. Sterling," Tom said. "This attests to his past experience and his detective abilities. Let's hope we can get a conviction, as much for him as for us and, of course, the victim. Anyway, folks, let's see if we can finish up early, so we can go for a drink in the Olde English Inn. I'd like to try a British beer for a change."

With her best poker face, Patricia asked, "By the way, Tom, do you mind if I wear the diamonds to the captain's dinner?"

Seeing the look on his face, she erupted in laughter. "Just kidding!"

♦   ◊   ♦

Earlier in the day, Jack told his wife that he'd like to see Vesna Gorenko one last time. Tomorrow was going to be busy.

With Sheila Turner along, Jack knocked on the door of cabin *A311* in late afternoon. Vessie Gorenko opened it and showed a surprise look on her face.

Jack said, "Hello, Vesna, is it alright if we come in for a minute or two?"

She nodded and stood aside to let them enter.

"I'm sorry to bother you, but I thought I'd come by and see how you are and to say goodbye. I'd like to tell you that I am not a member of the ship security section, nor even a member of the ship's crew, but a retired Canadian police officer, on a cruise. After the death of Mrs. Gessner was reported to the FBI in Miami, they asked me, because of my previous experience I suppose, to lead the investigation. When I talked to you, at the time, I could not reveal that fact to you. I sincerely hope you understand?"

Another nod from her.

"Are you okay?"

"I suppose so. I'm scared."

"Yes, I can certainly understand that. Just to let you know, when the ship docks Tuesday morning, you will be taken to the FBI office and then, sometime later, to a court. More than likely a lawyer will be appointed to speak on your behalf, and make an application for bail, which, given the circumstances, I feel will be granted and you will be able to return to your home. I'm afraid, though, that Rad will not likely be freed on bail.

"I can imagine what has been going through your head the last couple of days, and you're probably blaming yourself for what happened. What you did with the diamonds, of course, was wrong, as you realize, and I understand how difficult it must have been for you to tell ship security people and myself, about what happened."

"What will happen to me? Will I be deported?" she asked.

"Obviously I don't know for sure, but I could take a guess and it may be that you will receive a short time in jail and be placed on probation for a period of time. I will ask the FBI people to recommend that to their prosecutor. I'm fairly certain you will not be deported since you are a U.S. citizen. As for Rad, if he is convicted, he will spend a long time in jail, I believe. In any event, I wanted to wish you well, that you can get over this bad time, and get on with your life. So, I'll say goodbye and good luck."

A tear appeared in Vessie's eye and, saying nothing, she reach up and put her arms around Jack's shoulders, hugging him for a minute.

After leaving Vessie's cabin and before parting with Jack, Sheila Turner said, "How kind of you to say those things to that poor woman. I'll be sorry to see you leave the ship, Jack. For once, I'd like to shake your hand, sir," she said, reaching out and taking his. "I doubt that I'll see you tomorrow with all the busy-ness in preparation for debarkation. I wish you the best of luck and do hope our paths cross again in the future."

♦   ◇   ♦

That evening, Jack and Jean sat down in row F, seats 22 and 23 at 7:10. The theatre was already about half full. They'd wanted to get good seats. While formal wear for this evening was not mentioned in the ship's newspaper, everyone seemed to be well dressed. An opening night atmosphere prevailed. Those attending the show this evening were given a commemorative card by the ushers to mark the occasion of the first public performance of *North Atlantic*.

The premise of the musical was a light-hearted look at crossing the Atlantic Ocean on a cruise ship, surely most apropos for this ship's company. Promptly at eight o'clock, the house lights were darkened, talking stopped and in complete silence, a spotlight illuminated the cruise director, resplendent in a white tux, standing center stage.

"Good evening, ladies and gentlemen. Welcome to the première of *North Atlantic*. Think about this. Here you are, sitting in a cruise ship, on the North Atlantic Ocean, about to see and hear a new musical production of the same name. How appropriate is it for you, and for us, to be here on this auspicious occasion—the launch and sea trial of a wonderful musical. Your souvenir program provides you with many details: the composer is Howard Kind; lyricist, Samuel Silverman; and the director for this performance is Lyle Masters. This performance tonight will largely determine if the show is Broadway-bound.

"In the stage pit is our ship's orchestra, whom you've heard before on this cruise. The cast have practiced almost non-stop since we left Barcelona. It is my hope that you enjoy this gala performance, sponsored by World Cruise Lines for its guests on the *Seascape*.

"Please remember, if you have not turned off any cell phones and other noisemakers, kindly do so now. Also note, that due to copyright restrictions, the use of cameras or other recording devices is not allowed. Thank you and enjoy the very first production of *North Atlantic*."

As the maroon velvet curtains parted, the orchestra struck up with the show's signature tune: *Canary Islands*. The back of the set showed an island with a large volcano, a wisp of steam rising from its peak, and a cruise ship, with the WCL logo on the funnel, in the foreground. To many in the audience, it seemed a bit like the island of Bali in the South Pacific. Twenty chorus girls in line, dressed in sailor-style white and blue-striped tops, short skirts, sailor hats and dancing Can-Can style, were singing the first stanza to *Canary Islands*. The melody was catchy, stirring memories.

Canary Islands, in the Atlantic,
They are so… very romantic.
Come with me, and you will see,
On a cruise, across the sea,
Canary Islands.

Another musical piece, called *The Storm*, was projected in living color and action on the rear screen, the sound and fury of the Atlantic weather created by the orchestra using violins for the fast winds, trumpets and drums for the thunder, and cymbals for the crashing waves, eventually each kind of instrument joining in to contribute to a cacophony of noise at sea. The audience huddled in their seats.

The show, with five song and dance numbers and two duets, lasted an hour and twenty minutes, culminating in the male and female lead performers holding hands and walking along a backdrop of a painted golden sandy beach, watching a fiery-red sunset. Totally romantic. The performance received a standing ovation.

As Jean and Jack left the theater, she said, "That was a catchy little tune, *Canary Islands*. Reminds me a bit of that popular 1960s song—." Here she began singing the first line, *'I've got an island, in the Pacific, and everything about it is terrific.'* You remember that?"

"I do. *I've Got an Island, in the Pacific*. Wasn't it, um, Anita O'Day who sang it so coyly? This show should do well on Broadway. Fancy a night cap?"

Jean replied, "Sounds good. After that stormy *Atlantic Ocean* musical number, I almost feel I need to warm up."

"Alright. A quick one, and one last stroll under the moon, then to bed. How does that sound for a full warm up?"

SUNDAY, JUNE 1
At sea

This was the last full day at sea for the occupants of the Motor Vessel *Seascape*. At 9 a.m., the ship had 415 nautical miles to go to Miami, in 23 hours. Passengers and crew had not been given further information about the death of one of its passengers—and no one had asked. The silence imposed on those few crew members involved in the investigation had been maintained, an example of the respect for the *need-to-know-only* policy imposed by Captain Stuart. "Why cause concern among our guests when there's really no need?" he'd said to his staff captain.

Many more people seemed to be briskly walking the promenade deck this morning, almost as if they were preparing their sea legs for terra firma again. For most passengers, it was a day of mixed emotions: last day aboard ship, last day for great food and lots of it, last day with new and old friends, last day to shop for souvenirs, and last day for the final dinner tonight. Even a last visit to the casino—some determined to recoup their losses—before packing, and for many, late to bed tonight.

Jean and Jack Sterling were having a healthy breakfast: lots of fruit, drinking green smoothies.

She said, "We finally have a day together. The last one was when? Five, six days ago?"

Jack said, "That long, eh? Thank you for supporting me, Jean. I suppose I could have declined to help but if I had, I think I would have regretted the opportunity. There is a brotherhood among law enforcement people. In many ways, this has been a novel experience—quite unlike most, if not all, of the more mundane murders, if I can apply that word, that I've investigated."

"You should feel good about what you've done, Jack. I'm proud of you. It's too bad all the passengers on this ship don't know about this. It's certainly another tale to tell your grandchildren when you're old. What are we going to do for the rest of the day?"

Jack told her it probably wasn't necessary but he might do a quick, final check with the FBI team, as he would not see them again until the formal dinner with the captain.

Using her husband's baseball jargon, Jean asked, "So, Jack Sterling, how to you feel about scoring two home runs on this cruise? Two suspects collared."

"I'm not sure I'd put it quite that way, but thanks for the accolade. I feel good about being able to help. As usual, murder investigations always involve a variety of people. In this case, without being pretentious about it, I suppose, the Feds, and this cruise line for that matter, were a bit lucky I was here to be able to help. Maybe I should start a company for doing this kind of work—name it something like Cruise Ship Crime Investigations Incorporated or CSCII for short, and hire myself out. What do you think?"

"I have a short, one-word answer: NO. You're just kidding, anyway, Mr. Sterling."

"Of course. But let me try this on you. I was thinking of writing my memoirs as a detective."

Jean looked at him intently, trying to read his poker face.
She said, "Really?"

"I was just kidding—I think. The captain was telling me about writing down his naval adventures, including the Falklands War. Got me wondering about my past. What do you think anyway?"

"That's a novel idea, Jack. Pardon the pun! Why not go for it?"

"Well, first, I don't know that I can write well enough—."

"—You could always use a ghost writer," she interrupted.

"I suppose so. Second, I have a whole lot of tales to tell. How could I keep things interesting? Avoid repetition. Would my work just end up being a whole series of short stories? Lots to consider."

"I like the idea, sweetheart. Maybe Hollywood would pick it up for a movie, or NBC for a series or make it into a Monday Night Movie. You could be like *Columbo,* only Canadian and certainly better dressed. Being married to a clever, attractive writer. Hmm. George Clooney as you and Sandra Bullock for me!"

"Listen, I should go. It's getting close to ten. We should be finished by eleven or so I should think. I'll call."

♦ ◊ ♦

FBI agents Tom Bradley and Patricia Wilcox met Jack and Mike in the main security section office at coffee time, ten o'clock, to have a final discussion of the Rudman-Gorenko File. The other two agents were still busy with forensics. The tabletop was covered in paperwork. The 'manual' now consisted of a complete list of witnesses' names and addresses, the itemized list of evidence collected—the physical evidence now officially received by the FBI, and stored in boxes—photographs, diagrams, copies of notes, statements and so on. The three pieces of jewelry were in a sealed box inside the security section's safe. Anther item of evidence was in the locked cold storage: Rebecca Gessner's body.

The lead agent opened the discussion with, "So far, so good. Given our situation, there's little else to be done. We had Rudman in and tried to have a conversation with him, but he remained mute. He is scared though. Gorenko repeated essentially what she'd told you. Her evidence on the stand should help, unless she clams up. The evidence you've gathered, Jack and Mike, should go a long way toward getting a conviction of these two people if, of course, the forensic results turn out to be positive," Tom emphasized. "That is, particularly the found blood samples, and hair, if any of Rudman's fell out, especially in the scuffle on the bed. Too bad about the fingerprints—good try, Jack. As we know, the lack of a statement admitting to the murder, at least in this case, does not mean that the prosecutor will not lay charges, nor that a jury will find the defendant not guilty. I think we will have enough physical evidence to overcome the lack of what I call a backup statement. You can bet, Jack, that I'll have a robust discussion with our counsel. Given the unusual nature of this murder—on a ship at sea and the circumstances surrounding the investigation—to put it bluntly, it ain't going to be a sure thing. But, I'm going to remain optimistic. A conviction will set a good precedent."

"I'm of the same view, Tom," said Jack. "Either way, it's a case that needs to see the light of day, at least in the shipping world. In a way, if these two are found guilty, and this case receives its due public attention, that may cause the United Nations people responsible for *Law Of the Sea* matters to do some further thinking."

"You're right, Jack. As well, I think that would be a fitting epitaph for Mrs. Gessner, and maybe lead to a more comprehensive and legally-sound way of conducting sea-going criminal investigations. Before I forget, Mike, have you heard anything back about your injured seaman?"

"Yes. Got the news yesterday. The surgeons have managed to re-attached his hand, but he'll never be able to bend his wrist. They had to insert some metal for reinforcing. No one is sure how much dexterity and control he will recover, or how long rehab will take, but it is definitely better than no hand. He was a lucky man to have your plane available to get him to a top surgical hospital in time."

"Thanks. Good to hear that, and glad our jet could help. Alright, see you both this evening. Mind if we stay here a bit longer, Mike, taking up this space?"

"Be my guest."

◆ ◇ ◆

"Well, as the expression goes, Jack Sterling, *it's all over bar the shouting*—except maybe in the courtroom," said Jean. They were enjoying a coffee and pastry snack on the upper deck. Another hot day before them.

"I'm not at all sure, honey. Given the nature and circumstances of this investigation, a conviction could be difficult to obtain. Given that Rudman may go to trial, I'll be a chief witness for the prosecution. I'm certain he did murder that poor woman and I just hope all the evidence we obtained on the ship and with the FBI forensic unit's contribution, will be sufficient. Maybe not a good time for me to start a new job. Anyway, today's our last day and I want to enjoy it with you. We go to the captain's dinner tonight which will be fun. Otherwise, what would you like to do?"

"How would it be if we invite Hannah Goldman to lunch? Maybe cheer her up a bit. I imagine she's feeling a bit low."

"Yes, by all means. She seems like a very personable young woman. How about you call her?"

They met at the *Lido Café* on deck ten, at one o'clock. Dressed in a mid-length pale blue pleated skirt and a pastel pink and white striped top, Hannah looked young and beautiful, and composed.

"Hello once again, Hannah. How are you?" asked Jean as they sat down. "You look fabulous in this outfit."

"I'm okay, thanks. Nice to see you and Mr. Sterling again."

"Please, call us Jack and Jean. If you don't mind my asking, how long did you know Mrs. Gessner?"

"Just over a year. My father knew Mr. Gessner from way back. They met through the synagogue, I believe. My mother would meet Mrs. G. at Hadassah events and naturally talk about me and what I was doing. After I graduated from university, Mrs. Gessner asked me to be her personal assistant." Hannah looked down for a second or two to compose herself, and added, "I miss her."

"I'm certain you do. Is it too early to know what you're going to do next? Have you made plans, dear?"

"Well, I think I'll go back to my Alma Mater—the U of M—and take graduate studies, something to do with business. That part of helping Mrs. G.—assisting with her board of directors responsibilities—I found intriguing.

"Can you tell me, Mr. Sterling—I'm sorry, Jack—have you found out who… *did* this?" She could not bring herself to say *killed*.

"Yes, I believe we have."

"Is it a crew member?"

"Yes, he is," not wanting to implicate Vesna Gorenko at this time.

"Do you think he will be convicted?"

"Well, Hanna, that's difficult for me to say, but I believe we have a very strong case."

"Where is he now?"

"This is confidential, you understand? The suspect is in the ship's brig until we arrive in Miami. He'll be taken away by the FBI."

That bit of information seemed to placate her.

Jack explained there was a chance she would be called as a witness at the trial, though the probability was not large in his estimation.

'Time to change the topic,' said Jean to herself, directing the table talk to the production of *North Atlantic*. "Did you see the big show last night?"

"Oh, yes. Mr. Shuster and I went."

"What did you think of it?"

"I thought it was great. Very moving and lively song and dance numbers. I liked the backdrop showing the ocean in its various moods. Should be a success." She was grateful for the change in their discussions.

At the end of the meal, as they all stood to go, Jack reiterated their regrets about Hannah's companion, and wished her the best of luck with her graduate studies. They parted company with hugs.

♦　◇　♦

"Mrs. Donnelly, 'tis your husband callin'. How are you, me darlin'?

"Just fine, Michael Donnelly, and you?"

"I'm okay, love, better now that I'm speakin' to you."

"Not your usual cruise, this one, with a ghastly murder and all. Glad it's over?"

"Absolutely. It's been quite literally a bloody mess. Four people lost blood on this trip. I'll tell you all about it later. Boys okay? Good. We're on time to dock at eight tomorrow. As you know, leaving and arriving is always very busy for me but I'll try to call you again tomorrow evening. I have a captain's dinner to attend tonight, with Mr. and Mrs. Sterling and four FBI agents. Full mess kit with everything spit-and-polish. Looking forward to it. Extra hug for the boys. Bye, love."

♦ ◊ ♦

At 6:55, there were nine people seated at a large, round table, set in one corner of the chandeliered dining room.

They were: Captain John Stuart; to his right, Jack Sterling and Jean; and beside her, two FBI agents. On his left, his wife Susan, Mike Donnelly, and the other two agents. Both the ship's officers were wearing starched full-dress white uniforms—with gold epaulettes and braided aiguillette. The two wives wore long evening gowns. Jack was in a tux, the three male agents in suits and ties. Ms. Wilcox was dressed in a dark blue jacket and skirt and white, frilly, collard blouse—but no diamonds. In another corner of the dining room, a young Chinese woman was softly playing classical music on a white Steinway. This was the last night at sea and the place was filling up fast.

Water glasses were quickly filled, followed by vintage champagne poured into fluted crystal glasses. Each diner was given a large, dark brown leather covered menu, with the *Savoy Dining Room* name embossed in gold on the cover.

Pinging the lip of his wine glass just once with a spoon, so as not to disturb other guests, and remaining seated, the captain said, "Ladies and gentlemen, let me welcome you to dinner. Susan and I feel honored to have you present. This is the first time I've had such distinguished guests from the law enforcement community at my table. It's been a pleasure meeting you, although the circumstances that brought us together are regrettable. May I thank all of you for the time and effort you have put into this matter, handling it all with skill, discretion and diplomacy. Let us hope that the courts will not fail you for those efforts."

Raising his wine glass, he added, "Here's to you, my friends."

After taking a sip, as did his guests, John put his glass down and continued. "There's one thing left to do before we order. In recognition of your services, Jack, and the interruption of your and Jean's first voyage with World Cruise Lines, on behalf of the Company, I'd like to present you with this envelope, inviting you and Jean to go sailing with us again—this time, on the house, or rather on the ship," handing it to Jack.

Surprised, Jack took the envelope and opened it. The card read:

June 1, 2014

To: Mr. Jack Sterling

On behalf of WORLD CRUISE LINES, it is my pleasure to acknowledge our grateful thanks for your considerable efforts in assisting our Ship Security Section investigate the unfortunate death of one of our passengers.

Your company and that of your wife, Jean Sterling, is hereby welcomed to join us for any future cruise you may wish to choose, for 15 days, all expenses paid, staying in a luxurious Crown Suite.

It has been a pleasure to have you aboard,

With our sincere thanks,
Andrew Hollinger
CEO, WCL
Miami, Florida

Jack passed the letter to Jean and, waiting for her to quickly read it, said, looking at Captain Stuart, "Thank you, John, for your kind hospitality. This has been a remarkable voyage for us, and you as well, I expect. It was my first, and I hope my last, murder on the high seas. I don't wish to *work my passage* on our next cruise." This created a chuckle around the table. "I was very glad to offer my assistance and I have to say, unequivocally, that I enjoyed working with Mike Donnelly. He'd have made a good detective on any police force. I'd also like to acknowledge the presence of my new friends from the FBI, who will now have the task of taking this matter before the courts in Florida. I wish them luck.

"Also, it's been a pleasure to get to know you and your charming wife, Susan. Our two girls, if I may use that expression, got along very well.

"Hopefully, we shall meet again some day—perhaps you'll be the captain for our next cruise. To your continued good health, Captain," Jack finished, raising his glass, as did the others around the table.

♦ ◊ ♦

The captain's dinner was over. Jack and Jean were leaning on the rail of their small balcony, looking out on a full moonlit, silvery sea. For a few minutes, they listened to the sound of waves breaking on either side of the bow, as it sliced through the water creating a luminescent white froth.

"Let's go for a walk around the deck, Jack, one last time. We won't be here tomorrow evening. It's such a beautiful night."

As they did that, he put his arm around her waist and snuggled in close, feeling very contented. The gentle gust of warm wind ruffled her hair and in the moonlight, she looked lovely. He told her so and after checking their surroundings, they stopped momentarily for a kiss.

Back in their stateroom, Jean said, "Well, that was a pleasant evening for us. Very thoughtful of Captain Stuart, with his presentation and his remarks. We have something to look forward to next year. Maybe we could ask Avery along if she'd come on an 'old-folks' cruise. I have to say, Jack, that I've really enjoyed myself. This murder, unintentionally, opened up some nice experiences that I otherwise would not have enjoyed. You know, spotting the murderer, the tour of the crown suite, looking around the bridge, lunch with the captain's wife, and our final dinner with him. I didn't miss you that much, Jack Sterling…."

Picking up on the game, he replied, "Well, that's good, honey. Glad I was not in your way. I too didn't miss you too much either. With my mind in the investigative mode, not a lot of time for *other things*," he said pointedly. "Are you reading tonight?"

"No," she replied with a smile.

◆ ◇ ◆

Jean had finished most of the packing. Jack called Avery, telling her briefly about the events of the day, including being invited to the captain's dinner on their last night. He confirmed their arrival time in Toronto in five days and looking forward to seeing her.

She said, "So, Dad, you nabbed the guy. Haven't lost the touch, eh?"

"Thanks, Avery. I do feel a certain sense of satisfaction, a new kind of police experience for me."

"I'm proud of you, Dad."

It was now after eleven p.m. and he and Jean went to bed. They left the balcony drapes fully open to take advantage of a cool breeze.

The translucent moonlight entering their cabin, shining on their pure white bedspread, reminding them of the old song, *By the Light of the Silvery Moon.*

"Too bad we have to go home," Jean said. "I'm enjoying this."

"Well, we do have another chance—and in a crown suite! We just need to find time. Taking another job could certainly get in the way."

"By the way, what did Vesna have to say?"

"Not surprisingly, she was subdued. She's scared and asked me what would happen to her. I tried to soft-pedal my answer, and really could only guess, not knowing how the American justice system would deal with an offense like this, especially where a murder is concerned. As we parted, I noticed a tear roll down her cheek. She gave me a hug. I guess I'll find out what happened at some time."

"Jack Sterling, underneath all that no-nonsense, tough exterior you put on sometimes, you're really just a pussycat at heart. I love you."

World Cruise Lines ship, the MV *Seascape* gently nudged dock-side at precisely 0759 hours. Captain Stuart, watching the docking operation from the bridge wing on the starboard side, smiled to himself. 'Good. I'll be able to get underway for the next cruise on time today. Hell of a trip, this has been!'

Debarkation was set to begin at 8 a.m.

The morning had been hectic, for crew and for passengers, most of whom had been awake for at least three hours. By 5 a.m., the passageways were full of passengers' baggage, all appropriately tagged, waiting to be taken down to the hold on deck two, from where it would be offloaded. All of this activity was highly organized so that when luggage was taken ashore to the passenger shed, guests could easily find their belongings and be on their way.

Four suitcases, however, did not take that route. They had been taken to a side room near the passenger exit, to be turned over to FBI agents waiting in several vehicles on the dock. The baggage belonged to Canadian passengers Mr. and Mrs. Jack Sterling, and crew members Radovan Rudman and Vesna Gorenko.

Jack and Jean took their breakfast at six-thirty, after waiting in a long line at the serving counter. They then made their way to the security office to say their farewells to the people Jack had worked with so closely over the last six days. In spite of the virus thing, it was a long handshake he had with Mike Donnelly, saying he hoped to meet him again, inviting him to come to Toronto if he ever had the chance, and wishing his friend the best of luck. "Maybe I'll be hearin' your fine Irish voice again if this case be goin' to trial in Miami."

"Aye, that would be good, Jack, so it would. Nice to have met you, Mrs. Jean Sterling. Have a safe trip to the Everglades, will you? I've been there and am sure you'll like the place."

At 8:10 a.m., the Sterlings left the ship and were escorted to a nearby unmarked black vehicle, among several parked on the dock. As Jack was about to enter, he glanced to his left and saw the pale, frightened, face of Vessie Gorenko, sitting in the back of another car, looking at him. He waved to her and she gave a feeble wave back. He couldn't help himself: he raised his hand again, with his thumb up in encouragement.

Agent Tom Bradley was his driver. He told Jack that a full forensic team had gone aboard to conduct their own check of the murder suite, view the body, taking any other necessary samples and have them removed, along with all the pieces of evidence that Jack and Mike had collected over the past week. All these items had been signed over to the FBI technicians, who had to be off the ship before its scheduled departure on another cruise at 6 p.m.

Mrs. Rebecca Gessner's body would be taken for an autopsy to the Miami-Dade County Medical Examiner's facility a little later, in their long black vehicle. No need to have that transport come to the dock just yet and risk spooking the debarking guests—people generally knew what those kinds of vehicles were for.

♦ ◊ ♦

SAC Clive Lundgren stood up as his guests entered his office. Introduced by Tom Bradley, he shook their hands and said, "Very nice to meet you at last, Mr. and Mrs. Sterling. Tom, would you be kind enough to bring in the refreshments for our guests? Mary has it ready beside her desk."

As Tom left to do that, Clive gestured to some chairs at a coffee table on one side of his office.

"It's nice of you to come by. I know you're on the way to the Everglades and I won't keep you long. If you're not clear about the most direct way to go, go west to Highway 821 from here and turn south, all the way to Florida City. Go right onto the Everglades Highway, State Route 9336 and follow. The road curves to the south. Should take about two hours or so to get there. I'll write that out for you, although you'll have sat-nav display in your car, I should think."

"Yes, we do. Thanks for the directions though. I find it a bit unnerving to have a car talk to me."

"Just to let you know, we're about ready to move out of this office complex, and move into a very fancy all-glass structure up in Miramar. It's some place, I understand."

Tom returned with a small trolley bearing a variety of biscuits and a carafe of coffee. He filled the four dark blue mugs. These bore the FBI crest on one side and the three large, capital letters on the other, all in gold.

Clive said, "When you're finished, you may keep them. I'll have Tom escort you out of the building when you leave, so you don't get busted for theft of Federal government property," he said with a straight face.

They discussed the case a few minutes, asking for Jean's forbearance. "As you can appreciate, Jack, we very seldom get murders at sea, and, of the very few we've had to deal with, the bodies of the victims were thrown overboard, making them *corpus delicti* cases, if the case got to court. This is the first that I can recall, for our area at least, and it's probably true for other coastal areas of the United States, where the body was not disposed of that way. We may be lucky that it was found *in-situ* in the suite. It's going to be interesting to see how this progresses through our justice system, or not. Let's hope that our forensic evidence is solid. I'm well aware of our judicial problems and hope that our prosecutor is able to wade through the legal quagmire that this case may produce. It'll certainly be one for the books. Speaking of which, you really should write a book, Jack, about this and your past cases."

The Sterlings shared a quick glance.

The SAC looked at Tom, who got up and went to Clive's desk and stood there. Looking at Jack, Clive continued, "I have to say, Jack, that it's been a genuine pleasure to do business with you. Our agency certainly lucked out when Mike Donnelly found you aboard ship. God knows where we would be, or how this matter would have been resolved, if at all, had you not been on this cruise. I hesitate to think of the mess that may have been left for us. You, of all people, well know how satisfactory it is to find the killer and to bring that person to justice. We owe the victims the best of our efforts. And for you, Jean, thank you so much for your patience and good grace for sharing your husband's time on this voyage. And, I understand you identified the male suspect yourself. I'd like you to accept this small token of our appreciation," presenting her with an FBI gold lapel pin.

"Before I let you go, Jack, I have one last duty to perform but, before I forget, would you like your check in Canadian or American funds?"

Jack laughed. "Thanks, but no thanks to any payment, Clive. Let's just agree my services were *priceless,* okay? Nice gesture though."

After waiting for the appropriate cue, Agent Ralph Harkins entered the room and handed something to his boss.

"Jack, it gives me great pleasure to present this plaque to you for your services to the Federal Bureau of Investigation." Holding an 8-by-10-inch mahogany wood shield, embossed with the FBI crest in brass, Clive presented it to Jack, shook his hand, and simply said, "Thank you, Jack," while Ralph took a photo.

Tom took Jack's hand and, placing his left hand on top in a gesture of camaraderie, said, "It's been a pleasure. Hope we meet again, Jack."

Holding it up for Jean to look on, Jack read aloud the inscription on the brass plate under the agency crest:

PRESENTED TO
CHIEF SUPERINTENDENT
JACK STERLING (RET'D),
METROPOLITAN TORONTO POLICE SERVICE,
ON BEHALF OF THE FEDERAL BUREAU OF
INVESTIGATION, MIAMI, FLORIDA, FOR HIS
ASSISTANCE AND SKILL IN SOLVING THE
MURDER OF MRS. REBECCA GESSNER, AT
SEA, DURING A VOYAGE FROM BARCELONA
TO MIAMI, ABOARD M.V. *SEASCAPE*. MAY 2014

" Sentinel Corporation, Jack Sterling here."

"Jack, it's Tom Bradley calling from Miami. Good to hear your voice again. How's things in Toronto?"

"Fine, thanks. Whassup? Let me guess. You need my body down there to testify."

"Actually, we don't. It's taken almost five months of review and discussions, but Rudman's and Gorenko's lawyers, after pre-trial discussions with our prosecutor, agreed to plead guilty—Rudman to a reduced charge of manslaughter, and her to being an accessory after the fact, and possession of stolen property. You have similar offenses in Canada, I believe. Anyway, he was sentenced to eight years and she to a one-year term, suspended.

"Judge Pamela Reed, in her sentencing remarks, said that she agreed with defense counsel that when Rudman entered the suite, he did not have the intent to murder anyone, but to steal the jewelry. In the heat of the moment, when the deceased had rushed at Rudman and pushed him over, he overreacted by grabbing a knife and lashing out at the woman.

"I know what you're going to say Jack: 'Why did he have to cut her throat?' Maybe because she was screaming and he wanted to silence her, and she could become a witness if he left her alive. Who knows? Water under the bridge now, my friend. With respect to Vesna Gorenko, Judge Reed said that she was culpable in acting as an accessory to Rudman by her actions in colluding with him to hide the jewelry. Judge Reed said there might have been an element of intimidation by Rudman, essentially pressuring Gorenko to hide the jewelry—a consideration which lessened her sentence. I think I'm okay with that. What do you think?"

"At first blush, I suppose it's a fitting conclusion to the matter. I wonder though, and you probably do too, what might have happened if these two things occurred: *one,* Rudman's lawyer successfully making the argument that the U.S. District Court had no jurisdiction to try the matter, as the offense occurred well outside the territory of the United States; and *two,* if it went to trial, making a case for the evidence being inadmissible in view of the way the investigation was conducted and evidence collected, by two people—myself, who had no authority to do so and Mike, not a police officer but under the authority of the captain. A tenuous argument perhaps. It would have been good to know how the court would have ruled in a very unusual case like this one. In a way, I wish it had gone to full trial. It would have been interesting to hear what the judge might have said about jurisdiction and the right to act."

"Yeah, I see your point. But, we'll take what we can get, eh? Actually, Jack, you may like to hear this. I was in court when the judge, in her summation concerning the facts of the case, made reference to two things. One obviously was the lack of trained and experienced security people, and necessary equipment aboard ship, and the second, where the offense occurred—in mid-Atlantic. Using my words almost verbatim, Justice Reed related that you were discovered aboard ship and used your very extensive knowledge in matters of murder investigation, and that you ensured that the evidence was properly handled and guarded, with the proper procedures followed in handing them over to our agency personnel after they boarded the ship. As well, you ensured the rights of the two suspects were not abrogated. She made some complimentary remarks about your service and professionalism. She actually said, you did a 'sterling job,' with a very slight smile on her face. As the Aussies say, *'Good on yer, mate.'* A copy of the court transcript is on its way to you.

"I can't thank you enough," he continued. "I've also let Mike Donnelly know about the outcome. Oh yes, by the way, the spot of blood you found under the faucet handle in the bathroom was matched to Rudman's. And on the outer side and palm of the left glove, were matches to Rudman and the victim. Good thing you spotted that. You know, if it wasn't for your evidence, it's likely this could have resulted in one or two other results—the prosecutor feeling that there was insufficient good evidence to go to court or, if the prosecutor had decided to throw the case against the wall to see if it sticks like spaghetti, hoping to be successful—that both the accused may have walked free, due to the lack of a competent investigation. And that's no reflection on Mike Donnelly. Oh, by the way, our director has forwarded this case to the International Maritime Organization in London, as well as Cruise Lines International Association in Washington, for their review and possible future recommendations about dealing with issues like this one. So, my friend, all in all, job well done, *muchas gracias* as we say in *my* bilingual country."

"You are certainly welcome," Jack responded.

"One other thing. Do you still have any of that Delamain Cognac left?"

"Yes, I do. Why, you coming here?"

"Happy to say I am coming up to Toronto in about three weeks. There's an international symposium on drug enforcement my boss in Washington wants me to attend. Will you be in the city?"

"You bet I will, Tom. Confirm your arrival and we'll meet. Good of you to call me. Take care."

EPILOGUE ONE

MAY 20, 2015
Pacific Ocean

A year later, almost to the day, the Sterlings found themselves on a flight from Toronto to San Diego, California. Jack had completed almost a year of service with his new employer, and was taking his first vacation. They boarded a two-week cruise, from San Diego to the Hawaiian Islands, courtesy of World Cruise Lines.

They'd been at sea almost three full days, traveling over 1200 miles, well out in the Pacific Ocean, about halfway to their first stop, Honolulu. It was afternoon and they were lounging on the upper pool deck, in a bit of shade, Jean snoozing and Jack reading a new Joseph Wambaugh novel.

He heard a slight buzz and the PA system came on, waking Jean: "Attention, passengers. Would the following guest, Mr. Jack Sterling, please report to the purser's office. Mr. Jack Sterling to the purser's office, please. Thank you."

The Sterlings looked at each other in some surprise, and Jack said, "Oh, no! Not another one!"

EPILOGUE TWO

MAY 5, 2020
Port of San Diego, California

Five years had passed. They were shown to their veranda cabin by the steward. Bags would be delivered later. Jack and Jean were pleased with the stateroom layout, on deck 10. Not a crown suite, for sure, but certainly ample for the two of them. He went to the sliding door and, pulling the drapes wider apart, stepped onto the balcony for a quick look. He could see the whole of San Diego's tall, gleaming glass-and-steel skyline in the bright sunlight. It was a pleasant day to begin the 15-day cruise down the coast of Mexico, Central America, through the Panama Canal and across the Caribbean to Port Everglades. Back in the room, he briefly looked at several sheets of paper laid out on the bed cover and picked up the one labelled *Welcome from your Captain*, printed under the company logo and the name of the ship, M.V. *Ocean Waves*. He read the usual greetings and then noted the name underneath: *Michael Donnelly, Captain.*

"Oh my God! Jean, read this," giving her the paper.

Jean did and echoed the sentiments her husband had just expressed, "How about that!"

"You remember Mike, of course, from our cruise six or seven years ago aboard the *Seascape*, across the Atlantic. I'll call him later, after we've left the port and are underway. He'll be busy now."

◆ ◇ ◆

At 2000 hours, Captain Donnelly was in his quarters eating a late meal when his phone rang. He answered, "Captain speaking."

A voice said, "Faith and begorrah, if it's no' Captain Moikle Donnelly himself," in the worst imitation of the Irish language.

There was a slight pause, and Mike said, "Don't tell me. I know who's speaking. My former police detective mentor, Jack Sterling, is it not? How are you, my friend? I always review the passenger list, and noted yours and Jean's name. I was going to let you settle in and call you later."

"Yes, Jean and I very much look forward to seeing you when you have time. Congratulations on your master's appointment, sir!"

◆ ◇ ◆

At lunchtime the following day, the Sterlings met with Mike in his bridge cabin. Mike said that it was Moira he had to thank for pushing him to take the required courses and do the apprenticeship time, finally being promoted from staff captain to ship's master one year ago. He now had twenty years of service with World Cruise Lines.

After some reminiscing about the last momentous voyage they did together, Mike said, "I don't know if you've kept up with things *maritime*, Jack, but there have been developments in closing the loophole with respect to police authority for our security people. A resolution was passed by the IMO last year, designating international law enforcement authority to the chief of security aboard cruise vessels. I've been told that it is somewhat similar to the U.S. Federal Air Marshal Service or FAMS, but obviously with a much wider scope. I don't think it's quite as air-tight as land-based legislation though. I'm not sure that it could ever be. Training now includes a one-month mandatory course in criminal investigation through the auspices of Interpol. It's on-line, but better than nothing. Much better than the situation was six years ago. Problem, of course, is that the skills are so seldom used. But on my ship, I hold a twice annual review of that material.

"Security officers also have online access to experienced Interpol investigators to mentor them through anything complicated—not unlike how our onboard doctors can be walked through tricky surgical procedures by medical specialists on shore."

"Well, that's good to know, Mike. So, you won't be interrupting me in the middle of my cruise, calling on my services again?"

"No, I don't think so, Jack, so you and Jean can relax," he replied with a smile. "Now guess who is with me on this trip as my S.O.?"

Jack shook his head and replied, "Don't know. Who?"

"Sheila Turner. On her own initiative, she took a number of police college courses—inspired by working with you, Jack. Then she rose steadily through the ranks. We've had many trips now as master and S.O. together."

"And have you two had any further deaths at sea on your watch?"

"Yes, two. Natural causes in both cases. No murders, thank God. But don't worry, I'll do my best to make your cruise a pleasant and safe one regardless of deaths, be they foul or natural causes. Let's have a formal dinner together later in the voyage. I will send an invitation. Good to see you both again, and *'Welcome Aboard'* my ship."

The two friends stood, side by side, both saluting and grinning broadly as Jean pressed the button and the camera flashed.

CPSIA information can be obtained
at www.ICGtesting.com
Printed in the USA
LVOW04*1947200416

484568LV00010B/26/P